JUST PLEA

A NATE SHEPHERD NOVEL

MICHAEL STAGG

Just Plea

A Nate Shepherd Novel

For more information about Michael Stagg and his other books, go to michaelstagg.com

Want a free short story about Nate Shepherd's start as a new lawyer? Hint: It didn't go well.

Sign up for the Michael Stagg newsletter here or at https://michaelstagg.com/newsletter/

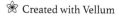

❀ Created with Vellum

PART I

PILLAR

1

They found Benjamin Trane crumpled beneath an oak tree, broken and dying. According to an article in the *Carrefour Courier*, a vehicle had run right up onto the sidewalk and hit Mr. Trane while he was walking a dog. The vehicle hadn't stuck around.

The woman who owned the oak tree, Mrs. Sharon Pepperstone, called 911. The rescue squad and the police responded, and Mr. Trane was rushed to the hospital. He died on the way.

Mrs. Pepperstone told the reporter that she hadn't seen the car or the driver who did it. She did recognize the dog, though: a small boxer who had belonged to a neighbor who had also recently passed, a man named Theo Plutides, God rest his soul. The dog was not injured.

When the *Courier* went to press on the Saturday morning after the accident, the police had no suspects and no witnesses. But, of course, they hadn't had much time to look yet.

I must not have seen the subsequent articles—I think I would have remembered a headline about the founder of Carrefour's largest charity being accused of vehicular homicide, especially one named Edgerton Fleece. It was big news locally, but I've been known to get focused from time to time and miss what's going on around me.

No, an oak tree, an uninjured dog, and a dead man. That's about all I remembered of the Benjamin Trane killing when Danny walked into my office two months later.

2

"Do you have a minute, Nate?" said Daniel Reddy.

"Sure." I typed a few more lines about jurisdiction, then looked up to see Danny still standing outside my door.

Daniel Reddy was my associate. He was tall and thin and about as smart a young lawyer as you would find at any big firm. I know that because he had followed me from a big firm to the two-man office that was just Danny and me.

I waved him in, and he hesitated a moment before taking his seat. Or attempted to take a seat, I should say, because he stumbled and kicked the chair leg before he untangled himself enough to sit down.

Danny's mind was always a little out ahead of his body. It got worse when he was nervous.

I tilted my head. "What's up?"

"I have a new potential case."

"Great! Another will?"

Danny looked down. "No." He took a deep breath. "It's a criminal case."

"Really?"

"I was hoping that you could take the lead. I wouldn't ask, but I got the referral through my church."

"No problem. What is it? Littering? Cursing in a public park?"

"Vehicular homicide."

I raised an eyebrow. "That's serious."

Danny nodded. "That's why I came to you."

I tapped my desk. "I can handle any hearings and it's a simple matter to plead—"

"He didn't do it, though."

Now I sat back. Danny shifted in his seat.

"A trial is a two-person job," I said.

"I know. I'll help."

I shook my head. "I thought you didn't want to represent accused murderers?"

"This is vehicular homicide."

"That's a pretty thin line, Danny."

"He didn't do it."

"That's a consistent comment from our clients."

"And Edge needs someone who isn't an idiot."

"I'm thinking of putting that on our business cards, 'The Shepherd Firm—We're not idiots.'"

"That's not what I meant, I know you're not an—I mean, you're really good at..." Danny took a deep breath, looked at the ceiling, and said, "He needs your help."

"Who is 'he?'"

"Edgerton Fleece." Danny looked at me expectantly.

I shook my head.

"He's the CEO of Pillars Outreach."

"The charity?"

Danny pursed his lips. "We like to say outreach organization."

"I stand corrected. I really don't know much about it."

"It helps a lot of people."

"Gotcha. What did Fleece do?"

"Nothing."

"Sorry, what is he *accused* of doing?"

"They say he hit and killed a man with his van and then left the scene of the accident."

"Okay, the first thing to do is to get him out of jail. I'll get ahold of Cade and we'll arrange for bond, then after that we can start to look..."

I stopped. Danny had looked a little embarrassed before, but now he looked down-right sheepish. "What is it?" I said.

"I already got him out."

"He's already had a bond hearing?"

Danny nodded.

"And entered a plea?"

Danny nodded again, then found something exceedingly interesting in the construction of our ceiling.

"And you did that?"

Danny shrugged and continued his ceiling inspection.

I sat back. "See, because I remember someone who came in to see me and said he didn't want to represent criminals anymore."

Danny shifted in his seat.

"And I believe I even helped that person start branching out into estate planning and business work."

Danny sighed. "Are you done?"

I smiled. "Except for the biggest question: what does Jenny think?"

"It was her idea."

"Really? Interesting."

"She doesn't think Edge did it either. And she knows good criminal lawyers are hard to find and...Would you quit grinning?"

"I agree with her. It's hard to find good criminal lawyers."

"You are so annoying."

"It's lucky she found one so quickly."

"Do you want to hear about the case or not?"

"I would love to hear a summary of the charges from a fellow defense lawyer."

"Vehicular manslaughter and failure to stop at the scene of an accident."

"When did it happen?"

"A couple of months ago."

"Really? And they're just now arresting him?"

Danny nodded.

"And your guy—what's his name?"

"Fleece. Edgerton Fleece."

"Fleece wasn't found at the scene, I take it?"

"No. I don't think he even talked to the police for a month."

"Interesting. So what do they have on him?"

"I'm not sure yet."

"Do you have any idea what happened? Who the victim was?"

Danny nodded. "It was a Pillars employee, a guy named Benjamin Trane."

"The victim was from Pillars too?"

"He was."

"You're as bad as a client."

"What do you mean?"

"Starting in the middle and giving me half the story. Start at the beginning."

Danny thought for a moment, then said, "Two months ago, Benjamin Trane was walking a dog at night when a car jumped the curb and hit him."

A bell rang. "Flung him into an oak tree, right?"

"You heard about it?"

"Read it in the paper. The oak tree and the dog left an impression."

Danny nodded. "Jenny and I volunteer at Pillars. We knew about the death at the time."

"But I take it there was no indication that Fleece might've been involved?"

"None at all. He even spoke at Benjamin's funeral. About a month ago, a detective spoke with them."

"Them?"

"Edge and his wife Carissa. Carissa had the impression that it was just a routine call since Benjamin had worked at Pillars."

"Apparently not."

"Right. So another month after that, last weekend, they picked Edge up and took him in. That's when they charged him. I arranged his bond and got him out."

"I didn't realize you knew how to do that."

"I'm not dumb, Nate. I just don't like it."

"All right. Sounds like I need to go out and see him. Is he at home?"

"He's at Pillars this afternoon."

I smiled.

"What?" Danny said.

"Nothing."

He ignored me and stood. "Four-thirty, okay?"

"Sure. I'll enter an appearance this afternoon. Jokes aside, you are staying on as co-counsel, right?"

Danny paused, but only for a moment, before he nodded his head.

"Good. Do you need to call him to tell him we're coming?"

"I've already set up an appointment. "

"Can't wait to get started, eh?"

Danny left.

3

Later that afternoon, Danny and I closed up shop and headed to the south side of Carrefour to meet with Edgerton Fleece, the CEO of Pillars Outreach of Carrefour. I had never been out there, so Danny gave me the address, and I plugged it into my phone.

Carrefour is a small city that sits on the Ohio-Michigan border near Indiana. The state line goes right through town, putting the northern third in Michigan and the southern two-thirds in Ohio. I live in the northern third on the Michigan side and my office is just barely over the line into Ohio. The Pillars headquarters is down on the south side in an area that was rural thirty years ago and suburban now.

It didn't take long to get there since the building was just off the highway. The exit led me to a traffic light where I turned into a four-lane private drive that ran between two large parking lots, both of which were mostly full. I came to an intersection with a color-coded directional sign welcoming me to the Pillars Outreach Center with arrows pointing the way to a food pantry, a childcare center, a loading dock, and corporate offices. I followed the arrow straight ahead to the corporate offices, found a place to park near Danny, and got out of my Jeep.

The asphalt parking lot led to a cement sidewalk from which arose a four-story building of green-tinted glass and chrome. At the top was the Pillars logo—the word "Pillars" sitting atop four white columns. Below it was written "Support for All."

"This place is huge," I said to Danny.

"You've never been here?"

"I don't get to the south-end much."

"You need to expand your horizons."

"Apparently. They built this?"

Danny shook his head. "The housing collapse of '08. A mortgage company went under right after they built this new headquarters."

"Ouch," I said.

"Pillars stepped in and took over the facility. The corporate gym makes a great daycare, by the way."

The two of us walked through a large reception area, filled with light and random seating, to a reception desk where an older gentleman in a sleeveless blue sweater vest sporting the Pillars logo directed us to the bank of elevators on the left that would take us to the third-floor corporate offices. We took the elevators and disembarked into another reception area, this time to meet a woman in her early fifties wearing a dress with a matching jacket.

She smiled and said, "You must be Mr. Shepherd."

"Yes, ma'am."

"And Daniel, I didn't know you were coming too. Wonderful."

"Hi, Mrs. Horvath."

"I'm so sorry, both of you, but there was an emergency down at the meal delivery center, so Mr. Fleece went down to help. He asked if you wouldn't mind meeting him down there?"

"Of course not. Where is it?"

"Excellent! You can head right down. Daniel can show you the way, Mr. Shepherd."

I glanced at Danny. "Oh?"

She nodded. "He's here every weekend."

"You don't say?"

Danny ignored me. "The back loading dock, Mrs. Horvath?"

"Just look for the freezer truck. Will we be seeing you at the fellowship breakfast this month?

"You couldn't keep me away."

"Wonderful!" she said, and seemed to mean it. "I'll mark you down."

We were headed back toward the elevator when it opened and a woman came barreling out. She was a little shorter than average and a little smaller, but the way she was carrying the binders under her right arm made it seem as if she was just as willing to run us over as go around. Fortunately, she chose the path between Danny and me instead of through us before stopping in front of Mrs. Horvath. "Edge missed our meeting," the woman said.

"He was called down to an emergency, Ms. Blackwell," said Mrs. Horvath.

"There's always an emergency."

Mrs. Horvath smiled and said, "I was just telling these gentlemen, these *visitors*, that Mr. Fleece is at the loading dock."

Ms. Blackwell barely looked at us. "Tell him I need to see him before he goes to the next emergency."

"Certainly, Ms. Blackwell." Mrs. Horvath's smile remained in place. "I'll tell him to call as soon as he gets back."

Ms. Blackwell didn't seem to notice. "The day care closes at six," she said and stalked off in a way that would have driven her heels through a less-reinforced floor.

Mrs. Horvath pivoted and indicated the elevator to us. "If you hurry, I'm sure you'll catch him."

As we took the elevator back down to the first floor, I said, "Every weekend? Really?"

Danny shrugged. "Mrs. Horvath exaggerates."

"Does she?"

Danny glanced at me, then shrugged again. "Most weekends, I guess."

The doors opened and Danny led us toward the back of the building.

"What do you do?" I asked.

"Jenny spends a couple of hours in the daycare, and I help load trucks for meal delivery."

"On Saturday?"

"People need to work and eat on the weekend too. They have a hard time filling those shifts."

I had always known that Danny spent a good amount of time at his church, but this was news to me. It was completely like him to volunteer at a charity every weekend and never mention it. I was about to ask him more when we pushed out an exit door and rounded the corner to the loading area.

A large semi-truck with the "Ready Meals" logo on the side was backed into the loading bay. A man with a green "Ready Meals" cap was standing there, arms crossed. Another man stood next to him, writing on a small pad. As we approached, the writing man tore out what had to be a check, handed it to the driver, and said, "Can we unload now?"

The truck driver nodded and said, "In advance next week."

"Sure." As the man headed for the back of the truck, he saw us and stopped. "Daniel, is it four-thirty already?"

"It is, Edge."

Edgerton Fleece detoured over to us. He was a little over six feet tall, with a wealth of dark brown hair that had a slight wave that might have been natural. He wore a dark blue pullover with the Pillars logo embroidered on the left chest and looked as if he would have no problem unloading boxes. As he shook my hand, he said, "And you must be Nate Shepherd?"

I nodded.

"Edgerton Fleece, Nate, but call me Edge." Edge looked from us to the truck and back again before pointing a thumb over his shoulder and saying, "I'm sorry but we really need to get this unloaded so the meals can go out and we're already running late. Can we reschedule?"

I looked at Danny and then looked at the truck. "We can help you unload if you like."

Edge's grin broadened. "Perfect." He gave my shoulder a clap and the three of us got to work.

We weren't the only ones. Two other men, teenage boys actually, were there waiting to unload.

"Here," said Edge and handed me a pair of work gloves.

I smiled. "I'm a lawyer but I'm not that soft."

Edge smiled back. "It doesn't look like you are. They're not for blisters, though, they're for the cold." He pointed as we climbed up into the back of the truck.

I saw that the stacked boxes of meals were frosting up and thought of those times you grab an ice cube out of the freezer and have it stick to your fingers. I pulled on the gloves, grabbed a double stack of boxes, and followed Edge and Danny as they did the same.

We walked down the truck ramp, through the loading dock, to an enormous walk-in freezer. "The corporate cafeteria was a perfect fit for our meal delivery service," said Edge over his shoulder.

"How many people do you deliver to?" I said as I set down my boxes.

"Two to three hundred, depending on the day." He shook his

head. "I wish it was more."

"That seems like a lot."

"It's just a small part of the food outreach program," said Danny as we walked back for another load.

"What do you mean?" I said.

Danny grabbed my arm and pulled me into another room. There were shelves, floor to ceiling, stacked with boxed and canned goods—I caught a glimpse of soup and tuna and rice and an entire section devoted to mac and cheese.

"Wow," I said, and meant it.

"This is the food bank," said Danny. The pride was obvious on his face. "Churches and charities contribute what they can, and Pillars buys the rest."

"And then the church members can come here?" I asked.

"Anyone can come here," said Edge. "There are an awful lot of people who need a hand."

"This is amazing."

Edge shrugged. "Like I said, I wish it were more."

We moved boxes for another forty-five minutes. As we worked, three women and three more teenage boys cut open boxes as fast as we could bring them in and stored the meals by type in the freezer. When we brought in our last load, Edge smiled and said, "That was a huge help! Why don't we head back up to my office and we can talk—"

"Hey, Edge!" A broad-shouldered man in the dark blue Pillars pullover jogged up. He had brown hair that was tight on the sides and long on top and a brown beard trimmed to a jutting point that somehow conveyed laughter instead of menace. "The Board is waiting."

Edge cocked his head. "I thought they weren't due here until five, Greg?"

Greg grinned. "It's five-fifteen."

Edge winced, then said, "Nate Shepherd, this is Greg

Kilbane, our head of community outreach."

Greg shook my hand. "You're the lawyer?"

"I am."

Greg looked at Edge. "Did you bring a retainer check?"

Edge pulled out the checkbook he'd pocketed earlier. "Ah, this is the corporate account." He shook his head. "I'm sorry, Nate, I left my personal checkbook back—"

Greg grinned. "Carissa thought you might forget. Here." Greg handed me a check. I saw the names in the upper left corner—"Edgerton Fleece and Carissa Carson-Fleece, M.D."

Edge looked relieved. "Thanks, Greg."

"No worries." Greg looked at me. "Danny says you're good."

I shrugged. "I sign Danny's checks."

"You're going to take care of this thing, right?"

"I'm still trying to learn about 'this thing.'"

"And you will," said Edge. "But I really do have to meet with the Board about our health clinic expansion." Edge put a hand on Danny's shoulder. "Why don't I come to your office tomorrow, that way you'll have my full attention."

"You're going to want to give it that," I said.

Edge nodded. "It's just been one of those days." He held out his hand and I shook it. It struck me more as the hand of a man who worked than one that sat at a desk.

"I'll see you tomorrow," said Edge as Greg Kilbane led him away by the elbow, talking rapidly in his ear.

Danny and I stood there for a moment in the wake of Edge's whirlwind and the wreckage of empty frozen food boxes. Then we walked back to the parking lot.

"He doesn't seem too worried," I said.

"Edge has a lot on his plate."

"He needs to empty it, or he'll be going to jail."

"There are plenty of empty plates already, Nate," said Danny. "That's why his is so full."

4

My trip to Pillars felt like a waste. Although I had served the greater good, I didn't feel like I had served my client at all. As I drove back to north Carrefour, I decided to salvage the night by stopping at the Brickhouse.

If you haven't been there in a while, you can find the Brickhouse near an abandoned spur of railroad track on the north side of Carrefour. It shares a parking lot with a restaurant called the Railcar and, as you pull in, you're confronted with an existential choice—turn left toward cold beer and tangy ribs surrounded by a view of the woods, the sound of a stream trickling among the rocks, and the sweet smell of hickory smoke; or turn right toward hard angles of iron and concrete to be besieged by the driving bass of music that demands action and cruelly maniacal encouragement. If you knew the owners of the Brickhouse, you might just think that they'd set it up that way on purpose.

The Brickhouse is owned by Olivia and Cade Brickson. The siblings spent most of their spare time at the gym when they weren't working in their day jobs as an investigator and a bail bondsman. I walked in the front door of the used brick building carrying my gym bag because I didn't have the energy to face Olivia by entering without it.

Olivia was standing in front of the main desk. I stopped. "My goodness," I said.

"What's the matter, Shep?" she said. "Haven't you ever seen someone look amazing before?"

"No, did I miss someone?"

Olivia had short, bleached white hair that was tight on the sides and longer on top. Normally, she let her hair swoop down around the left side of her half-mirrored glasses, but today it was styled up and back. Usually when I saw her in the gym, she was dressed for work in a tank top and running pants, but today she was wearing a sleeveless black dress. If you're curious about the designer of the dress, you're talking to the wrong guy, but I can tell you that it was short and it was black and it was sparkly.

And while Olivia might have been right, it would never do to let her know.

"Liar," she said. She pointed at the gym bag. "Does that mean you're getting some work in tonight?"

"A couple of kinds. I was going to ask you about an investigation before I started."

A set of headlights flashed across the door. "Be happy to, Shep. I have to run now, though. Email me tomorrow?"

"Sure." I pointed at the black Escalade that had pulled up outside. "Financial advisor/ultra-racer?"

She grinned. "Cardiologist/rock-climber." Then she wiggled her fingers goodbye and slipped out the door.

I smiled, swung my gym bag over my shoulder, and headed back to change.

~

It was dark outside when I got home and dark in the house when I entered. I flicked on a few lights, dumped my gym bag in the laundry room and my laptop on the island, then stood in front of the fridge for a couple of minutes before preparing a feast of plain chicken breasts, white rice, and canned corn. I ate it while reading the latest book about a big guy who served justice by beating up the bad guys and enjoying it.

Don't judge me. He's decent company.

I finished my dinner as the big guy learned that something was seriously amiss in a small town. I gave him a break while I cleaned up the dishes, then rejoined him as the big guy followed his leads and whooped a series of asses. Then I set him aside and flicked through the high-def channels and Netflix and Hulu and Apple TV and Amazon before deciding there was really nothing on. I settled on a seven-season sitcom from the early 2000s and watched three episodes before calling it a night and heading to bed, exhausted from all the excitement.

5

When I arrived the next morning, Danny was already working away in his office. I stuck my head in and said, "You need to straighten your friend out."

Danny looked up. "Good morning."

"He's in serious trouble."

"That's why I took you out there."

"We don't have time to spin our wheels. We need to get to work."

"I agree. I've texted both Edge and his wife and confirmed with Mrs. Horvath. He'll be here at two o'clock today." He folded his hands, waiting.

"Well, then, let's get to work."

Danny flourished his hands across a desk filled with notepads and briefs. "If only someone would let me."

I nodded and went to my office.

~

I EMAILED OLIVIA FIRST, asking her to look for information on the victim Benjamin Trane, our client Edgerton Fleece, and any reports of the accident and Edge's subsequent arrest in the news that she could find. I thought about calling the prosecutor's office but then decided it was too soon since I didn't have the slightest idea of what happened or what my client was accused of.

I pulled up the police report next. The accident had occurred about two months earlier on the evening of February 17. Although it had snowed a couple of days before, the conditions that night had been clear with no rain or ice. From the looks of the scene, one vehicle had been involved; it appeared to have run across a driveway, onto the sidewalk where it had hit Benjamin Trane and threw him into the tree. From the diagram on the back page, it appeared that the tire tracks arced off the street and back onto it without stopping. Benjamin Trane was alive when the police arrived but died en route to the hospital.

There were a few handwritten witness statements, but none of them identified a driver or a car. There was nothing else in the report identifying the driver, which meant the prosecutor or the police had done an investigation afterward that had found evidence linking it up to Edge.

I needed to find out what that was.

THAT AFTERNOON, Danny stuck his head in. "Edge is here."

I checked the time. "Five minutes early even."

Danny smiled. "That's because his wife is with him."

I raised an eyebrow.

"You'll see."

I grabbed a legal pad and a couple of pens and went out to meet them.

Danny already had them set up in the conference room. Edge was sitting there, legs crossed, leaning back in his chair and turning it from side to side as he smiled and said something to Danny about meal deliveries. A woman was sitting to his left. She was thin, with straight brown hair pulled back with a clip so that it fell to her shoulders. She stood as soon as I walked into the room and strode around the table, hand extended.

"Nate Shepherd? Carissa Carson-Fleece."

I remembered the title on the check as I shook her hand. "Nice to meet you, Dr. Fleece."

She waved. "Carissa, please. I'm sorry about the confusion yesterday."

Edge smiled. "I apologized to Nate after we unloaded the truck."

Carissa looked at him. "You made Nate unload the truck?"

"I volunteered," I said.

"People need to eat," said Edge and turned to me. "Carissa thinks I need to prioritize."

"I don't think it," she said. "You do."

As we all sat down, Carissa put a brown file on the table and pulled out a stack of manila folders. "Did Greg get you the retainer yesterday?"

"He did. Thank you."

"I assume there may be charges for experts?"

"I don't know for sure yet, but there's a good possibility."

"You'll let us know an estimate in advance?"

"Absolutely."

"Make sure that you send any bills to me. They'll get paid faster."

"Sure."

"And if you want to make sure something gets to Edge, or that he arrives somewhere on time, you'll want to copy me in, and probably Mrs. Horvath, too."

I glanced at Edge, who smiled and said, "I'm more of a big picture guy."

I nodded. "You know this is probably a good time to talk about—"

Carissa Carson-Fleece raised her hand. "I'm very aware of privilege, Nate, and that you're going to have to work with Edge on his own and have confidential conversations with him. I have similar issues in my practice. What I'm saying is that if you have something that needs to be done, and you need to make sure that Edge does it, you'll want to let me know."

I looked at Edge, who shrugged. "She's not wrong."

Carissa put a hand on the manila folders. "What do you know about what happened?"

"Virtually nothing."

"This will help you get started, then. Here is a copy of the accident report. Here's a copy of the registration and insurance information for the minivan Edge was driving that night. It's registered to Pillars, but it's a company car that he uses exclusively."

With each statement, she slid me a folder. She slid me another and said, "Here is the insurance claim form that was filed for damage to the van."

Alarm bells. "Why was there damage to the van?"

Carissa looked me straight in the eye. "Edge hit a deer."

"When?"

"The day before Benjamin's accident."

"I see."

"Here's the bill from the auto body shop that fixed the van and the name of the mechanic."

"What part of the van was damaged?"

Carissa looked at Edge.

"The front bumper and hood," he said. "I think the right headlight too."

I was beginning to see our problem.

"Finally, here's the personnel file for Benjamin Trane. He worked for us, for Pillars I should say."

"What did he do?"

"He was part of our seniors outreach program. He had a list of folks he checked in on regularly and helped them with anything they needed to maintain their independence."

Edge shook his head. "We miss him very much."

Carissa Fleece stood. "I expect you have some things to discuss. I need to stop over at St. Isidore's. I'll be back in an hour."

I stood along with her. "I may have some questions for you."

"I expect you will. But you won't want to do that in my husband's presence, right?"

"That's right."

"And the answer is 'no,' by the way."

"What's the question?"

"I wasn't with my husband the night of the accident. I was working a shift at the St. Isidore's emergency room."

I nodded. "So no easy alibi testimony."

"If there were, we might not be here. See you in a bit, Edge."

"Thanks, Care."

With that, Carissa Carson-Fleece left the room by what I assumed was the shortest, most direct way out.

I sat back down and shuffled through the manila folders Carissa had left before sliding them to the side in a pile that I'm not sure she would have found to be satisfactory. I flipped a page on my legal pad and said, "So, where were you at the time of the accident?"

"I don't know exactly—I was home most of the day but sometime between six and seven, I went over to Snyder Funeral Home."

"Why's that?"

"Theo's funeral had been the day before and a number of people had donated checks to Pillars in his name. The director called and asked if I'd like to pick them up, so I did."

I scribbled. "Who's Theo?"

"Theo Plutides, one of the seniors Benjamin worked with at Pillars. Theo had died a few days before and his funeral was held the day before Benjamin died. It was Theo's dog, Roxie, that Benjamin was walking when he was killed."

I looked up. "I'm lost, Edge. You need to start at the beginning."

Edge raised a hand. "Sorry. Pillars has an independent living outreach program. There are a number of folks in our community who have physical challenges but can still live on their own if they have just a bit of help. Theo Plutides needed a hand. Benjamin Trane worked for us and helped Theo out."

I looked at Carissa's folder marked "Benjamin Trane." "So Trane worked for Pillars in the independent living outreach program?"

Edge nodded. "He had a knack for it."

"What did he do?"

"Just about anything. He had a list of people he checked in on every day and he would just do whatever needed to be done."

"Like?"

Edge smiled. "It would be easier to say what didn't he do. Small household repairs, pick up medications, arrange for lawn mowing or snow shoveling or major repairs, taking pets to the vet. And good Lord, you would not believe how much time he spent fixing settings on smartphones and computers." Edge's smile faded. "He was a good man."

Edge looked up, "So anyway, one of the people on Benjamin's list was Theo Plutides. Theo had always been a big supporter of Pillars, but in the last few years he'd had more health challenges and Benjamin stepped right in to help. Benjamin took it pretty hard when Theo passed."

"And that was right before Benjamin died?"

Edge nodded. "A little less than a week. Theo's funeral was the night before Benjamin was killed. Like I said, that's why I was out—Theo had requested that all memorial donations be made to Pillars, and I was going over to pick up checks that people had left at the funeral home the day before."

"So you were out driving the night that Benjamin Trane was killed?"

"For a little bit, yes."

"Where?"

"From my house to Snyder Funeral Home and back."

"Did you go anywhere else?"

"Not that I can think of, no."

I looked at Danny.

"Routes, got it," he said.

"What time?" I said.

Edge held out his hands. "I really don't know, between six and seven probably."

I looked at another folder Carissa had left. "So tell me about this deer."

Edge shook his head. "That was something, let me tell you. I was coming back from work late, we're trying to get financing for a healthcare clinic, and a deer shot out of nowhere and jumped right into my van."

"Driver's side or passenger?"

"Passenger side, in the front though."

"What did you do?"

"I stopped, but it took off. The van was drivable, so I went home."

"Did you call the police?"

Edge frowned. "The deer wasn't there and no one was hurt. Should I have?"

"Not necessarily. Just looking for things we can use."

"Ah. Well, no, I didn't."

"So this was late on the night of February 16?"

"Yes."

"The night before Benjamin Trane was killed?"

"Yes."

"Did you tell Carissa about it when you got home?"

"No, she was working a shift at the hospital."

"I see. How about the next morning?"

Edge shook his head. "She was still at the hospital. She picked up a second shift."

"Okay. Did you call anyone about the van during the day on February 17?"

"No, we were under the gun with the health clinic financing proposal, so I went to work on it first thing."

"At the office? Did you drive the van in to the office?"

"No. I worked at home that day. I get interrupted all the time at the office and I really needed to work through the proposal. I talked to a few people if that helps."

"On the phone?"

"Yes."

"Who?"

"Dawn Blackwell. Lynn Horvath. Greg Kilbane. Maybe Carissa but I try not to bother her at work."

"Did you tell any of them about the deer?"

Edge sighed. "I was really focused on the financing."

"So no?"

"No."

"Did anyone see the van that day? Did you show it to anyone?"

"It was in our garage all day until I went over to the funeral home that night."

"Did someone see it then?"

"Not that I know of. Maybe the director, Robert Snyder, did."

I set down my pen. "You know this is a problem, right?"

"I'm beginning to see that. But I didn't kill Benjamin."

"I understand. But I'm looking for ways to prove it. We're going to need to put our hands on everything we can that shows where you were and—"

Edge's phone buzzed. "Excuse me." He scrolled through and then looked up, embarrassed. "I'm really sorry, but I have to get back. We've had a, well, it's just a situation."

"We have more work to do Edge," I said.

"I know, but so do I. Besides, I told you the most important thing."

"What's that?"

"I wasn't there and I didn't do it."

"Right."

"Wait," said Danny. "Didn't Carissa just take your car?"

"She did. Greg Kilbane is going to pick me up." Edge stood and stuck out his hand. "I appreciate all your help, Nate. Tell my wife that we finished, will you?"

"Edge, anything you tell me is confidential and I won't reveal it to anybody else. But I also won't lie for you."

Edge smiled. "Good to know. Then tell her that Greg took me back to Pillars."

"Aren't you going to tell her?"

"Eventually. But I bet she checks in with you first." His phone buzzed again. "He's here." Edge waved again and left.

Danny waited until the door closed then said, "What do you think?"

I looked at Danny. "A deer? Working from home?"

Danny slouched. "I was hoping it was just me."

"This is usually when you say *I* sure know how to pick them."

"True," said Danny.

"Danny, you sure know how to pick them."

"I don't think he did it."

I grinned. "I'll expect more respect from you the next time I say that." I thought. "I already have Olivia on Plutides and Trane. You'll re-create Edge's routes for the day before and the day of the accident?"

Danny nodded, wrote on his pad, then said, "I have a referral source meeting this afternoon. I'll get on it first thing in the morning."

"Referral sources? For criminal cases?"

"Estate planning."

"Are you sure this isn't tempting you to rethink the whole trial lawyer thing?"

"Not even a little."

I smiled. "Have fun."

"Thanks."

Danny had just gone to his office when my phone buzzed. There was no name attached to the number, but that was just because I hadn't entered it yet.

"Hello, Carissa."

"Is Edge there, Nate? He's not picking up."

"He left just a bit ago."

Silence.

"He said to tell you Greg was picking him up."

More silence, then, "I see. Did he stay for the whole meeting?"

"Most of it. I understand you didn't see him the night of the deer accident or the next day before Benjamin Trane was killed."

"I worked a shift the night before, then a doc called off, so I picked up another one the next day."

"So you didn't see the van after the deer accident but before Benjamin's accident?"

"No, I was at the hospital the whole time."

"Carissa, I'm going to need any information, anything at all, that shows where Edge was the day before and the day of the accident. Texts, emails, calls, receipts, anything."

"I understand."

"Anyway you can help will, well, it will help."

"I'll work on it."

"Thanks."

As we hung up, I had no doubt that she would.

6

I went to the Brickhouse that night after work. A new guy I hadn't met before scanned my card and went back to checking his phone. When I asked, he said that Olivia would be back around eleven to lock up and that Cade was off for the day.

I thanked him. He nodded without looking up.

I changed in the locker room then came out and grabbed a bench. Turnout was light that night—there was one woman working on the heavy bag and a guy pedaling aimlessly on a stationary bike but there was no one in the free weight area. The scrape and clang of plates onto the bar echoed in the big space of the empty gym.

It took the clattering of plates for three more sets before I figured out the problem and said, "Hey, Gage!"

The young man at the desk stared down at his phone for a couple more beats before he looked up.

"How about some music?"

He nodded and turned in that pointing circular way of somebody looking for something that had been shown to him some time before. Then he ducked down and, a few seconds later, sound blasted out of speakers and a bass rhythm pulsed through the concrete.

I didn't recognize the song, but it filled the space.

7

When I came to the office the next day, Danny jumped up from his desk and came out to meet me. He stumbled, caught his balance on the doorjamb, then said, "So I was at the reception and didn't think much would happen but then I started talking to Spencer and it turns out he has a bunch of contacts that need estate planning services, and he's not happy with the people he's referring them to and he'd heard of us, well, he'd heard of you, and I mentioned that we were branching out and he said he'd send us something and if we were responsive and the client was happy, he would be sending us more so—"

I didn't want to interrupt him, but I had no idea what he was talking about. I raised my hand. Danny stopped.

"Where did you go, Danny?"

"To a young lawyer and financial planner cocktail hour."

"Who did you meet?"

Danny took a deep breath. "Spencer Martel."

"And he is?"

"He runs a financial services company, Martel Financial. Maybe more than one."

"He's young?"

"Not really. He's probably forty."

I was closer to thirty than forty, but barely, so I smiled at Danny's description of my fleeting youth.

Danny didn't notice as he continued. "Spencer was there to meet new estate planners. He said he always has potential clients who need estate planning services, and he likes to find people he can work with who will refer back to him for other financial services."

"That's how it works. Sounds promising."

Danny nodded. "We hit it off, but I figured it was just polite conversation. Except then I had an email first thing this morning. I think he's going to refer us some work!"

"That sounds like a great lead. Let me know if I can help."

"You've done estate planning?"

"Not a lick. But I will sign checks if you need more training."

"Thanks!"

"Let me know when the first file comes in and we can talk about how to set it up."

"Perfect."

"I know it's not as exciting as drafting a will, but we have vehicular homicide to discuss."

"Right, right." The glow went out of Danny's face. "I haven't done any work on Edge's routes yet."

"I didn't think you had. Why don't you start with that, and I'm going to call Olivia to get her on board."

Danny nodded and, now that the excitement from his new lead had dissipated, made it back to his desk without incident.

I grabbed some coffee, went to my office, and gave Olivia a call.

"Hey, Shep," she said. "I see you weren't a total slacker last night."

"Saw it?"

"I check the membership scans. Look like you cut it a little short but at least it was something."

"Actually, my all-seeing fitness overlord, I added some things. Attendance was light, so I didn't have to wait for anything."

"Likely story."

"You'd know if you'd been there. What were you up to?"

"I had another engagement."

"Oh? Did it involve a cardiology consult?"

"If it did, that would be confidential doctor-patient information."

I chuckled. "For him, not you."

"Damn lawyer."

"So that's a 'yes'?"

"Of course. So I have your Fleece and Pillars research. I haven't gotten to Benjamin Trane yet."

"That's okay. You're probably still focused on your heartbeat."

"My cardiologist certainly is. So Edgerton Fleece goes to Baylor University for undergrad, majors in philosophy and economics. Comes up to Northwestern, gets an advanced degree in the economics part. Hops from there over to Princeton and gets a Ph.D. in the philosophy part."

"So a professional student?"

"At that point, it sure seemed like it. From there, he bounced around between some churches and some service organizations."

"Doing what?"

"That's not clear. He was never on the actual staff at any of these places, but there are plenty of pictures and mentions that show he's always around. And then, for about two years, he just disappears."

"How do you do that?"

"It's not easy, I can tell you, but he did a good job. For two years, he's just gone. No social media, no mentions in any staffing, nothing. Then he shows up out of nowhere in Nashville, meets Carissa Carson, who six months later becomes Carissa Carson-Fleece, and the two of them move up here to Carrefour."

I did the math. "Was she in medical school?"

"She'd just finished at Vanderbilt. She landed a family practice residency up here with LGL University and while she did that for the next year, Edge established the base for Pillars."

"I see what you did there."

"It's the little things that get you up in the morning."

"Clever. What was the base?"

"From what I can see, he started a food pantry. He rented a small space over by Route 484, recruited a few volunteers, and started passing out food. What's really interesting, though, is how Pillars started to grow."

"Oh?"

"From what I can see, Edge pitched churches directly and sold them on the idea that they can do more good collectively than standing alone. He gets churches to fund the pantry—with food, money, volunteers, whatever they can spare—and by the time Dr. Carson-Fleece was done with her residency, Pillars was the biggest food pantry in Carrefour. From there, Pillars started a daycare where single parents get the services for free. And a rideshare to take seniors to doctors' appointments. And before too long, it expanded into a meal delivery program and an independent living program and, most recently, a couple of free clinic days per month where Carissa provides free medical care."

"Wow."

"How do they do all that, you ask?"

Silence.

Finally, I said, "How did they do all that, Liv?"

"Glad you asked, Shep. Donations."

"Seems typical for a charity."

"It is. Except Edge has the foresight to incorporate and create a board that is made up of his biggest church sponsors."

"So there's more buy-in for his mission?"

"You got it. And it just keeps growing. Then flash forward to a month ago and you have one of the biggest providers of charitable services in the city with one of the biggest bodies of volunteers in the city that's moved into one of the biggest charitable facilities in the city that's now looking to make a run at starting the largest free medical clinic of its kind in the city."

"Okay?"

"And then its CEO kills a man with his car."

"Allegedly."

"Allegedly."

There was silence for a few moments. Liv knew me well enough to let it sit there before I said, "It sounds like Pillars' footprint is everywhere."

"Footprints. And yes."

"How have I not known more about this?"

Liv laughed. "Have you met yourself?"

"Apparently not." I thought. "Did Pillars put out any posts related to the accident?"

"Not directly. It put out a statement regarding the tragic passing of beloved employee Benjamin Trane and the obit certainly mentioned Benjamin's association with Pillars and all the ways he helped but nothing that indicated there was any relationship between Benjamin's death and Fleece's car until two months later when he was arrested."

"What do you have on Trane?"

A sigh from the other end of the phone.

"Right, right, right, you said you hadn't gotten to him yet. Sorry."

"I mean the information genie did just magically grant you two informational wishes."

"She did."

"Jumping right to three seems greedy."

"Can I wish for more wishes?"

"You'd have to rub the lamp first."

"Seems to me the genie might rip my arm off if I did that."

"Certainly if you didn't buy her dinner first."

"Thanks, Liv. I owe you."

"Don't worry. The bill's on the way."

Liv reminded me that one workout on one day did not prevent a person from becoming a jelly-filled dough ball, I promised I'd stop by the Brickhouse that night, and we hung up.

I took a moment to digest the information the Liv-genie had just delivered. It was interesting that Edge had grown one of the biggest independent charities in Carrefour, but it really didn't matter one way or the other for what I had to do, which was defend him from the accusation that he'd run down Benjamin Trane and killed him. Although I was just diving into it, it seemed that there were two big issues on that score—where Edge had actually been at the time of the accident and the convenient collision with a deer the night before.

I'd had two meetings with Fleece and didn't think a third would give me any more information on where he'd been. So I decided to see someone who might.

8

When I arrived back at Pillars this time, I didn't have Danny to guide me, so I followed the signs that led me from the visitor section of the parking lot through the lobby and past the man in the vest to the side stair, then up to the administrative offices on the third floor. Mrs. Horvath smiled at me as I came through the door, lifted one finger slightly, then turned back to the woman standing in front of her.

"I'm sorry, Dawn, but he has the service luncheon that day."

The woman standing in front of Mrs. Horvath's desk could not have been more than five feet tall. Her blonde hair fell around her shoulders, and she was dressed in the dark pants and dark blue Pillars pullover that was the unofficial uniform of the place. I recognized her from the last time I had been here; not so much by her face, but by the oversized binder she held crossed in her arms. Her eyes looked tired, with the faintest hint of dark circles, as she tilted her head to the side and said, "How about after?"

Mrs. Horvath looked at her computer. "He has a facility meeting for the health clinic."

"And after that?"

"Story-time at the daycare."

"And after that?"

"He's visiting patients at St. Wendelin's."

"When will he be done?"

"He's scheduled to be done at seven but you know how he is. I wouldn't plan on anything before eight-thirty p.m. Do you want me to schedule you for eight forty-five?"

"Lynn, you know the day care closes at six."

Mrs. Horvath nodded. "You said this was important, so I didn't know if you could make an exception."

The blonde woman didn't lift her foot, but she certainly ground her heel into the floor. "I've already used too many late pick-ups. I should be able to get a meeting with our chief executive officer during business hours to discuss our audit and taxes."

"Of course, Dawn. That's why I suggested two weeks from Tuesday."

The blonde woman shook her head. "That's too far away."

Mrs. Horvath looked at her computer screen. "Do you really need the whole afternoon?"

"To go through the books of a multi-million-dollar organization with a budget of"—the blond woman stopped and glanced at me before she continued—"Yes, I really need his whole afternoon. Or a morning."

"Then it really will be two weeks."

The woman looked as if she were biting the inside of her cheek. "I need Edge to prioritize this."

"I think that's exactly what he's done, Dawn."

Dawn had the appearance of someone counting before she said, "Put me in for that Tuesday then. But you have to let me know if there's a cancellation."

"Of course." Mrs. Horvath fingers clattered across the

keyboard before she flipped a finger at me and said, "This is Mr. Shepherd, Mr. Fleece's attorney."

Dawn turned to me, and the binder seemed bigger and the circles under her eyes seemed blacker when I faced her straight on. She held out a hand around the thick binder and said, "Dawn Blackwell."

"Nate."

"Well, I hope Edge's attorney has more luck than his CFO, Nate."

"I could cancel story-time," said Mrs. Horvath. "But I know how much Dana likes it."

Dawn Blackwell pursed her lips. "Low blow."

Mrs. Horvath's serene smile stayed in place, and she shrugged.

"Nice to meet you, Nate," Dawn Blackwell said, and hustled off with her binder.

"So, you're the guardian of the schedule?" I said.

Mrs. Horvath turned to me without a second glance at the retreating CFO. "I'm afraid I am. But you didn't have to come down to make an appointment, Mr. Shepherd. You can call me anytime."

"I'm not here to make an appointment, Mrs. Horvath. I'm here to see if you can fill me in on Edge's schedule from a couple of months back."

Mrs. Horvath smiled. "That's easy enough. What date are we looking for?"

"February 16 and 17."

Mrs. Horvath's face became suitably grave. "The accident, of course." Her mouse moved in tiny circles and clicked once, twice, three, times before she said, "There we go."

"Great. Could you print me a copy?"

"Already done." A small printer hummed on top of her desk.

"I've emailed you a copy as well," she said as she handed me the paper.

I glanced at the little hour blocks for the two days. "The 16th looked busy."

"It was going to be normal, but Mr. Plutides' funeral was that day so I had to stack everything up before and after."

"I see. Did the meetings go all the way until ten that night?"

"At least. I left then, but Edge was still working."

That was consistent with Edge telling me he'd been on his way home that night at eleven-thirty when he hit the deer. I looked at the next day.

"The 17th looks pretty clear."

"Looks can be deceiving. Edge was home all day working on getting the health clinic financing proposal done."

"Did you talk to him?"

"Oh, yes. Many times. I had to move quite a few things around."

"Did he mention any other reason for staying at home?"

"Why would he need another reason?"

"Oh, he didn't, I just wondered if he mentioned one."

"I'm not surprised Mr. Fleece decided to stay home to finish up. Everyone is always looking for him when he's here."

"Like Ms. Blackwell?"

Mrs. Horvath nodded. "Exactly like Ms. Blackwell."

"How about the night of the 17th?"

"I didn't schedule anything for that night either."

"Edge mentioned going to the funeral home?"

"Oh yes, Mr. Snyder did call and tell me about the donations. I called Mr. Fleece and told him. I offered to pick them up, but it was after office hours, so he said he'd do it."

"Anything else he was doing that day that you can think of?"

"No. None of his regularly scheduled monthly meetings were set for that night and I don't see any events listed."

"Do you handle Dr. Fleece's scheduling too?"

Mrs. Horvath straightened, her face neutral. "Dr. Carson-Fleece manages her own schedule."

"I suppose that makes sense with handling call and such."

Mrs. Horvath nodded.

"Thank you, Mrs. Horvath. I appreciate your help."

"You are most certainly welcome, Mr. Shepherd."

"It seems like you're the one to call if I need time with Edge?"

She nodded. "Mr. Fleece says you are to have the highest priority."

"Thanks," I said.

"Support for all," she said with a smile, and I hadn't made it more than two steps before the phone rang and Mrs. Horvath answered, "Pillars Outreach, how may I help you?"

I decided to take the elevator down the two floors, and I promise not to tell Olivia if you don't. As I went, I looked at Edge's schedule for February 16 and 17. On the 16th, every hour had an appointment, including lunch, until ten o'clock at night. I didn't try to puzzle out what they all were—some were obvious, and some had abbreviations that I would have to ask Edge about, but the fact was that every hour was scheduled from seven-thirty a.m. until ten p.m.

And then on February 17 there was nothing.

Not a single thing to show what Edge might have been doing instead of killing Benjamin Trane.

9

I stopped back at the office on the way home. I touched base with Danny, who was excited because he had received some more materials from that guy Spencer Martel that he'd met at the young lawyer's reception. I told him that I hadn't had any luck establishing where Edge had been, which reminded him that I had a message on the general number from the prosecutor's office from a lawyer named Ryan Pompeo.

I think I mentioned that we don't have a secretary, at first because I couldn't afford it and now because we'd managed so long without one. Most people reach us by cell phone or email now anyway, but we kept a general number that we used to unofficially screen calls. It was unusual for a lawyer to call the general number and I didn't recognize the name as I hit the button for the message.

"Hey, NATO, this is Ryan Pompeo over at the prosecutor's office. I saw your appearance in the Fleece case. I'll be handling that one so I was touching base to see if we can move this thing along and free up all of our time. Give me a call."

Two things were unusual about the message. First, prosecutors never reached out first. They were always too busy and most of them thought it was a sign of weakness.

Second, no one ever called me NATO. I mean, come on.

I called.

"Pompeo here."

"Ryan, Nate Shepherd."

"Hey, NATO! Thanks for calling me back. So, you're on this Fleece disaster?"

"I don't know that I would call it a disaster, Ryan."

"Really? Running over a man and scaring his dog doesn't seem like the *best* way to start your day."

"I'm not aware of any evidence that my client did that."

"No, I don't suppose you would be since you haven't received our file yet."

"We don't have to wait for the file, Ryan. If you have a witness or video or something that you want to tell me about, I'm happy to listen."

"Ha! I'm sure you are. And if you have any alibis or witnesses that put Fleece somewhere else, I'm happy to listen too."

"I'm not the one who has to prove anything."

"Okay, so I take it you don't have any alibi evidence."

"I didn't say that."

"I know you didn't say that, but you didn't say that you have some either."

"I don't have to."

"Easy, NATO, we're not in front of a judge here. I was just calling to find out if you have any information for me that'll move this case along."

"What do you mean?"

"I mean, do you have any information that would make me want to drop this from a vehicular homicide to vehicular manslaughter?"

"Are you offering that?"

"Would you accept that?"

"I can't say that I would right now."

"Then I can't say that I'm offering it right now. You let me know though if you gin up some evidence to make this go away or if you're interested in pleading it out."

"I won't do the first. Sure on the second."

"No reason we can't cut through the bullshit and move this case."

"Okay."

"I'm not going to yank your chain just to yank it."

"I appreciate that."

"This town is too small, and life is too short."

"True."

"Okay, NATO. Thanks for calling back. Let me know if you think of something."

"Will do, Ryan."

We hung up. When we did, I could not say that I felt any better about Ryan Pompeo, our case, or the use of treaty organizations as nicknames.

AFTER RYAN'S call I was ready to wrap up for the day, so I turned off the lights, locked up the office, and headed over to the Brickhouse. I did my thing and afterward talked to Cade for a while. Cade is Olivia's brother, owns the gym with her, and runs a bond business. We hadn't seen each other in a couple of weeks so we were catching up and he was telling me about a client who broke bond because he absolutely, positively had to see Eminem in concert and if you're going to see Eminem in concert you really have to get some weed and you can't smoke all that weed by yourself so you pretty much have to pick up your cousins who live practically next door just over the state line which, you have to admit, is invisible so how, just how, can going to an Eminem concert be a bond violation?

Cade was still chuckling at his own impersonation when his phone buzzed. He looked at it and said, "Sorry, Nate. Gotta go."

"Sure. Emergency?"

"For someone. Grab a beer tomorrow?"

"Sure. See you."

Cade waved and was out the door. I gathered my things and headed out too.

I thought about walking over to the Railcar, but I had already eaten barbecue twice that week. Nothing on my way home appealed to me either—I didn't feel like being good in the neighborhood or having it my way or seeing if, in fact, they had all the meats, so I kept on driving.

I arrived home to a dark house and was staring into the fridge contemplating subsistence on chicken breasts—again—when my phone buzzed. It was my sister-in-law, Izzy.

"Brother of my husband, you do not return my calls."

"I certainly do, Iz."

"Not lately. Mark and I need a favor."

Mark was my youngest brother.

"Sure. What's up?"

"We're going to a Red Wings game Saturday night with a few couples. Are you available?"

"Izzy, I appreciate it, but I don't really want to go to Detroit with someone I haven't met—"

"Well, look who's all full of himself! I wasn't calling to ask you to go—I was calling to see if you could babysit the boys. They always love it when you come over and James said you're halfway through whatever that sword and sorcery book is that you've been reading to them."

I was glad she couldn't see my face over the phone. "Sorry, I thought you meant—"

"I know, you think I might know some woman whose idea of a good time is spending a Saturday night with a morose lawyer, but I'll be damned if I do. I can see how you could get confused though."

"I mean, you're always—"

"Yes, I am always trying to ruin my friends' perfectly good Saturday nights. So, are you available?"

"For the boys? Of course."

"Great! Can you be over around five? The game's at eight."

"Sure, Iz. I'll see you then."

I hung up, relieved that Izzy wasn't trying to set me up again and looking forward to spending some time with my three nephews. Then I went back to contemplating what the contents of my fridge proved about the fundamental nature of my existence.

For the record, I made an egg stir-fry and decided to live the bold life by adding some peppers to it.

10

My meetings with Edge and Mrs. Horvath hadn't revealed an easy alibi that would establish that Edge was somewhere else when Benjamin Trane was killed. So the next morning when I arrived in the office, I dug into everything about the accident itself.

I started with the police report that was drafted the night of the accident. At six-thirty p.m. on February 17, multiple witnesses reported hearing a crash. The first 911 call was made by the property owner where the accident occurred, a woman named Sharon Pepperstone. Responding officers found Benjamin Trane lying on the ground beneath an oak tree, bleeding, semi-conscious, and alive. A dog was next to him, barking. The rescue squad arrived simultaneously and transported Mr. Trane to the hospital. I already knew that he died on the way.

Although it had snowed a few days before, the weather that night was clear, warm for February in Ohio which meant right around freezing, and the road was dry. There was no indication why the vehicle may have lost control.

I don't know if you've ever read a police accident report but there's a section at the back where the officer draws a simple picture to re-create what happened. Here, it just showed a rectangle, labelled as "#1," swerving off the road, up Mrs. Pepperstone's driveway, along the sidewalk, and into Benjamin Trane, who was marked with a "#2." There was a dotted line, then the "#2" was written again next to a squiggly circle representing a tree. The drawing then showed the car continuing in a semicircle back onto the road. Though the roads themselves were clear, there had been enough snow on the ground to see the tire tracks.

Besides Mrs. Pepperstone, the responding officer took statements from two other witnesses, who were neighbors. Although all of them heard the crash and the barking dog, none of them saw the accident, none of them saw the car, and certainly none of them saw Edgerton Fleece.

I set the report aside and hopped onto the court's online docket to check the filings in the case. The prosecutor, Ryan Pompeo, had filed an indictment against Edge, which meant that he had presented the case in secret to a grand jury, which had found that there was enough evidence to support a charge against Edge of vehicular homicide and failure to stop at the scene of an accident.

Here's the screwy thing—the State of Ohio can accuse you of killing someone and arrest you, but it doesn't have to say how you did it or include any particular facts about what happened or why in the indictment itself. Instead, the indictment can just read, like the one here, that "the grand jurors, by the authority of the State of Ohio, do find and present that Edgerton Fleece on the 17th day of February in the city of Carrefour did negligently and recklessly cause the death of Benjamin Trane while operating a motor vehicle and subsequently failed to stop at the scene of that accident contrary to the form of the statute in such case made and provided and against the peace and dignity of the State of Ohio."

That's it. No description of what happened, no description of why, and certainly no description of the evidence that the indictment was based on. No, the State can start this whole process without telling you a damn thing and that's what it had done here.

To be fair, a lot of times the lawyer can still tell how his client is linked to the crime. You know, the police arrested the guy at the gas station with a gun in his hand or broke up a fight outside the bar, or, with car accidents, found the defendant in a wrecked vehicle at the scene. In a case like Edge's, though, where the arrest was made a couple of months later and the accused is uncertain of his connection to the crime, or is unwilling to discuss it, it's a lot more difficult to figure out what's what. Sure there are ways for the defense attorney to find out what the State has—bills of particulars, discovery, *Brady* disclosures, all those procedural things. But they have one thing in common—they all take time.

Edge had told me that he wasn't involved. Pompeo, though, had presented something to the grand jury connecting Edge or his van or both to the crime that night and the grand jury had decided that it was good enough for them.

And I'm not going to lie—Edge's story about hitting a deer was making me very, very nervous.

I pulled out Carissa's folder on the "deer accident." It held a copy of an insurance claim form for the damage. It listed February 16 as the date the deer was struck. I checked the date the claim form was submitted.

February 18. The day after Trane was killed.

The "deer folder" also contained an invoice from an auto body shop called Carrefour Collision. It listed repairs to the front fender, right headlight, hood, and right quarter panel. All consistent with hitting a deer.

Or a man.

I set aside the "deer folder" along with my concern and spent the rest of the morning drafting requests for disclosures from the prosecution. It would take them a while to get me the information, but I wanted to get that clock ticking. I checked the court's docket sheet, saw that it had scheduled a pretrial for that Friday, and calendared it up.

It was almost lunchtime when I heard someone come in the main office door. I was on my way out to our small reception area when I heard Danny's voice. "Mr. Wernicke, Mrs. Wernicke, I'm Daniel Reddy, so nice to meet you. Did you find the office okay? Yes indeed, the elevator is slow for only going up three floors but you're here now. Fantastic."

I came out to find Danny offering to take the coats of a couple who looked to be in their early eighties. The man wore a blue sport coat and the woman a print dress that both looked as if they were in the regular rotation for going to church. I smiled, unable to help myself. There was a generation that still believed that was how to dress when they went to see their lawyer.

Danny had a pair of London Fog trench coats hung over one arm when he said, "Nate, this is Mr. and Mrs. Wernicke."

I smiled, introduced myself, and shook their hands.

"The Wernickes are here to make some changes to their estate plan."

Mr. Wernicke, a short man with large glasses, said, "Mr. Martel over at Martel Financial said Mr. Reddy here is the man to see for that kind of thing."

I smiled. "He certainly is."

"Would you all like some coffee or water?" said Danny.

"Coffee for me," said Mr. Wernicke.

"Water would be delightful," said Mrs. Wernicke.

Danny froze, realizing he had two London Fogs in one hand and a note pad and pens in the other.

"Why don't you all get started in the conference room," I said as I took the London Fogs off Danny's hands. "I'll bring you the drinks."

Danny gave me a quick smile and ushered the Wernickes into the conference room. I hung up the coats, delivered the drinks, then excused myself and went to start my own inspection of 5436 Sunnyfield Drive.

11

Harvest Township is in the southernmost section of Carrefour. It's technically part of the city, but it's somehow carved out its own services and school board and taxes. There's no sign marking the border and there's no clear line from one street to the next except that, after you've traveled a little ways into Harvest, you realize that the houses are a little bigger and the speed limits are a little lower and, when you pass the high school, you'll notice that the student parking lot is filled with vehicles that are inordinately nicer than any sixteen-year-old should be driving.

Sunnyfield Drive was a good portion of the way into Harvest Township, not among the smaller houses on the border but not quite all the way into the massive estate section either. Sunnyfield was also one of several "through drives," roads which the common folk, such as lawyers from Michigan, might use within Harvest Township when getting from one part of Carrefour to another, as opposed to some of Harvest's more isolated, winding roads where outsiders were more recognizable.

About half a mile from my destination, I stopped at a traffic light at the intersection of Sunnyfield and Coulter. I waited then proceeded, noticing a number of side streets with names like Orchard and Grove and Turtle Dove and Poppy Bloom.

There were no address markers out on the streets, presumably because you weren't meant to stop if you didn't know where you were going. I slowed a little so I could read the numbers on houses, which wasn't easy given their distance from the road and their frequent obstruction by bushes and trees. I caught the odd number, though, so I had a sense of where I was and figured I was getting close. Then I saw the enormous oak tree up on the right and knew I was there.

I slowed down a little more. The road ran straight at this section, continuing on to a traffic light in the distance. There was a sidewalk on the right between the road and the oak tree. There were streetlights spaced evenly along the road but not precisely here.

I turned into the cement driveway of 5436 Sunnyfield, which was right before the oak tree when you came from this direction. I idled up the drive, which was a good length and lined with ornamental pear trees, to the walk that led to the front door.

The house was a sprawling brick ranch, built in a style that was on the rich side of respectable in the 1960s and a little on the modest and dated side now. The yard was filled with oversized trees that were probably planted with the house.

I had barely stepped out of my Jeep when a woman shot out the front door onto the porch. She was using one of those hand-carved wooden canes, the kind with no cushion on the handle and a gnarled, rugged shaft, and before I could say hello, she was halfway down the walk.

"Mrs. Pepperstone?" I said. When she kept coming, I broke into a half jog to try to meet her halfway.

She didn't stop at the end of the walk but instead turned down the driveway. "Keep up," she said.

"Mrs. Pepperstone, that's not necessary."

"You're here about the accident, aren't you?"

"Yes, ma'am."

"Well, how are you going to learn about the accident if you don't see where it happened?"

"That does seem best."

"Hmph. You figured out how to tie that tie this morning, so I suppose you're not a total skull-rattler." She cocked her head at me. "You did tie that tie, didn't you? Not one of those derelicts that leave it tied up in a knot and slip it over his head in the morning?"

"No, ma'am. I mean, yes ma'am, I did tie it."

"Hmph," was all she said, and I found that I had to increase my pace to keep up with her cane-assisted gait.

"Are you going to introduce yourself or not?" she said.

"Of course, I'm sorry. I'm—"

"It seems like the least you could do when you show up unannounced in my driveway."

"Yes ma'am, of course, I'm—"

"I'm an old woman. You could be dangerous."

"I'm Nate Shepherd. I'm a lawyer."

"Ah, so not dangerous. Just annoying."

There didn't seem to be anything to say to that, especially since it seemed that I'd done nothing to disprove her experience so far.

She continued, punctuating each sentence with a clack of her cane. "Although you're not as rude as the last one, calling me Sharon as soon as he knocked on the door. Is that good manners where you come from?"

"No, ma'am."

"No indeed. My Johnny would've popped him on the spot, God rest him."

That seemed to be all she had to say for the moment, so I followed the verbal whirlwind that was Mrs. Sharon Pepperstone down the drive. She was of middling height and broad in a way that didn't convey the softness of age but rather the strength to step up in her dear departed Johnny's stead and pop you one if you deserved it. Her golden-brown hair likely came from a box, and I can't imagine that anyone would ever say so. Fine lines covered the corners of her eyes and descended like starbursts down her cheeks. I knew from the police report that she was seventy-six years old, and I would have said that she looked it except that the energy with which she excoriated me made her seem twenty years younger.

"All right," she said, pointing her cane. "That's the oak tree, which I assume you're not too dense to figure out. The car came from *there*"—she pointed back up the way I have driven in—"and hit him *there*, in the middle of the sidewalk, and threw him *there* into the side of the tree we're looking at."

"You didn't see it, did you?"

"Of course I didn't see the accident. Didn't you read the accident report?"

"I did."

"Then you know I didn't see it!"

"How do you know? What happened, I mean?"

Mrs. Sharon Pepperstone rolled her eyes. "Because there was snow on the ground and I could see the tracks coming in and I could see the tracks going out and I could see the blood in the snow and the body by my tree. Cripes-sakes alive, you youngsters need to see everything on your phone, or it didn't happen." She raised an eyebrow at me. "Aren't you going to write this down?"

My mouth twitched. "I'll take notes on my phone when I leave."

She stared at me for a full beat before she said, "So I heard the crash, and I wasn't sure what it was, but then I heard Roxie bark and I knew right away it was her."

"Roxie?"

"The dog! Are you sure you tied your own tie this morning? Do you think a man was out here barking? It was the dog."

"I didn't know her name was Roxie."

"For cripes-sakes, I said 'bark,' didn't I? That's a pretty good clue I was talking about the dog, don't you think?"

"Yes, ma'am, it is. I meant, how did you know her name was Roxie?"

Mrs. Sharon Pepperstone rolled her eyes. "Because I knew her, of course. The kids didn't call you Sherlock growing up, did they?"

"No, ma'am."

"No kidding."

I decided to ask my question and take my beating. "How did you know Roxie?"

"A dog walks by your house twice a day for seven years, you get to know her."

I blinked. "Benjamin Trane walked by your house for seven years?"

"Are you deaf and slow?"

"I'm trying to speed up, ma'am."

"Try harder. I didn't say Benjamin Trane walked by my house for seven years, did I?"

"No, ma'am."

"I said *Roxie* walked by my house twice a day for seven years."

"Yes, ma'am, you did. And who was with Roxie all those years?"

"Theo, of course."

"Theo Plutides?"

"Is there some other Theo that has a service dog named Roxie that Benjamin Trane worked for?"

"No, ma'am."

"Then of course, Theo Plutides! At least until he couldn't walk so good anymore. Then Benjamin took over."

"Where's Theo's house from here?"

"What do you mean…I already told Pompino or Pumpateo or whatever his name was."

"Pompeo?"

"That's the one, Pompeo—I already told him all about this. Don't the folks in your office talk?"

"I'm sure they do, but I'm not with his office."

Mrs. Sharon Pepperstone straightened. "I thought you said you're a lawyer?"

"I am. I represent Edgerton Fleece."

Just that quick, the tip of a gnarled wooden cane was pressed against my chest. "You should've said so in the first place. Get off my driveway."

"If you could just tell me—"

"The next thing I see better be your tail headed in the other direction."

Mrs. Sharon Pepperstone gave me a jab with her cane and seemed more willing to channel her dear departed Johnny than spend one moment more with me, so I turned my tail in the other direction.

I climbed into my Jeep and decided that any phone research could wait until I was gone. I backed out of the driveway, making sure I avoided Mrs. Sharon Pepperstone, who stood in her front yard and watched me go the whole way.

12

I drove up to the next traffic light, figuring it wouldn't do to stop in the road with Mrs. Sharon Pepperstone on patrol. I turned, then went up another mile, turned again, and found an EveryGround Coffee just outside the invisible line of Harvest Township where I could get a cup and do some quick research on my phone.

Once I had started the caffeination process, I looked up "Theo Plutides, Harvest Township." It took me a few tries to get the spelling right, but I eventually found an address, 333 Plowshare Drive, and a map. Plowshare Drive intersected with Sunnyfield Drive not more than one hundred yards from Mrs. Pepperstone's house. One turn to the right after her house would take a dog-walker down the street to the cul-de-sac where Theo Plutides had lived.

I took a last sip of coffee, then headed back to take a look.

I was coming to the Plutides' house from the opposite direction, so I didn't have to pass Mrs. Pepperstone again. I turned down Plowshare Drive where the houses were still old, but the lots were larger and the homes bigger and more eclectic.

I didn't have to drive far. At the far end of the cul-de-sac sat house number 333. There were stone walls on either side of the driveway that did not support a gate but sent the message that you'd best have a good reason for coming past. If the drive had been empty, I might have gone in except I saw a van in the driveway that said "Northwest Auction" on the side.

I stopped at the end of the driveway and looked. The house was a square, white two-story with a green slate roof and a large triangular pediment supported by four columns that covered the entire front porch. It was set far enough back from the road that I knew the lot must be bigger than it appeared from where I sat. The house seemed quiet except for the van, which I could now see read:

Northwest Auction
The Premier House for Fine Estates
Call BEST-BID today!

I looked at the house, then looked back up the road. All told, we weren't more than three hundred yards from Mrs. Pepperstone's house, well within dog-walking range. I took a last look, then headed out to see a man about a deer. I hoped.

CARREFOUR COLLISION WAS BACK in Carrefour proper, tucked away on a main road right next to a huge metal scrapping operation, which I suppose made a certain amount of sense. Its one-story building had faded red sides with a shiny silver roof, and it had a fenced-in back lot filled with dented and smashed vehicles of all sorts. A long sign ran along the roof line, announcing in bright yellow letters that Carrefour Collision was Your #1 Auto Body Shop. There were ten parking spaces out front, half of which were filled. I parked, went in, and got in line.

A man wearing a red ball cap with two yellow, interconnected “CCs” and a matching red shirt with a “Carrefour Collision” patch emblazoned on the left chest stood behind the counter. The man was helping each customer with a smooth efficiency, running down each item in the bills, pointing out each repair, and matter-of-factly explaining each item’s necessity and cost.

The man was unfailingly patient and explained any item, no matter how small, until the customer understood it. At the same time, he was steadfast and not the least bit defensive about any charge, no matter how outrageous the customer thought it might be. As I watched him work, it suddenly struck me that auto body shop owners experienced the same skepticism about the value of their services that lawyers do.

When it was my turn, I stepped up and said, “I’m looking for Rick Dalton.”

“You got him.” He turned and clicked a new screen open on his computer. “Are you picking up or dropping off?”

“Neither.”

“How can I help you then, sir?”

“I understand some detectives have spoken to you about the Edgerton Fleece repair. I’m here to talk to you about that.”

Rick Dalton didn't blink. He just glanced at the line behind me, which had grown to three customers, and said, “I have some folks waiting on their cars. I can give you a little time at lunch if you can wait...forty-five minutes or so.”

“Sure.”

He looked at me directly. “I’ll come out to your car.”

I supposed that there were better things for your business than to talk about homicides in your lobby.

“Will do. It’s the Jeep.”

Rick Dalton nodded, looked past me, and said, “Dropping off or picking up, ma’am?”

I took the hint and went out to my car.

The forty-five minutes turned into an hour, but I used it to put the finishing touches on a brief that Danny had drafted in another one of our cases and to listen to the talk radio's latest opinions on what the Detroit Lions should do in the upcoming draft—personally, I thought they should take an edge rusher instead of a quarterback but a collection of "insiders" seemed to differ. If the last twenty years were any indication, none of us really knew.

The front door opened, and Rick Dalton strode out. He was average height but thick in a move-hunks-of-metal kind of way as opposed to a lift-plates-of-iron kind of way.

I rolled the window down as he approached and said, "Thanks for—"

"I only have a couple of minutes. Ask what you need."

"Sure. I saw an invoice for work your shop did to repair a van for Edgerton Fleece. Do you remember that?"

"I do. The van was part of Pillars fleet, though, not Edge's own vehicle."

"Right. What did you do?"

"Replaced the right front quarter panel, pounded out a dent in the hood. Did the invoice say we replaced the headlight?"

"It did."

"Then that too."

"Do you remember who brought it in?"

"Yep. Edge."

"How do you remember that? Did you know him before?"

"I did."

"How?"

Rick Dalton squinted. "I don't know that that's your business."

I nodded. "Is the date on your estimate correct? It says February 18th."

"If that's what it says, that's when it was."

"That's the day he brought it in?"

"That's right."

"Do you know when it was done?"

"A couple of days later. I know we turned it around pretty quickly."

"How so?"

"I know he's pretty busy on the weekends, so we tried to get it back to him by then."

I nodded. "Did Edge tell you what happened?"

"He said he hit a deer."

"Does that happen this time of year?"

"Mister, it happens all year round."

"You've seen a lot of car versus deer accidents?"

He pointed at the sign. "They practically built the place."

"Did this look like one?"

"What do you mean?"

"The damage to the van. Did it look like what you see when a car hits a deer?"

"Sure, I mean the front right end was all banged up, there was some denting on top, and the headlight needed to be replaced."

"Was it drivable?"

"Yeah. It looked to me like the deer wasn't going that fast. Edge was lucky."

"That it didn't do more damage?"

"No. That it didn't come through the windshield and kill him."

The front door opened and another man in a red cap stuck his head out. "Rick! Bob's on the phone."

"Be right there! Gotta go," he said to me and started to walk away.

"Rick."

He stopped.

"How do you know it was a deer accident?"

"I told you, because the dents were right. And because of the blood."

"The blood?"

"It gets into all the cracks and crevices. You can't get it all out even if you wash it."

Then he walked away.

13

I was on my way back to the office when the phone buzzed with a number I didn't recognize. I hit the hands-free and answered.

"Nate Shepherd."

"NATO! It's Ryan Pompeo."

"Looks like I'm going to have to add you to my contacts, Ryan."

"You're not going to start ducking my calls now, are you?"

"Wouldn't dream of it."

"Good. Because then you'd miss all the sunshine and plea deals I bring."

"You haven't offered me a plea deal."

"I hope you're not this literal at parties, NATO. It would be a real drag."

"So I've been told."

"I haven't offered you a plea deal. I'm offering you one now."

"What's that?"

"Aggravated vehicular homicide based on recklessness and failure to stop after an accident resulting in death."

"Any sentencing recommendation?"

"The maximum five-year sentence but served concurrently with the fleeing charge. And a lifetime driver's license suspension, of course."

"Of course. That doesn't sound like a plea offer, Ryan."

"No?"

"No. It sounds more like your best day at trial."

"I suppose you could look at it that way. The other way to look at it is that you and I can avoid all this trial business and move on with our lives."

"It doesn't seem like my client would get to move on with his, though."

"Sure, he would. In five years. With the help of Uber, of course."

"I appreciate the call, Ryan, but that's not a serious offer."

"It is a serious offer, NATO. You know how serious?"

Silence.

"How serious, Ryan?"

"So serious that you have until the pretrial on Friday afternoon to accept it."

"So you're saying I have until this Friday for my client to accept an offer of a plea deal that would be your absolute best day at trial?"

"Exactly. Let me know what your client wants to do before the pretrial starts."

"This is a joke, right?"

"No joke. I told you, I'm serious."

"Then I can give you our answer right now."

"No, no, no, NATO—hey, I like that, it sounds like a song. No, I'm serious, which means you have to take the offer to your client."

"I think we both know what his answer will be."

"You never know. Things can change. By the start of the pretrial, NATO. Or call me now that I'm in your contacts."

Then he hung up.

I tapped my thumb on the steering wheel all the way back to the office.

~

As I was walking in, Danny was walking out.

"What's up?" I said.

Danny grinned. "Late lunch meeting with a new client."

"Oh, yeah?"

"Yeah. Another estate plan."

"From Martel again?"

"Yep."

"Congratulations!"

Danny's grin broadened. "Thanks!"

"Do you have a second before you go?"

"Literally that."

"Pompeo offered us a deal on Fleece."

"What was it?"

"Aggravated vehicular homicide and failure to stop at an accident resulting in death."

Danny cocked his head. "Those are both felonies, right?"

I nodded. "And he's looking at five years and a lifetime driver's license suspension."

"But that's what he'd get at trial!"

"That's what I said."

"We can't take that!"

"Exactly. Which begs the question."

"Why would he offer it?"

"Right. And with a deadline by Friday's pretrial."

"This Friday? No way!"

"That was my thought."

"Did you tell him no?"

I shook my head. "He made it clear it was a serious offer, so I have to present it to Edge."

Danny fidgeted. "So present it, get your no, and reject it."

"I will. But the why of it bugs me."

Danny shifted his weight again.

"Right, right," I said. "Estate plans await. Good luck."

"Thanks!" he said and shot out the door.

He didn't stumble at all.

THE FIRST THING I did when I sat down was call Edge. Voicemail. I tried Carissa. Voicemail. So, I went with the nuclear option.

I called Mrs. Horvath.

"Mr. Shepherd! What can I do for you today?"

"Hi, Mrs. Horvath. I've been trying to reach Edge."

"Certainly, Mr. Shepherd. Mr. Fleece is in an executive committee meeting right now, which I expect will last most of the rest of the afternoon."

"I see. Could you make sure that he calls me after?"

"Of course. Can I tell him what this is regarding?"

"An important personal matter."

"I will make sure that he calls, Mr. Shepherd. Is there anything else I can help you with?"

"I've also been trying to get a hold of Carissa. Do you know if she's available this afternoon?"

"I'm not involved in Dr. Fleece's scheduling, Mr. Shepherd."

"Okay. Thanks for your help, Mrs. Horvath. I appreciate it."

"Of course, Mr. Shepherd. Have a nice day."

As soon as I hung up, my phone buzzed again. I thought it was Mrs. Horvath calling back, but it wasn't.

"What's up, Liv?" I said.

"Your body fat percentage," said Olivia.

"You know you really should charge extra for these motivational sessions."

"I do. Check your bill."

"Sorry, too weak to open the envelope."

"Figures. I have some information on Trane."

"Shoot."

"He has a criminal history."

"Really?"

"Really. Turns out seventeen years ago, Benjamin Trane robbed a convenience store."

"Whoops."

"And an amusement park."

"What?!"

"Yep. He robbed a ticket booth over in Sandusky. Probably figured there would be more money and less security there."

"How did that work out?"

"With an immediate arrest and a plea deal that sent him to prison for five years.

"I didn't see anything in Pillars' personnel file. I wonder if they knew."

"They knew if they did a background check. It wasn't hidden. He didn't change his name or anything."

"Interesting." I did the math. "That would mean he started working for Pillars shortly after he got out. I'll be sure to check."

"Let me know what you find, and I can follow-up."

"Thanks, Liv."

"I just won't be able to next week."

"No rush. What's next week?"

"I'll be out of town."

"Oh yeah? Torturers' convention?"

"No, that's in the fall. Just a vacation."

"Great. Where?"

"Red Rock. Nevada." A pause. "Brad has a place."

"Brad?"

"The cardiologist."

"Oh, right. Good places to climb there?"

"I guess some of the best this time of year."

"Good. Have a great time. This will all wait till you get back. Happy climbing or don't fall or whatever the hell you say to someone who's decided to leave a perfectly good swimming pool and scrabble up a mountain."

"It's a cliff face and I will. And just because I'm taking a vacation doesn't mean you can. I'll check your card log when I get back."

"I'll be sure to send Danny over to swipe it for me every day. Have fun."

"Always."

As we hung up, I added Benjamin Trane's criminal history—for armed robbery, of all things—to the facts I didn't understand about the case.

14

My phone buzzed at four-thirty p.m. Edge. Chalk one up for Mrs. Horvath.

"Sorry I didn't get back to you, Nate," he said. "I've been in meetings and meetings to schedule meetings all day."

"No problem. Is it always like that?"

"Not this bad. We've been working on a couple of big projects—a new health clinic and a childcare expansion—and we've hit some snags."

"Yeah?"

"Yeah, the usual, increased construction costs and financing hiccups. We'll work through it. But I can't imagine that's why you called me."

"No, it's not. I won't keep you. I got a call from the prosecutor today."

"Why didn't you say so? Is he dropping the charges?"

"No. He called to offer a plea deal."

"What's a plea deal?"

"When the prosecutor offers an arrangement where you

plead guilty to a crime, usually one that's less than the one you're charged with."

"Why would I do that?"

"The defendant does it when there's a good chance that he'll be found guilty of the crime he's accused of."

"What does the prosecutor get out of it?"

"The certainty of a conviction and saving the time and expense of trial."

"Well, I didn't kill Benjamin, so there's no reason for me to plead guilty to anything."

"I understand. But I am ethically bound to relay the terms of the offer before you reject it."

"Relay away. But the answer is going to be no."

"Fine. The prosecutor's offering a deal where you plead guilty to aggravated vehicular homicide and failure to stop at the scene of an accident. There are some legal intricacies involved but essentially, he'll recommend that you be sentenced to five years in prison and have your driver's license permanently suspended."

There was silence at the other on the line before Edge said, "That's *less* than what I'm charged with?"

"No, that's exactly what you're charged with."

"Then why would I accept that?"

"There's no reason to unless you want to avoid the expense and publicity of a trial."

"But the publicity would be just as bad with my conviction, trial or no, right?"

"Exactly."

"And money's not the issue, so there's no way I would take this. Am I missing something?"

"No, I agree. I recommend you let me reject it."

"Please do! What happens next?"

"I'll tell the prosecutor we pass on the deal, and we'll meet with the Court on Friday to set a trial schedule. I'll let you know how it goes."

"Thanks. Was there anything else?"

"No. Oh wait, yes—did you know Benjamin Trane had a criminal record?"

"I know that everyone has a past before they come to Pillars."

"Did you do a background check?"

"I'm sure we followed whatever procedures we were supposed to follow for his position."

"You know he served time for armed robbery?"

"I know that Ben worked for us for many years, did a fine job, and that we miss him very much. Is that all you had?"

I thought. "Yeah, for now. Thanks."

"Good. So, how are you?"

I paused. "I'm fine, thanks."

"Are you sure? Is there anything we can do to help you?"

"No, we have the case under control, Edge. Don't worry, we'll handle it."

"I'm not talking about my case. I'm talking about you. Personally."

I blinked. "What?"

"Is there anything you need?"

"Why? Should there be?"

Edge laughed. "No, Nate, no. But we don't know if our brother or sister needs help unless we ask, do we?"

"I guess we don't, Edge. But I'm fine. Thanks for asking."

We said goodbye and, as I prepared for the pretrial on Friday, I wondered in passing why it would seem so unusual for someone to ask, genuinely, what someone else needed.

15

Our pretrial was set for one-thirty p.m. on Friday afternoon so I arrived at one o'clock to talk to Ryan Pompeo ahead of time. As I was standing in the central lobby outside of Courtrooms 5, 6, 7, and 8, I realized that I had no idea what Pompeo looked like.

One o'clock turned into one-fifteen, and I still hadn't seen him when the elevator dinged and a man who had to be Ryan Pompeo came striding out straight toward me.

He was tall, slightly taller than me, with black hair cut tight on the sides and long on top so that it swooped up and to the side in a style that required some form of artificial support system. He wore a dark blue suit with pants that were a little too tight and shoulders that were a little too wide so that he reminded me of a kite.

If I had any doubt about who he was, it vanished when the man grinned and wound up his arm before he stuck his hand out and said, "NATO! Nice to finally meet you in the flesh."

I shook his hand. "Hi, Ryan."

"Jesus Christ, what happened to your ear?!"

It had been a while since anyone had mentioned it and I had

long since stopped seeing it in the mirror, so I paused for a second before I said, "Old football injury."

"What, did the kicker use it as a tee? Jesus, that's bad. Must've hurt like hell."

"I guess I forgot about it."

"I don't know how you could. So did you convey my offer to your client?"

"I did."

"And will he accept it?"

"Of course not."

"Are you sure? It's a bargain."

"I don't see how."

"Seems to me that five years for killing someone is a pretty light sentence. Shoot, your man behaves himself, he'll probably get out even sooner."

"If he had killed someone, maybe. Since he didn't..." I shrugged.

"My office doesn't see it that way."

"I'm sure you don't. But you also haven't given me anything to change my mind."

Pompeo smiled and smacked my shoulder. "Same goes for you, NATO. Any alibi evidence that you have for me? Anything to put your Mr. Fleece anywhere besides a big ol' oak tree on February 17th?"

I shook my head. "Not my burden, Ryan."

Ryan checked his watch. "One twenty-eight, sport." He pointed to the courtroom. "The deal doesn't walk through those doors. What do you say?"

"After you."

~

Judge Stephanie Jurevicius was new to the bench, so I had never met her before. Jurevicius was a famous political name in Carrefour, going back at least three generations. I seemed to remember that Stephanie Jurevicius had cut her teeth as a magistrate over in domestic court for a few years before a seat had come open here in Common Pleas after Judge Burroughs had suddenly passed away. Stephanie Jurevicius had been appointed by the governor to fill the seat—three generations of family connections, remember—and would have to run this coming fall to keep it.

Which is all a long way of saying I had no idea what to expect from her when we entered her court.

Judge Jurevicius was on the bench handling another matter, so I caught the eye of the judge's bailiff, a stern-faced woman named Mickey Fields, waved, and slipped into one of the benches in the gallery. Pompeo rattled through the swinging gate to the court side of the room, told Bailiff Fields in a stage whisper that the attorneys were there on Fleece, then stood with arms folded by the bailiff's desk.

I saw the bailiff's lips move but couldn't hear her. Pompeo's head jerked, then he took four steps back and took a seat.

Waiting gave me a few minutes to study Judge Jurevicius. I knew she was young for a judge, meaning about my age, but I hadn't expected her to look as young as she did. She had straight brown hair and one of those youthful faces with smiling eyes and a turned-up nose that would make her look young for decades. She wore a lace collar outside her robe, like the kind that Ruth Bader Ginsburg wore, and a string of pearls. The conservative accessories didn't make her seem older, though; instead, they exaggerated her youth.

I wasn't really paying attention to the case she was handling but after a few minutes, Judge Jurevicius said, "Trial is set for

June 13. Bailiff Fields will send out an order with the rest of the dates." Then she banged her gavel with a sharp rap.

I started, as did everyone else in the courtroom, everyone except Bailiff Mickey Fields who just moved a brown file from one pile to another. Contrary to what you see on TV, judges almost never bang their gavels. It was startling.

"Bailiff Fields, please call the next case," said Judge Jurevicius.

"State vs. Fleece," said Bailiff Fields.

I stood and walked through the gate to one counsel table as Pompeo took the other and Bailiff Fields brought the file up to the judge.

"Counsel is here for the pretrial, Your Honor," said Bailiff Fields.

"To set dates?" said Judge Jurevicius.

"Yes, Your Honor," Bailiff Fields said and went back to her seat.

"Yes, then, we are here on the case of State vs. Edgerton Fleece for a pretrial to set dates for a trial schedule. Also appearing are...Will counsel please state their appearance for the record?"

"Ryan Pompeo for the State, Judge."

"Nate Shepherd for defendant Edgerton Fleece, Your Honor."

"Good afternoon, Mr. Pompeo, Mr. Shepherd. It appears that we are here on charges of aggravated vehicular homicide and failure to stop at the scene of an accident involving the death of a person. So this would be a...felony level trial...so we will reserve...one week for trial? Is that sufficient counsel?"

"Sure," said Pompeo.

"Yes, Your Honor," I said.

"Excellent, then we will reserve one week...."

A ding came from Judge Jurevicius's computer. She turned,

clicked, looked at her screen, nodded, turned back to us, and said, "I should inquire, counsel, does Defendant Fleece's plea remain not guilty?"

"It does, Your Honor," I said.

"Yes, Your Honor," said Pompeo. "The State made a good faith offer of a plea deal promptly in this case, which has been rejected by the defendant."

"Does the State intend to continue negotiations for a plea agreement?"

"No, Your Honor," said Pompeo. "The state intends to dismiss the case."

I kept my face blank but couldn't stop myself from glancing at Pompeo.

He was grinning.

Judge Jurevicius blinked once, looked at her computer screen, blinked again, then picked up her gavel. "Very well, Mr. Pompeo, based on your representation, the Court will not set a trial date. This pretrial is—"

"Actually, Judge?"

The gavel paused in mid-strike. "Yes, Mr. Pompeo?"

"The state will be dismissing this indictment because it will be filing a new one with additional charges against Mr. Fleece."

Now I did look at Pompeo. He looked back and kept grinning.

"What...charges are those?" said Judge Jurevicius.

Pompeo didn't take his eyes off me as he said, "Murder."

I kept my face flat and stared back. "Defense counsel has not been made aware of these charges, Your Honor. Or their basis."

"Judge, we've presented additional evidence to the grand jury, and they've concluded that Mr. Fleece's killing of Benjamin Trane was intentional. We'll dismiss this case and file our new indictment this afternoon."

"I haven't been provided with a copy of that document, Your Honor."

Pompeo held his hands out. "Like I said, Judge, it hasn't been filed yet. I was just letting everyone know what's going on."

The judge's computer dinged. "Counsel," Judge Jurevicius said, her eyes still on the screen. "Do you anticipate the defendant's plea to remain the same?"

"I haven't seen the indictment yet, Your Honor, nor have I seen any evidence that my client was even at the scene, let alone that he intended to kill Benjamin Trane—"

"Defense counsel has not requested discovery or a bill of particulars and our time for *Brady* disclosures hasn't passed yet, Judge," said Pompeo.

"—so at this point, yes, the defendant's plea remains not guilty. I expect we'll enter the same plea when the new charges are filed."

"Judge, if I may?"

Judge Jurevicius's eyes were a little wide but her voice calm. "Yes, Mr. Pompeo?"

"I know between the dismissal and the new filing, Mr. Shepherd and I will have a whole bunch of procedural details to handle, disclosures, all that stuff. But, as long as we're here and have our calendars, maybe the Court could set a trial schedule for the new case?"

"A trial schedule for a case you haven't filed?" I said.

"It's no different than this one."

"You're adding a murder charge."

"Your client was already accused of killing Mr. Trane. It's the same case."

"You know it's not."

"Dead is dead."

The judge's computer dinged. "Counsel will address the Court, not argue with each other."

We stopped.

Pompeo turned to the bench. "Judge, we're here already. The Court could just pencil it in—that would save the Court's time and it would let us hit the ground running since we'd all know what the schedule is we're dealing with in the new case."

"Mr. Shepherd?" Judge Jurevicius said.

"I think the State should file its case and give us an opportunity to see it before we schedule a trial date, Your Honor."

"Like I said, Judge," said Pompeo. "You could just pencil it in and set some disclosure deadlines too, so that Mr. Shepherd gets his information even sooner."

Judge Jurevicius twisted her gavel.

"And, if the trial date doesn't work down the road, Mr. Shepherd can always seek a continuance. Heck, we'll even join it. This just seems like the most efficient use of the Court's time all the way around."

Judge Jurevicius paused, then said, "How does our August look, Bailiff Fields?"

There was some back and forth as we all checked our calendars before Judge Jurevicius nodded and said, "Excellent. Bailiff Fields, please pencil in a trial date of August 22."

"Of course, Your Honor." Bailiff Fields turned to her computer and clicked away for a moment.

"Very well, counsel," said Judge Jurevicius. She lifted her gavel again. "Our trial date of August 22 is confirmed. The State will provide its file to the defense by next Friday and the defense will provide its preliminary disclosures the week after. Bailiff Fields will issue the appropriate scheduling order."

Judge Jurevicius rapped the gavel on the sounding block so that it cracked across the courtroom. "What is our next case, Bailiff Fields?"

I gathered my things and walked out after Pompeo who was

already at the door. After I pushed through, he turned and smiled. "I told you it was a good deal."

There was only one way to treat a guy like Pompeo. In court anyway.

I shrugged. "It wasn't my guy."

Pompeo's grin broadened. "Oh, that defense works all the time."

"Are you going to tell me the basis for the change?"

"You'll get the indictment."

"Which won't tell me anything."

Pompeo's face looked like it was about to split. "Ask your client who benefited the most from Benjamin Trane's death."

"Who?"

"Ask Fleece." He slapped my shoulder. "Well, I gotta bolt. Have an indictment to file."

As he walked away, he waved with his back to me and said, "See you in August, NATO."

16

Some things need to be handled in person. Telling your client that he's being charged with murder is one of them.

I went back to my office and, sure enough, at four fifty-five p.m. I received an electronic notice from the Court. I checked it. True to his word, Pompeo filed an indictment for murder.

In Ohio, murder is the purposeful killing of another, which is what a lot of other states call second degree murder. Pompeo hadn't gone for aggravated murder, which other states call first degree murder, but the sentence in Edge's case could still be fifteen years to life.

Not something you want.

The indictment was just as general as the one before. Basically, Pompeo said that Edgerton Fleece had killed Benjamin Trane by hitting him with a car and then failed to stop after. This time though, he said the killing was purposeful instead of reckless; that's why he'd filed the new charge.

It was time to have a come-to-Jesus meeting with Edge.

I'd called Mrs. Horvath right after the pretrial and she'd told me that Edge would be at the Pillars food pantry that evening if I needed to reach him. I drove over to the Pillars campus, followed the signs, and found the section for "Food Patron Parking." I parked a little further away and walked in.

Edge was there with two women and four teenagers. The teenagers were counting boxes and cans as they stacked them on shelves while the women followed behind and marked an inventory list. Edge was off to the side, cutting open the paper seal on a large cardboard box.

"Rice here, Kelly," he said.

"Got it, Edge," said one of the women and ticked her sheet.

"Hi, Nate," Edge said. "I'll be just a few more minutes."

"I need to see you now, Edge. Privately."

"We have a pickup in the morning so let me just finish—"

I turned to the woman. "Excuse me, Kelly, is it? Can I borrow your pen for just a second?"

"Of course," she said.

I took her pen and circled one word on the piece of paper I was holding. "Thank you very much."

Kelly smiled and went back to her inventory. I handed my piece of paper to Edge. His eyebrows furrowed as he took it. Then his head snapped up.

"Mur—" he stopped and glanced at Kelly and the others.

I pointed to the door. "May we?"

"I'll be right back, Kelly."

Kelly nodded and kept ticking boxes.

We went outside and walked a little farther from the door before Edge said, "Murder? This has gone from an accident to *murder*?"

I nodded. "They filed this today. They've recharged you."

"What does this mean?"

"It means that instead of accusing you of killing Benjamin Trane by accident, they're accusing you of doing it on purpose."

"But I didn't do it at all."

"I understand that. But they seem to think you did."

"Why?"

"I don't know any of the details yet. They have to provide me with some of the evidence next week so I'll know more then, but I need anything you can tell me now."

Edge looked me right in the eye. "I wasn't there Nate. I don't know what happened to Benjamin Trane."

"Then let's approach this from another angle. I asked the prosecutor why he was charging you with murder. He said to ask you who benefited the most from Benjamin Trane's death."

"What in the world does that mean?"

"It means that he thinks you had a motive to kill him."

"But I didn't kill him at all."

"Let's leave that aside for a moment. Why would the prosecutor think you have a motive to kill Benjamin? Who benefited from Benjamin's death?"

"Nobody benefited from Benjamin's death! Not me, not Pillars, not anyone! Thank goodness Theo passed first because I don't know how we would have replaced Benjamin for him."

I shook my head. "That's not the right answer, Edge. There has to be something."

"It's the only answer, Nate. I didn't kill Benjamin Trane and I don't know anyone, anyone in the world, who's better off because he died. We miss him terribly."

It was clear that, right now, Edge wasn't going to give me anything on motive. There was another angle though. "Edge, to represent you, I need to know the truth."

He blinked. "Of course."

"If I know the truth, we can craft our defense around it."

"Alright."

"So I need you to tell me—did you really hit a deer?"

His head rocked back. "Yes, I told you that."

"Because it looks like an awfully big coincidence."

"I don't know what to tell you, Nate, except that I hit a deer."

I remembered something that Rick Dalton had said. "Edge, did you wash the van before you took it to Carrefour Collision?"

He nodded. "Yes."

"Why would you do that?"

Edge's brow furrowed. "Because it had blood all over it."

"And you wanted to clean it off?"

"Of course."

"Why?"

"Because hitting a deer leaves a horrible mess. There's blood and hair and it's disgusting. Carrefour Collision gets paid to fix my van, not clean up my mess."

"When do you think you washed the van?"

"I'm not sure. Right before I took it in, I think."

"Where did you get it washed?"

"I did it myself. There's one of those hand-washing places a mile or so from our house—you know, where you put the quarters in and use the foamy brush and the big squirt gun."

"You hand-washed it?"

Edge nodded. "I wasn't sure if one of those auto washes would get it all out."

"I imagine you paid with quarters."

"Sure. That's what it takes. Why?"

"Meaning there's no credit card receipt?"

"No, I don't usually turn in expenses that small. This would've been under ten bucks."

I didn't mention to him that a lack of a credit card receipt would also make it harder to prove that he'd been there washing the van.

I was beginning to see one of the angles Pompeo would be taking.

Edge looked over his shoulder at the pantry door. "Nate, I

have two hundred people coming tomorrow morning. I need to get these empty shelves stocked."

"You know there's more to this, right, Edge? On motive, where you were, all of it. They wouldn't have brought these charges if there weren't."

"I know they think so, but I also know I didn't do it. You'll have to sort it out. I really have to go now. We'll talk soon."

Edge went inside and I left, not knowing much more than when I got there.

Which could only mean that, when I did find out what was going on, it was going to be bad.

PART II

FIXATION

17

On Saturday at exactly five o'clock, I showed up at my brother Mark's house to hang out with my nephews while Mark and Izzy went to a Red Wings game. If you haven't visited in a while, Mark and Izzy have three boys whose names all start with "J": Justin, James, and Joe. A while back, James had broken his leg pretty badly and his recovery had led to a series of regular visits that included group video games and group readings of high fantasy adventure. James's leg had improved quite a bit, but I was still more than happy to come over so that Mark and Izzy could get a night out.

I didn't know what virtual arena my nephews intended to humiliate me in that night, but I had brought the DragonLance Chronicles' *Time of the Twins* for my contribution. And for those of you who think that the conflict between Caramon and Raistlin was a little too violent for my nephews' consumption, I can only say 1) they will have disemboweled me dozens of times in their video game before we read a single word; and 2) what else are uncles for?

Judging from the cars, it looked like most of the Red Wings group was already there, so I hustled up to the front door carrying a stack of four pizza boxes with the book on top. Izzy opened the door before I got there.

"On time, with pizza? I'm in love. Boys! Uncle Nate is here!"

Justin, the oldest, swooped in like a hawk and hit the pizzas. "Hi, Uncle Nate," he said, grinning as he skittered away with the boxes.

I had just enough time to swipe the book off the top box before Joe, the youngest, came tearing around the corner and plowed straight into my leg. "Uncle Nate!"

I picked him up, flipped him around, and held him upside down by both ankles. "You need to reset your traps, Iz. The mice in your house are getting bigger."

Joe laughed and punched me upside down in the thigh. I flipped him around, put him in a bear hug, and dug my chin into his chest while tickling both sides.

"Not the chin of doom!" said Joe, laughing.

"What?" I said, and tickled harder.

Joe tried to talk but kept laughing until I set him down. When he caught his breath, he laughed one more time, then said, "You're going to be mad," and sprinted after the pizzas.

As Joe went out, James came in and, although it might have been my imagination, it seemed like he was limping less.

"Hey, troll," I said, and went to pick him up. He shot right under my arm for a perfect single leg takedown. That kind of effort needs to be rewarded, so I let him pick up my leg before breaking his grip, picking him up, and cracking his back. He laughed once before I set him down, then he grabbed the DragonLance book out of my hand and said, "We'll mark how far we get."

"What?"

He grinned. "You're going to be so mad."

"James!" said Izzy. "Go get some pizza."

Still grinning, James yelled, "I get pepperoni!" then hustled into the kitchen.

I looked a question at Izzy. Now that my hands were empty, she gave me a hug, kissed my cheek, and said, "Come on in."

My brother Mark met me at the kitchen entrance and handed me a beer. "Hey," he said.

"Hey." I looked at the beer. "I don't know that I need one of these while I'm watching the boys."

Mark gave me a little smile. "Yes, you do," he said, and stood aside as Izzy put a hand on my back and guided me in.

There were a good number of people milling about, so it took a moment to take it all in. The boys were standing around the kitchen table, tearing pizzas apart and putting them on paper plates. A teenage girl I didn't recognize was standing with them, trying to make sure the pizza hit the plates instead of the table and filling plastic cups with a two liter of Pepsi.

Three adults were standing around the kitchen island, which sported a bucket of beers on ice, bottles and mixers for drinks, and a pre-made tray of meat and cheese.

"Nate," said Izzy, her hand still on my back. "You know Doug and Zoe Kirkland."

A tall, dark-haired man tipped a beer and a short blond woman waved from the other side of the island.

"And this is Kira Freeman."

A woman in a Red Wings jersey and jeans stood with her back to me on this side of the island, her dark brown hair long enough to touch the top of the number "2." She glanced over her shoulder and raised a seltzer can. "Hey," she said.

I nodded and waved. "Brother and babysitter."

"Yeah, about that...," said Izzy.

If you have followed along with me before, you know that I can be slow on the uptake in situations like these, but I'm not glacial. It finally clicked. A teenage girl with the boys. My nephews' grins. The beer in my hand. Two couples. Kira.

And me.

"I thought I was babysitting," I said.

"I thought Brenda was coming," said Kira.

Izzy smiled, green eyes sparkling. She looked at Kira. "Brenda called an hour ago—her mom fell, and she has to take her to the ER."

She looked at me. "You were already on the way and Haley lives right across the street and is saving for a band trip to Disney World." Izzy tilted her head back. "How much more do you have to go, Haley?"

"One hundred and fifty dollars, Mrs. Shep."

Izzy looked at Mark. "Make sure you tip her extra." Back to me. "It seems to me like everybody wins."

Kira's face was neutral, but her mouth might have ticked up. "Well, it will take more than that for me to miss a game."

"It sounds great, but you know I didn't bring—"

Mark tossed me a Red Wings pullover.

"Thanks," I said and slipped it over my head.

"Great," said Izzy. "Now finish those drinks. We need to get going."

There was a flurry of drink-finishing, island-clearing, and instruction-leaving before Izzy herded us to the door and Mark went out to start the car. Doug, Zoe, and Kira, who apparently all knew each other, went next. I hung back and whispered to Izzy, "You know we can find out if Brenda's mom really fell."

"Oh, she fell," said Izzy.

"We can also find out if you pushed her."

Izzy smiled, scrunched her nose, and shrugged. "Get in the van, Nate."

~

Izzy directed Kira and me into the back seat of the van because, of course. Mark and Doug sat in front and Izzy and Zoe sat in the middle row of captain's chairs, which allowed Izzy to lean around the seat and direct our conversation toward anything except the fact that she had awkwardly forced Kira and me into the back seat together. Through that managed introduction, which reminded me of an opening statement, I learned that Kira had met Izzy through work and that they had gone out now and again, usually with Zoe and the mysteriously-disappeared Brenda.

Izzy had just recounted the story of when the four of them had gone to Nashville for Zoe's bachelorette party and included a fact that was apparently unknown to the then groom-to-be Doug sitting in the front passenger seat. This refocused Izzy and Zoe's attention forward for the moment.

"Oops," said Kira, smiling.

"Damage control." I smiled back. "Izzy said you met at work. Are you at Lounge King too?"

She shook her head. "I run an auction company. One of the executives at Izzy's company died a few years ago and our company handled the estate sale. I met Izzy as we were sorting things out."

Kira paused for a moment as Zoe proclaimed that she had absolutely without question told Doug the whole Nashville story before. Izzy bore witness and was insulted, to her core, that Doug doubted them.

Kira smiled. "We hit it off."

"You do estate auctions?"

"We do."

"What's the name of your company?"

"Northwest Auction. It's a family business."

The name clicked with the van I'd seen. "You're doing the Plutides estate?"

She blinked. "How would you know that?"

"I drove by the house earlier this week and saw one of your vans."

She nodded. "That was me. We've been hired to sell his house, his houses I should say, and all of his personal property." She shook her head. "It's as big an estate as we've handled in a while."

"How so?"

"Well, not big, exactly. Complicated more like. We have to sort through all his things to find what we can evaluate on our own and what needs to be appraised."

"Does that take a while?"

"It does if you do it right. You don't want to put some valuable piece up for pennies or junk up for a lot—you'll lose your credibility."

"And money."

"Exactly." She tilted her head. "Why were you going by? Do you live near there?"

"No. It was work for me too."

"Right, you're a lawyer. Are you working with Manny on this?"

"Who's Manny?"

"Manny Amaltheakis, Theo's attorney—well, the attorney for Theo's estate now. He's helping the executor with the sale."

This was the first I had heard of Manny Amaltheakis. "I may need to get in touch with him," I said. "Could you give me his information?"

"Sure. So you still haven't said."

"Said what?"

"Why were you going by the house?"

"I represent the guy who's accused of running over the guy who was walking Theo's dog."

I hadn't really noticed Kira's eyes until right then when, I swear, they cooled from light blue to gray.

"Your client almost killed Roxie, too," she said.

"The dog?"

She nodded.

"My client didn't do it."

"You have to say that, don't you?"

"No. If I thought he did it, I wouldn't have said anything."

She thought for a second, then nodded, but our conversation stalled like it tends to do when someone brings up attempted-dog-murder. Fortunately, the conversation in the front seat was getting animated so we could hear the outraged conclusion as Zoe convinced Doug that she had fully disclosed the details of the Nashville trip years ago but that she forgave the man for his poor memory and unfounded doubt.

I smiled and said out the side of my mouth, "There's no way Zoe told him everything."

Kira smiled. "That's not the half of it."

THE RED WINGS had been rebuilding for a while so Little Caesar's Arena wasn't full, but it was full enough that the crowd was loud and raucous when the Wings went up 1-0 in the first period. Mark sat on my right and Kira on my left but with Izzy on the other side of her, there was enough crosstalk that it didn't feel awkward keeping up a conversation, and Izzy especially kept us laughing whether it was stories about my nephews, or observations about the couple over in section 110, or the fact that the executives at Lounge King wouldn't know HR if it grabbed them by both cheeks and I swear to you that she said it without the least bit of irony.

I also learned that Kira knew more about the team than I

did, which I should have suspected from the fact that she wore a Jiri Fischer jersey, and he hadn't played since 2005. It wasn't long before Mark was talking past me to her when he needed to make an intelligent hockey point.

We spent the third period yelling as the Red Wings lost the lead, got it back, then held off a power-play to win at the horn. We cheered and celebrated with each other and with our new-found best friends in rows 13 and 14, and the buzz of energy continued on the Detroit streets all the way back to the parking garage.

It was as much fun as I'd had in a while.

IT WAS after midnight when we piled out of the van. There were shared hugs and thanks and comments that we'd have to do it again. Mark and Izzy headed in to check on the boys and Doug and Zoe waved as they pulled out of the drive. Kira and I were parked at the curb and we stopped between the front of my car and the back of hers.

She glanced over as Mark and Izzy went in the front door, then gestured. "Do you watch your nephews often?"

"Once a week or so."

She cocked her head. "Really?"

"Ever since James broke his leg."

"Oh, right. Well, I'm sorry you missed them."

"Next time. Tonight was a lot of fun."

"It was."

We both paused.

I know, I know, it was the obvious opening, but I was uncertain and had no idea how she thought about being thrown into this thing and goddammit I was way out of practice and not at all sure about how I felt.

The moment passed.

Kira smiled and said, "It was good to put a face to Izzy's stories, Nate. I'll text you Manny's info."

"You too, Kira. Thanks."

Then we got in our cars and left.

I know. Smooth.

I DROVE HOME, tapping my ring on the steering wheel in time to Chris Stapleton, and pulled into the driveway. It had been light when I left so I'd forgotten to turn on the porch lights again. I pulled into the middle of my two-car garage and, as I got out, I realized that it was a tighter fit than it had been before, that the projects and junk and random things were starting to pile up on the sides.

I went in the house and found that I had forgotten about the lights in there too. I turned one on in the kitchen and one in the hall, then tossed my keys into a bowl, where they landed with an echoing clang. I started to charge my phone when I saw that I had missed a text from Kira sent twenty minutes before.

Here's Manny's info. Had it in my car.

The Wings play St. Louis next week.

Twenty minutes. It was late, but if she'd sent it before she left, she should just be getting home too.

I opened the fridge and contemplated a snack. Nothing jumped out at me. It was all the same stuff.

I shut the door, picked up my phone, and typed:

Thanks!

I stared at the screen, then typed:

Would you like to go?

I hopped out of the message so she wouldn't see three blinking dots staring at her. I went back to the fridge and suddenly had a taste for a late night omelet, which, in case you're wondering, can be tricky because you need to chop some peppers and dice some ham and grate some cheese and beat the eggs until all of the white is completely folded into the yolk while butter melts in a pan but you need to bring the pan up to temperature slowly so that it won't burn the butter or scald the eggs because once you pour the eggs in you need to run the spatula around the outer edge so that it doesn't stick and you really need to watch carefully so you can see the exact point when the pan side of the eggs are firm but the top side is still runny because that's when you flip them but I don't have the skills to just flip it out of the pan so I just slowly work the spatula underneath until it's all the way to the center of the egg circle and then flip it quickly so that it doesn't break but you only have a few seconds then to cover the whole thing with cheese but just one half with the peppers and ham before folding it over gently and turning the heat down just a little bit so that the cheese melts and the peppers and ham cook but the eggs don't burn and once it melts down you flip it over to even things out until, more by sense than by any particular timer, you know that it's done and slide it onto a plate where it awaits a bath in Frank's hot sauce. Like I said, tricky.

I put the plate next to my phone, which showed a text coming in, exactly twenty minutes since I'd responded.

No, the game's on Wednesday so I won't be out of work in time.

Then a second message.

But we could watch it somewhere.

I immediately replied. *Sounds great.*

She liked my text and the three dots disappeared.

I went back to the fridge, grabbed a beer, and took a sip. Then I sat down and ate my omelet.

18

On Monday morning, I used the information Kira had given me and contacted the office of Manny Amaltheakis. I spoke to a pleasant woman who encouraged me to come down that afternoon because, although she couldn't schedule an appointment for me with Mr. Amaltheakis, she was almost certain he would be there between three and five, right after lunch, and would be happy to speak with me about whatever my legal needs were.

I spent the rest of the morning working on other cases, then went over to the office of Amaltheakis Law, Ltd. that afternoon.

The Amaltheakis law office was in a small columned building in Harvest Township. I've mentioned before I hadn't spent much time in Harvest, but his building seemed to mirror the style of the area—small standalone buildings that housed boutique practices for the odd lawyer or accountant or orthodontist.

The inside was old school. There was a lot of dark wood and plush furniture, highlighted by accents of brass and gold. It would have seemed dated except that everything was new and, as I looked closer, I suspected that the wood was exotic, the furniture custom, and the gold not painted but, well, gold. It dripped money and appeared to be a recent, deliberate choice as opposed to long-standing indifference to change.

A polite woman behind the reception desk greeted me, remembered our call, and, upon finding out that I was a lawyer, asked if I would be more comfortable waiting in the conference room. That was fine with me, so I took a seat and a moment later was given a cup and saucer with coffee that was concentrated, strong and delightful.

The conference room was more of the same; the wood table looked like some sort of custom piece and there were paintings on the wall—one of a woman and child, one of a harvest scene complete with sheaves of wheat, and one of a vineyard on rolling hills—that I presume were original and would impress me if I knew enough to be so.

The most unusual piece was set along one wall on a credenza. It was a sculpture of an honest to goodness cornucopia, a horn that seemed so real that I had to walk over and touch it. An array of fruits and small tasty baked things were stacked in the opening.

"A piece from my mom," said a man. "She is long gone so I do not have the heart to get rid of it, but I never know what to do with it either. The fruit is fresh, just arrived this morning. Help yourself." He reached over and grabbed a couple of dried dates that were sitting amid apples and oranges and pears.

The man was of medium height and broad, with a wealth of hair that had gone white save for a touch of black at the temples. He sported a gloriously thick mustache, which was also white, and wore a gray silk suit with a white broadcloth shirt that was open at the collar. He popped a date in his mouth, then extended his hand and said, "You must be Nate Shepherd."

"I am. Mr. Amaltheakis?"

"Manny, please." Manny Amaltheakis popped a second date into his mouth and said, "So what can I tell you about Theo?"

"How do you know that's what I'm here about?"

"Kira gave me a call." He reached out and took a small sweet roll. "Told me you might stop by. Ida!"

The receptionist swept in and deposited another cup and saucer on the table for Manny.

"You are divine, Ida, divine."

She nodded and left.

Manny waved us to the table, sat, and raised his cup. "You had the coffee?"

"I did."

"You did not put anything in it, I hope?"

"Never."

"Good. It is straight from Brazil. Best you are ever going to drink. Theo and I invested in a farm down there years ago. Took most of two decades to get the plants right, but I think you will find it was worth it."

He took a sip that was only slightly slurpy and said, "So, Theo."

I nodded. "I represent a man named Edgerton Fleece."

"I know him well. Do you represent him corporately for Pillars or personally for his murder trial?"

I took a sip myself. "In the murder trial. Mr. Fleece is accused of killing Benjamin Trane."

"I am aware of that. Both of them were very important to Theo."

"That's part of why I'm here. I don't understand the relationship between all of these folks. I wondered if you would be willing to fill me in."

Manny Amaltheakis rattled the cup into the saucer. "We should establish a few things first, so that there are no misunderstandings later."

"Sure."

"I was Theo's lawyer. We go back decades, to Detroit, before we moved down here in the '70s."

That surprised me. Manny didn't look older than his early sixties, but if he was a contemporary of Theo's, he was probably closer to eighty.

"While he was alive, I was Theo's business lawyer—I helped him do deals, joined him in a few, and drafted up his estate plan before he died. Now that he is gone, I am working with his executor, his great-nephew, to help him weave his way through the maze of his uncle's dealings, and I am working with Kira Freeman to liquidate the things that Theo didn't designate a home for. I take it you have known Kira for a while?"

"Not really. Why?"

"Because she called for you. No matter." Manny took another date. "Like I said, Benjamin Trane was very important to Theo. So was Pillars. I know your client is accused of murdering Benjamin, but I also have not read anything yet to conclude that this is true, so I have not been able to make up my mind, yet, whether your client did it. I do know that your client founded the organization that helped Theo maintain his independence in his last years so, when Kira called, I was willing to talk to you today. But just so you know, if it ever appears to me that Mr. Fleece killed Benjamin, I will help the prosecution bury your client in any way that I can. This is fair?"

"Very."

"Good," said Manny. "What do you want to know, Nate Shepherd?"

"How was Theo Plutides connected to Benjamin Trane and Pillars?"

"Pillars really came first," said Manny. "Years ago, Theo's church got involved with donating to the Pillars food pantry. Food security was always a big deal to Theo; he hated the idea of people going hungry, especially in this country where we have so much. He went over, checked out what Pillars was doing, and was impressed with the operation your client had up and running. Once Theo got to know more about Pillars and then saw firsthand the difference the pantry was making, Theo had a few meetings with your client to see how he could help."

"Could he?"

"Help? If you have to ask, then you did not know Theo. He made regular donations, big ones, to make sure the pantry was staffed and stocked and helped fund the expansion into meal delivery." Manny sipped his coffee. "By the way, you can tell your client that Theo set up a trust that will fund the Pillars' food pantry for the foreseeable future.

"Really?"

Manny waved a hand. "It will not fund until Kira has liquidated the estate and the property but, yes, Pillars is not going to have to worry about where its food is coming from anytime soon."

"That's very generous."

Manny shrugged. "Theo was a generous man. Anyway, Theo began to struggle physically as he got older—he had always fought epilepsy and his vision was never good, and, once he dislocated his hip, he just could not get around well at all. So Edge sent Benjamin Trane over to help even though Theo did not want it. Theo could afford to hire his own help, but Benjamin started coming over and Theo took a liking to him, and their friendship just grew from there."

"What did Benjamin Trane do?"

Manny shrugged. "All the things you do when you look in on someone—ran Theo around on errands, charged his scooter, fixed annoying little things around the house. And helped Theo get Roxie her walk, of course."

I smiled. "The famous Roxie."

Manny smiled back. “She is indeed. She was Theo’s, hmm, one, two, third service dog. For his epilepsy.”

“Theo was still walking Roxie?”

“Have you ever been around a service dog?” asked Manny.

I shook my head.

“You have to be careful that she does not create a bond with anyone except the person she is taking care of. If someone else becomes the source of support or food or fun, the dog will start paying attention to that person instead of the person who needs the help. Over the last couple of years, Roxie needed walks, but Theo could not be trusted to be outside alone anymore, so Theo would wait until Benjamin came over and then take Roxie out with his scooter with Benjamin following along behind to keep an eye on them.”

I nodded. “One of the neighbors mentioned seeing them.”

“They were quite a trio—I saw them a couple of times a year when Benjamin brought Theo over for meetings. Benjamin was attentive and conscientious, and Theo appreciated it.”

“Did Theo say that to you?”

“He did. And of course, he remembered Benjamin in his will.”

“If I may ask, what did Theo leave Benjamin?”

“The Ford Mustang they liked to tool around in. And his wallets.”

“His wallets?”

Manny smiled. “Theo had a bit of a sense of humor. He wanted Benjamin to have some walking around money.”

“Do you know why Benjamin was walking Roxie the night he died?”

“Benjamin was taking care of Roxie after Theo passed. Benjamin lived in an apartment that did not allow pets, though, so Roxie was still staying at the house while that got sorted out.”

I thought and decided to push it a little farther. "Would you mind if I stopped over at Theo's house?"

Manny's eyes narrowed. "Why?"

"To get a sense of the route, check out the car—"

"Generally snoop around?"

"—Exactly."

Manny smoothed his mustache and ran his thumb along his chin before he said, "I guess there is no harm as long as Kira is there. But remember what I said earlier—if I am ever convinced Fleece did kill Benjamin, I will see to it that he is buried myself."

"Understood."

Manny waved a hand. "But in the meantime, tell him that I'll be in touch to discuss the food pantry foundation once the estate is liquidated."

"I'll be sure to tell him."

Manny waved a hand. "All this talk of food makes me hungry. Do you want to eat?"

"Sorry, I have to get back to the office. Thanks, though."

Manny stood. "Make sure you eat. Here, take some dates. Yes, yes, and the bowl too."

Before I knew it, I was walking out of Manny Amaltheakis's office with some more information and a bowl of dates.

I wasn't sure what to do with either.

19

When I went to the office the next morning, I told Danny what I had learned from Manny Amaltheakis. Danny listened and nodded and took notes. When I finished, he tapped his notepad with the back of his pen and said, "I still don't see how Fleece benefits."

"From what?"

"You said Pompeo told you to ask Fleece who benefited from Trane's death, right?"

"Right."

He wrote "Theo" on his notepad, then drew an arrow down and to the left and wrote "Trane." "We know how Benjamin Trane benefited from Theo's death."

I nodded. "Trane gets a car and some walking around money from Plutides. Or will once the estate is finalized."

"Right." Danny drew another arrow down from the word "Theo," this time to the right, and wrote "Fleece/Pillars." "And Manny Amaltheakis told you that Pillars benefited from Theo's death since Theo set up a trust for the Pillars food pantry."

"Right." Danny then drew a horizontal line between Trane and Fleece that formed the base of the triangle. "None of that gives us this, though. Nothing you just told me indicates any benefit that *Fleece* would've received from *Trane's* death."

I nodded. "Which Pompeo thinks gave Fleece a motive."

"Right. These are all intertwined in some way, but I don't see it yet."

"Me either."

Danny shook his head. "We sure know how to pick 'em."

"We? This was all your idea, remember?"

"I suppose you're going to keep reminding me of that until this trial is over?"

"Every day."

"Excellent. Do we even have anything on the accident yet?"

"We know our client was driving in that part of town around the time of the accident in a van covered in deer blood."

Danny looked at me. "You're kidding."

"I'm not." I'd told Danny about Pompeo's plea deal but not about my visit with Rick Dalton, so I filled him in on what I knew about our client's damaged, bloody van.

"That doesn't sound good."

"No, it doesn't. Neither does the fact that he hand-scrubbed it in a self-serve car wash the next morning."

"Pompeo still has to have more though—a witness, a picture, something."

"We should know when Pompeo gives us his file Friday. I don't know that there's much more we can do right now, especially with Olivia out of town."

"Oh? Where'd she go?"

"She's climbing red rocks as we speak."

"Where?"

"Red Rock."

"You know that's irritating, right?"

"What?"

"Never mind. Anything else you want me to do right now?"

"Not that I can think of."

"Mind if I leave for lunch a little early?"

"Of course not. What's up?"

"I'm meeting with a financial planner from Martel Financial, another young guy just getting started. Spencer thought that it was good to start building a referral network of people my own age."

"Perfect. Make sure you pick up lunch and bring back the receipt."

"What for?"

"So we can start the Shepherd Firm Client Entertainment Account."

Danny grinned. "Lobster it is."

SINCE I WASN'T EATING lobster on my boss's tab with a financial planner, I was sitting at my desk munching a sandwich when my phone buzzed.

"Hi, Edge," I said.

"Nate, these new charges are a problem."

"I agree."

"No, not that. Well, that, but not in the way that you're thinking. I'm sitting here with Dawn Blackwell, our CFO."

"We've met."

"Do you mind if I put you on speaker?"

"I can't talk to you about the case with someone else in the room, Edge."

"This isn't about the case, Nate. Well, it involves the case, but it's not about the case, but...can I put Dawn on with us?"

I looked at the ceiling. "Sure."

There was a click, then, "Can you hear us, Nate?" in that distant echo that indicates a speakerphone.

"I can."

"So there's a story in the *Carrefour Courier* today about the new murder charge. Did you see it?"

"No, but I believe you. I'll check it out when we hang up."

"We've received two calls—"

"Three," said Dawn.

"—three calls from churches who are withdrawing their sponsorship of several of our outreach ministries."

"Okay."

"It's jeopardizing our daycare expansion and our health clinic build."

"I see."

"We can't afford to lose that money. Too many people are counting on us."

"I understand."

"So, what are we going to do about it?"

"What do you mean?"

"Legally, what can we do to stop them from pulling their support?"

"They're mostly pledges," said Dawn.

"Which are legally binding, right?" said Edge.

"Edge," I said, "I can't advise you on this."

"What do you mean? You're my lawyer, aren't you?"

"That's right, Edge, I am. I am your personal lawyer. That means I represent you, Edgerton Fleece. I can't represent Pillars in any of its disputes with any of its sponsors—"

"Patrons," said Dawn.

"—patrons about your case. It's a conflict."

"What do you mean it's a conflict?" said Edge. "I founded Pillars."

"But you're incorporated, right? And have a board?"

"Sure, but the Board does what I say."

"The corporation is its own entity, Edge. I can't represent it and you."

"Why in the world not?"

I was silent for a moment, then said, "Edge, I need to have this conversation with you privately."

"Because one way Pillars could react to all this is by firing, Edge, right?" said Dawn.

I was silent.

"But the Board would never do that," Edge said. "The board members are from all our biggest churches. They've been with us from the beginning.

I didn't say anything.

"So what do we do?" said Edge.

"I'll get you the names of a couple of lawyers you can talk to," I said. "They can look at the pledge agreements and advise your board."

There was brief muttering, then Edge said, "Okay, Nate. Thanks. We'll look for it."

"How much are we talking about, by the way?"

"Ten percent of our budget," said Dawn. "But even that amount puts our financing for the health clinic and childcare expansion at risk."

"And we're still a ways from trial," I said and immediately regretted it.

"When's the trial?" said Dawn.

"This August."

"But that's four months!"

"Right. That's pretty fast for a murder trial, but I can always ask for more time."

"No! I'm saying that's too long to wait! Do you know how much money we could lose by then?"

"No."

"All of it!" said Dawn. "And we need that clinic. And the extended childcare. If we don't keep this together..."

"Dawn, you're going to have to take my word for it, four months is about as fast as it gets."

"I don't want any continuances then, Nate," said Edge.

"I won't ask for one, Edge. We'll have the case ready to go by then. Dawn, I need to talk to Edge alone, but I can give you some good news on the finance front before you go."

"I could use some good news, Nate."

"I met with Manny Amaltheakis yesterday. He said that Theo's estate includes a bequest to form a trust that will permanently fund the Pillars food pantry."

"That's great!" said Edge.

"It won't start paying out until the estate is liquidated but, from the way he spoke, it sounded like your pantry will be overflowing with food for the foreseeable future."

"That could be just what we need!" said Edge.

Dawn's voice cut in. "Edge, if the pantry is fully funded, then that's money we could divert to the childcare expansion while we wait for..." She trailed off.

"It is a blessing for sure," said Edge. "Dawn, why don't you go ahead and run those numbers and I'll catch up with you after I finish up with Nate."

"Okay."

Dawn said her goodbyes, and the phone switched to that particular closeness that tells you the speaker has been switched off.

"Well, that's good news anyway," said Edge.

"It is," I said.

"Manny has always been a good friend of Pillars."

"Did you know Theo was going to leave this bequest to Pillars?"

"He had talked vaguely about it once in a while, you know,

that he might want to leave us something to help, but we never talked specifics."

"You know he left some things to Benjamin too."

"You mean the car? Benjamin told me all about it." Edge sighed. "I keep forgetting he's gone."

"Well, you're going to be getting some reminders this week."

"What do you mean?"

"I mean the prosecution is going to turn over its file Friday. I fully expect them to either make a statement to the press or leak information about the evidence that's included."

"Why would they do that?"

"So that the potential jury pool hears it and is prejudiced against you."

"But I didn't do it."

"I know, Edge. But it's the prosecutor's job to convince them that you did. And that's one way to do it."

"I thought I was innocent until proven guilty."

"That's exactly what Pompeo is trying to do."

"I see. Is there anything I should be doing?"

"If there's an article or a report, don't respond. Don't issue a statement, don't talk to a reporter, don't talk about it in your building. If anyone contacts you with a question, you refer them to me."

"I understand."

"Just keep your head down and I'll let you know what I find out at the end of the week."

"Right. Thanks, Nate."

We hung up. I gave that advice to my clients all the time but it usually wasn't followed as much as I'd like. I hoped Edge would keep the clamps on this one, though, because it was going to get worse before it got better.

20

On Wednesday afternoon, I sent a quick text to make sure Kira was there, then went over to Theo Plutides' house to look around. It was also the day we had kinda, sorta texted about doing something after work. I figured it was a good day to go over, just in case.

This time I followed the route that the killer had used the night Benjamin Trane had been killed: I came straight down Sunnyfield Drive, stopped at the traffic light at the intersection of Sunnyfield and Coulter, then drove down the straight away until I slowed down by the big oak tree at 5436 Sunnyfield Drive. There was no sign at all that a man had died there, just an unscathed oak whose branches reached out over an unstained sidewalk.

I accelerated again until I reached Plowshare Drive, took a right, and followed the road to the house number 333 on the cul-de-sac.

I pulled into the driveway, parked next to the Northwest Auction van, and walked up the path to the front door.

It was only April so things were just starting to blossom, but I could see that the grounds were immaculate. The grass had shaken off its winter brown and looked as if it had already been cut at least once. The bushes were in sharp order and off to the right were two rows of what looked like dwarf apple trees. A weeping cherry to the left had buds but not blossoms. I heard the soft trickle of water as I walked past the columns to the double front door and knocked.

The doors opened and Kira walked out to meet me. She wore jeans with a button-down shirt and low-heeled boots, and her dark hair was haphazardly bound in a low, loose ponytail.

I pointed. "Glad to see you kept the fountain running. The place was going to hell."

Kira smiled. "Lots of people have fountains."

"Honestly, I don't know how people live without them."

Her smile broadened as she shrugged. "I'd rather sell a place with a fountain than without it. So Manny gave you the run of the place?"

"He said I could take a look at the things you were setting aside for Benjamin Trane. Or his estate now, I should say."

"No problem. Do you want to start with the big-ticket item?"

"The car? Sure."

"Come on." Kira gave me a wave and led me into the house.

"Whoa!" I said.

Kira stopped. "This is the 'gets worse before it gets better' stage of things."

The house of Theo Plutides was huge, its ceilings were high, and the rooms were far larger than any single old man would ever need, but I couldn't tell you the first thing about how it was laid out or decorated because every square inch of space in every direction was covered in stuff—furniture and boxes and bins and rows of tables strewn with the flotsam of a long life stretched in every direction. There was a faint sense of order—I think a room contained nothing but couches and divans while another was filled with lamps and chairs—but you had to cross your eyes and let go to see it, like with one of those magic eye pictures.

"We have to inventory everything," said Kira. "Then we decide what gets auctioned individually, what gets sold in lots, what gets sold online, and what gets donated. You're looking at a few weeks of work."

"Really? I mean, wow."

"Some estates are more challenging than others."

She led me through the front rooms to a long kitchen where the order made a little more sense—plates and silverware and appliances covered every inch of island, counter, and table space —and from there through a hall to a large mudroom, which I'm sure the good people of Harvest referred to by another name like le vestibule la dirté. We then went through the garage and out a side door where we followed a path that led to an outbuilding that had the look of a second garage. Kira keyed in a code and the door went up. Unlike every other space I had just seen, this area was pristine. There was nothing in it except two cars, one red and one silver, and a motorcycle.

"It's this one," said Kira, pointing at the red one.

"Is that a Mustang?"

Kira nodded. "1966 convertible. Signal flare red. Its engine—"

I raised a hand. "Telling me anything beyond 'it has an engine' would be a waste."

Kira smiled and tapped my chest with her finger. "Then let me tell you what makes this one special. There's an outfit down in Florida that remakes 1966 Ford convertible Mustangs—they use the original chassis and put in a new engine with modern amenities. Benjamin loved taking Theo on errands in this one in the summertime."

"And Theo left it to Benjamin?"

"He did."

"What's it worth?"

"You're looking at a couple hundred thousand."

"Really?"

"Really. What?"

"Just thinking about all that money that's one texting teenager away from the scrap heap."

She smiled. "Feel free to skip my auctions."

I pointed. "What about those?"

"The Aston Martin and the Harley go to the nephew. He's still deciding whether to keep them."

"The nephew?"

"Rory Dennison. Nephew, sole heir, and executor of the estate of Theo Plutides. And ultimately my boss."

"I thought it was Manny?"

"Manny hired me, but Mr. Dennison decides what to sell and what to keep."

"Seems like that could take a while."

"Usually. But here, it's not too bad.

"Why's that?"

"Because he wants to sell everything. Or just about everything."

I remembered the state of the house. "That seems like a lot."

"That's why it'll take a few months. Mr. Dennison wants to make sure that he gets every dime out of the sale." She pointed. "Need to see any more?"

"No, thanks."

"There's one other thing to show you then."

Kira led me back through le vestibule and the kitchen, through the room with the chairs and lamps, to another that was filled with paintings, books, and bins. Judging from the bookshelves lining of the two walls, this was Theo's study. Framed paintings were stacked three and four deep along one wall, books from other rooms were stacked in front of the filled bookshelves, and stackable bins lined the remaining wall. As we walked past the bins, past labels of "CDs" and "Drives" and "Phones" and "Tablets," I realized that they were alphabetized. We stopped at the end of the row, in front of one labeled "Wallets."

"This is the other," said Kira.

"Theo really left Benjamin his wallets?" I said.

"And the contents therein."

"Isn't that unusual?"

Kira smiled. "You wouldn't believe the instructions I get sometimes. This is nothing."

I looked in the bin. "Manny said Theo wanted to leave Benjamin some walking around money. What's the total?"

"So far we've found four wallets totaling $9,439.00."

"Not a bad walk."

"Not at all."

Kira's phone buzzed. She looked, gave a sigh, and said, "That's Mr. Dennison. I need to take this, but it might take a few minutes. Stick around 'til I'm done?

"Sure."

Kira nodded, answered her phone, and said, "Good morning, Mr. Dennison...Yes, we're making progress...Yes, I uploaded the updated inventory last night."

Kira mouthed "Thank you" and walked back out toward the kitchen.

I turned back to the plastic bin with the four wallets sitting inside. Actually, it was three wallets and a money clip. The wad of bills in the money clip seemed thick and the outer bill was a one hundred but somehow it didn't seem appropriate for me to rifle through it, so I just looked. Ten thousand dollars and a fancy car seemed like a generous bequest and my estimation of Theo Plutides went up a notch.

I wandered across the room to the paintings. I saw that some were in cases and some had glass coverings and some just frames and bare canvas. I flipped through one row, which seemed to feature a woman in yellow robes with red flowers or sheaves of wheat, then another, which consisted of maritime battles during the War of 1812. They were all paintings as opposed to prints and I was beginning to see what Kira was talking about—sorting through all of these things to value them properly would take months.

I was flipping through another set of paintings, this time of landscapes, when I came to one of those signs that you find in lakeside tourist shops all over Michigan. It was a rectangular piece of gray slate with a rustic rope (meaning frayed) running through two holes drilled into the top so that you could hang it lengthwise. I picked it up. A poem was painted in white script that read:

Seek hope, young orphan.
Reject despair, old father.
Grow wisdom, innocent youth.
Guard wonder, wise age.
Play music, make love,
drink wine, toast life!

Two wineglasses were tilted toward each other in one corner and musical notes floated upward in the other.

I couldn't say it fit with the other pieces but I had also been in enough lake-side shops with my wife Sarah back in the day to know that sometimes these things just follow you home. I put the poem back and checked out the books.

I was leafing very carefully through a book by Ralph Waldo Emerson that seemed very old when Kira came back.

"Sorry about that," she said. "He calls just about every day to check on the progress."

"No problem." I waved around. "This place is a treasure trove."

Kira smiled. "Sixty percent of this place is a treasure trove. Forty percent is complete crap. That's what's taking so long."

I laughed. "That's why you get paid the big bucks."

"Right."

Kira's mood had changed after the call, and I could see she was preoccupied.

"Hey, thanks for showing me around. I'll get out of your hair."

"Thanks, I mean—"

I smiled. "I know what you mean."

We were walking through the couch room when she said, "I'm sorry, Nate, but I can't meet you tonight—I have an art appraiser coming at seven. The guy's some sort of Commodore Perry expert and I need him to assess some works of his landing in Japan and it's just been impossible to get him here—" She paused, caught her breath, and pushed a stray lock behind her ear. "Can we reschedule?"

"We don't have to."

"No, I want to. Things are just stacking up."

"Sure. I'll have to check the Red Wings schedule, though. I'm not sure when they play next."

Kira looked relieved. "I don't need the Red Wings, Nate. How about dinner? Friday?"

"That sounds great. Pick you up at seven?"

"Perfect." She touched my arm. "Thanks for understanding."

"No problem. I'll see you then." I had taken three steps down the walk when I turned. "Where do you want to go?"

She smiled. "Surprise me."

"That's just cruel."

"I know." She smiled and shut the front door.

21

Friday was the day the prosecution's discovery was due, the day we were going to learn just how Ryan Pompeo was going to justify a murder charge. The business day doesn't end until five p.m. and, in this age of electronic filing, Pompeo technically had until eleven fifty-nine p.m. to deliver the documents to us, but I showed up at the office that morning with the hope that maybe Pompeo would want to get out of town early that weekend.

I arrived to find Danny in our conference room with a young couple, the Perrys, who recently had their second child and so were biting the bullet to make an estate plan. It turned out they had a standard insurance policy and some modest assets, and it would have been a simple matter to handle were it not for a gap, slightly deeper than the Mariana Trench, over just which of their sisters should be named guardian of their two angels. Danny patiently defused the situation and gently brought them around to think about which solution would cause the least disruption for their children if the worst, God forbid, were to happen. Once they thought of it in those terms, the Perrys agreed that Las Vegas was awfully far away and that

Kalamazoo, Michigan would be easier for the kids to deal with.

I could hear most of it from my office. I hated to say it, but that type of work really seemed to suit him.

Since I didn't have any emails or packages from the State of Ohio regarding Edgerton Fleece, I spent some time working on other matters and fretting about where in the hell I was supposed to take Kira for dinner.

I had spent the last couple of years making meat and vegetables for one out of the fridge, ordering in, or going to restaurants that I chose based on the game that was on TV or the Scoville rating of its hot sauce. Before that, Sarah and I had gone to places where we had—and stick with me on this—really liked the food. I hadn't had to pick a restaurant and worry about the impression the choice itself made in more than a decade. Was formal trying too hard? Was informal being lazy? Was French cuisine pretentious or pedestrian? And gastronomical goodness be damned, why in the hell would you deconstruct anything when it was a perfectly good meal in the first place? And listen, before you suggest it, social media was no help at all since every time I checked, I found a dozen restaurants I'd never heard of and every one of them contained at least one review from someone who'd almost died of food poisoning.

I flipped my phone on my desk in disgust and wished the evidence of the murder I was going to spend the next four months of my life on would just get here already.

I heard Danny wrapping up and went out to join him in the main office to say goodbye to the Perrys. They were young, maybe five years younger than me, so I introduced myself and said, "Great to meet you both. Once he has the documents finished, you'll have to let Daniel and his wife Jenny take you out to dinner to celebrate."

"A night out?" said the wife. "That would be wonderful."

"You know, somewhere really nice but not stuffy or old, so you can relax away from the kids but get some really good food."

"Like Althouse?" said the wife.

"Exactly like Althouse," I said.

Her face lit up. "I've heard such good things, and I wanted to go there, but we just can't get away with the kids."

"Well make sure you schedule a sitter now. What do you think, two weeks, Daniel?"

Danny stared at me for a beat, then smiled and said, "Two weeks should do it."

"Wonderful," said the wife. She turned to her husband. "My mom could babysit."

"I'm sure my mom will want to weigh in on that," said the husband, and the two of them continued their conversation on the way out the door.

After Danny shut the door behind them, he turned back to me. "Do you want to tell me what that was about?"

"Business development for you. I'm sure they have friends your age who need the same service."

"Uh-huh."

"And make sure you use your new client entertainment account."

"Right."

"I'm always there for you, Danny. Remember that."

I had gone back to my office because there was no sense in letting that conversation go any farther when I heard the front door open again.

A courier service was standing there with two Bankers boxes. Danny and I relieved him of them, signed the receipt, and took the boxes into the conference room.

The top of each had a printed sticky-label that said, "*State vs. Edgerton Fleece—Prosecution Disclosures.*" We opened them and got to it.

You can tell a lot about lawyers by the way they produce documents, and I don't mean the knee-jerk characterization of good vs. evil that your mom attributed to neat and sloppy people. What I mean is that some lawyers will give you an itemized production, with each individual document labeled and cross-referenced in an index that makes things easy to find so that everyone was dealing with the same documents at trial. Others will label the types of documents, like expert reports or medical records or witness statements, but don't identify the documents that are in each category. And some just hand you a box and say, "Here, this is how I found it, have at you."

It's really the lawyers in the second group that you have to keep your eye on. The first group wants to make sure that they can prove at a moment's notice that they provided you with everything. The third group has better things to do and figures we'll all just work it out as we go. The second group, though, the second group wants to be able to say that they provided you with a document but not be bound to an actual index of production if a document mysteriously turns up later. Those are the ones you have to watch.

You guessed it—Pompeo gave us a letter with broad categories but no itemization.

If it had been a lawyer I'd dealt with before, like Jeff Hanson or Tiffany Erin or even T. Marvin Stritch, I wouldn't have been too concerned about it—we'd built up a certain level of trust and I'd found that, on this sort of thing, those lawyers were always on the up and up. But Pompeo? We had no history, and what I'd seen in this case so far didn't give me the slightest level of comfort. So we'd have to itemize and index everything ourselves.

"Are you ready for an inventory?" I said.

"No, I'm just Reddy," said Danny.

"That was terrible."

"I learned from the best."

"We each take a box, then you make a master list?"

Danny was already opening his. "How did I know that's how this would go?"

"You learned from the best."

So we started pulling out the evidence Ryan Pompeo had assembled against Edgerton Fleece that supported a charge of murder.

I PULLED a brown folder out of my box and started creating piles. There was one for the accident report, another for the paramedic's run sheet when they responded to the call, then piles for the medical records, the coroner's report, the police accident report, the witness statements, from Mrs. Pepperstone and her two neighbors, and some more statements from people I didn't recognize yet.

I started a new pile with the bill from Carrefour Collision and a statement from Rick Dalton, then sorted through a bunch of documents that looked like Pillars' financials. Finally, there was a drive at the bottom simply labelled "Pictures/Videos" that I assumed had pictures of the crime scene and the autopsy which I'd leave for Danny to sort through.

I'd hate to disappoint him.

That was it for my box. Not that that wasn't enough.

I looked up. Danny only had two piles, one fairly large and one quite small. "What have we got there?" I asked.

"The prosecutor's theory on motive."

"Which is?"

Danny was scanning the four or five pages from the little pile. "Just a second."

It was barely that before Danny put it down.

"And?"

Danny put one hand on the big pile. "This is the estate plan of Theo Plutides—his will and a series of trusts and the supporting documents. I haven't gone through it for the details—"

"Slacker."

"—but we know from your meeting with Manny what Theo left to Benjamin."

"The '66 Mustang and the wallets."

"Exactly." Danny put his other hand on the tiny pile. "This is the will of Benjamin Trane."

"He had a will? I didn't think he had any family."

"I don't think he did. The will is a form like you could get for any of the internet legal services companies."

"Okay. And?"

Danny flipped to the fourth page and handed it to me. "Benjamin Trane left everything he owns to Pillars."

22

The two of us stared at the documents, one big and complex, the other small and damaging.

"Wait a minute, though," I said. "We know what Theo left Trane—the car and the wallets."

"How much was that?"

"A little under ten thousand dollars in the wallets."

"And the car?"

"It was a Mustang that Theo had refurbished or retrofitted or something like that, but let's just say it's two hundred thousand dollars. Are you going to kill someone for that?"

"You know people have done it for less."

"Sure. But for an organization with a budget of millions? Because remember Trane's estate doesn't go to Fleece, it goes to Pillars. This doesn't seem like enough.

"It's definitely something. But you're right, it doesn't seem like enough."

I shook my head. "I'm calling Pompeo."

Danny tapped Theo's huge estate plan. "Want me to read this first?"

"That'll take days. I want to catch him before the weekend. This seems like bullshit. Let's see what he says."

I called Pompeo on my cell and put it on speaker between us.

"NATO! Calling to plead guilty?"

"No, Ryan. I'm sitting here with my associate, Daniel Reddy—"

"I am ready to talk to him."

"—and we were just going through the materials you sent over."

"Good, good. Thought I'd send you some light reading for the weekend."

"Yeah, we received two boxes, but we didn't get the third."

"I only sent two boxes."

"Really? Huh."

"Why do you say that?"

"Because you still haven't given me any evidence of motive."

"Didn't you get the will?"

"I did."

"Pretty convenient that Trane left everything to Fleece's organization when he died, don't you think?"

"Ryan, Pillars is a big organization. Do you really think Fleece would kill someone over ten thousand dollars and a car?"

"Ten thousand dollars?"

"I talked to Theo's lawyer. That's how much cash was in his wallets."

Silence, then, "That's a lot of cash to some people."

"Come on."

"And it *is* a nice car."

"Tell me there's more."

"There's plenty, believe me."

"I guess if you want to argue to a jury that ten thousand dollars is enough for a literal pillar of the community to commit murder, that's up to you."

"There's more than enough in those wallets for me to show a jury, NATO. I've got your man at the scene and a motive for murder."

"At the scene? I didn't see any evidence of Edge at the scene."

"Fine, I thought we were talking man to man but, if you're going to be a stickler about it, I have your man's vehicle at the scene and your man destroying evidence the next day."

"Destroying evidence?"

"You saw the vehicle repair bill, right?"

"From when he hit a deer? I did."

Ryan chuckled again. "That's certainly what the insurance claim form says. Which I have to give Fleece credit for because it takes some pretty big stones to turn in an insurance claim after you damage your vehicle killing someone."

"Deer are a menace."

"They sure are. But usually in the fall during the rut. So yes, I call scrubbing blood off a van and repairing a dent from a man's body destroying evidence." He chuckled. "Feel free to call it routine vehicle maintenance, though. That'll be fun."

"It still seems pretty thin to me, Ryan."

"I tell you what, take some time, go through the file, take a good look at what we have. I don't have any authority from my boss yet but if you take a plea to murder, I think our office would recommend a sentence closer to the fifteen-year side than the life side. Think about it."

"Not much to think about from my end."

"Take the time anyway. Life's too short and your client will probably want to leave prison at some point."

"Not happening."

"Then it sounds like we're in for a fun summer. Don't let him work you all weekend, Steady Reddy. Later."

Pompeo hung up.

"Is Sir Bro-heim always like that?" said Danny.

"Pretty much."

"Yeah, we're not losing to him." He tapped the big pile. "I'll dive into this."

"It can wait until Monday. We still have plenty of time."

"Okay."

"Are you almost finished for the day?"

"Just about. I have to put my notes together real quick on the Perrys' estate plan from this morning, you know, since my boss committed me to having it done in two weeks."

"Prompt service is paramount in our industry."

"Right. I heard you, you know."

"Heard me what?"

"Make a reservation at Althouse right after the Perrys left."

"I don't know what you're talking about."

"You're saying that if I called Althouse right now and cancelled the reservation for Shepherd, nothing would happen?"

"I didn't say that at all. I said I don't know what you're talking about."

Danny looked at the ceiling. "The reservation was for two, so that eliminates your mom and dad or Mark and Izzy or Tom and Kate. Olivia is out of town and Cade, well, I don't think you'd be asking a woman, a young woman, where she would like to eat to impress Cade."

"Who said anything about impressing anyone?"

"No, you're right. Your exact words were 'somewhere really nice but not stuffy or old? Where you can relax and get some really good food.'"

"I don't recall saying that."

"I can have the court reporter read the transcript back if you like."

"I thought you hated trial work."

"I do."

“Then quit the cross-examination, Counselor.”

“Fine. May I ask who this person is that you're not going to dinner with that you don’t want to impress?”

“An acquaintance.”

Danny grinned. “Good luck, NATO.”

“Don’t even.”

23

When I was in high school, the last game of the regular season was against our rival Carrefour South, which was led by a hotshot, all-state quarterback named Mitch Pearson. I remember standing at one end of the field, arms linked with teammates on either side, swaying back and forth to "Enter Sandman," waiting for the PA announcer to say "the Carrefour North Panthers" so that we could tear through a paper banner and sprint onto the field.

Or there was the time when I watched my brother Tom's team play for the high school football state championship against Edwardsburg. I had watched that game on TV and remembered drinking some coffee right before kickoff and then thinking it was a big mistake because it felt like my heart was going to jump right out of my chest.

And, of course, there was that moment in my first solo murder trial, where my client was facing the death penalty, and Hank Braggi and I had stood, and we had faced the jury and we had waited for agonizing minutes as the Court went through its pain-staking procedure before it announced the verdict.

Sorry, that was a bit of a ramble. What I meant to say was,

that Friday night, I got out of my Jeep and walked up to the front door of Kira Freeman's townhouse.

When Kira opened the door, her dark hair hung loose and straight down around her shoulders. She wore a black shirt that was tight at the top and loose at the wrists and black pants that fit the same way over heels that made her quite a bit taller.

"Wow," I said before I realized it. "I mean, hi."

Her mouth ticked in a small smile. "That," she said, "is an acceptable response. Come in. You can meet my roommate before we go."

I waited as she closed the door, then followed her in.

Right, the townhouse. It was very nice. Wood floors, white trim and walls, neat, with fine decorative pieces scattered about. That was about all that registered with me at the time.

She led me into a living room with a small couch, a large comfy chair, and one of those set ups where the TV was above the fireplace. Kira walked around the couch to a wide, flat pillow. "Nate Shepherd, this is Roxie."

As I rounded the couch, a dog hopped off the pillow and sat at attention next to Kira. It was a boxer, with the square jaw and drooping ears that gave her a sadly intense expression. She was a little smaller than other boxers I'd seen, probably just under fifty pounds, and her color was different too—dark, almost black but with a mix of brown, and a single irregularly shaped white blazon on the center of her chest. I could also see some faint white around the muzzle that was probably the result of age.

"Hello, Roxie," I said. Her ears perked for a moment at my voice, then drooped again.

I pointed. "May I?"

Kira nodded. "Roxie, free," she said, and Roxie came trotting over. I let her sniff my fist and, when she seemed comfortable, squatted down and scratched Roxie under one side of her jaw.

Kira said, "Let me grab my purse."

"Sounds good."

As Kira went upstairs, Roxie leaned into the scratching and closed her eyes.

Kira came back down.

"She's so calm." As I said it, Roxie lost interest and walked back to her bed, lay down, and curled up.

"She is. That's the service dog in her. But I think she misses Theo and Ben too."

"Yeah?"

Kira nodded. "That was about as active as she's been since she came here. Ready?"

"I am."

"So, where are you taking me?"

"The Althouse."

"Interesting."

"Have you been there?"

"No. You?"

"I hear great things."

"So, no?"

"Right."

"Then let's go find out together."

"This looks interesting," said Kira as she turned the page.

"It does," I said.

I was staring at a menu where I only recognized about half the terms. Vegetables like cauliflower and mushrooms I understood, but I didn't understand the pairings, like nettles and chives, and there were some things, whether they were grains or plants or herbs, that I'd simply never heard of before.

"How did you hear about it?" she said.

"A client recommended it."

I continued to stare. Everything had an explanation for how it was sourced, which I appreciated because it sometimes gave me a clue what the heck it was, but I had to say I had read less sourcing of material in briefs to the Supreme Court.

The front server took our order. Kira looked entirely comfortable ordering a first of season salad and a purple barley risotto with cauliflower. With both of their eyes on me, I defaulted to the most familiar looking thing on the menu. "I'll have the mushroom steak with lentils and garlic sauce."

"Excellent," said the front server. "Chef cooks it to a medium rare texture. You'll love it."

"Great."

We ordered another round of drinks—a locally distilled, cucumber and mint infused vodka for her and the closest thing to a house lager they had for me. To her credit, the front server was able to almost entirely hide her disdain when I ordered it.

After our renewed drinks arrived, I said, "So how long have you been doing estate auctions?"

Yes, I am just that smooth.

"It's the family business. Well, my dad's business, actually. Mom's a molecular biologist at the University."

"Yikes."

"Exactly. I came up helping him. Auctions wound up being more in my wheelhouse than molecular biology so that was the path I took."

"Is he still involved?"

"No, he passed eight years ago."

"Oh, I'm sorry. You took over after he died?"

"I did. Have you always practiced criminal law?"

I shook my head. "I started in the prosecutor's office here in Carrefour to get some trial experience, went to a big firm for a while to practice on the civil side, then left and went out on my own. The first big case I landed was a murder case and now that seems to be what keeps coming in my door."

Kira nodded. "Big estates are the same way. Once you get one, it leads to the next, and before you know it, you have a bunch of them."

"It's exactly like that."

"That's how I got the Plutides estate. I worked with Manny Amaltheakis on a different estate and he was happy enough with the money we raised that he referred this one to us."

The front server came with a cutting board of Ezekiel bread that had been kneaded by poets or something and a pat of sunflower butter.

I took the cutting board by the handle with my left hand and offered Kira a slice. As she picked one, I noticed my hand.

I should say that I noticed my wedding band. I hadn't even thought about it.

I put the cutting board back down and put my hands in my lap.

Kira took a dollop of butter and spread it on the bread. "I know about Sarah."

I cocked my hand. "You do?"

"Izzy," she said and took a bite.

"Of course."

"No, not at the hockey game. Back when it happened. We've been friends for a long time."

I nodded. "Oh, right."

"I say that just so you know it doesn't have to loom out there. And you don't have to be self-conscious about mentioning it. Or her."

I held up my hand, showing her the ring. "I should've thought to take it off—"

Kira shook her head. "You forget what I do for living, Nate.

People always have a hard time parting with things from someone they love. I get it."

"Thanks."

"Now if that's from a new wife I don't know about, I'll be pissed."

I smiled. "I've been meaning to tell you—"

She pointed the knife at me.

"—that I'm glad we could reschedule."

I took my own knife, for the butter not self-defense, and the two of us marveled how much sunflower butter tasted like, well, butter, before I said, "Speaking of rescheduling, can I mention one work thing?"

She nodded. "I don't mind."

"We received the prosecutor's evidence disclosures today in the Fleece case. Benjamin Trane apparently left his estate to Pillars."

"Okay."

"They're saying that Trane leaving his estate to Pillars was Fleece's motive for killing him."

Kira scowled. "The car and the wallets?"

"Apparently."

"That doesn't make much sense."

"That's what I said. But they're relying on it, so I expect you'll get an order at some point to hold on to those things."

"Okay. Thanks for the heads up."

The mushroom steak and purple barley risotto arrived, and we dug in.

Oh, and in case you're wondering, my mushroom steak was actually a giant mushroom, but in fairness, it was delicious.

~

We talked the rest of the evening, discovering people we both knew and places we both went and a common disdain for pumpkin pie which had subjected us both to Thanksgiving Day scorn. Before I knew it, the mushroom steak and purple barley risotto had turned into lavender ice cream and sustainable coffee, which then led to an easy, laughing ride home.

As I walked her to the door, she said, "Thanks for dinner, Nate."

"Thanks for going."

"It was...enlightening."

I smiled. "Who knew nettles grew in Carrefour?"

"How about I pick the place next time?"

It took me a beat. "Next time?"

She shook her head. "Nate, you could give a girl a complex."

"I think that's a great idea. Dinner, I mean."

"Good. You pick the time." She smiled, put her hand on my waist, kissed my cheek, and said, "Don't feel like you have to wait too long."

Then she opened the door and went inside.

I stood there and stared at her house number for a few seconds, knowing there was something I was supposed to do. Then I remembered, walked back to my car, and drove home.

24

On Saturday morning, I was two cups of coffee into my day when my phone buzzed. Danny.

"Hey," I said. "Is everything okay?"

"Yes, I mean no, I mean yes everything is okay with me personally, no something is very wrong with our case."

"Fleece?"

"Of course."

"I thought you weren't working this weekend?"

"I wasn't, but then I thought I could use the Plutides estate plan as a learning tool and see how some of these big estates are set up, so I brought it home for the weekend."

"Who wouldn't?"

"It's a free chance to learn."

"I get it—who doesn't want to snuggle up on a rainy weekend with a good estate plan?"

Danny didn't rise to the bait. At all. Instead, he said, "Can you meet me in the office this morning?"

"Can't you just tell me?"

"I think I need to show you."

"Really?"

"And I need you to make sure I'm right."

"It's that serious?"

"It's that serious."

"Okay. Forty-five minutes?"

"Let's make it an hour. I have to wait for Jenny to get back from her Pilates class to watch Ruth."

"No problem. But make sure you tell her that you called this meeting, not the evil boss man."

"I will. See you in an hour."

I hung up. This was completely out of character for Danny. He rarely called me on the weekend, and he never told me to come to the office, so I couldn't imagine what it could be about.

I went to the office to find out.

After we sat down in the conference room, Danny flipped open the big binder that held the Theo Plutides estate plan and said, "There are a bunch of documents in here, but there are only a few we need to worry about."

"Okay."

He flipped open to a tab. "This is Theo Plutides' will. In it, he leaves specific things to specific people and specific charities. This first section is monetary bequests—see here's one to St. Wendelin's Hospital, here's one to the Carrefour Theater, and here's the one to fund the trust that will support the Pillars Food Pantry."

"Wow. That's a lot of mac and cheese."

Danny nodded. "The next section is where he leaves specific property to people—see he left some paintings to the museum, an ATV to a buddy's son, things like that."

"Got it."

"And here, toward the end, is where he mentions Trane."

I looked over Danny's shoulder and read. "'To Benjamin Trane, I leave my 1966 Mustang and all wallets, hot and cold.' Right. We knew that. The wording is a little funny, but I get it."

I studied the list, then said, "Okay, so far that's what we thought, right? That Theo gave Trane the car, which was worth maybe two hundred thousand dollars and the wallets, which have around ten thousand dollars in them?"

"That's not the part I'm worried about," said Danny. "So from what I can see, Theo owned a whole lot of stuff scattered over at least three states, which would normally be a nightmare for someone to track down."

I thought about just the things I'd seen in Theo's house earlier that week. "Still with you."

"So to help his nephew Rory Dennison and his lawyer Manny Amaltheakis know where to find things, Theo created an inventory." Danny flipped to a new tab in the binder, then held up that section between his finger and thumb. It was more than two inches thick.

"You wouldn't believe all the things that are in here—bank accounts, brokerage accounts, bond holdings, property titles and descriptions, shares of private businesses, you name it. Theo lists the asset followed by the account number or other ID so that Rory and Manny can find it."

"Okay."

"The first section is financial holdings, which he classified as cash, currencies, and bearer paper."

"I see it."

"For example, here's the first one. You have 'Currency–US dollars; Amount–$159,322.00; Account–First Carrefour' and then the address and account number for the bank."

"I see. Wow, that's a lot of accounts." I traced one finger down the "amount" column and saw an awful lot of cash. "I think nephew Rory is going to be just fine."

Danny ignored me and flipped two pages. It was still the currency section, but it looked like the amounts were getting progressively smaller.

Danny tapped the page, right in the middle, and said, "This is the important entry:

Currency–Bitcoin (100);
Amount–$22,331.00;
Account–cold wallet.

The term caught my eye. "Cold wallet?"

"Do you know what that is?" said Danny.

"I feel like I'm about to learn," I said.

"Think of a cold wallet like a special thumb drive. It holds the keys to your digital currency, cryptocurrency like Bitcoin, completely offline where it can't be hacked."

"So, the wallet is a physical thing?"

"Yes, it's a physical device that holds the keys to your cryptocurrency."

I saw where Danny was going. "This terminology matches the will exactly, Danny, so yes, I think you're right—Theo left Benjamin this cold wallet with the Bitcoin in it too."

Danny nodded. "Which means the money in this wallet went to Pillars when Benjamin Trane was killed."

I did the math, then nodded and put a hand on Danny's shoulder. "I appreciate your concern and showing me right away, Danny. But I think we can manage the extra $22,000.00. I don't think that amount will matter that much to the jury."

To his credit, Danny remained patient. "If it were $22,000.00, I would be at my daughter's play date right now." He put his finger on the column that said "Bitcoin (100); Amount–$22,331.00" and said, "I wasn't sure what 'Bitcoin (100)' meant, so I checked the date of the inventory, which was January of 2015."

I don't know a lot sometimes, but I knew enough to know that I was getting a very bad feeling about what Danny was showing me.

"Then I went back and checked, Nate. You could buy Bitcoin in January of 2015 for $223.31 a piece. So one hundred Bitcoin was worth $22,331.00 back in 2015."

"Okay. Did you check what it was worth in February of this year?"

"I did."

"What?"

"$52,173.50."

I exhaled. "That's not much more than the forty-four thousand then. We can still manage that."

Danny shook his head. "Not fifty-two thousand total, Nate. Fifty-two thousand a piece."

I gripped the back of the chair. "If each Bitcoin was worth that much then..." I paused at the math.

Danny finished it for me. "Then this account was worth $5,217,350.00 on the day Benjamin Trane died. And he left it all to Pillars."

25

I sat down. "This has to be a mistake. There's no way Theo gave Trane 5.2 million dollars."

"He might not have thought he was," said Danny. "He might've thought he was giving him twenty-two thousand."

I pointed at the binder. "That doesn't strike me as the work of a careless man."

"Not careless exactly but look at all these things." Danny rifled through the pages of the inventory. "Nobody can keep track of all this. What if he just didn't pay attention to a bunch of these things after he made his estate plan in 2015? He looks at all of his accounts back then, itemizes everything, decides where it's all going to go, and forgets about it. Or at least only pays attention to the things he's actively managing. One little cold wallet?" Danny shrugged. "It would be easy to lose track of."

We both sat there staring at the binder, which had become an enormous turd sitting in the middle of our conference table.

"I still think it's a mistake," I said finally. "I'm calling Manny Amaltheakis."

"Mind if I sit in?" said Danny.

"You better, you're going to be doing a lot of the talking." I dialed Manny's number, put my cell on speaker, and placed it between us.

I got Manny's voicemail, which shouldn't have surprised me since it was Saturday morning. His message left his cell number in case of emergencies, and it seemed to me that I had 5.2 million of them, so I dialed it.

"This is Manny's phone," said a woman's voice.

I paused, then said, "May I speak to Manny, please?"

"I don't know. Let me check."

I heard some muttering. Then, the woman again. "Who is this?"

"Nate Shepherd. It's about the Plutides estate."

More muttering. Then a giggle, something scraping across the phone, the sound of it being dropped, then "Yes, Nate Shepherd?"

"Sorry Manny, but something's come up with the Plutides estate."

"I do not see how that is possible since Theo is already dead."

"There's an item in the inventory of his estate plan—"

"How do you have Theo's estate plan?"

"The prosecutor produced it yesterday. Did you give it to them?"

"I guess I did. What is your question?"

"Do you remember the inventory?"

"If you have seen the inventory, then you know that it is lengthy and that I will not remember everything in it."

"I appreciate that, Manny. There's one entry I need to ask you about."

"You are taking a very long time to do so."

"In the cash and currency section there's an entry that says, 'Bitcoin (100); Amount—$22,331.00—cold wallet.'"

A pause then, "Nate Shepherd, I am naked in my kitchen

and the *froutalia* is almost done. If you have a question, pleas ask it."

"Danny and I read that entry to mean that there are or hundred Bitcoin in a cold wallet."

"Who is this Danny?"

"Hi, Mr. Amaltheakis. I'm Daniel Reddy, Nate's associate."

"Daniel Reddy, are you the one who read the inventory mean that there are one hundred Bitcoin in a cold wallet?"

"I am, Mr. Amaltheakis."

"Then have you read the inventory correctly."

I motioned and Danny went ahead. "Mr. Amaltheakis, took the $22,331.00 to be the amount the Bitcoin was worth ba in January of 2015."

"Once again you have hit the nail with the hammer, Dar Reddy."

"So it's now worth—"

There was a voice in the background, then Manny said, " yes, it is worth whatever one hundred Bitcoin is worth to Now, things are getting cold here."

"Sorry, Manny," I said. "Last question—Theo left Benja Trane all of his wallets, hot and cold. Is that really this one tc

"Daniel Reddy seems like a good lawyer, Nate Shepherd. should trust his conclusions."

"That has to be a mistake."

Manny chuckled. "Theo Plutides was a capricious man. thing he left to Benjamin Trane could just as easily have tu to nothing. I would bet that if you have Daniel Reddy through that inventory, you will see that as many things tı bad as turned good. Now, I must flip my *froutalia*. Goodbye.

He hung up.

"So, it's not a mistake," said Danny.

"It's not a mistake." I tapped the table. "I don't think would believe that Edge killed someone for two hundred sand dollars. It will believe he could have done it for five million."

"They'll believe anyone could have done it for five million."

"Especially someone who acted suspicious."

After a minute I realized that we were both just sitting there, staring at the binder. "Good work, Danny, thanks. Why don't you go home and see if you can catch the end of that play date."

Danny seemed to snap out of it too and nodded.

"And don't forget to tell Jenny that *you* called *me* in."

He smiled. "I already did."

"And remind her that this whole case was your idea."

He picked up the heavy binder with both hands. "Right."

"Have a good weekend."

I WAS HALFWAY home when I realized there was another problem. Well not a problem exactly, not with my case, more of a time-bomb of an issue that I didn't want a friend to stumble into unawares.

And also a problem.

I thought about driving to Kira's house but my recent call with Manny making naked *froutalia* reminded me that everyone needs their privacy on Saturday mornings. I called.

Kira answered. "Playing hard to get, eh?"

"We have a problem. Not a problem. An issue."

"Oh?"

I heard her tone cool. I took a mental step back, realized what I had just sounded like, and said, "I mean, good morning, Kira, I had a great time last night. I didn't mean to call you so early, but I got a call from work this morning that there was an emergency related to the Fleece case and in the process of investigating that, I realized that you need to be aware of what I discovered this morning so that you can manage the Plutides estate properly."

"Boy, you sure know how to make a girl feel wanted."

"I am the smoothest. I didn't want to bother you, but I think you need to know right away, so I called."

"Seems like if you're going to disturb my Saturday morning you could at least buy me coffee."

"Done. Dine in or delivery?"

"Delivery. One cream no sugar."

"On the way."

Half an hour later, I was standing at Kira's door, coffees in hand. She ushered me in, and I totally didn't notice her hand momentarily on my shoulder as she guided me back to the kitchen.

As we sat down, I said, "Sorry again about the call."

Kira smiled. "I'm not that sensitive."

"Still sorry though."

She took a sip of coffee and smiled. "Forgiven. So what's the issue that's not exactly a problem but might be a problem?"

"There's a possibility that there might be a thumb drive floating around Theo's house with more than five million dollars in it."

Kira set down her coffee. "What do you mean?"

"I mean that I learned this morning that there is a cold wallet with one hundred Bitcoin in it that Theo left to Benjamin Trane."

"I see."

"Do you know what a cold wallet is?"

"I do."

"Have you seen it?"

"This one? No."

"Did you know about it? It was in the inventory."

"I didn't. I'm mostly dealing with assembling and appraising the physical items and preparing them for sale. I usually only check the financial list if I find something like stock certificates or bonds."

"Who assembles the financial assets?"

Kira shrugged. "I assume Manny."

I heard a rustling and then the click of claws on hardwood as Roxie walked over from her bed to me, then sat at attention, staring. I reached out and scratched under her jaw.

"Roxie, lay down," said Kira.

Roxie did and rested her head on my foot.

Kira smiled. "It's your voice, I think."

"Why?"

"She's used to living with a man."

I pet Roxie, because of course, then said, "So that's why I called."

"Because Roxie is used to living with a man?"

"No, because I thought you might not know about the cold wallet. And I suddenly had a vision of one of your employees throwing away the drive with the pens and the stapler without knowing what it was."

"That would be embarrassing. I know the difference between a wallet and a thumb drive but I'm not sure that all my employees do."

She took another sip, then said, "It's not five million by the way."

"No?"

"No, today it's closer to 4.2 million."

I smiled. "Oh, well that's a relief then."

"The value changes like bungee cord." She took a long sip of her coffee, then stood. "Well, sounds like I need to get to work."

"Now?"

"If someone came to your house and told you that there was

a bag with five million dollars sitting on your conference room table all by itself, would you go to the office?"

"Right. Sorry to ruin your Saturday. Need help?"

She thought for a moment then shook her head. "I don't think we should cross the streams on this one more than we have. I'll let you know if I find anything."

Roxie stood as I stood and I gave her a scratch goodbye. Then Kira said, "Roxie, bed," and Roxie walked over, head down, and lay down.

When we came to the door, Kira said, "I'll follow-up with Manny to see if he knows anything about where it might be."

"Sorry again for the intrusion."

"Not at all. Thanks for thinking of me."

She kissed my cheek, and I left. I had a lot to learn quickly, so I knew right where to go.

26

Olivia was standing behind the desk as I walked into the Brickhouse. "I don't see a gym bag," she said.

"Welcome back."

"Did you lose weight while I was gone?"

"No."

"Huh. Looks like you went down a shirt size or two."

"Not a one."

"Well as long as you're comfortable with yourself, that's what's important."

"Thanks. How was the trip?"

"Fantastic. Climbed every day."

"Looks like you got a lot of sun."

"Climbing in the desert will do that. So if you're not here to work out, what do you need?"

"Maybe I just missed you terribly."

"Of course. And?"

"And I have a Bitcoin problem."

"Personal or work?"

"Work."

"Head back to my office. I'll be right there."

I made my way through the gym to Olivia's office, which was a curious mixture of gym class office, library, and cybercrime lair. She had a beat-up desk like you would find in any gym with rows of worn books stacked on old shelves. In front of them were four monitors, a laptop, and a desktop computer all arranged like an air traffic controller for a super criminal. I took a seat in an egg-shaped plastic chair and waited.

Olivia came in and shut the door. She pulled a tracksuit jacket on, ran her hand back and forth through her hair to spike it back up, and said, "So, bring me up to speed."

I told her about the developments while she was gone—about the discovery that Benjamin Trane had left everything in his will to Pillars, that Benjamin Trane had inherited a car and all of Theo's wallets, and that one of those wallets contained one hundred Bitcoin.

That got Olivia's attention. After a couple of clicks on the keyboard, she said, "That was worth over five million dollars when Trane died."

I nodded.

"So what do you need to know?"

"I'm not sure yet, I don't know what I don't know, you know?"

"I know."

"I guess to start, I need to know what one of these cold wallets looks like."

Olivia reached into her desk and pulled out a small oblong case, a little bigger than an egg. She unzipped it and pulled out a rectangular drive that was shorter than a stick of Wrigley's gum. "Here you go."

"You have one? Here?"

"Obviously."

"Why?"

"Because sometimes I make payments for things with one."

"You pay for things with cryptocurrency? Like what?"

Olivia stared at me with her mirrored glasses like a sphinx.

"Right," I said. "So how does it work?"

"Flip it open."

I rotated the drive out from its metal casing. "Okay."

"Looks just like a thumb drive, right?"

"Right."

"Except see that small screen in the middle?"

"I do."

"When you connect that drive to a computer, that screen will light up. See the two buttons on top?"

"Yep."

"That will let you enter a PIN number. Once you enter the PIN, you have access to any cryptocurrency associated with this particular wallet."

"So this is a cold wallet?"

Olivia nodded. "A physical drive like that is a cold wallet."

"What's a hot wallet?"

"A hot wallet is an online account, more like a bank account or brokerage account. You store your currency in the cloud."

"Seems easier."

"It is. And less secure."

"Why?"

"Do you want the easy answer or the computer security answer?"

"Why don't you give me the easy answer."

"That cold wallet you're holding isn't connected to the internet. When you login with it, none of the information you used to access your currency is online where someone can see it. Instead, it's all right there in your hand. That means hackers can't get to it and empty your account."

I held the drive up between my thumb and forefinger; it couldn't have been more than three inches long. "But this would be so easy to lose."

"The assumption is that if you put five million dollars in it, you'll be careful where you put it."

"But what if someone takes it?"

"They would still need your PIN to log in to the wallet."

"But what if someone has your PIN?"

"If you're foolish enough to give someone your PIN and give them your cold wallet, they can plug in your cold wallet, enter the PIN, and transfer every cent of currency to wherever they want. And once it's transferred, you're never getting it back."

"You can't track it down?"

"That's kinda the point. Let me make this easier. If you put five million dollars in a safe, left the door open, and taped the combination up on the wall, would you be surprised if someone reached in and took the cash?"

"No."

"It's the same thing with that wallet and the PIN."

I stared at the tiny thing in my hand that couldn't have weighed more than a few ounces. "There really could be millions of dollars in here?"

"No. There could be *billions* of dollars in there."

I swore.

"Right." She pointed. "It seems to me that Pompeo is going to be able to point to a motive."

"He sure is."

I handed the cold wallet back to Olivia. She held it up and said, "So who has the wallet now?"

"I don't know. It appears to be missing."

"And you said the PIN was in the estate plan inventory?"

"It was."

Olivia shook her head. "Amateurs. So Manny Amaltheakis has the PIN?"

"Yes."

"And the people in the prosecutor's office?"

"Yes."

"And the people with the auction house?"

"Right."

"Let's assume for the moment that you and Danny are trustworthy. That's still an awful lot of people who have had access to the information."

"Right, but nobody has the wallet."

"Nobody has the wallet *now*. If somebody finds the wallet and has access to the PIN, that money will disappear, and nobody will even know."

"Kira wouldn't do that."

Olivia cocked her head. "Kira?"

"The head of the auction house."

"And how do you know that?"

"She's handled big estates before."

"And how do you know *that*?"

"We talked about it at dinner the other night."

Olivia grinned and sat back in her chair. "Nathan Shepherd, did you get back in the saddle while I was gone?"

It would not do for Olivia to see that I was embarrassed, so I shook my head. "I'm not even in the corral, Liv. It was just dinner."

Her grin widened. "So where did you go for just dinner?"

"Althouse."

She laughed. "You're kidding."

"I'm not."

"What kind of false front was that?"

"I'd call it more of an honest mistake."

"What in the world did you eat? No wait, let me guess—the mushroom steak."

"How did you know that?"

"Ha! I went there with that vegan cyclist a couple of times last year. I bet that's the only thing you recognized."

"Pretty much."

"So. Spill."

"We just went to dinner the one time."

"You only went out once?"

"Yeah, after the hockey game with Mark and Izzy."

"So you've gone out twice."

"No, the hockey game was kind of a group thing."

"With other couples?"

"Yes, but—"

"So twice."

"—we weren't a couple then."

Olivia nodded. "But you are now."

"No, you mirrored Inquisitor, we are not."

"But you're going out again?"

There's no pleading the Fifth with Olivia, there's only distraction and avoidance. "We haven't made any plans."

"Hmph," she said, and turned toward her computer.

"No, wait, I don't want you to do research on her."

"Oh, it's not for you."

"You're awful."

"As far as you know." Her smile dropped a bit. "I'm not kidding about the wallet. If you let people know there's a drive floating around with that kind of money on it, you're going to get yourself a *Mad Max Fury Road* situation. You can't put the genie back in the bottle, but just be careful who knows it's missing from now on."

"Got it. Thanks for your help."

She waved. "Go away. I have stones to overturn." Her fingers began to clack over the keyboard.

You can't stop some things, so I left.

27

I texted Edge and Carissa that I had to see them, preferably together. When I didn't hear from either of them for a couple of hours, I texted again and said it was urgent. Carissa texted back right away this time and said she could meet at six o'clock at Pillars. I told her I hadn't heard from Edge. Fifteen minutes later, she texted that she'd corralled him too but that we'd need to push it to six-fifteen. I told her I'd meet them then.

I tapped my phone, thinking. I was seeing prosecution's picture now. The damaged car, washing it before the repair, the lack of an alibi—all that was bad enough, but five million dollars? It wasn't going to take Pompeo too much to push the jury toward finding that Fleece had an awful lot to gain from Benjamin's death. I needed to find out right away how much the Fleeces knew.

~

I MET the Fleeces at Edge's office an hour later. I was surprised how busy the Pillars facility was on a Saturday night until I remembered that most of their outreach operations ran seven days a week.

Carissa was dressed in hospital scrubs and had her hair pulled back in a barrette. Edge wore the usual dark blue Pillars pullover and khaki pants.

"Thanks for meeting me on such short notice," I said, shaking both their hands.

Carissa nodded. "You said it was important."

"It is."

"But I have a shift starting in forty-five minutes at St. Isidore's."

"A shift?"

"I do traveling work there in the emergency room."

"Until we get our clinic up and running," said Edge.

"If," said Carissa.

"When," said Edge, smiling. "My wife can be a little pessimistic."

"Realistic."

Edge kept smiling and actually seemed to mean it. "So, you wanted to see us, Nate? Something with the case?"

"Yes, but I need to ask you a couple of questions first."

"Fire away."

"Did either of you know that Benjamin Trane had named Pillars in his will?"

Edge and Carissa looked at each other and shook their heads. "No," said Edge. "But I'm not surprised."

"Why's that?"

"Benjamin didn't have any family that I knew of. And he was at one of our planned giving seminars late last year."

Some days it just doesn't pay to get out of bed.

"What do you mean a planned giving seminar?" I said.

"It's one of the ways we fund our projects," said Edge. "We

started doing it a couple of years ago and it's been really effective."

"Edge, what is it?"

"We give a little presentation on all of the ways we reach out to the community, explain our operations, present testimony from some folks who have been positively impacted from our outreach. Then we explain that you don't even have to donate now to make a difference in people's lives. Instead, you can remember one of these projects in your will or you can make a general bequest to Pillars and we'll put it into a special projects fund and allocate the funds for you."

I rubbed my forehead. "Do you speak at this seminar?"

Edge nodded. "I explain our mission and then introduce each group leader to talk about their operation—the meal service, the childcare, the independent living assistance, all that. Then at the end, I tell them how they can help."

"Is this on video?"

"Sure. We upload it to our YouTube channel, and I think a couple of other platforms."

"Nate," said Carissa. "What's this about?"

I watched them both as I said, "Trane left his entire estate to Pillars. The prosecutor is going to use that as evidence of motive for the killing."

Edge laughed. "Then you should have no trouble winning this case, Nate," he said. "Benjamin didn't have anything.

I nodded.

"In fact, his passing has left us with a gap in our staffing that we're having a hard time filling. His death makes it harder for us to fulfill our mission, not easier."

"I'm afraid that's not the case, Edge. Benjamin got an inheritance from Theo Plutides before he died."

Carissa frowned.

Edge shook his head and said, "Are you talking about the

car? I mean, Ben was thrilled about the car but that's not enough to matter, is it?"

"He inherited some money, too."

Edge nodded. "I know Theo appreciated Benjamin. I'm not surprised he left him a little something."

"It was more than a little something."

"How much more?" said Carissa.

"About five million more."

Edge was leaning back in his chair, smiling, when I said it. I watched the information sink in—his smile turned to a scowl which turned to shock as the front legs of the chair came back to the floor. "Are you saying Theo gave Benjamin five million dollars?"

"I'm saying Theo gave Benjamin something in an account that started out modest and grew to be worth five million dollars by the time he died. Did either of you know?"

"No," said Carissa.

"Of course not," said Edge.

I didn't mention Bitcoin on purpose. Neither of them asked what the account was. At the time, I wasn't sure if that was good or bad, so I just said, "You see the problem, don't you?"

Carissa's nod was curt. "By problem you mean the fact that Edge pitched Benjamin on donating to Pillars in his will and then supposedly killed him right after Benjamin came into five million dollars?"

I nodded. "That's the one."

"It's not a problem," said Edge.

"Why's that?"

"Because I didn't do it."

"Right. I need all your materials on this planned giving seminar you gave and the links to where it's been posted."

Edge seemed unaffected as he said, "Mrs. Horvath isn't in

today, but I think I did see Dawn and her daughter. We can ask her on the way out."

"Great. Edge, Carissa, I need to know, now, if either of you had any knowledge that Theo had left Benjamin this kind of money."

"No," said Carissa.

"None," said Edge. "And I would think that I would've heard about it."

Carissa looked at her smartwatch. "I need to get to my shift. You were right to tell us today."

"Don't mention this to anybody," I said.

"You don't have to worry about that." She put her hand on Edge's shoulder, bent down, and kissed his cheek. "Did you hear Nate?"

He smiled. "I heard him."

"Don't mention the money."

"I won't."

She patted his shoulder and headed for the door, then stopped. "Do we get the money? Pillars, I mean?"

I thought. Ohio has something called a slayers statute which prevents someone who was convicted of killing someone from profiting from the death. Since Trane's money was going to Pillars, I didn't know if it would apply to this situation. It also wasn't my job to figure that out, so I said, "I'm not sure."

"That amount of money would help a lot of people, Nate. And solve a lot of problems."

"I'm sure."

"See you in the morning, Edge," Carissa said to her husband.

"Love you," Edge said. He turned to me as the door clicked shut. "You seem to think that this is bad."

"That's because it is. It adds an element that complicates things and changes the notoriety of the case."

"Well then, we better get you what you need. Let's go see if

Dawn is still here so we can get you back home for the weekend."

"Don't worry about me. This is my priority."

"I appreciate that, Nate, but work should never be our top priority. We have to tend to our families and ourselves too. What's wrong?"

"Nothing. You're right. Let's go find Dawn."

28

"Normally I would have you talk to Lynn Horvath since she runs all the seminars, but she's not in today," Edge said as we walked down the hall. "Dawn Blackwell is, though, and I'm pretty sure she'll be able to put her hands on the materials."

"Perfect," I said. "Thanks."

"I'll just tell her—"

"Actually, Edge, I'd prefer that we don't tell her anything."

"No, right, of course not. We won't tell her anything." He said the last bit as if he were reminding himself. "You just want the planned giving seminar materials, right?"

"Right."

"She's just around the corner here."

Before we reached the corner, a green-clad comet shot into us. With a squeal of laughter followed by a high-pitched shriek, the green comet turned out to be a young girl with a green jumper, black tights, and a stuffed monkey that was missing one eye and had fluff poking out of the seam on its back.

"Sorry, Mr. Edge," said the girl.

"That's okay, Dana."

"Mom says I should look both ways."

"Your mom is right. Is she up here?"

"She's in her office fixing the numbers."

"Oh, yeah?"

"Yeah. She says the morons never put them down right."

Edge nodded. "That is a problem."

I heard a ping and Edge pulled out his phone. "Agh, I have to get down to the loading dock. Dana could you—"

Dana blinked up at him.

"No, that's not a good idea," said Edge. He held out a hand. "Let's go see your mom."

Dana grabbed Edge's hand and pulled him around the corner to another set of offices. I followed.

Right as we entered, Dawn Blackwell came out of a small office on the right, yelling "Dana! I told you to stay...Oh, hi, Edge."

Edge smiled. "I believe I found something that belongs to you."

Dawn looked at her daughter. "Dana, I told you stay in this office."

Dana leaned forward and tipped her head up. "Mr. Cheever said there were bananas in the hall."

"You can't listen to Mr. Cheever, you have to listen to me."

"But we want bananas!"

"Naturally." Dawn looked up. Her short blonde hair was a little messy and she looked tired, tired in that way I had seen with both of my sisters-in-law when their kids weren't sleeping solidly through the night and made up for it by barreling around every which way during the day.

Dawn took Dana's hand and said to us, "She's in daycare enough during the week. I thought since no one was in today..."

Edge waved. "Don't think twice about it. I have to go down to the loading dock. Could you give Nate here the materials for the planned giving seminar and a link to the video?"

"Sure. Why—"

"Thanks! Gotta get down there. Thanks for coming in Nate!" Then Edge shot off.

"We talked on the call the other day, right?" Dawn said.

"We did."

"Nice to meet you in person."

I figured it was counter-productive to say we'd met when she'd stormed away from Mrs. Horvath's desk a while back, so I just said, "You too."

"Are the seminar materials for Edge's case?"

"No one has asked for them yet, but we're trying to be thorough."

"Good. Can you hang on a minute? I don't have one of the brochures, Mrs. Horvath keeps those, but I can print one for you real quick."

"Perfect."

While Dawn was printing the brochure, I talked to Dana about where Mr. Cheever was from—Madagascar, in case you're wondering—whether he had any brothers and sisters—he did not, he only had a mommy—and what his favorite food was—chicken nuggets. I asked if they had McDonald's in Madagascar and she said that no, his mommy likes to make them herself. When I asked what Mr. Cheevers liked to do for fun, Dana said he liked to draw and sing and swing, and when I asked if he sang along with songs on the radio, she told me not to be silly—monkeys don't have radios. Which was really an impossible point to argue.

True to her word, Dawn was back quickly with the brochure. "The link to the video is in there. You can call Lynn if you have any questions."

Dawn looked over her shoulder at Dana, who was bouncing

Mr. Cheevers on a chair, then said, "Do we still have to wait until August for the trial?"

"It's looking like it. Donations still tough?"

"Our expansion project is on life-support," she said. "And if this trend keeps up, we'll be cutting back services soon. Like daycare hours. We can't get that Plutides money soon enough."

"The food bank grant still hasn't funded?" I asked.

Dawn turned back to me. "What? Oh, no, not until the estate closes."

There was a crash, followed by a "Mr. Cheevers!" and I noticed that Dana was gone. So did Dawn, who waved goodbye, yelled "Dana!" and ran back into her office.

I left Mr. Cheevers hanging and made my escape.

29

During the summer, my family cooks out every Sunday afternoon at my parents' cottage on Glass Lake. Through football season, we get together to eat, watch the Detroit Lions, and commiserate. There's nothing regular that goes on in the late winter and early spring—the kids have sports, my parents take off for a while to Florida, and we get together here and there to do odd projects on each other's houses.

On this particular Sunday, it being April and my dad being a fishing maniac, I went up to Glass Lake to help my dad put in his dock and get his boats out of storage.

The whole crew was there. My older brother Tom and his wife Kate had brought their girls Reed, Taylor, and Page and their boy, little Charlie, while my brother Mark and Izzy had brought all three of their miscreants—Justin, James, and Joe.

My dad had the dock all ready to go, so we paired off and soon my dad and Mark, Tom and me, and Justin and Taylor were grabbing sections and heading into the water with encouragement from shore by James and Page. And if you're thinking April seems a little early and are wondering if the water in Glass

Lake would still be freezing cold, you'd be right—the water was freezing, and it didn't help at all that it was cloudy with a bit of a breeze. My dad, darkly tan from his time in Florida and, more importantly, wearing waders, stood hip deep in the water without a care in the world, while Tom, being the uber-prepared football coach that he was, lorded it over us in a wetsuit. I mean, the guy didn't even scuba dive, for Christ's sake.

While Mark and I shivered along with the kids as we adjusted the legs on the dock, Tom said, "I see it all the time, Dad," said Tom.

"What's that, Son," said my dad.

"No matter how many times we do something, some kids just make the same mistake over and over and over again."

"You can only work with the players you have, Son."

"I know but, as a coach, it's frustrating. You wonder, will they ever learn?"

"Probably not but what can you do?"

"Have you ever noticed how old people are ungrateful?" I said to Mark.

"You mean how they get to be too feeble and weak to do basic chores at home and then grouse and mock the people who are young and strong enough to do it?" said Mark.

"Exactly."

"No, I hadn't noticed. You know what I have noticed though?

"What?"

"That oldest children always seek their dad's approval."

"Disgusting, isn't it?" I said.

"Mostly just insecure, I think."

"Hey!" said Justin.

"Don't worry, Son," said Mark. "I was talking about the oldest."

"I am your oldest!"

"Huh. So you are. Well, hopefully *you'll* grow out of it."

After a wholly unnecessary extra fifteen minutes that involved a carpenter's level, we eventually finished installing the dock and went inside to change into dry clothes, an activity my dad and Tom crowed about having little need for. Then we all gathered for a lunch of crock-pot chili and fresh bread.

It wasn't a formal meal, so we were scattered about at the counter and a couple of different tables, and I made the mistake of sitting down first. Kate and Izzy promptly sat down on either side, surrounding me.

"So what did you do this weekend?" said Izzy.

"Not much," I said. "Worked yesterday."

"How about Friday?" said Kate.

"Yeah, I worked then too. I have a case that's—"

Kate shook her head. "How about Friday night, ass—" Kate glanced at the far table with her daughters, "—dear brother-in-law?"

I shrugged into my chili. "Just had some dinner."

"Where?"

"A restaurant, over on the south side."

"With anyone?" said Kate.

"A friend of Izzy's."

"A friend of Izzy's or a friend of yours?"

I smiled. "I guess both."

"How'd it go?" said Izzy.

"You probably know better than me."

"Actually, I don't." Her green eyes glittered. "I'm very good about boundaries."

"Right. I forgot."

"So are you and Kira going to see each other again?" asked Kate.

"How do you know it's Kira?"

Izzy grinned. "Kate's family. And her question was, are you and Kira going to see each other again?"

"Probably. She told me to pick a time, and she'd pick a place."

"So when are you going?"

"I don't know. I haven't thought of a time yet."

"You haven't thought..." Izzy set down her spoon. "You went out on Friday?"

"Yeah."

"She asked you to call her?"

I nodded around a bite of chili.

"And you want to?"

I chewed, then, "I think so."

"But you haven't given her a time?"

"No. But it's only been two days."

People have told me that French baguettes are not weapons. I can tell you that they are, especially when wielded with speed and anger to smack your ear.

"Why wouldn't you call her?" said Izzy. The baguette remained in hand.

"I did! I talked to her for work yesterday."

"You called her for work?" said Izzy. "And you didn't give her a time?"

"So?"

I made a mistake. I was looking at Izzy. Kate hit me in the other ear.

"Out," said Kate. "Now!"

"Where?"

"Outside. Call."

"At least let me finish—"

Kate literally took my bowl. "Goodbye."

I walked past the table where Tom and Mark ate chili in peace with my mom.

"You two really are no help," I said.

"Mom, this chili is delicious," said Tom.

"I'm getting seconds," said Mark.

"They're not wrong," said my mom.

Everyone has an opinion.

I WENT OUTSIDE, not because Kate said to but because there was no way I was doing this from inside the house. I called Kira.

She picked up right away. "Nate, I was just going to call you."

"Oh, yeah? What's up?"

"I can't find it, the wallet."

"No?"

"I've gone through everything that we've organized so far. We're not done inventorying but there's no wallet anywhere in the house that we've found so far."

"Could Theo have hidden it?"

"He might have, but you'd think he would know that if he hid it too well, it wouldn't be found after he died. Typically, people have a stash of important papers and valuables; I'd expect to find it there."

"Have you found Theo's stash?"

"That's just it, we've found several, but the wallet wasn't in any of them."

I thought. "You know, it wasn't worth five million when he put it away."

"That's my thought too. We've found where he kept his highest value assets. I'm thinking there may be a couple spots where he squirreled away stuff that wasn't quite as important."

The irony of talking about twenty-two thousand dollars as if it weren't much money wasn't lost on me but everything's relative.

"What's next?" I said.

"I'm going to check Theo's safe deposit boxes when the

banks open on Monday. That will take a while because he had more than a few. If that doesn't turn anything up, I'll just keep looking."

I shook my head. "This is crazy, isn't it?"

"I've never seen anything like it."

"Same."

"I'll look for a little while yet before I call it a day. What about you?"

"I'm up at my parents' place with the family getting the place ready for summer."

"Sounds fun."

"Mostly."

"I'm sorry, I jumped right into my news. Why the call?"

"I realized I hadn't gotten back to you on a time. How's this Friday?"

"I'm traveling the end of this week. How about the next Friday?"

"Works for me."

"Perfect. I'll pick the place."

"But what if I have a taste for mushrooms?"

"We'll find you a side dish."

"Great."

"And two things, Nate."

"What's that?"

"I already told you I'm not that sensitive. And say 'hi' to Izzy for me."

I smiled. "Got it. And I will."

"Good. I'll talk to you later in the week. Sooner if I find five million dollars."

"Thanks, Kira. Bye."

I hung up, steeled myself, and walked back into the house.

I ignored my mom and my brothers as I grabbed another bowl, refused to make eye contact with Izzy and Kate as I filled it, and sat down next to my dad who was at a table with Reed, Taylor, Justin, and James.

As my dad nodded, my teenaged niece Reed said, "So, what did she say, Uncle Nate?"

"You too, troll?"

"Is she pretty?" said Taylor.

"You know your parents have done a terrible job of raising you both."

Justin and James laughed into their chili.

I raised a hand and said so all could hear, "Next Friday. We're going out next Friday."

Mark shook his head. "Have you ever noticed how some people need to broadcast everything they do?"

Tom nodded. "Middle kids. Always needing attention."

I pointed at Taylor and James. "You know they're talking about you, right?"

Justin snorted in laughter as Taylor asked if you can have two middle children while Kate and Izzy nodded sweetly from a table away.

"Eat your chili," said Pops.

30

On Monday morning, I walked into the conference room and looked at the documents spread out all over the table. It was hard to believe that only three days had passed since we'd opened the boxes and called Pompeo. I felt a wave of irritation and embarrassment as I remembered my call to him Friday, rattling on about how ten thousand dollars wasn't sufficient motive for a murder, when I knew now that he had been sitting there smirking with the knowledge of five million motives. I dove back into the piles to see what else I'd missed. By the end of the morning, three things stood out.

The first was a witness statement I'd skimmed over. Robert Snyder, the director of the funeral home where they'd held the services for Theo Plutides, had confirmed that Edgerton Fleece had indeed come to Snyder Funeral Home at approximately seven p.m. on the night of February 17 to pick up donations. The statement was bare bones, but it confirmed that Edge had been there about seven p.m., just after Benjamin Trane had been killed.

It also confirmed that the front right part of Edgerton Fleece's van was dented.

The second was a video clip from the thumb drive in the bottom of the box. The video was saved as "Alert Shield Video—3901 Sunnyfield Drive." It was a quick clip, maybe ten seconds, and the date stamp showed it was taken at about six twenty-eight p.m. on February 17. It showed a Pillars van driving westbound on Sunnyfield Drive. A quick search showed me that the address where the video was taken was about a mile away from the accident site, heading directly toward it at exactly the right time.

The third was another video, but this one substantially longer, saved as "U-Wash Security Video." It showed Edge in one of those do-it-yourself car washes, washing his Pillars van. Actually, scrub is a better word. Over and over again.

It was one thing to have Edge tell me he'd washed the van before he'd taken it to Carrefour Collision. It was quite another to watch that painstaking way he did it.

So Pompeo had Edge's van on the way to the scene of the accident right before it happened, he had Edge and a dented van at Snyder Funeral Home right after the accident had happened, and he had Edge methodically scrubbing the van and taking it in for a rush repair job the next day. It wasn't a bad case for Pompeo for a hit and run. I thought it was a stretch for murder.

Except for the five million dollars. Viewed through that lens, all of the evidence didn't look negligent; it looked sinister.

I went into Danny's office to talk about it and found him poring over the Plutides estate planning binder.

I sat down. "Got it memorized yet?"

Danny shook his head. "There's so much here. I don't know how he kept it all straight."

"I don't know that he did." Then I told him about my conversations from the weekend—that Kira hadn't found the cold wallet yet, that Trane had gone to a seminar where Pillars convinced him to name Pillars in his will, and that Edge claimed that he knew Theo Plutides had left Benjamin Trane a car but didn't know anything about any five million dollars. Then I told him about the evidence Pompeo had produced that put Edge all around the scene of the accident and cleaning up afterward.

Danny listened, then nodded. "The five million dollars makes all of that worse. A lot worse."

I nodded. "That was my thought."

"You know, I was thinking about this over the weekend—"

"You and me both."

"—about how volatile Bitcoin is, that it's worth one million less today than it was at the accident and could be worth millions more by the time of trial."

"Or nothing at all."

"That's right. But it really doesn't matter how much the Bitcoin is worth when we go to trial, does it? It could crash tomorrow and be worthless at trial but what would still matter is that, on the day Benjamin Trane was killed, it was worth five million dollars. That's the motive."

I thought, then said, "You're right. It's okay for us if it goes down between now and then but the value could go up, too. I want you to draft a motion limiting the prosecutor from mentioning a value in excess of what the Bitcoin was worth on the day of Benjamin's death and hang onto it just in case. We don't want Pompeo strutting around the courtroom talking about ten or twenty or fifty million dollars if the value skyrockets."

"So a good idea that creates work for me? Shocking."

"Job security, my friend." I stood. "Keep poring through that estate. I feel like there are still parts that we can't see moving."

"Agreed," said Danny. "Speaking of which."

"Speaking of what?"

"Parts we didn't see moving that are about to bite us."

I sighed. "Hit me."

"Did you read Trane's will?"

"I was storing that in your head."

"That's what I figured. Lynn Horvath is the executor."

"Our Mrs. Horvath?"

Danny nodded.

"You're saying Fleece's secretary is the executor of the estate of the man Fleece is accused of killing?"

"If it makes you feel any better, she's also the official Secretary to the Pillar's Board."

"It does not." I resisted the urge to rub my temples. "So Fleece's secretary is the one who would sign the check giving Pillars five million dollars?"

"See, people say you're slow sometimes, but I tell them you catch right on. Eventually."

"Good work."

"Thanks. There's more."

"Naturally."

"Have you looked at the video of the Pillars planned giving seminar yet?"

"The stuff that Dawn gave us? I skimmed the materials. Seemed pretty typical. 'Remember Pillars in your will, here's some language to do it,' sort of thing."

"Not the written materials. The YouTube video."

"No."

"I assume that you're not going to put Edge on the stand at trial?"

"Of course not."

"Well, the jury is going to hear from him. For about twenty minutes. About all the things that Pillars does for the community."

"Okay."

"And about how their donation, their individual, special donation left in their will, can 'keep the Pillars' mission alive.'"

I stared at Danny. "He says 'alive?'"

"Emphatically."

"Well, shit."

"An accurate summary."

"I guess I should watch the video."

"I guess you should."

"It sounds bad."

"It's not good."

"Okay. Thanks for the heads up. I'll watch it and think about how to deal with it."

"That's why they pay you the big bucks."

I went back to my office and sat, thinking. You know, what lawyers call working, which would cause my father to put one callused hand to his head and wonder where he went wrong. And it began to sink in just how bad this all looked.

Over the weekend, I'd been focusing on the location of the money but, for purposes of my case, that really didn't matter. What mattered was that as soon as Benjamin Trane had come into some money, a lot of money, he had been killed. And once he was killed, all of that money went straight to Pillars. Just like it was planned.

Pompeo's opening statement wrote itself.

PART III

RESISTANCE

31

It was June before I figured out that Pompeo was holding out on us. Actually, it was Olivia who figured it out and it's a good thing because I don't know that I would have, but for the love of all that's good and holy, don't tell her that.

When I arrived at the Brickhouse that day, Cade was standing behind the desk. He wore a black T-shirt that looked like someone had stuffed softballs under it on top of his shoulders and black sunglasses pushed up into his short black hair. He looked exactly like what he was, the most dangerous wrestler, and maybe the most dangerous man, Carrefour North High School had ever produced, and I was continually grateful that he was on my side.

"Olivia's looking for you," he said.

I checked my phone. "I don't have a message."

He shook his head. "No, she said that if you managed to roll your soft ass in here to send you to the office."

I should have said that Cade was *usually* on my side.

"I'll head back. Thanks."

Cade nodded and kept on doing whatever it was he was doing.

I poked my head into Olivia's office, where she was rapping away at the keyboard.

"You wanted to see me, Liv?"

"Oh good, your conscience did get the better of you today."

"Every once in a while, you know."

"Take a look at this," she said and tilted her monitor toward me. "Do you know much about the Alert Shield camera system?"

"Is that the one that goes on people's doorbells?"

"One of many. Different systems seem to populate in different towns and Alert Shield is the one that's taken root here in Carrefour."

"Okay."

"So, the police can't get direct access to homeowners' videos but they can send a request to Alert Shield owners to check their footage for a certain date and time to see if they can find any video that's related to a suspected crime."

"It's up to the homeowner to turn it over?"

"Most of the time. Any guesses on what our good friend Mitch Pearson did?"

Mitch Pearson was the Chief Detective in Charge of Serious Crimes for Carrefour, Ohio. We had a long history. I was surprised I hadn't bumped into him earlier on this case. "He made the request?"

"He did. For our date between six and seven p.m."

"Did he get anything?"

"He did." She clicked open a window. "There was one taker who uploaded this video."

Internal alarm bells went off, so I raised one hand and looked away from the screen. "Liv, where did you get this?"

Olivia turned on me. "What are you suggesting, Shep?"

"I'm not suggesting anything. I'm asking if you got this in a way that would allow me to use whatever is on it."

"If you must know, the Alert Shield company policy is that the police need to request the footage publicly. Then owners can upload it voluntarily through the app where it is available for the police and for all other members of the community to see, which in turn shows how the Alert Shield cameras are making the world an idyllic and safer place."

"So you're a member of the Alert Shield community?"

Olivia shrugged. "It seemed like the best way to get access to footage I sometimes need around town."

"Doesn't that mean you would have to install a camera?"

She smiled. "We have a very interesting, twenty-four-hour view of the cleaning supplies in our storage closet."

"Not the outside of the gym?"

"Number one, I'm not recording people coming in and out of here, ever. Number two, if anyone's dumb enough to steal from me and Cade, they'll get what's coming to them."

"Fair enough. So, what's on the video that was uploaded?"

"More than you've been told. Or shown, I should say."

Olivia didn't explain that, so I watched as she clicked her mouse. "This is a map," she said. "The video was uploaded to Alert Shield from 3901 Sunnyfield Drive."

I frowned. "That's the address from the video the prosecution gave me, right?"

"It is." Olivia clicked again, and the address filled the screen:

3901 Sunnyfield Drive–Uploaded Videos (2)

"Two videos?" I said.

"Yep. I think you'll recognize the first."

A video played that took about ten seconds. It showed a silver minivan with a blue Pillars logo on the side door roll by the camera.

"That's the video Pompeo produced to me," I said.

"Right. Then there's this one." She clicked on the second and I saw a "00:08:00" pop up next to it.

"Does that mean it's eight minutes long?" I asked.

"It does. You'll see that there's a cat frolicking on the porch, so it kept the system tripped." She clicked.

The same view of Sunnyfield Drive appeared on the screen. A car passed on the far side of the road, then another car. A little later, the silver minivan with the blue letters drove by on the far side, right to left.

"That's the Pillars van," I said.

"That's *a* Pillars van," said Olivia.

I opened my mouth, she raised her hand, and I shut up. Thirty seconds or so went by. Then a second Pillars minivan drove past on the far side, right to left.

"Did the video just loop?" I said.

"Nope," said Olivia.

"That's a second van?"

"That's a second van."

I characterized Pompeo.

"You owe Mrs. Pompeo an apology," said Olivia.

I shook my head. "Are there anymore?"

"No more Pillars vans but four more vehicles." Olivia dragged the cursor across the screen so that the video ran in fast forward. "There's a gap after the second van, then cars every couple of minutes. It doesn't look like the road was very busy."

"How could he do that? Pompeo's obligated to produce everything he has—"

"He'll say he doesn't have it." Olivia clicked a couple of more screens. "Here's the chat in the app." She pointed. "See, here's where Pearson asks for the video. And here, a couple of days later, 'ladyshark330' replies with the upload of the eight-minute video we just watched. And here is Pearson's reply."

I read aloud, "'Thank you ladyshark330. That video is too

large for our system. Could you just upload the part at 6:28 pm?'" I looked at Olivia. "Can you do that?"

"You can. The homeowner can upload all or part of any video. Then the next day from ladyshark330—'Here you go, Detective. Thanks for all you do!'"

"And that's the ten-second video?"

"That's the ten-second video."

"Can we—"

"No, you can't blow it up for license plates. There isn't sufficient resolution."

"How about—"

"No, not faces either. The system's designed to focus on a face at your door, not on a car in the street. If those minivans didn't have 'Pillars' emblazoned on the side, it would be hard to identify them at all."

"And we can't see the right side of the van at all because of our angle?"

"Correct. The camera is where it is."

"Because if the dent was already there, it would verify Edge's deer story."

She turned to face me. "I'm no lawyer, but even though you can't see the dent, the fact that there's another van there within the window seems like reasonable doubt."

"You're no lawyer, you're better than one."

"True."

I nodded. "Any vehicle there in the window could raise reasonable doubt. A second Pillars van is a shit-ton of it."

"Is that the legal term?"

"They don't teach it until third year. Do me a favor?"

"No. I will do you a remunerative service, though."

"Can you—"

Olivia handed me a thumb drive. "The full video, the video clip, and copies of the messaging."

I pocketed it. “Thanks.”

“Always. Still seeing Kira?”

“When I can. She’s been traveling a lot for some estates over the last month, and I’ve been fairly busy too. How’s Dr. Rock Climber?”

“You could learn his name.”

“I could.”

She stared.

“Fine,” I said. “If he makes it to the Fourth of July.”

“He will. We’re going to Yosemite this summer.”

“Sounds like fun. But not in August.”

“The trial’s on the calendar.”

“Excellent.”

“Now quit avoiding your workout.”

“I’ll get going.”

32

The next morning, I called the Chief Detective in Charge of Serious Crimes for Carrefour, Ohio, Mitch Pearson. He answered, "This is the Chief Detective in Charge of Serious Crimes for Carrefour, Ohio."

I mean, sweet Jesus.

"Would that be Mitchell Pearson?"

A pause, then, "What do you want, Shepherd?"

"Good morning."

Silence.

"I'm calling about the Fleece case."

"That's with the prosecutor now."

"Right, but you're still investigating it and your file's not up to date."

"What do you mean?"

"I see you've been requesting video from Alert Shield patrons, but I didn't get all of it in the prosecutor's disclosures."

"We've provided all videos that we downloaded."

"And I didn't see any recordings of your interviews with any Alert Shield patrons."

"There weren't any recordings."

"Just interviews?"

Silence again, then, "Nothing on the record."

"Pearson, everything with a police officer in a murder case is on the record. You know that."

"You trying to tell me how to do my job, Shepherd?"

"Only if you're not handing over interviews and videos to the prosecutor. Especially if they would help exonerate my client."

"It's not my job to do your job."

"I thought your job as Chief Detective was to find who actually committed a crime?"

"It is. I have."

"I look forward to seeing your video. All of it."

"I look forward to your client going to jail."

Pearson hadn't been much help, but it was good to know that there are some things you can rely on.

I knew I had something here, but I needed some expert advice before I went too far down this road to make sure I didn't screw it up. I looked in my contact information and found the number for Edgar Sprite.

Edgar Sprite was an engineer turned accident reconstructionist who I had recently used in a case to show that an arrow hadn't pierced the body of a victim. He was engaging, he was smart, and he had a love for math that people usually reserved for puppies. Although he had testified in my case about the flight trajectory of an arrow, auto accidents were his bread-and-butter so this should be right up his alley.

He answered right away. "Hi, Nate!"

"Edgar, how are you?"

"Couldn't be better. Just figuring out whether a motorcycle braked before an overpass or if the overpass braked for the motorcycle. So, do you have something for me?"

"I do."

"Excellent! Arrows again? Bullets? Very small rocks?"

"No, just a run-of-the-mill auto accident."

"Great!"

"But with a murder charge attached."

"Even better! What do you need?"

"My client is accused of hitting a man with a minivan and throwing him into a tree."

"Ouch! I take it the tree won?"

"It did. There's no question the man was killed that night when he was hit by a car. The question is whether it was my client in his minivan that did it."

"I take it there aren't any direct witnesses to the accident or we wouldn't be having this discussion?"

"That's right."

"So I need to make sure the accident happened the way they say?"

"Partially. One of the ways that they're putting my client at the scene is through an Alert Shield video from a person's porch."

Edgar Sprite practically cackled. "Now we're talking."

"They're saying that my client's minivan is passing by at the right time in the video to have caused the accident. But there are other cars and a second minivan in the video too. I need you to—"

"Compare the cars with the scene to determine if any of the evidence matches any of the vehicles?"

"Yes."

"And you know, depending on the video, I may be able to determine which car caused the accident for you."

"Really? How's that?"

"Math! I may be able to estimate the rate of speed and if I can estimate the rate of speed, I can tell you the time it would've taken to travel the distance to the accident site, and if we have the time to the accident site, bam! You have the vehicle that caused the accident."

"That would be amazing," I said. "So, are you interested?"

"Of course! Send me the materials and the video and I'll get started on it right away."

"Excellent. Thanks."

We hung up.

I've said this before, and I'll say it again—I went to law school because there was no math involved, but Edgar Sprite always made me feel as if I were missing out on something.

Next, I went over to Danny's office. "I think Pompeo is holding out on us."

Danny was staring at the Plutides binder. "Good," he said absently. Then, "Wait, what?"

I told him about Pearson's request on Alert Shield, the uploaded videos, and our good fortune that Olivia had found them both.

"Pompeo wouldn't withhold disclosures, would he?"

"I'd bet he's going to argue that he never possessed the full video so he wasn't obliged to produce it."

"That's cutting it awfully thin."

"Right. So let's get discovery requests out for all videos they've requested, regardless of where they're kept, and notes from any interviews, and see what they say."

Danny scribbled on a pad. "Done. When do you want it served?"

Before I could answer, Danny raised a hand. "I'll get it served today so we can set up the motion as soon as possible. Any other progress?"

"I have Sprite on board to see if he can help us with the video or the scene. My next step is to find out who else had use of the vans. How about you?"

Danny flipped some pages back and forth. "Just swimming in the Plutides accounts. Nothing new." He sighed, then looked at his smartwatch. “Oh, shoot.” He stood. “I have to meet with the Haughtons.”

“The who’s?”

“A new estate client. Lunch. I’ll draft the discovery when I get back.” Then Danny gathered his file and his coat and shot out the door with nary a stumble.

I smiled as the door shut, then looked at the Plutides estate planning binder sitting open on his desk. I hadn’t spent much time in it since Danny was the estate planning expert, so I flipped to the table of contents. I saw that it referred to a few documents that I was familiar with—the will of Theo Plutides, the Theo Plutides trust, the Theo Plutides Food Security Foundation—which funded the Pillars food pantry—and then a couple of other foundations he’d set up that I hadn’t heard about yet. Then, I saw the inventory list with all of its many accounts.

The farther down the list I went, the more unintelligible the accounts became. It started with savings and checking and money market accounts, but then it shifted to IRAs and 401(k)s and HSAs, and from there devolved into columns of ETFs and BIP39s and DRIPS. I mean, if I had a dollar for every acronym I saw on that list, well, I would still have a lot less dollars than Theo Plutides.

Adrift in a sea of random letters and numbers, I gave up, shut the binder, and decided to spend my afternoon finding out just who had access to those Pillars vans.

33

I thought about who I should call to follow up on the vans and there was really only one answer.

"Good afternoon, Pillars Outreach executive offices. How may I direct your call?"

"Hi, Mrs. Horvath."

"Hello, Mr. Shepherd! I thought that was your number. I'm afraid Mr. Fleece is in a meeting right now."

"Actually, I was calling for you."

"That's a happy coincidence then! How may I assist you today?"

"With the corporate vans, do you maintain a log sheet?"

"For who's using them each day? Of course, our insurance company requires it. There's a terminal where you sign in down by the key rack."

"If I come down, could someone show the logs to me?"

"I can do better than that." I heard the clacking of keys in the background. "What days do you want?"

"A week before and a week after the accident."

"I tell you what, I'll give you a month on either side, just to be safe," she said, typing. "That's February 17, minus thirty, plus thirty and"—I heard a tap, tap, tap—"there you go. It should be hitting your inbox momentarily."

"Great. How many corporate vehicles are there, by the way?"

"Vans and delivery trucks?"

"Just vans."

"Six. Mr. Fleece has one on a permanent basis and then another five that have a number of drivers."

The email appeared. "There it is," I said.

"Will there be anything else today, Mr. Shepherd?"

"No, I think that's it, Mrs. Horvath. Thanks."

"Certainly. Support for all, Mr. Shepherd."

"Goodbye" seemed like an inadequate response, but it was all that I managed.

I opened Mrs. Horvath's email and scanned the log sheet. For Van 1, "Edgerton Fleece-Primary Driver" was listed for each day. For the remaining five vans, there was a calendar-type log broken into half-hour increments. Vans 2, 3, 4, and 5 had a regular pattern to them—each one was signed out all day every day from seven in the morning until eight at night. It looked like, typically, one person would take a driving shift from seven a.m. to two p.m., then someone else would step in from two p.m. until eight p.m. When I studied it closer, I saw that certain people had regular shifts—so John Smith might drive Van 2 in the mornings on Monday, Wednesday, and Friday while Jane Doe drove it on Tuesday and Thursday afternoons.

Van 6 was different. For most of January, it was on the same sort of rotating driver schedule as the others. But then around mid-February, February 8 to be exact, a guy named Greg Kilbane had taken over the vehicle. It was signed out to him all day, every day, like Edge's van, until the middle of March. I knew I'd heard Greg's name before, but right then I couldn't place him.

I studied the sheets, and it took longer to notice the other anomaly, this time with Van 5. Van 5 was signed out by different drivers all day, every day, from seven in the morning until eight at night. Every day except for one day—February 17.

On February 17, Van 5 was signed out until two p.m. and the afternoon shift had never come on. Instead, all those half hour blocks for the rest of the day were empty, including the exact time of the killing. Then the entries picked up again the next day, but not until noon.

I printed out a couple of copies of the log sheets and was still studying them when Danny came back from his lunch meeting. I called out and he came in.

"What's up?"

I handed him a copy and explained what they were. As he scanned it, I said, "Van 6 is signed out to Greg Kilbane. Remind me who he is?"

"Big guy, pointed beard," said Danny.

"Right, right. Smiles a lot?"

Danny nodded. "That's the one."

"What's he do again?"

"Officially, he's the community outreach liaison. He works with all of our participating churches and business leaders to coordinate contributions and outreach. Unofficially, he's Edge's right-hand man. He does whatever needs to be done that Edge can't get to."

"Like what?"

"Lately, I know he's been spending a lot of time on the health clinic project. I think he's involved in the fund raising for the construction."

"Any idea why he'd have a Pillars van?"

"None. He's always working there though, so I'm not surprised."

"So Kilbane had Van 6. Now look at the log for Van 5."

Danny scanned, then flipped the pages back and forth. "This

is the same as...oh, yeah. The night of February 17 stands out a bit."

"Right."

"It looks like..."—he flipped back a page again—"Neil Carter normally drove the Wednesday evening shift. We'll need to check with him."

"Do you know him?"

"No. Do you want me to track him down?"

"That's alright, I'll handle it."

Danny shook his head, then held up the log sheet and laughed.

"What?" I asked.

"When you think murder weapon, you think gun, knife, cyanide. You don't leap to minivan."

"We didn't choose the minivan life; the minivan life chose us." I stared at him for a moment, then said, "What are you hearing within your church about its support for Pillars? With the charges and all?"

Danny nodded. "My church is still committed to volunteering in the areas we've been helping in. That's not really dependent on Edge. He really serves more as an organizer and motivator so that his moral status is not really a key to that mission. If someone's hungry, they're hungry, regardless of what Edge has done. *Allegedly* done."

He tapped his pen on the table. "But I don't think anyone's too keen on giving them new money while this is going on."

Danny and I had a good relationship. He didn't probe too deeply into my life, and I didn't delve into his. I knew there were some things that he was not in line with me on, but it never mattered because we were friends, we respected each other, and most of our time together was spent in frantic work. Which made this next question tricky.

"Are you still comfortable volunteering there? I guess what I mean is, don't feel like you still have to go there to look good for the case."

Danny waved a hand. "Pillars' philosophy meshes with ours."

"Which is?"

He smiled. "Support for all."

"That seems a little generic to send you there every Saturday."

Danny paused, and now he appeared to be choosing his words carefully. "I don't know exactly what the next world holds, Nate, but I know that an awful lot of people need help in this one."

I was reminded, and not for the first time, that Danny was a far better man than me.

"Hey, how'd the lunch meeting go?" I said.

Danny smiled. "Great! They want me to draft a will, a trust, healthcare stuff—the whole package!"

"Was that a Martel referral again?"

Danny nodded.

"We have to send him a very, very nice Christmas present this year."

Danny grinned. "I'm liking this Shepherd marketing account thing."

"Good work."

Danny left to draft discovery and wills, and I was thinking about vans and felonious drivers when my phone buzzed. Kira.

"Hey!" I answered. "Are you back?"

"Just," Kira said. "And I figured I'd better call before you stack up appointments to avoid me."

I smiled. "I'm not the one who fled the city at the thought of dinner."

"True. So how about tonight?"

In the weeks since our dinner at the Althouse, Kira and I had cancelled and rescheduled over and over, but I'd had two emergency hearings come up and she'd been traveling all over the country with the Plutides estate and believe me, you can't say anything to me about excuses and advancing age that Izzy hadn't said to me on Memorial Day. Since then, Kira and I had managed a quick pre-work coffee one day and a standing meal-truck lunch, which wasn't much but was enough that we had kept trying.

"I'm in," I said. "But since you're picking the time, does that mean I pick the place?"

"Not after last time." She laughed. "I mean, I have some ideas."

"Excellent."

"Why don't you stop by the auction house after work, and we can go from here?"

"I'll see you then."

34

The Northwest Auction facility was not at all what I expected. The front lobby looked more like a theater or an opera house, complete with a bar, a coat check area, and an enormous screen on one wall. A pair of ten-foot tall, double wooden doors stood closed in the left wall while an open room on the right gave me a glimpse of plush chairs, a raised dais, and a wall lined with glass cases and stands.

It was quiet, which meant sound traveled, even through stout wooden doors.

"Just sell his shit!"

Muttering.

"There's no way it takes this long! Just put it online and click a button!"

More muttering.

I couldn't make out the words, but I felt the soothing rise and fall of their rhythm.

"Of course, I want the most money possible! That's what I hired you for!"

Soothing muttering.

"Do you think I'm stupid? Do you think I'm one of the dumb

fucks from this shit town that you can fleece? I know you two are just dragging your feet and milking the bill, so get a move on and get shit done!"

The double doors opened, and a man stormed out. I had a brief impression of a light suit and an open shirt with no socks and loafers as a man flipped his floppy hair out of his eyes, huffed at me, and stomped the rest of the way out.

A moment later, Kira and Manny Amaltheakis walked out.

"And now Nate Shepherd appears," said Manny Amaltheakis. He gave me a rolling wave and turned to Kira. "Apparently, it is a Plutides day for you."

"Every day is," Kira said. "Manny, you know—"

Manny raised a finger. "Kira, I have already given Rory Dennison more cash out of the estate than he has ever had in his grasping little life and it is still not enough. I have told him that selling an estate as big as his uncle's takes time, but the ignorant little..." Manny took a deep breath, exhaled, and said, "I cannot snap my fingers and turn the Plutides estate into cash and neither can you. You do not have to worry about me, Kira. Just keep doing your job because you know who the first one will be to shriek if you miss something valuable."

"I appreciate that, Manny," said Kira.

Manny waved it off and turned to me. "You know, I still have not decided if your client killed my client's friend."

"I understand."

"Do you have proof yet that he did not?"

"I still don't think the prosecutor has proof that he did."

Manny sighed. "I am long overdue for whiskey." Manny waved to Kira, ignored me, and left.

Kira took a deep breath and said, "So. Dinner."

"Where to?"

"I've been cooped up and it's nice out tonight." She grinned. "Have you heard of a place called the Railcar?"

You know my feelings on the Railcar. It's particularly pleasant when the weather's nice enough to sit out on the covered patio, next to the stream. It was nice out that night—a little warm for June but not too muggy yet—so the waitress led us to a small table in one corner and took our drink orders.

"Interesting choice," I said.

Kira smiled. "I do better research than you."

"We didn't have to come here."

"Who says I don't like barbecue?"

The waitress returned with a beer for me and a vodka for Kira and I was convinced that she just might like barbecue when she ordered without looking at the menu.

As we each took a drink, Kira visibly relaxed, and I said, "I have to say, your auction house wasn't what I expected."

She arched her eyebrows. "Let me guess—you were picturing a man in a cowboy hat fast-talking into a megaphone?"

I smiled. "Product of my upbringing."

She took a sip of her drink. "Most of our business is online or at the home of the estate. Every once in a while, though, we need to hold the auction ourselves or throw a reception to remind people that we exist. The people I deal with expect a certain environment."

"Speaking of people you deal with, Rory seems like a prince."

"Sorry you had to walk in on that."

I waved. "We've all been there.

Kira shook her head. "He calls every day wondering when we're going to start liquidating."

"Yeah? When will that be?"

Kira looked at me as if she were fully capable of putting a drink straw through my eye.

I laughed. "Sorry, sorry. No more work."

She smiled. "Thank you. And in that case, probably in July or August. I think I'll be tethered to Sunnyfield Drive most of the summer, which is too bad because I won't get up north."

"Where to?"

"Our family has a place on the lake in Glen Arbor."

"Really? Are you on Big Glen or Little Glen?"

"You know it?"

"You don't forget that water once you see it."

"Little Glen. South shore. How about you? How do you spend your summers?"

"Mostly stick around here. I have a pool."

"Hmm. Lake people versus pool people. Not sure I should be eating with someone on the other team."

"My parents' place gets me a guest pass to the lake people convention."

"I'll have to check ID on that one."

The waitress stopped by to offer us another round of drinks, we accepted, and as she left, I said, "So where did you go the last couple of weeks?"

Kira took another sip. "Plutides had a house in Sanibel Island, so I went down there first. It took an extra week, but we got most everything squared away and ready. Then on the way back, I stopped in western New York for a meeting about the valuations on some paintings."

"Oh yeah? Was that for Plutides too?"

"Do you remember the maritime paintings?"

"Is that the stack of sea battles with the cheesy 'live, drink, love' poem thrown in?"

"Those are the ones. Turns out it's worth a lot more as a complete set than the paintings are worth individually."

"The frayed rope really adds value, eh?"

"Yes, that's exactly it."

Kira sipped her drink and gave me a half smile as she said, "I admire your restraint by the way."

"About?"

"The Sanibel Island house."

"What about it?"

"No, I did not find the cold wallet down there."

I shrugged. "I figured when I didn't hear from you."

"My, aren't you trusting."

"I also didn't hear a report that you'd disappeared."

Kira shook her head. "It's driving me crazy. I went through the entire Sanibel house, every room, every drawer, same as up here in Carrefour. Nothing. He has one more property in Harbor Springs I have to inventory so I'll be checking that one next."

"Maybe it'll turn up there."

"Hopefully. I'm running out of places to look."

"How'd the Sanibel trip go otherwise?"

"Pretty well actually. Since it was a vacation home, it was pretty easy to inventory and get in order. I have a fishing boat to move but nothing too complicated."

"Yeah, what kind of boat?"

"A Hatteras GT65."

I choked. "That's not a boat, it's a yacht."

"A sport fishing yacht."

"Good lord, don't tell my father about it."

She raised an eyebrow. "He'd want to buy it?"

"No, he'd never want to stop talking about it."

Kira tilted her head over her drink. "Are you saying I'm going to see your father at some point?"

I smiled. "I doubt we could schedule it."

Right on cue, her phone buzzed. She held it up, and I saw a series of text notifications from "Dennison."

"Yikes."

"And that doesn't include missed calls. So, I turn this off and put it away"—she turned off the phone, put it in her purse, then touched the bottom of her glass to the top of my bottle—"and you tell me about Glass Lake."

So I told her about Memorial Day at Glass Lake and by the end of dinner that had somehow morphed into her accepting an invitation to join us on the Fourth of July that I didn't exactly remember giving but made me glad just the same.

35

The next afternoon, I met Edgar Sprite out at the Pillars headquarters. We were in a metal outbuilding that served as the company garage, staring at a row of six silver Dodge Grand Caravan minivans all with the blue Pillars logo decaled on their sides.

He looked at me. "Is the minivan Fleece was using in this group?"

"Right there," I pointed, "in the middle."

Edgar Sprite was a wiry man in his sixties, and I don't think I had ever seen him walk anywhere. He sprang to the minivan in the middle, squatted down, then strode around to the right front corner and put his hand on the metal. "They did a good job with the repair. I don't see any evidence of it just looking at it with the naked eye."

"Can you tell how big the dent or damage would've been?"

"Not now. Did anyone take any pictures?"

"Not that I know of."

"You usually would for insurance."

"Right. What about the video from the car wash?"

Sprite nodded. "That let me see some from the front, but I

didn't have a great view of the wheel-well." He frowned. "I've looked at the repair bill too. The damage was pretty light for hitting a deer."

"How about for hitting a man?"

Sprite ran a hand along the right edge of the hood, looking at damage that was no longer there. "It depends on whether the man, or the deer, was stationary or moving, the angle, whether it was direct or glancing. It could have been either."

He looked at me. "But it's on the light side for a deer."

I nodded.

He bounced back and motioned. "Come around with me."

I hustled to keep up with Sprite as we came around to the left side of all the vehicles. He pointed. "See, the Alert Shield video was taken from the left side, the driver's side. We can't see the right front at all."

"So, if the damage was already there from hitting a deer, we wouldn't be able to see it?"

"Exactly. We have a view of the far side of the hood, but I just can't say if that would show anything or not."

I stared at the vans. "I'm bad with cars, but they all look the same to me."

"That's because they are," said Sprite. "Same color, same make, same model. Probably got some kind of fleet deal from a rental company. What do they use them for?"

"Mostly transporting people to appointments or kids to and from childcare."

"I saw the logs. Have you talked to any of the drivers to see where they say they were?"

"That's my next stop."

Sprite stared at the vans nodded. "I'd run that down. I don't know that we're going to get any evidence from the scene that distinguishes one of these vans from the other."

"Okay."

"I haven't run my calculations from the video yet to see if I can tell which vehicle might've caused the accident. I'll let you know what I find. Hopefully, I can at least narrow it down."

"Anything will help."

Sprite snapped me a nod. "Let me take some pictures and I'll be out of your hair."

I let Edgar Sprite do his work and walked over to the far corner of the garage where two men and two women stood in front of an industrial counter. There was a computer sitting on the countertop, a key rack above it, and cabinets underneath. Most importantly, however, there was an old school coffee percolator sitting there with the orange light on and the four drivers stood around it, mugs in hand, like it was a campfire.

"May I?" I asked.

One woman smiled, one man pointed at the contribution can, and the other two kept watching Sprite.

As I put a five in the can, one woman said, "How much longer is he going to be?"

"Just a couple of minutes, I think."

"Because I have three baseball diamonds and a dialysis appointment to get to."

"He'll hurry."

The woman looked unconvinced as I found a cardboard cup and poured.

"Is this for the murder trial?" said the other woman.

"It was no damn murder, and you know it, Gabby," said one of the men.

"I didn't say it was a murder," said Gabby. "I said it was a *murder trial*. Which it is."

The man who hadn't said anything nodded upward to me. He looked to be in his early seventies with short white hair and thick brown glasses. "Mrs. Horvath said you wanted to talk to me?"

"Neil Carter?"

He nodded.

"If you have a minute," I said.

Neil Carter gestured to the vans with his cup. "Not going anywhere."

I motioned and the two of us stepped outside. The other three drivers watched us go.

"I wasn't driving that night," Neil Carter said as I opened my mouth. "I wasn't anywhere near Sunnyfield Drive."

"I know, Mr. Carter. That's—"

"I don't know anything about what Mr. Fleece was doing either."

"I understand, Mr. Carter. I just wanted to ask why you weren't driving that night."

Neil Carter blinked behind his thick lenses. "What do you mean?"

"From the logs, it looks like you drive every Wednesday from two to eight, right?"

He nodded. "That's one of my days."

"So why not on the 17th?"

"The 17th?"

"The day Mr. Trane was killed."

"Where's my mind, I know that, Mr. Trane left us on the 17th. So the day before, the 16th, was Mr. Plutides' viewing and funeral and I had a full load of folks who were going—three loads actually because there wasn't a person who knew him who didn't want to pay their respects—and I have one little girl who spills her fishy pretzels and one woman, Mrs. Prescott, who's so upset her blood sugar spikes and so she eats half a banana and forgets the other half, and someone—I still don't know who—brought a bag of Oreos, but I swear only got half in their mouth. I was more than a little upset that day—there wasn't a person who wasn't, especially after poor Roxie wouldn't leave the casket

—so I have to admit I didn't look at the van much after I dropped off my last patron. Then, when I came in for my shift the next day—that's the 17th then—Marcy—that's the morning driver—she tells me that little Emma Dalton got carsick all over the back seat and I see that this van of mine is an all-fired mess. So I call Mrs. Horvath and tell her what's what and she tells me not to worry, she'll see that it's detailed that day. I tell her that I have pickups, and she says not many, and she'll see that they're all covered. I say I can do the detailing, but she says it's already handled." Neil Carter paused, then said, "Do you know Mrs. Horvath?"

"We've met."

"Then you know if she says it's handled, it's handled."

"Seems like."

"And that there's no arguing with her once she's set her mind."

"I get that impression."

"So I went home, went with Mrs. Carter to the grocery store, and came back the next day to a sparkling clean van."

"That's it?"

"That's it."

"Do you know who cleaned the van?"

"I believe we have a company that does that, but you'd have to ask—"

"Mrs. Horvath?"

He pointed around his coffee mug and grinned.

Just then, Edgar Sprite bounced out the garage door. "All done, Nate. I'll call with a report," and before I could lift my hand to wave, he'd strode halfway to his car.

Neil Carter craned his head and looked in the garage. "I have to get to my pickups. Are we done?"

"We are. Thanks, Mr. Carter."

As Neil Carter ambled back into the garage, I went into the Pillars building to see Mrs. Horvath.

36

When I arrived on the third floor, the ever-present Mrs. Horvath was behind the reception desk. "We're all done out in the garage, Mrs. Horvath, thank you."

"Excellent, Mr. Shepherd. Did you find Mr. Carter?"

"I did. Thanks."

"Did you get the information you needed?"

"Mostly."

"What else can I help you with?"

"Mr. Carter mentioned that his van needed to be cleaned on the 17th?"

Mrs. Horvath nodded. "My goodness, it certainly did."

"He said you arranged for it?"

"I did." She turned to her computer. "Just...a... moment. And there we go." A small printer whirred at her desk and then she presented me with a sheet.

"What's this?"

"The receipt from the detailing company that cleaned the van that afternoon. I believe they listed Kirk as the man who handled the call."

I glanced at the receipt. "I see that."

"Do you need me to contact them?"

"No, I don't think so."

"I do remember him saying that banana and Oreo was quite a combination—"

"I bet."

"—but that carsick vomit was 'its own special hell.' I understood the sentiment though I didn't appreciate the language. It took him most of the afternoon, I believe."

"I don't think I need to talk to him, Mrs. Horvath, thanks. Is Greg Kilbane around though?"

Mrs. Horvath checked her book. "He is. Would you like to see him?"

"If he has a moment."

Mrs. Horvath rang him, found that he did indeed have a moment, and led me back to Greg Kilbane's office, which was in the same small suite as where I'd run into Dawn Blackwell and her daughter Dana before.

"Thanks, Lynn," said Greg Kilbane as he rose from his desk.

Now that I saw him, I remembered him—tall, wide shoulders, with a sharp beard and a big smile.

"Hi, Nate," he said as he shook my hand. "I have a finance meeting in ten minutes, but I can push it back if you need me."

"Thanks, Greg, but I won't take longer than that."

Greg Kilbane gestured for me to take a seat and I noticed as I did that Mrs. Horvath was already gone.

"This is for Edge's case, I take it?" he said.

"It is."

"Anything I can do to help, you just ask."

"You're the community liaison?"

Kilbane nodded. "I am."

"So how's the case affecting your community support?"

Kilbane's smile stayed on his face, but his eyes dimmed.

"Our board has members from ten of our largest contributing churches and then rotates another five members. The board members believe in our outreach. Their support hasn't wavered."

"But some non-board churches have withdrawn their support?"

Kilbane's smile disappeared into his beard. "I'd say instead that they're not going to offer any new support right now."

"Like the health clinic?"

He nodded. "Exactly like the health clinic."

Kilbane's phone buzzed. "Speak of the devil. Let me just handle this real quick."

I nodded as Kilbane took the call.

"Care? Yeah, those are the new numbers. Hey, I'm meeting with Nate about your husband's case...I agree...Yep, I will before the meeting starts...Bye." Kilbane hung up, and the smile was back. "Carissa's deeply involved in the health clinic project as you might imagine."

"I see."

"That's the topic of the finance committee meeting today, to see where we are."

"I understand that's where the donations are really being affected."

"It is. The sooner we can get past this, the better."

"We have another couple of months yet."

"No delays though?"

"Not right now."

"Good."

I stood. "I don't want to keep you from your meeting."

Kilbane stood too. "Was that it?"

"I was following up on the vehicle logs too."

"Sure. What's up?"

"You have a company van?"

Kilbane nodded. "Sometimes."

"Do you have your own car?"

"I do. But we wear a lot of hats around here."

"You have to haul people around?"

"Like you wouldn't believe."

"You had one on the night of Benjamin Trane's accident?"

With each question, Kilbane's eyes narrowed further, but his smile remained the same. "I didn't hit anybody, Nate."

"No, no, no, of course not. All you have to do is look at your van to know that."

Kilbane's eyes turned quizzical.

"There's just more than one van that looks like Edge's floating around, is all."

"And that matters?"

"For some of the evidence the prosecutor has. He's using video of a Pillars van to put Edge at the scene of the accident, but I'm not sure it's Edge's."

"You can't tell which van it is?"

"Not right now, no."

"That's too bad."

"Do you know where you were driving that night?"

"Four months ago? No, sorry Nate, I don't."

I nodded then looked at the time. "I better let you get to your meeting. Thanks, Greg."

"Any time. Call if you need anything else."

We shook hands and I left. I turned out of the doorway, took a few steps, then checked my phone. I'm not going to lie, I just flipped to random screens as I listened to Greg Kilbane.

"Yep, he just left," he said. "You have the numbers? We don't have much time." And then he started into a discussion of the latest revenue projections.

I pocketed my phone, felt moderately guilty, and left.

I MADE my way out of the building and was crossing to the parking lot when I saw a small woman struggling to juggle a computer bag, a purse, a backpack, and a Banker's box all while maintaining a hold on a small girl's hand.

I hustled over and said, "Can I take that box, Dawn?"

"No, I've got it," Dawn Blackwell said.

The backpack slid from her shoulder to her elbow, which made the box tilt and papers slide out as she gripped her daughter's hand to keep the little girl from stepping into the traffic lane.

I caught the papers and steadied one corner of the box. "Please?"

Dawn's shoulders slumped. "Okay."

I took the box and waited as Dawn Blackwell slid the papers back in, then rearranged the backpack, her purse, and her daughter's hand. Hands still full, she gestured with her head. "The white Kia Sportage over there."

As we walked a couple of aisles over, I hefted the box. "Homework?"

"Loan documents," she said. "I'm pulling together financials to get approval for our expansion."

I nodded. "The health clinic?"

"And the childcare expansion."

"Isn't there a finance meeting right now?"

Dawn Blackwell winced. "I'm joining it later by Zoom. We have a doctor's appointment."

"My ear hurts!" said Dana.

"The doctor will make it better," I said.

Dana smiled. "She gives me suckers!"

"Ask for sour apple."

Dana made a face.

I smiled, then said to Dawn Blackwell. "Greg said our case isn't making it any easier, the financing."

"No, it's not," said Dawn Blackwell. "But we have to find a way to fill those needs."

"Why's that?"

"Because nobody else will."

As we came to the Kia Sportage, Dawn Blackwell popped the back hatch. I slid the box in as Dawn opened the back passenger door and had her daughter climb into a car seat.

"I want on the other side, Mommy!"

"The car seat's on this side, Dana."

"But I like to look in the mirror!"

Dawn buckled her in. "This side's fine."

"But I like it the way it was before!"

I shut the hatch and noticed a license plate holder from Tri-State Auto Store that dared me to "Just Tri to Beat Our Deals!"

Dawn closed the backseat door, took a breath, then seemed to remember I was there. "Thank you, Mr. Shepherd," Dawn said.

"Nate."

She nodded, gave me a half smile, then hurried around to the driver's side and climbed in. I stepped back out of the way as Dawn pulled out, vicariously exhausted from my short walk with the Blackwells.

37

I was back at the office finishing up for the day when Kira called me.

"Hey," I said. "Did you find it?"

"Nate Shepherd, I'm beginning to think that you're only interested in my wallet."

"That's not true at all, Kira. I'm only interested in your *cold* wallet."

"I'll be happy to give you something cold."

"Ah, straight to the heart."

"And no. I haven't found it. It's driving me crazy. I'm off to his Harbor Springs property next."

"Good luck. When are you going?"

"This weekend. Which is actually why I'm calling. I was wondering if you could do me a favor?"

"Sure."

"You'd better hear it first. Would you be willing to look after Roxie while I am gone? I took her to a kennel when I went to Sanibel, and I swear to God she seemed pretty down when I got back. She knows you and, honestly, I think that you feel more like Theo and Benjamin to her."

"I'll have to go to work during the week."

"She's fine during the day. Just a brief walk at night should do it."

"Then sure."

"Great. I'll plan to drop her off before I go."

"Speaking of plans, are you doing anything tonight?"

"I'm still a little stacked up here, but I could eat."

"We don't have to go out if you don't want," I said. "I could bring some takeout over and we could just eat and watch Netflix or something."

A pause, then Kira said, "And just sort of chill out?"

"Yeah, if you want."

There was a shorter pause before Kira said, "I'm up for that."

"An hour?"

"Make it two, I have a few things to wrap up here."

"See you then."

I KILLED some time at the office and then some more deciding on what food to pick up. It took me longer than it should have because I realized that I had failed once again and had no idea, despite two dinners, what Kira actually liked on the whole takeout thing. I started to text, decided that was a bad look, then ordered Thai with the knowledge that it would be a huge hit or a colossal failure.

I arrived at Kira's townhouse a little later with two bags, a fervent hope that I hadn't screwed the pooch, and the number for the nearest Marco's Pizza loaded on my speed dial.

Kira opened the door. "What have we here?"

"Spicy green papaya salad, Pad Thai, and mango sticky rice for dessert."

She leaned forward, expressionless, and inspected the "Som's" restaurant label on the bag. "Any green curry in there?"

"No, I thought it might be too spicy."

"Hmm. Should have told them it was for me, they'd have added it. Still," she smiled, "good instincts."

As I followed Kira in, Roxie trotted over with the click of claws on hardwood. The very good girl allowed herself to be scratched, then plopped down next to the table as we set out the food.

We started with the papaya salad and a general discussion of our days. As we made our way through the Pad Thai, we took a pleasant detour into our respective families (three sisters for her, one in town, one up north, and one in Colorado), but by the time we were splitting up the sticky rice, Kira said, "It's driving me crazy, you know."

I paused mid-chopstick. "No more discussion of family—got it."

She smiled. "No, I love going to visit my sister in Durango. No, I mean that there is five million dollars sitting in one of my estates that I can't find!"

"No work rule?"

"I'm allowed to break it, obviously."

"Maybe you'll find it in the Harbor Springs place."

She shook her head. "I think that's going to be just like Florida. There's no reason that Theo would store the wallet up there in a vacation home."

"So maybe it's here?"

"I've gone through every part of the Carrefour house. More than once."

I took a bite of the sticky rice with a little mango on top then clicked the ends of my empty chopsticks together. "Have you checked the library for secret doors?"

"What?"

I shrugged. "It always worked on *Goosebumps*."

Kira's light blue-gray eyes went a shade grayer as she said, "Funny." She stabbed a piece of mango instead of grasping it. "I just can't think where else it could be."

I straightened. "What if he already gave it to him?"

"What do you mean?"

"Theo. What if Theo gave the cold wallet to Benjamin Trane before he died?"

Kira was silent as she ate the mango.

I continued. "Theo's health was failing for a while and maybe, from what he knew, the Bitcoin was only worth twenty thousand dollars."

"*Only*."

"I know but Theo was worth a ton so twenty thousand is a number he might just hand to somebody and not think twice about it. Maybe the wallet is at *Trane's* place."

Kira nodded. "It's worth checking. Where even is Trane's place?"

"I have no idea. But it seems like I should take a look."

I thought about the possibility that Trane had the wallet all along for the first time. Then I realized that since Trane was the victim of a crime, the police may have already been there, looking for a connection with Fleece. But I hadn't received a disclosure from the prosecutor showing that there had been an inspection, which then made me wonder if this was one more thing Pompeo was keeping from me.

I looked up.

Kira was smiling. "Thinking it through?"

"Enough for tonight. Sorry."

"Don't apologize. I brought it up."

"Done?"

She was, so the two of us cleaned up the dishes, which didn't take long since half of them were cardboard boxes. She offered me another beer, which I took, poured herself a glass of white wine, and we made our way over to her common room. I hesitated for a moment, then took a seat on the couch about a third of the way in. She did the same from the other side, sitting with one leg tucked underneath her, facing me.

I was woefully out of practice in doing couch calculus but Roxie seemed to support the decision on our placement when she got up, walked over, and flopped down on the floor between our feet, which made something else occur to me.

"One more work thing?"

She arched her eyebrows, then nodded.

"Why do you have Roxie?"

Kira smiled. "I'm in charge of inventorying and disposing of all the assets of Theo's estate. As part of that, I'm supposed to take any steps necessary to preserve the value of his possessions, like the way I'm storing the paintings."

Kira moved closer to me and reached down to pet Roxie behind the ears. "Technically, Roxie was Theo's property. He didn't make any arrangements for her in his will, which means I need to arrange for her care until she is disposed of—that sounds terrible, let's say placed—like any other asset."

I was a lawyer, so I was used to the law putting things in categories but as I looked at Roxie looking up at Kira with those forlorn eyes, I had a hard time putting her in the "disposable property" category.

"Will the service dog company take her back?"

"A lot of times. But Roxie is too old."

"How old?"

"Nine. So they said I was better off just finding her a permanent home. I could have kept her in a kennel while we organized the estate, but I decided that would cause me to burn in hell."

"Very possibly."

Kira stopped petting her and Roxie put her head down and

closed her eyes. As Kira straightened, I reached over to the coffee table and grabbed the remote.

"So how do you get to Netflix?"

Kira looked at me. "We're watching Netflix?"

"Isn't that what we said?"

"It... is."

"We can watch something else if you want."

Kira sat back, then smiled. "No, Netflix is fine."

"I think the Wings are on if you'd rather."

Kira looked at me. "Sure, Nate, if we're going to watch something, I'd rather watch the Wings."

"Red Wings it is." I turned on the Wings, who were up in the first against the Minnesota Wild.

We made it to the end of the second period before Kira said, "You know, Nate, I have to get an early start tomorrow."

"Sure, sorry, I didn't notice the time."

"No need to apologize. Thanks for dinner."

"You bet."

I pet Roxie goodbye, then Kira walked me out. She gave me a quick kiss and, as she shut the door, I thought I heard her sigh.

38

The next morning, I stopped in Danny's office first thing. "Has Pompeo responded to our discovery requesting all of the Alert Shield videos?"

Danny shook his head. "Not that I've seen."

"So we know he's holding back the longer video Olivia found that shows all the cars. Now I'm wondering if there are results of a home inspection he hasn't given us either."

"What home inspection?"

"Trane's." I told him about my conversation with Kira and my theory that Theo might have given the cold wallet to Benjamin Trane directly. Then I said, "Once I went down that road, I started thinking about what Pearson, and later Pompeo, would have investigated once they decided this was a murder. They had to have searched Trane's house looking for evidence of who, or in the case of Pillars, what, he had a relationship with."

Danny nodded. "And we haven't been given the results."

"Or the opportunity to take a look there ourselves."

Danny knew right where I was going. "I'll draft a motion to compel production of the Alert Shield video and the results of their search of Trane's home. I'll join it with a motion for leave to inspect Trane's property ourselves." He shook his head. "I should've thought to do that before."

I shrugged. "I didn't think of it either." I thought. "I don't know that we need a motion for leave to inspect. Call Mrs. Horvath, she's the executor. Find out where Trane lived and set up a time for us to go over there with her."

"Done. When do you want this filed?"

Before I could answer, Danny raised his hand. "Never mind. File the motion, then call Horvath."

"Reverse that."

Danny tilted his head.

"Trial isn't for another two months. There might be five million dollars lying around Trane's house right now."

"Which isn't exactly our responsibility."

"No, but I'll feel a lot better once I know where it ended up."

"And you are going to do what exactly?"

"I'm going to keep coming up with these great ideas for you."

"Fantastic."

My phone buzzed. "I mean, I'll be consulting with our experts." I held up the phone. "Sprite."

I stood and picked up as I went back to my office. "Edgar, how are you doing?"

"Are the witness statements our best estimate of the time of the accident?" Edgar Sprite said without preamble.

"I think so," I said. "There's no video of the accident and the paramedics and police didn't arrive until after they were called. I suppose the 911 call would put it within a couple of minutes."

"Mrs. Pepperstone was the first one to call. Did she call right away?"

I thought back to my meeting with her. "It took her a little while to figure out what was going on and a little more to get outside. She walks with a cane."

"And the other neighbors called after her."

"From what I can see."

"So the best evidence of the exact time is when the witnesses say they heard the crash?"

"Right."

"See the problem is that they're all going to have different devices telling them what time it is, if they even looked at all."

"I agree. But we have a good general time. I think it's listed as, yes, six twenty-eight p.m. That should be it, give or take, shouldn't it?"

"Yes, yes, but it's the give or take that's the problem."

"How so?"

"I can calculate the two vans' speeds from the video by measuring the distance between landmarks on the video and then timing how quickly they traverse the distance. I can then take a measurement from the area of the video to the area of the accident and tell you how long it would've taken each van to get there. Actually, I can put the eight vehicles from that long video at the accident scene within about a ten-minute window."

"Great."

"But the problem is, without an exact time of death, I can't say mathematically which one caused the accident, not with the necessary certainty. The variable is too large."

"Could anyone say with certainty which vehicle caused the accident?"

"Not from the video, no."

I thought. "We can use that then."

"How do you mean?"

"We can argue that no one can tell from the video alone which of these eight cars caused the accident."

"I think that's the key—from the video alone. And remember, just being on this video doesn't mean any of them caused the accident. It just means that they were on Sunnyfield Drive a mile and a half away in the right window of time."

"Got it. How about the vehicles themselves? Can you tell anything about those?"

"I think all I can give you is negatives in this case, Nate. There's no way to tell from the video if any of those vans were damaged on the front right so the prosecution can't use it to *disprove* Fleece's deer collision. And there's nothing from the site that affirmatively links back to Edge's van."

"That's something."

"But there's also nothing at the site that affirmatively links to any other vehicle."

"Sounds like things I'll be using on cross rather than calling you directly, Edgar, but keep the materials. I still may need you depending on how the prosecutor approaches things."

"Will do, Nate. I'll keep looking and see if I can come up with more for you to work with."

"That's great Edgar, thanks."

"No problem. Back at it."

I had just hung up when Danny walked in. "We're going to look at Trane's place this afternoon."

"That fast?"

"Mrs. Horvath is very efficient."

"That she is."

"I'll send you the address. It's a little apartment closer to downtown."

"Where all the millionaires live."

"I'm sure that's exactly what we'll think when we see it."

39

That afternoon, Danny and I met Mrs. Horvath at Benjamin Trane's apartment. It was on the south side of Carrefour too but nowhere near Harvest Township. He was closer to the central city in a building of twelve or so units that would have been new in the 1960s. The exterior was blue and in need of paint, while the roof had the streaked white of faded black shingles that needed replacement.

Mrs. Horvath was waiting for us by the front glass door. "Good morning, Mr. Shepherd. And Daniel, what a pleasant surprise. How is little Ruth?"

Danny smiled. "Great, Mrs. Horvath, thanks."

"So," she put a key in the door and opened it as she spoke, "Benjamin was on the second floor. I contacted the landlord and paid rent for the next two months so that we have time to manage things with the estate. He was happy to do it. Mind the can."

She led us up a see-through stairway, the kind with runners but no risers, around the abandoned soda can, and up one floor to the second door on the right. "This was Benjamin's place," she said, opening the deadbolt, then the door.

I walked in and froze. "Mrs. Horvath, what happened?"

The place was neat and clean and organized. A row of boxes lined the far wall of the single common room, each one labeled in black marker with clear, neat handwriting—things like "dishes," "pants," "shoes," and "game system." There was nothing lying out, anywhere. And the place was spotless.

"It still needs a good cleaning, I know," said Mrs. Horvath, "but we put everything in order."

"We?"

"Greg Kilbane and me. Benjamin didn't have people, you know, that's why he picked me to take care of his affairs. Now Benjamin was a good man, and he took care of our patrons just about as well as anybody could, but he just did not make tidying up a priority." Mrs. Horvath shook her head and "tsk'd." "It took some elbow grease from me and some muscle from Greg, but I'd say things are ready for disposition now."

"When did you do this?" I asked.

Mrs. Horvath rocked her foot between the hard toe of her shoe and her sensible two-inch heel, making a little clicking sound. "Let's see, it was after he died, obviously, but before the funeral. I'd have to check my calendar to be sure."

"Why before the funeral?" asked Danny.

"Greg was hoping to find a few pictures that we could put up at the funeral home and, since I knew I would be managing the estate, I wanted to see if there was any mail to make sure that I didn't miss any bills that might be coming due."

"Did you find anything?"

Mrs. Horvath shook her head. "Nothing but electric and water bills."

"When you were organizing, did you find anything unusual? Anything that you weren't sure what it was?"

"I don't know that I did, Mr. Shepherd. What do you mean?"

"Did he have a junk drawer or a computer case? Any unusual electronics?"

"There's a video game system in that box over there. That was the only computer-type thingy that I saw."

I nodded. "When did the police come?"

"I would say it was a week or so later. Maybe two."

"Did they take anything?"

"Not that I know of, but I don't know that I would."

"What about the will?"

"Oh, they didn't take that. I gave it to them along with his lease and some bank account information. They thought it was important."

I ignored that. "And did they tell you that it was okay to get rid of his things?"

"They asked me to wait for a while but then they called me a few weeks later and said they wouldn't need anything else.

I pointed at the boxes. "What's the holdup now?"

"The lawyer, the one who did the estate plan, he's marshaling the assets or some such thing before he tells me how to dispose of them."

I decided to test her knowledge. "Is there much to marshal?"

Mrs. Horvath shook her head. "Well, Mr. Shepherd, you know from the reports in the paper that there will be five million dollars at some point, along with the car, but I haven't seen any of that. I assume Mr. Amaltheakis will let me know when that's appropriate."

"You've spoken with Manny Amaltheakis?"

"Several times. He's most helpful."

I had a thought. "Do you know if he ever spoke to Benjamin?"

"Oh, yes. Mr. Amaltheakis told Benjamin about the car. Benjamin was so excited about that."

"He was?"

Mrs. Horvath nodded. "The minute Mr. Amaltheakis told him that he would be getting the car, Benjamin told just about anyone who would listen. He was thrilled."

"Did Benjamin mention anything else that he was getting from Theo?"

"A little bit of gas money, no, walking around money, that's what Benjamin called it but nothing like what it turned out to be."

I nodded. "Has Amaltheakis said there is any difficulty with the funds?" That was as close as I wanted to come to mentioning that the cold wallet was missing.

Mrs. Horvath shook her head. "No, Mr. Amaltheakis just told us that it would take a while to wrap up Theo's estate and get back to me, but you know lawyers."

"I do."

"Oh, goodness, Mr. Shepherd, I'm sorry. I always forget with you."

"Do you mind if I look in a couple of these boxes? I won't take long."

"You go right ahead."

I looked in what I thought were the most likely boxes—the ones marked "game system" and "miscellaneous" and even one labelled "tools," which held a surprising number of them. There was nothing in any of them that remotely resembled a cold wallet.

There was also surprisingly little paper and what there was had been well-organized by Mrs. Horvath. I skimmed through the bills and some junk but didn't find anything from Theo Plutides or Manny Amaltheakis or anyone else that would indicate that Trane had received five million dollars.

I looked at Danny, who shook his head, and we each folded up the last box that we'd been looking through.

"Thank you, Mrs. Horvath," I said. "I think that should do it."

"I hope that was helpful."

"It certainly was."

We left, with Mrs. Horvath locking up behind us after having reached another dead end.

~

I WAS STILL STEWING about the missing five million dollars in general and the terrible optics of Mrs. Horvath serving as Benjamin Trane's executor in particular, and how I was going to handle all of that at trial, when I stopped at the Brickhouse that night. Olivia was working the desk while Cade was hanging new "Brickhouse" gear—T-shirts, tanks, sweatshirts—on the wall behind it.

Olivia smiled, took my membership card, and blew on it.

"Dust keeps the card reader from working," she said and swiped it.

"So does wear and tear."

She nodded. "I have seen that with other members."

As she handed the card back, I said, "Hey, I'm filing a motion to get any more video that the police have on Fleece."

"Good, although I think I've found everything they pulled from Alert Shield."

"Just making sure. And I included a demand that they produce anything that they may have found at Trane's apartment."

"Trane's apartment?"

"Kira and I realized last night that the police have probably checked there, too. I'll let you know if we find anything that needs follow-up."

Olivia smirked. "You and Kira last night?"

"Nothing major. She was working late, so I offered to bring dinner over and watch some TV."

Olivia's smirk broadened into a grin. "A little Netflix and chill?"

"No, we were going to watch Netflix but then the Wings game was on, so we watched that instead."

Olivia froze for a moment, then she started to laugh.

"What?"

She held up one finger, then said, "Cade! Come over here."

Cade pulled an earbud out, and when Olivia waved him over, stepped down off the footstool. By the time he joined us, Olivia had stopped laughing. She cleared her throat, put her hand on her brother's arm, and said to me, "Did you offer to bring Kira dinner and watch Netflix last night?"

Cade opened his mouth. Olivia shushed him and pointed back at me.

"Yeah," I said.

She pressed her lips together, cleared her throat again, then said, "Did you offer to chill out too?"

I frowned. "No. I think she did. Yeah, I asked if she wanted to eat-in and watch Netflix, she said 'just watch Netflix and chill out?', and I said sure."

Cade opened his mouth. Olivia tapped his arm rapidly until he shut it, then gestured to me. "And what did you do?"

"I told you, I turned on Netflix but then we decided to watch the Wings game instead."

Olivia put her head on the counter and laughed. Cade shook his head and went back to hanging shirts. I stood there, confused. Olivia refused to tell me what was so funny. In fact, every time I asked, she just laughed harder so eventually I went back to the locker room and changed to work out.

Before I came out, I pulled out my phone and did some quick research. You know, because I'm this super smart lawyer guy. When I found it, I just stared at my screen and reinterpreted my entire dinner with Kira the night before. Then I put my phone away and went back out into the gym.

Olivia started laughing again as soon as she saw me.

I went to the equipment on the far side of the room. It would only make things worse if Olivia saw me blush.

40

Two days later I was standing in Judge Stephanie Jurevicius's courtroom. Danny was with me. Bailiff Mickey Fields was scowling.

"Did you serve Mr. Pompeo with your motion?" she said.

"I did."

"Did you ask him to voluntarily produce what you're asking for?"

"I called a couple of times, and we weren't able to connect. I emailed as well and didn't get a response. That's why I filed the motion."

"Let's give him a few more minutes—"

"Sorry, Mickey," said Ryan Pompeo as he plowed through the door. "I was at a sentencing down in Judge French's court."

Bailiff Fields didn't nod, and she didn't say it was okay and, in fact, she didn't acknowledge Pompeo's excuses at all. Instead, she said, "I'll let the judge know you're ready," and went back into the judge's office.

"NATO, what gives?" said Pompeo. "A motion to compel? Why didn't you just ask me for it?"

"I did, Ryan. Twice."

"We didn't talk."

"No, and when you didn't call me back, I emailed you a couple of times."

"I don't think I ever got those."

"Okay."

"Do we really have to go through this today?"

"Did you send over the videos you have?"

"I'm sure I've sent what I have."

"You only have a ten second video of one van?"

Pompeo waved. "Do you have any idea how many cases I'm handling? Why don't we just—"

Bailiff Fields came out of the judge's office. Ryan walked past me to her. "Is the Judge ready to see us now? I'm sure we can—"

"All rise," said Bailiff Fields.

Pompeo stopped short, a surprised look on his face. Bailiff Fields just stared at him. When she didn't move, and then Judge Jurevicius came out of her chambers, Pompeo hustled back to the other counsel table.

Judge Stephanie Jurevicius took a seat and said, "Good afternoon, Counselors. We are here on the motion of defendant Edgerton Fleece to compel the State to produce videos and any evidence found in its inspection of the victim's residence." She looked up. "Is this your motion, Mr. Shepherd?"

"It is, Your Honor."

"I have read your brief, Mr. Shepherd, and believe I understand your position. Do you have anything you wish to add?"

I stayed standing. "Your Honor, the prosecution has not served us with a brief in opposition, so we ask that the Court grant—"

"I received the State's brief this morning, Mr. Shepherd," said Judge Jurevicius. "Didn't you?"

Pompeo stood. "Judge, if I may, we didn't have much notice of this hearing, so we just filed our response this morning. I have a copy for counsel here," Pompeo handed me the brief without looking away from the judge. "Basically, Judge, it's our position that these videos are publicly available so it's not necessary for us to produce them."

Judge Jurevicius looked at me. "Is that true, Mr. Shepherd?"

"Your Honor, the videos are only available if you are part of the Alert Shield network. I'm not but Olivia Brickson, whom I've employed in this case, is. Fortunately, she was able to access this particular video. However, it was pure happenstance that she found it. We ask that the prosecution produce any videos that they have which are related in any way to the events of this case. We also ask that they disclose any videos they have which show other people or vehicles in the area around the time or place of the scene of the accident."

Pompeo held out his hands. "Judge, we've produced any videos in our actual possession."

"Your Honor," I said. "I would include any video which the prosecution or law enforcement requested from the public that is being maintained on a public server."

Judge Jurevicius looked at me.

"I think the State might be making a distinction between what it actually has and what it has access to," I said.

She turned to Pompeo. "Are there any such videos, Mr. Pompeo?"

"I would have to check, Judge."

"We would want a representation on the record one way or the other, Your Honor," I said.

"Is that a problem, Mr. Pompeo?"

"Not at all, Judge. Like I said, I'll have to check."

"Was there anything else, Mr. Shepherd?"

"Yes, Your Honor. We've learned that the prosecution has inspected Benjamin Trane's apartment. We would ask that the State disclose any items it took, pictures taken, or evidence procured in that part of its investigation."

"Mr. Pompeo?" Judge Jurevicius said.

"We definitely looked there, Judge, but I don't recall offhand whether we found anything. I'll be happy to check and produce it to Mr. Shepherd if we did."

"Mr. Shepherd, is that everything you were looking for?"

"At this stage, Your Honor."

"Very good. If that is all—"

Pompeo raised a hand. "Judge, the executor of the victim's estate is a Pillars' employee and in fact works directly with the defendant. I assume Mr. Shepherd learned about the search from her. We would ask that the Court restrict the executor's access to Mr. Trane's property and only allow her to do so under the supervision of a police officer or the prosecution."

"What in the world is the basis for that?" I said.

Pompeo didn't look at me. "The defendant should not be allowed unfettered access to the victim's house and property. There's a great risk of spoliation of evidence."

"You said you didn't find anything, so apparently there isn't any evidence there to spoliate."

Pompeo smiled but kept his eyes on the judge. "You can never be too careful."

Judge Jurevicius's computer dinged. She stared at us for a moment before looking at her screen, then saying, "The Court believes it is reasonable for defense counsel to have access to the property, the same as law enforcement, but defense counsel must do so in the presence of an officer or prosecutor who will then log any items that are taken.

"Your Honor," I said. "Mrs. Lynn Horvath is the executor of

the estate for Benjamin Trane. I assume this order only applies to me and not to her as she fulfills her duties as an executor."

"She's Fleece's assistant, Judge. She should be supervised too."

"That's not tenable or practical. She has to dispose of the estate."

The computer dinged. A moment later, Judge Jurevicius said, "Mrs. Horvath, is it?"

"Yes, Your Honor."

"Mrs. Horvath may do her duties without supervision. However, she must give the Court and the prosecutor fourteen days' notice before she disposes of any property to make sure that it is not related to the case."

"Understood, Your Honor."

"Now, Counselors, if that is all—" Ding. She paused, looked, then said, "The Court does not appreciate having discovery disputes brought to it, especially with basic things like this. I expect you to meet with each other and make a good faith effort to resolve these disputes prior to seeking Court intervention. Do I make myself clear?"

"Yes, Your Honor," I said.

"Sure, Judge," said Pompeo.

"Very well. Have a good day, gentlemen." Judge Jurevicius banged the gavel and went back to her office without making eye contact.

"I'll check for any Alert Shield videos by the end of the week," said Pompeo.

"And any other videos you have."

"Yeah, right, right. I gotta bolt. I have another hearing upstairs." With that Pompeo was out the door.

Bailiff Fields was busy writing something in the Court's scheduling book.

"I'll see that Ms. Horvath gets the order, Mickey."

She didn't look up and continued to write. "Sure, Mr. Shepherd."

"Thanks for your help today."

"Don't thank me," she said. "Thank the judge."

41

It was the end of the week, three days after Olivia had so gently explained my screwup at dinner, and I still hadn't called Kira. She was leaving for Harbor Springs, though, so it was time to bite the bullet. I called.

"Hey, stranger," she answered.

"Hey, Kira. Are you still headed to Harbor Springs?"

"Tomorrow. Are you still good to watch Roxie?"

"I am."

"Great. Okay if I drop her off about eight?"

"Sure. Did you want to eat or anything?"

A pause, then, "I'd love to, Nate, but I have a lot of things to get organized for tomorrow yet. When I get back maybe?"

"You bet. You know what we were talking about at dinner the other night?"

"Remind me."

"About Theo giving Trane the wallet before he died?"

"Oh, right."

"I don't think he did. I went over to Trane's place and went through his things." I explained my visit with Danny and Mrs. Horvath. "So, we struck out again."

"We certainly did."

I decided to assume she meant with finding the wallet.

Silence. Then Kira said, "Or he had it and someone took it."

"I haven't seen any sign of that so far, but I suppose it's possible."

"It's on to Harbor Springs then. Eight tonight, okay?"

"See you then."

I ARRIVED home right at eight and had just set my keys down when I saw the flash of headlights in the driveway. I took a peek, then went out to see if Kira needed any help. She was juggling a bag, a bed, a bowl, and a leash, so I grabbed the bag and the bed and let her guide Roxie into the house.

There was a little bit of a scramble as the bed was plopped onto the family room floor, the bowl was placed in the kitchen, and an array of supplies from the bag were explained. It had been a while for me on the whole dog thing but we'd had a couple at home through my teenage years, so I wasn't a stranger to it either. Roxie watched it all from the family room, forlornly skeptical.

Kira had brought a food bowl but forgotten the water bowl, so I pulled one out of the cupboard and was filling it from the sink when Kira said, "Is that Sarah?"

I looked over my shoulder. Kira was looking at a picture on the fridge. Two of them actually.

"Yes."

"She's pretty."

"She was."

Kira turned away. "There's a cup in the food bag. One in the morning, one at night. You saw the lead for walks. And she can make it in the house until dinnertime if you let her out before you go to work in the morning."

"Got it."

"I walked her before I came, so you should be good until tomorrow." She turned both ways, looking around, checking. "I think that's it."

Roxie stood in the family room, staring. Kira pointed. "Roxie, bed."

Roxie stared another moment, then walked over to the bed and lay down.

Kira turned back to me. "I'm not sure how long I'll be gone but I'll call as soon as I have a better idea. Or when I find five million dollars."

"No worries."

"And I owe you dinner when I get back."

"Yeah, about that, I'm sorry if I screwed that up."

"I told you, I love Thai food."

"I mean, if you didn't want to watch the Wings."

Kira smirked and said, "I already told you, Nate, I'm not that sensitive. Besides—" She kissed me and, as she pulled back, gave me a small smile and said, "Next time I'll pick what we watch."

Then she hustled out the door.

Roxie watched me from the family room. I went to my room and changed, came back to make some dinner and still she just lay there, watching. Then I realized something. "Roxie, come."

She popped right up and came over. She'd been under command on the bed. "Heel," I said, and took her on a tour of the house.

She followed me from room to room, investigating, sniffing, and generally muffling about. Each time, though, when I left a room, she followed.

Eventually, we made our way back to the kitchen, where I ate some cold chicken and rice and Roxie flopped down next to my chair. I cleaned up when I was done, then made my way out to the couch and flipped through the channels.

I kept an eye on Roxie, who finally ate a little from her bowl and took a drink. Then she came around to face the couch and stared.

I stared back. Then I patted the couch and said, "Okay."

Roxie hopped up and curled into the far side of the couch, which seemed like as good a place as any.

And that was how Roxie came to stay at my house.

I RECEIVED a call from Edge over the weekend. Actually, that's not quite accurate—I missed a call from Edge late Saturday morning. I'd gone for a run and then tacked on a little extra when I took Roxie for a walk and, when the two of us returned, I saw he'd called and called him back right away.

"What's going on, Edge?"

"What are the chances that we get the money from Benjamin's estate?"

"I'm not in love with that question, Edge."

"We lost two more churches and a non-profit. Expansion has been put on hold and we're fighting just to keep funding the services we provide now. I'm looking at all options to keep the doors open. One of those is the potential recovery from Benjamin. So what are our chances?"

"What does Pillars' corporate attorney say?"

"I can't get a straight answer out of him. He keeps saying it depends."

"It does."

"You're as bad as he is."

"Occupational hazard."

Edge took a deep breath. "I'm sorry. What do you mean?"

"Two things. First, there are rules that prevent a person from benefiting from the death of someone they killed. I don't know if they apply in this case."

"Okay. But what if we win?"

"Then there's no reason that the estate shouldn't pass exactly as Trane wanted. Second, there's a practical problem."

"What?"

"No one can find the cold wallet where the money is stored."

"Do we have people looking for it?"

"Yes."

"All right, if we find it, how soon can we get it?"

"If by we, you mean Pillars, there's no way it gets any money before the Plutides estate is settled."

"When is that? August?"

"Maybe later."

"I see."

Edge was silent for a moment, and I let him digest it. Then he said, "You're saying we shouldn't count on the money at all and should just look at it as a windfall if we receive it."

"If you're making financial plans then, yes, I think that's the way to approach it."

"But Pillars should still get the foundation grant from Theo for the food pantry, right? Win or lose?"

I thought it through. "That's right. Theo left a grant to fund the food pantry. That goes directly to Pillars. There's no claim that you had anything to do with Theo's death, so the grant from Theo to the Pillars food pantry should still be valid."

I heard a sigh on the other end of the line. "So we should be able to keep providing food, no matter what?"

"That's right."

"Well, that's something."

"That's a lot of something. Anything else you need?"

"A way to fund a health clinic and a childcare expansion."

"Absolutely. Anything else?"

"No, I think that does it. Have a good weekend, Nate."

"You too, Edge."

Roxie was sitting next to me, looking up. I pet her and tried to set aside the fact that my client had just called asking when he could get money from the person he was accused of killing but found that I wasn't ready to do that yet. I had brought the Plutides estate binder home and decided to take a quick look at the food pantry foundation Theo had set up for Pillars to double check what I'd told Edge. I looked, and the language was as I remembered it, and I felt pretty sure that the result of our trial wouldn't affect this particular gift from Theo Plutides.

Of course, that brought me back to the cold wallet, so I flipped to the inventory tab, past the cash accounts, and stared at the entry for the wallet filled with Bitcoin. Again.

No account number. No location. Just an eight-digit pin number that would unlock the wallet for whomever was holding it in their hands.

I scanned the entries before and after it. Most of the other accounts had addresses too—the brokerage accounts listed online addresses and passwords, the 401(k)s and the DRIPS and the ETFs all included the online trading account or the financial advisor who had access to it. The BIP39 account was a little different but even that had a series of three sixteen-digit account numbers to identify it.

Nothing for the cold wallet though. Just that damn PIN with no location.

I kept leafing through the back few sections of the binder, out of pure curiosity now. Under "real estate assets," I found the houses in Carrefour, Sanibel Island, and Harbor Springs, along with Theo's interest in a variety of commercial properties. Then under "tangible personal property", there were sections for all sorts of things, including jewelry, artwork, and rare books. There was even an interest in an honest to God racehorse which, from the look of things, made more in stud fees than I did practicing law which provided evidence of either the complete randomness or the sublime purpose of the universe, depending upon your perspective.

I was getting nowhere so, eventually, I put Theo Plutides' estate plan away. If there was a clue to the location of the physical wallet, I didn't see it.

Roxie did fine over that weekend, by the way. She was calm and she slept a lot, but she perked up noticeably when we went for a walk. I completely forgot a poop bag, so we did have to hustle back to the house to get one before my neighbor, Mrs. Nygard, noticed but I think we escaped unscorned. Roxie was happy to lay on her bed in the family room as long as I was within eye shot. If I strayed too far, I soon heard the familiar click-click-click, and a moment later, the snuffling nose of the brindle boxer.

I chalked it up to the old habits of service dogs dying hard.

The biggest adjustment was at night and honestly, I should have anticipated that. I went to bed, thinking that Roxie would just sleep in hers like she had all day. I had no sooner gone to my room than the click of paws coming down the hall alerted me that this arrangement was not satisfactory. When she stood in the doorway, sadly staring, I figured it wasn't very sportsmanlike for me to have a bed and her to have none, so I went back to the family room and brought her bed down. She seemed content with its placement in the far corner, curled up, and went to sleep. So did I.

I was fast asleep when I was awakened by a sharp bark and a dog's nose in my face.

I glanced at the clock. Two thirty-two a.m. "Jesus, Roxie, how about we sleep?" I said.

Roxie stared at me from beside the bed then, apparently satisfied that I was now awake, went over, lay back down in her own bed, and closed her eyes.

I didn't think anything of it and went back to sleep myself.

42

On Monday morning, I got Roxie settled and then went to the office. Danny was waiting, paper in hand. "Sleeping in today?" he said.

"The dog ate my homework. What's that?"

"Ryan Pompeo's expert witness disclosure."

"Any surprises?"

"I'm not sure." He held out the paper and the two of us looked at it together.

I read out loud. "Alan James Hackett, accident investigator/police officer. Not surprising. Scott Swayze, a financial advisor and cryptocurrency expert. I suppose if they're going to use the five million dollars in Bitcoin as a motive, they have to make sure the jury knows just what the hell cryptocurrency is."

Danny nodded. "That's what I thought."

"Kevin Donald, paramedic. Cause of death." I looked at Danny. "I think we know what the cause of death was."

"Right, I imagine it's to make sure to get some shock value testimony in."

I jiggled the paper. "You're right, Danny. All in all, I don't think it's too bad."

"Except I'm not sure about this," he said and pointed to the bottom of the page.

In an expert disclosure, lawyers always throw in some catchall phrases because we're paranoid and we want to make sure that we can elicit any kind of testimony from any kind of witness that we want. There are two ways to do this. One is that you name categories of people, like "any doctor who treated the victim at any time," or "any expert disclosed by any other party." The other way is to name a fact witness who might have a particular expertise that you also want to elicit information from.

Ryan Pompeo had listed a lot of the usual catch all phrases at the bottom of his expert disclosure. There was one in particular, though, that had caught Danny's eye and now it caught mine:

> The prosecution may elicit expert testimony regarding financial accounting and cash flow from Dawn Blackwell, CFO of Pillars.

I looked at Danny. "Now would be a good time to tell you I got a call from Edge this weekend."

"Oh, yeah?"

"He wanted to tell me that Pillars' cash flow is in the toilet. Their expansion financing is stalled and they're tapping everything they can just to keep the doors open."

Danny frowned.

"What is it?"

"I wonder if Spencer Martel could help."

"With what?"

"Pillars' financing. Either through Martel Financial or with another one of the companies he works with."

"A referral to Martel is fine, Danny, but don't get involved in any of it."

He looked the question.

"We represent Edge, not Pillars. You can't get involved in anything for the company."

"But I can tell Edge to reach out to Spencer Martel to see if he can help?"

"Yes, and you can call Martel to make the introduction, but that's it."

"It's worth a shot then. I'll call them both today." Danny tapped the expert witness disclosure. "Regardless, it sounds like Dawn Blackwell can paint a pretty bleak picture."

"And I would guess that she'll be able to show that five million dollars would solve those problems.

Danny bit his lip. "That would be pretty damning coming from Pillars' own CFO."

"I think I better have a meeting with Dawn and find out just how damning it will be."

WITH THE ASSISTANCE of Mrs. Horvath, I was able to get a meeting with Dawn Blackwell that afternoon. Mrs. Horvath showed me to a conference room at the appointed time. At five minutes after, she stuck her head in to apologize that Ms. Blackwell was running just a few minutes late. At fifteen minutes after, she thanked me for my patience, told me it would be just a few minutes more, and asked if I wanted a refill for my coffee, which I accepted. And, at twenty-five after, she told me that Ms. Blackwell was just about here until, at thirty-two minutes after, Dawn Blackwell came in, weighed down with thick binders and profuse apologies.

"Sorry, Mr. Shepherd—"

"Nate."

"—-Nate. I had a conference call go long. We're still trying to put together the health clinic financing."

"How's that going?"

"About how you'd expect when your founder is accused of murder." Dawn raised a hand. "Sorry. The call didn't go great. The bank homed right in on our cash flow issues."

"Cash flow issues are why I'm here. You were disclosed as a witness today by the prosecution."

Dawn's eyes widened. "What? Why?!"

"They're going to elicit expert testimony from you about Pillars' financial status. And its cash flow."

"Can they do that?"

"Yes."

"But I didn't agree to testify!"

"You don't have to. They can subpoena you."

"Can't you stop them?"

"I can try. But I don't think it will do any good."

Dawn pressed her lips together. "Don't waste our money then."

"It's that bad?"

She nodded.

"Why don't you show me what I'm dealing with."

For the next hour, Dawn Blackwell took me through the numbers. She had short blonde hair and an upturned nose that would have made her seem pixie-ish except for two things—her dead serious regard for the numbers and the dark circles under her eyes. As she showed me red number after red number, I began to understand why.

It was bleak. General donations had fallen off dramatically since Edge had been arrested and they expected the drop to continue through trial. Donations were their lifeblood, Dawn explained, and without them, they only had a few small grants and dedicated endowments to keep the doors open.

When she was done, I said, "I talked to Edge a little bit about this. He thought Pillars would be able to make it through trial?"

"Maybe. It depends on if the donations level off or keep falling." Dawn looked up, her eyes tired. "But the Trane donation will come through, right? I mean, that would save everything.

I decided not to mention that the cold wallet was still missing and said, "You realize that reaction is why the prosecutor is calling you, right?"

Dawn tilted her head. "What do you mean?"

"Your relief that the money from Trane's estate could save Pillars. They're using that as Edge's motive for the killing."

Her face went white. "I didn't realize..." Dawn looked at her ledger. "Edge would never think like that."

I nodded. "That's what we'll want to convey. Is there anything else you should show me about the finances?"

"Not that I can think of."

"They may ask you about conversations you've had with Edge about the financing."

"Okay."

"And probably Carissa too. Do you ever talk to her about any of this?"

Dawn Blackwell's face became flat. "I only talk to Dr. Carson-Fleece about how our finances affect building the new health clinic."

"Nothing else?"

"That's all she's interested in. Well, that and reimbursement for marketing expenses to raise money for the new health clinic."

"Is that an issue?"

"It is when you don't have money to burn. And we don't."

I thought about the old adage that you have to spend money to make money in business, then remembered that Pillars was a charity and saw Dawn's perspective as she kept rolling.

"I can't tell you how many dinners they've expensed, how many events they've attended, to get this thing built."

I nodded. "Carissa and Edge?"

Dawn shook her head. "Carissa and Greg Kilbane. He's the liaison, so he's the one with the relationships and the one who attends most of the functions. They just went to another one last week, and of course, Greg ran another red light on the way."

"What do you mean?"

"Greg Kilbane has never met a red-light camera that he hasn't run through. I get those little City of Carrefour envelopes almost every month."

"Why would you get those?"

"Because he always does it in the company minivan. It's registered to Pillars, so Pillars gets notice of the fine, which means me."

I had a vague feeling of uneasiness, the kind you get when you think something might mean something but you don't know that it means something and there's really no reason it should mean something but you're afraid you're just going to have to check even though that something was probably nothing. "Does Pillars pay those?" I said before I thought it all the way through.

"We used to. Not anymore—there are too many and we don't have the money. Now if anyone gets a ticket, I just give it right to them to pay. Do you need them?"

Here's the thing—if I asked Dawn to search for that information, say for whether any Pillars minivan got a red-light ticket on the night Benjamin Trane was killed—she could be asked to produce it to the prosecution or worse yet, testify about it on the stand. The prosecution hadn't asked for any such records, and, at this stage, I didn't know that any such evidence existed. Right now, I had a hunch, and I would want my own person to investigate hunches.

"No, thanks. I don't need Greg's red-light ticket from last week."

Which, of course, was absolutely true.

Mrs. Horvath stuck her head in. "I'm so sorry to interrupt, Dawn, the daycare called. It's closing early today."

"I made arrangements for them to stay open late today!"

"Amanda's son is sick so she can't come in for Brandy who can't stay because her mom has an appointment... Do you really want the whole daisy chain?"

"Why make me fill out the late pick-up form if they're not going to stay open?!"

"I know, dear."

Dawn sat back in her chair. Hard. "I just want to do my job, Lynn."

"And you do it very well. Fifteen minutes."

"Are we done?" said Dawn to me.

"We are. Thanks for your help."

Dawn was already gathering her books. By the time I stood, she was hustling out the door.

"Dawn's keeping a lot of balls in the air," I said as I gathered my things.

"She certainly is," said Mrs. Horvath, looking after her. "The expanded day care can't come soon enough." Mrs. Horvath looked back to me. "How did she hold up?"

"As well as can be expected."

"I suppose that's all we can do, isn't it, Mr. Shepherd?"

"Very true, Mrs. Horvath."

I thanked Mrs. Horvath, who was making me rethink my whole position on hiring an administrative assistant, and left.

As I pulled out of the parking lot, I made a call.

"This line is not available for excuses," answered Olivia.

"You'll be happy to know it's related to work."

"I'm always available for that. What's up?"

"Research."

"Our topic?"

"Traffic light cameras."

PART IV

CRITICAL LOAD

43

Early on the morning of July 4th, I pulled into the driveway of Kira's townhouse and hustled up the steps. She opened the door before I knocked, said, "Just about ready," and gave me a quick kiss before heading back in. "Can you grab Roxie?"

I didn't have to since Roxie came trotting around the corner, tail wagging, and said hello. I petted her hello back and the two of us went into the kitchen where Kira was putting a beach bag on the island alongside a dog bag and a covered tray.

"There'll be plenty of food," I said.

"We're not coming empty-handed, freeloader."

"I have a cooler in the car."

"Beer doesn't count."

"You haven't met my brothers."

Kira put on a Tigers ball cap and sunglasses to complete the T-shirt, shorts, and flip-flop ensemble, then slid the beach bag over her shoulder and grabbed the tray. I clipped the leash on Roxie and took the dog bag in the other hand.

"What about the bed?" asked Kira.

"I brought the one from my house."

"Perfect."

Then the three of us loaded up and headed to Glass Lake.

"So, is it straight north from Carrefour?" asked Kira.

"North and a little east," I said.

"Pretty drive."

"It is once you get out of town. Thanks for coming. I know you're busy with the auction."

"Thanks for inviting me. I don't have time to go to all the way up to Glen Arbor, so Roxie and I would've been celebrating at the townhouse."

"Can't have that. Are you working tomorrow?"

"I am. Getting into the last dash toward the Plutides auction."

"How's it going?"

"Pretty well. All the appraisals are in, so we're down to setting opening bids and determining floor values. I have cleaning crews hitting all three properties over the weekend so that we can stage it all next week."

"They're working on the Fourth?"

Kira nodded. "They were willing to do half a day today and half a day tomorrow for double-time." She smiled. "And yes, the estate can afford it."

"I'm aware."

We turned off the main state route to a two-lane road that wound over hills and around other lakes.

Kira looked out the window. "So who all is going to be there?"

"My mom and dad, of course. Mark and Izzy you know, and their three boys."

"Right."

"My older brother Tom and his wife Kate with their kids Reed, Taylor, Page, and Charlie. Reed and Taylor will love you, by the way."

"Oh? Why is that?"

"Because you're you and they're teenage girls."

"Flatterer."

"Truth. I talked Danny and his wife Jenny into coming out for the afternoon, too."

"Oh, good."

"Then Olivia and her cardiologist and Cade and someone."

"And someone?"

"There's honestly no way to know."

She smiled and nodded. "So, I finally get to meet the famous Bricksons."

"I know, with the three of you running in so many different directions, it's been hard to put anything together."

She smiled and nodded. "Sounds like fun."

"Come in, come in," said my mom. "Here, let me take that tray. We'll just put this over here, perfect, and there we go. Welcome, Kira," she said, and gave Kira a hug as soon as both of her hands were empty.

Kira smiled and, before she could get a word in, my mom continued, "I'm so glad you were able to make it. I understand you've been burning the candle at both ends."

"Oh, it hasn't been too bad."

"No need to be modest, dear. Isabella has been telling us all about what a wonderful auctioneer you are."

Kira smiled. "Izzy has?"

My mom gave me a hug and said, "I've long since given up

getting any information out of this one. Always hiding behind that attorney-client nonsense."

"You don't say?"

"Exactly. I'm not telling you anything you don't know. And who is this?"

"This is Roxie."

My mom magically produced a treat from somewhere and made a friend for life. "The kids will love to see her."

My mom straightened. "Your brothers are already here. I think your dad is putting together a water ski run before the jet skiers start. Make yourself at home, dear," she said to Kira. "It's open season on anything in the refrigerators or coolers—we'll just be grazing until the cookout tonight, so help yourself."

Then my mom bustled back to the kitchen.

I smiled and put my arm around Kira's shoulders. "Ready to run the gauntlet?" I said.

"Ready," said Kira.

~

"Roxie!" screamed Joe and came tearing over as soon as we came out the back door. James, Page, and Charlie weren't very far behind.

I had brought Roxie over to Mark and Izzy's the week Kira was out of town and she'd been a huge hit. As a service dog, she was naturally patient with the kids and her exposure to them made this a pretty safe situation, but I was caught there with the kids as Roxie became reacquainted with James and Joe and met Charlie and Page, who were already hugging her and nuzzling her neck.

I was standing there making sure nobody was poking anything that shouldn't be poked or mouthing anything that shouldn't be mouthed when I looked up and saw that Kira had kept right on walking toward the group of adults standing down by the lake. She smiled, waved, and said, "See you down there."

A moment later, there was a shrieking "whoo-hoo" that let me know Izzy would handle the introductions.

I wasn't sure that was helpful.

It took a few minutes for Roxie and the kids to settle down. Eventually, though, I was able to take her off lead, and she was free to roll and play fetch until her nine-year-old bones became tired of it. I did know that as long as I was in the yard, she wasn't going to run away, so, with a last pet for her and claws of doom for Charlie and Page, I went down to the lake to mitigate whatever damage my brothers had done.

Kate and Tom and Izzy and Mark were standing around a cooler talking to Kira. My dad, the tan guy with the stark white hair, waved to me, then went back to supervising the hauling of skis onto the boat by Justin and Taylor.

Kate and Izzy were wearing shorts over swimsuits, while my brothers wore board shorts with an air of superiority.

"Tell the truth, Kira," said Tom. "You lost a bet, right?"

She smiled. "No."

"So, it's community service?" said Mark. "How many hours do you still have to go?"

"Hush," said Kate. "You'll scare her off."

"Thank you, Kate," I said.

Kate smiled. "She clearly has a soft spot for abandoned puppies and wounded birds."

"There was a time when you were my favorite."

"Hey!" said Izzy, and gave me a back-handed slap, hard, in the middle of the chest.

I looked at Kira. "Kira, everyone. Everyone, Kira."

Izzy waved a hand. "She's already met everyone, and everyone can already tell she's way too good for you."

"Don't tell her," said Mark.

"You think she doesn't already know?" said Tom.

This had gone far enough. I decided to play dirty. "Where's Reed, Tom?"

Tom scowled and Kate frowned before he said, "She'll be up this afternoon."

"With her boyfriend?"

Tom's scowl deepened.

Kate nodded. "Yes."

"Did you give them directions? Wait, he's a senior, isn't he? Never mind, I'm sure they'll figure it out."

Tom stared. Mark laughed.

"Anybody want to take a once around the lake before I start pulling the gremlins?" said my dad.

"Want to go?" I asked Kira.

"Love to," said Kira.

"We'll go too," said Tom.

"Absolutely," said Izzy, and the four of them joined Kira and me as we tramped down the dock to the boat.

After everyone else was onboard, I was slipping the ropes off the cleats when I heard a car pull up by the cottage.

"I do believe that's Danny and his wife," said Tom.

"Seems like you should go meet them since you invited them and all," said Mark.

Kira grinned. "I'll see you in a little while."

I stood there for a moment, holding the rope in my hand, keeping the boat from drifting.

My dad looked at me, gave me his white-toothed grin, then gunned the boat in reverse.

I tossed the rope into the bow and made my way back up to the house.

In case you're wondering, cackles travel quite a distance over water.

I MET Danny just as he and Jenny were unloading their little daughter and all the assorted gear that entails. My mom came bustling out at the same time, hugging them both, thanking them for the lovely fruit salad which they in no way should have brought, and cooing that the pictures her son had shown her of their little Ruth certainly didn't do justice to this beautiful girl before her. Jenny beamed and Danny smiled, and they both allowed themselves to be helped, which was no small feat. As my mom helped Jenny carry all their things into the house, Danny pulled me aside and said, "Do you know about the 120-hour rule?"

"I know about the five second rule."

"Nate, I'm serious."

"So am I, Danny. What's the 120-hour rule?"

"It's a statute that says you have to survive by one hundred and twenty hours."

Danny was talking like he sometimes walked. "Danny, I don't have any idea what you're talking about. Slow down."

Danny took a deep breath, then nodded. "It's an estate rule. In order to receive something through a will, a person must survive the person who wrote the will by one hundred and twenty hours. If he doesn't, he's considered to have predeceased the person who wrote the will."

"Dumber, Danny," I said. "Make it dumber."

Danny pointed to his car. "Say I leave you my car in my will. And I die."

"We're all very sad."

"Nate!"

"Sorry."

"If I leave you my car in my will, you have to live for one hundred and twenty hours after I die in order to inherit it. If you die within one hundred and twenty hours of me, the law treats you as if you died before me."

"Okay."

"And the car passes to someone else under the will."

"Got it," I said. "So if you die and leave me your car, but I die twenty-four hours later, the car doesn't go to me and my estate; it stays with your estate and goes to someone else under your will."

Danny sighed and put both hands out. "Exactly."

"That's great, Danny. Why do I care?"

Danny doesn't swear, so he didn't then, but spoke to me with the patience he'd developed from caring for his baby daughter.

"Because Benjamin Trane died one hundred and eighteen hours after Theo Plutides."

44

It took a moment for that to sink in. Danny waited.

"Is that true?" I said finally.

Danny nodded. "Theo died on February 12 at 8:55 p.m. Benjamin Trane died on February 17 at 6:52 p.m. That's one hundred and eighteen hours."

"How in the world did you figure this out?"

"It was yesterday. Spencer Martel forwarded me another client, but this time it was an estate to administer. He told me to make sure I checked on the death of one of the beneficiaries of the will. When I asked why, he told me about the 120-hour rule, which I'd never heard of before. So I checked and, sure enough, the beneficiary he was thinking of had died the day after the person who had written the will, so the estate was going to proceed as if the beneficiary had died first. I didn't think any more about it until I woke up this morning and realized that the deaths of Theo Plutides and Benjamin Trane happened awfully close together. So while Jenny was feeding Ruth, I hopped on my computer and checked the death certificates for them both and, sure enough—one hundred and eighteen hours."

"That's great work, Danny."

Danny was excited. “That eliminates the motive for the murder case, doesn’t it?”

I thought. “Not completely, but it sure helps.”

“What do you mean?”

“Listen, you’re a lawyer and you’ve been drafting wills, right?”

Danny pursed his lips and nodded.

“Had you ever heard of this rule before yesterday?”

Danny thought, then slumped.

“Right,” I said. “And you can be damn sure Edge hadn’t either so Pompeo can still argue that Edge *thought* Pillars was getting five million dollars when Trane died.”

Danny slumped further.

I slapped his shoulder. “But it sure gives us something to talk about. This makes a huge difference, Danny. Great work!”

He nodded, still looking a little glum.

“I mean it, we can really use this.”

“Thanks.”

“Now let’s get your daughter some beach toys.”

I MADE it down to the water just as my dad’s boat was pulling away again. Kate, Tom, Mark, and Izzy had disembarked and were walking up the dock while the boat went back out with Kira, my dad, Justin, and Taylor. Kira and Taylor waved.

“Dumped you already,” said Tom.

“Didn’t take long,” said Mark.

“They’re going to ski,” said Izzy. “Pops wanted a spotter.”

Mark, Tom, and Izzy scattered to cottage activities and kid-checking while Kate stayed behind. “I think Kira found a new best friend in Taylor,” said Kate.

“Yeah?” I said.

"Yeah. Talk to Taylor if you're curious about where Kira's sunglasses, swimsuit, or flip-flops came from."

"I'll keep that in mind when I'm looking for a new one piece."

Kate gestured to the yard. "Roxie's a hit."

I watched as Charlie, Page, Joe, and Roxie rolled in the grass together. "She's great with kids."

"She's going to sleep soundly tonight."

"Good. Maybe she won't wake me up."

"She does that?"

"Every couple of nights. Same time."

"Does she have to go or something?"

"No, she'll just wake me up for no reason and then go back to sleep."

"Service dogs are pretty sensitive. Didn't you say that her owner had epilepsy?"

"Great, so now I have epilepsy?"

"No, but she's probably been trained to recognize sleep disturbances."

"What's disturbing my sleep is a dog's nose in my face..."

I stopped before I said, "at two thirty-two a.m."

Kate didn't notice as she laughed. "I suppose that would do it."

Charlie squealed and Kate said, "I better check on them," and went to see who needed a juice box.

I admired my sister-in-law once again for how conscientious she was about checking on her family.

The lake was calm that morning and it looked like Pops was putting it to good use as I saw what looked like Taylor's head bobbing up and down between a set of skis. I figured they would be out there for a while, so I went up to the garage and grabbed a paddleboard. That was of significant interest to Roxie, so she followed me back down to the water's edge.

There was about a six-foot strip of sand between the grass and the lake, and Jenny and little Ruth were sitting in it. Ruth was sitting in Jenny's lap giggling as Jenny let sand trickle across little Ruth's feet.

Jenny looked up at me, smiled, and said, "Did Danny talk to you?"

"He did."

"I told him not to bother you on the holiday, but he was pretty excited."

"It's no bother. Part of the job. Just remember, this case was his idea."

"I know." She smiled. "And mine." Her face grew serious. "Thank you, by the way."

"For what?"

"For letting him switch."

I shrugged. "He's doing all the hard work to make it happen."

"Mr. Martel has been sending him so many clients and you can just see the difference in him doing that instead of being mired in...," she looked up, "the other stuff."

I thought about how he'd acted during his meeting with the old couple the other day. "He is different when he's doing that kind of work. More comfortable with himself."

Jenny smiled. "And he's not so..."

"Distracted?"

"Exactly."

"I'm going to have to distract him one more time, you know."

"I know," she said. "And, as you've pointed out, several times, it's our fault. But thank you anyway."

I shrugged. "He's a good man."

Jenny smiled as Danny returned right on cue, bearing a blue

bottle. "I found some SPF 50 instead of the 30," he said and squirted some sunscreen on little Ruth's arms.

"But don't tell him that," I said.

"Tell me what?" said Danny.

"That we needed a juice box, too," said Jenny.

"Shoot, I forgot," he said, and handed the sunscreen to Jenny. She smiled at me, I winked, and then I put the paddleboard into the water.

I HADN'T GONE MORE than twenty yards before Roxie started barking like a maniac. I stopped but she didn't seem to calm down, so I turned back to shore. That stopped the barking and when I ran the board aground, it started the tail-wagging.

That's when I had my "Why don't we put the peanut butter in the chocolate, Mr. Reese," moment. I put the paddleboard right next to her in the shallow water, then helped her on. It took her zero seconds to find the front middle balance point and sit at attention. I guided the board gently away from the shore then, once the fins cleared the sand, stepped up quickly and caught my balance. Roxie sat there, nose to the wind. I smiled and started paddling.

ONE OF THE things I love about paddleboarding is how close you can get to things. Somehow, it just doesn't disturb the birds or the fish or the turtles and you can get far closer to them on the water than you could walking up on them on land. I've come right up to a loon, just floating there calm as you please, when it never would've let me get near it otherwise.

I discovered that morning that a row of ducks is not at all

interested in having a barking dog glide up on them but honestly, with all of their quacking, they kind of had it coming.

Since this was Roxie's first trip, I hugged the shore, just in case, but I didn't need to worry. Once her duck-scattering duties were done, Roxie lay down and tucked her head between her paws, her brindle coat glistening with the water and the sun as we paddled.

As the sun grew hotter, I warmed up to Danny's discovery. If Danny was right, if the law treated Benjamin Trane as if he had died before Theo Plutides, then all of that money in the cold wallet would not pass to Benjamin Trane. And if the money didn't pass to Benjamin Trane, then it wouldn't pass to Pillars after Trane died. Instead, the money would go back into Theo Plutides' estate and would be distributed in the catchall provision to Rory Dennison. I wasn't crazy about Rory Dennison getting more money, but nobody ever said that the rich deserve it. Well, actually, they say it all the time, but that doesn't mean it's true.

No, the important thing, the thing I could work with, was that Trane's death didn't give money to Pillars. It actually took money away. My first instinct was to blast that information at Pompeo next week to shake things up, but that would just let him adjust his strategy to this new information. Then I realized that it gave me a chance to set a trap for Pompeo at trial.

Danny had found an obscure rule. My bet was that Pompeo either didn't know about it or was ignoring it because his case was sexier with Pillars getting the five million dollars. If Pompeo figured it out on his own—no harm, no foul. We'd be prepared for it. But if he didn't figure out the rule, and if he told the jury over and over and over again that Pillars gained five million dollars from Benjamin Trane's death and that wasn't actually true? His case, and his credibility with the jury, might not recover.

As I turned around, I realized that Danny and I needed to keep this rule to ourselves. A lot could still happen between now and trial and we'd have to see how this played out.

I thought about something else on the way in—about what Kate had said about Roxie's service dog training and about Roxie waking me up at night. There are certain things I don't talk about much, even with you, and I'm not going to go into it here because it didn't really have anything to do with my case involving Edgerton Fleece. I'll just say that, at the time, I had thought that I was past most of it, not the loss but the raw unmanageability of it, and Roxie waking me up at that particular time told me that I might still have a ways to go.

We glided in and I hopped off at shore, right before the paddleboard's fins grounded into the sand. Roxie sat up, then jumped off like a pro.

I pulled the board through the sand onto the grass and flipped it over, fin side up. Then I walked over to where Danny sat digging a moat in the sand with a tiny blue plastic shovel, bent down, and said, "Don't tell anyone about the one hundred and twenty hours. We need to surprise them."

Danny nodded.

Then I pulled up a plastic chair and waited for the boat.

45

bout half an hour later, just before noon, Taylor came running down the dock. "Uncle Nate, Kira dropped a ski!"

"Did you make her pick it up?" I said.

"No, dufus. She kicked it off her foot and skied on just one!"

"Wow."

"Then Pops turned the corner so hard that she shot way outside the wake. She was going so fast!"

"That's amazing!"

"It was!"

Once my dad had eased the boat into the lift, I went over to the turn wheel and cranked it 'til the hull was out of the water. Kira was unclipping a ski lifejacket with one hand while holding her phone in the other. She gave me a smile and kept talking. "We're all set? Okay...No, that's fantastic...Yes, focus on the outside tomorrow then."

I looked at my dad. "She gets to take her phone?"

My dad is a maniac about cell phones out on the boat—something about peace, tranquility, and monkey minds. He shrugged. "She's a guest. And she can slalom."

I shook my head at yet another childhood betrayal as Kira slipped out of the lifejacket and grabbed a towel. "No, I'm out-of-town today...Tell you what, just leave it all right there in the foyer and I'll pick it up and take a look...No thank you, your crew is amazing...Happy Fourth to you too."

She hung up. "Thanks, Dave. It won't happen again."

"No worries," said my dad.

"Who are you and what have you done with my father?" I said.

My dad shrugged. "When you can slalom, you can bring your phone."

"Unfair."

Kira slipped on her flip-flops, grabbed her t-shirt, and ignored my hand as she stepped onto the dock.

"See what you've done?" I said. "You've started a skiing arms race."

She laughed. "The water was perfect. There's usually a lot more traffic on Little Glen, so I had to give it a try."

I pointed at the phone. "Everything okay?"

"Yeah, it was the cleaning crew at the Plutides house. Since they were working on the holiday, I had to take the call. They finished the inside today and will do the outside tomorrow."

"What was that at the end?"

"They have some of Roxie's toys and a few other things. They weren't sure what was trash and what was still good, so they left it for me in a bag. Mind if we pick it up on the way home?"

"No problem."

My dad walked with us up the dock. "There's plenty of food out," he said to Kira. "Can I get you a sandwich?"

I stared. "Honestly, who are you?"

My dad shrugged. "She knows boats too."

As much as the adults were happy to duck in and out of eating, the kids had regular mealtime expectations by God, so around noon most of us gravitated to the house, filled a plate, then grabbed a spot on the deck or the lawn. My mom and Kate were managing kids at the table on the deck, so Kira and I found ourselves taking two empty lawn chairs in the yard with Tom and Mark and Izzy.

My brothers behaved themselves at first. They asked about Kira's job and that led to a discussion of some of the amazing cars she had auctioned off in the past. I don't know a DB7 from an XKR so most of the conversation was lost on me, but Mark seemed impressed by the fact that she had had the chance to drive them and even more impressed by her precise knowledge of their value.

I was halfway through a sandwich when Kate came down the deck steps, holding her cell phone out in front of her like a scorpion. "It's your daughter," she said, and pressed the phone into Tom's hand.

"What is it, Reed?" Tom said. He listened, then put his plate in his lap, leaned back, and rubbed his forehead with his other hand. "Is it drivable?"

"Uh-oh," said Izzy.

"No, just leave it there. We'll have your mom drop us off on the way home and see if we can drive it to Barry's for an estimate...Well, you're just going to be without one for a while... You're okay, so there's no reason to cry...No, I'm not worried because you're going to pay for it...That's actually entirely fair...I expect you and Hunter to be here in forty minutes...Drive safe...Bye."

Tom sighed and hung up the phone.

"Is she okay?" I said.

"She's fine. She hit the cement base of a light post at Target. Kate, did you tell her she could go to Target?"

"She needed a new swimsuit."

"How's the car?" said Mark.

Tom shook his head. "Not drivable."

"She did that kind of damage in a parking lot?"

Tom nodded his head, joining Mark in amazed marvel at the scientific impossibility of it all.

"Did you say you're taking it to Barry's?" said Mark.

Tom nodded. "It usually takes about a week, though."

"I've had good luck at Complete Rebuild if the wait is too long," said Mark.

"We always take our vehicles to Southside Auto Shop," said Kira.

That talk made me realize that I had missed a major part of our case investigation. I got up and walked over to one of the coolers sitting by the deck and, as I did, texted Olivia. Then I put my phone back in my pocket, opened the cooler, pulled out one for myself and said, "Need one, Tom?"

"No, not yet."

"Hunter is the boyfriend?"

"Yes."

"So where's he going to college next year?"

Tom held out both hands. I tossed him one. After that, it only seemed polite for the rest of us to join him.

46

Reed and her boyfriend arrived at the same time as Olivia and her doctor, and both were met with a melee of inquiries. As everyone made sure that Reed was okay and thanked Hunter for picking her up, Olivia introduced Dr. Brad Isaac all the way around. It was rare for me to meet one of Olivia's boyfriends because they typically weren't around that long, but the cardiology/rock-climbing bit must have been a winning combination. He was over six feet tall with the lean, lanky build of someone who could hold himself on a sliver of stone. His hands were callused when I shook them, which surprised me but of course shouldn't have, all things considered. He smiled as he said, "It's great to finally meet you, Nate."

"You too, Brad. How was Yosemite?"

"Amazing. We got Olivia on Snake Dike and the Regular Route and..." He trailed off, then waved. "Sorry."

"Not at all, sounds like a blast."

"It was. It really was. And Olivia took right to it."

"This couch potato?" I said as Olivia walked up. "You must be a great teacher."

"Good Lord, Shep, put a shirt on," Olivia said. "People are still eating."

"Liv, this is Kira. Kira, this is Olivia."

Olivia smiled. "It's nice to meet the patient woman I've heard so much about."

"Likewise."

"All right, enough yakking," said my brother Mark.

"Mark!" said my mother.

"It's time for the cornhole tournament."

If you haven't spent much time in the Midwest or southern United States, you might not have come across cornhole before, also called "bags" in some godforsaken, aberrational places in Ohio. It's a lawn game, similar to horseshoes or jarts, where you try to toss beanbags into a hole in a rectangular wooden board about twenty-seven feet away. There are two boards and two teams of two people and the first team to twenty-one, exactly twenty-one, wins.

Technically, it's a game of skill and hand eye coordination. In reality, it's an excuse to stand in the sun with your friends, drink beer, and mock each other.

Kira and I teamed up against Olivia and Dr. Brad. For the first game, Olivia and I stood at one board while Dr. Brad and Kira stood at the other as we started.

"Green or white," I said to Olivia.

"Green," said Olivia, taking the four green beanbags. She tossed the first bag, which landed with a thump and a slide. "I got your text on the way up here. You want me to look into body shops?"

I threw. "I realized I'm missing a whole angle on the Fleece case investigation." Thump, slide. "We should be looking for other repair bodywork around the same time."

"What do you mean?" Thump, slide.

"Let's just assume that Fleece didn't do it." Thump, slide.

"Okay."

"That means somebody else hit Trane, so somebody else's car had damage."

"Right."

"So what if we checked body shop records for that same week? Maybe we get lucky."

"Didn't the cops do this?"

"If they did, they're not sharing."

"Seems like a long shot."

"I'd call it a medium shot. There aren't that many body shops, especially in southern Carrefour, and we're only looking for a limited window of time."

"They aren't going to just give us that information, you know."

I glanced at her. "I suspect you can be pretty persuasive."

"Of course, I can. I just need you to acknowledge that I'm the only one who can do it."

"You're the only one who can do it."

"See that wasn't so hard, was it?" She tossed her last bean-bag, then I threw mine and watched it slide off the board.

"1-0, green," Dr. Brad called out.

Olivia smiled sweetly. "Neither was that. Speaking of my stellar investigation, I still haven't heard back on my requests for traffic cameras tickets in the area."

"Thanks. Let me know when you do."

Just then, Izzy dragged a lawn chair over and plopped down with a hard seltzer. "Kate, get your chair over to this game. There's a goddamn turtle shell convention going on down here."

Dr. Brad looked over at Izzy.

"You have one more beanbag to pick up over there, Dr. Brad," said Izzy with a grin, then sipped her seltzer.

Dr. Brad looked at Olivia, startled, as Kira patted Dr. Brad's shoulder. "You get used to it."

Kate brought a chair over next to Izzy and took a sip out of a tumbler with a straw. "Don't mind us, you four," she said. "Play on."

~

It took about two rounds for Dr. Brad to get used to the commentary from the peanut gallery before he rebounded. He and Olivia had clawed back to an 11-9 lead when Olivia turned to me and said, "Your text about the auto body shop completely diverted me. I had something else to tell you."

"What's that? Nice toss, Kira!"

"Why didn't you tell me Fleece's wife was having an affair?"

I snapped my head around. "What?"

"I was checking the social media feeds of Pillars volunteers and contributors and all that, just to see what was what, and I ended up down a rabbit hole about Edge's wife having an affair. His wife is Carissa, right?"

"Carissa Carson-Fleece, yes."

Dr. Brad put a bag in the hole. Kira did the same. I didn't comment on the great cornhole play but instead said, "What were they saying?"

"I was checking posts about Edge and the murder charge and it was about what you'd expect—some people coming in to support him and his work, others posting that he should step down and be locked up, with a few sprinkling in that it was all a terrible tragedy that's part of a greater, unknowable plan."

"None of that's a surprise with a murder charge."

"No, what surprised me was when someone chimed in with a 'between his murder and her affair, they're quite the pair.'"

"Did people push back on that? The affair?"

"They acted like it was an old criticism. There were a bunch of variations on 'that's been going on for months' versus 'you know that's not true.' It's clear that the affair rumors have been circulating for a while."

"I hadn't heard anything about this."

"You're not looking in the right places. So I went farther back, and it looks like last fall there were a flurry of posts about Carissa and a guy named Greg Kilbane."

"I know him."

"People were posting pictures of the two of them at different events accompanied by what passes for subtle comments on social media like 'interesting,' or 'they seem close,' or 'spending more time together.'"

"Anything else on them?"

"Isn't that enough?"

"It's plenty. I just wanted to make sure that was it before I talk to my client."

"That's what I've got."

"Score?" said Dr. Brad and Kira.

I realized it was the second time.

"Oh, sorry. Wow, you both put it in the hole twice?"

Kira looked from me to Dr. Brad. "Can you get me a referral for an appointment?"

Dr. Brad cocked his head. "You need one?"

"My back is killing me from carrying this guy."

Olivia and Dr. Brad won the first game before Kira and I won the second. The argument of who was carrying whom continued, so that we switched to boys versus girls for the third game, which had me standing next to Kira.

"You two were deep in conversation," Kira said.

"Work. She's been doing investigations in the Fleece case."

"How long have you all known each other?"

"Junior high. I went to school with her brother."

Olivia smacked Dr. Brad's butt as he tossed. Izzy and Kate ruled that it was not a foul but in fact encouraged.

"Have they been dating long?" said Kira.

"Liv and Dr. Brad? I'm not sure. Sometime around the beginning of the year."

"And Liv was friends with your wife too?"

"Great friends. Her brother was too."

The deep thrum of a powerboat had been growing in the distance and now thundered as a black and red ski boat rumbled its way over to my parents' dock.

"Is that a Scarab?" said Kira.

I nodded. "Cade's here."

The cornhole broke up as we strung some bumpers and tied Cade's boat off. Then Cade picked up a huge cooler and put it on his shoulder, because, honestly, what good is an engine-throbbing entrance without an accompanying feat of strength? He walked up the dock onto the grass and introduced us to Molly, the woman who was with him, as Izzy cackled that the day was just getting better.

Have you ever noticed that good days are more boring to describe than bad ones? On that particular Fourth of July, after Cade arrived, my dad took the kids out tubing while the adults alternated between cornhole, swimming, and hassling each other in the heat of the mid-summer Michigan sun. Danny and

Jenny called it a day in the late afternoon and took little Ruth home for a well-deserved nap while Roxie had the same idea in the family room.

Eventually, my dad got the grill fired up for the chicken and the oil fired up for his fish fry and we all kept on rolling. I came out of the house from checking on Roxie and went over to see my dad, who had four trays of chicken arrayed on a table before him like a king as the grill warmed up.

"Need any help?" I asked, knowing the answer.

"Not with the chicken, Son, but my hand's empty."

I smiled and filled it from a cooler.

"Thanks," he said.

As he took a sip, he picked up a big plastic shaker bottle and sprinkled his homemade mix of spices over rows of skin-on, bone-in chicken.

"What's the heat gradient today?" I asked.

My dad smiled. "Grandchild level." He picked up a smaller shaker bottle, this one with a black top. "I'll leave this one out if you want a little extra once it's done."

"Perfect."

I watched him sprinkling a coat of spices that was uniformly even from long practice. As he flipped the chicken to hit the other side, he said, "So your friend is selling a Hatteras GT65, eh?"

"I warned her not to let that slip."

"I behaved myself." He smiled and took a sip. "No promises if she comes back though."

"Fair."

Then my dad snapped his tongs like lobster claws and started loading leg quarters onto the grill.

~

Reed and her boyfriend Hunter were sitting on one side of the table next to Olivia and Dr. Brad while Kira and I sat next to Cade and Molly on the other.

"You were just hanging there?" said Reed.

"I was roped off," said Olivia.

"And it was how high?"

"I don't know, what did you say Brad, seven hundred feet?"

"Eight," said Dr. Brad.

Reed's eyes widened. "That's almost a quarter of a mile!"

"More or less," said Olivia.

Dr. Brad leaned around Olivia to Reed. "The cool thing is that by the time you're at the top, you're almost five thousand feet up. It's a great view of the valley floor."

"Aunt Olivia, that is so bad ass." Reed looked at Hunter. "Wouldn't you love to do that?"

"Uh," Hunter said around a mouthful of chicken.

Reed grabbed his arm. "Wouldn't you?"

Hunter looked unconvinced and took another bite.

I took the black-topped shaker my dad had squirreled away and added a bit to my chicken.

Olivia straightened. "Is that Pop's hot stuff?"

"Yep."

"Gimme."

I handed Olivia the shaker, and she immediately put it to use.

"What's that?" Kira said to me.

"The spicy version of Pop's rub."

"I'll take some," Kira said.

"It's pretty hot," said Olivia and handed it to her.

"I can handle it," said Kira, then sprinkled a generous portion on her chicken and dug in.

~

I BROUGHT in a couple of trays, one with chicken and one empty.

"Thank you, dear," said my mom and took them from me. Before she could protest, I took a spot at the sink and started washing a serving bowl from the stack.

"You get back out there," she said.

"If you want to get me back out there faster, you can dry."

My mom grabbed a towel, smacked me with it, and dried the first serving bowl.

"The pasta salad was good," I said.

"Don't try to flatter your way out of this."

"I wouldn't think of it."

"Good."

"Because all I can think of is how good that rhubarb pie was."

She shook her head, stacked the bowl, and said, "So when is this next trial of yours?"

"Middle of next month."

"And it's another one of these murders?"

"Alleged murder, Mom."

She tsk'd. "You know I'm not wild about that, but our church has been working with Pillars for years."

"Yeah?"

"Yes, indeed. It would be a shame if Mr. Fleece got it shut down."

"I'm working on it."

"I know that dear. You just make sure that you eat better this time. You looked like you lost ten pounds during that football player's trial."

I had long since given up on convincing my mom that I wasn't losing weight every time I tried a case. I mean, I was, but it was only a little and it came right back. "I will, Mom."

"If you made your meals in advance, you could just heat them up."

"Sure."

"Why don't I bring you a few this time?"

"That's really not necessary."

"You could just store them in the freezer and then pop them in the oven when you get home."

I could tell my mom that there really isn't time to cook something in the oven at midnight when you have to be back at the office at five. Instead, I just said, "Thanks," and appreciated the fact that I'd have a freezer full of meals for the week after the trial.

"I'll bring them over the week before."

"Great."

I finished the last bowl, then grabbed a thermal cup, and poured myself some coffee.

"You and Kira are welcome to stay," she said.

"Thanks, Mom but I think we'll head back after the fireworks. We both have to work tomorrow."

She tsk'd again. "On Sunday? Over the holiday weekend?"

I shrugged and gave her a kiss on the cheek.

"You need to get your priorities in order."

That one stung a little bit, but I knew she didn't mean it in the way I took it. "Probably," I said, and went out to see the fireworks.

47

It was about midnight when we crossed the state line into Ohio on the way to Kira's place. Roxie was stretched out in the backseat, snoring and occasionally giving a high-pitched whimper that I assumed was a response to dream-squirrels. Kira, who had been scrolling and responding since we'd left Glass Lake, hit one more button, sighed, and turned off her phone.

"I'm sorry. They just piled up all day."

"I usually ignore them when I'm about to sell a multi-million-dollar estate but that's just me."

"You're just better at it than me, Patches."

One of the disadvantages of taking your date to an all-day gathering with your family is that far, far too many stories come out including childhood nicknames that a boy might've accumulated when he constantly tore the knees of his jeans.

"You shouldn't listen to my brothers."

"Fine, Natty."

I sighed. "Or my mom."

Kira stretched out, then laid her head back on the seat rest and smiled. "Your family's nice."

I smiled. "They couldn't stand you. Except my dad. I think he might have written me out of the will for you today."

"I'll leave you a little something."

"Appreciate it."

I'd promised Kira we would stop at the Plutides house so she could pick up the bags that the cleaners had called her about, so I detoured to Sunnyfield Drive and stopped at the traffic light at Sunnyfield and Coulter. We passed Mrs. Pepperstone's house with its famous oak tree, then turned on Plowshare Court to Theo's driveway at house number 333.

"Need help?" I said as we stopped.

"No, he said it wasn't too much. I'll just be a second."

Kira hopped out of the car, went up to the front door, and let herself in. The light came on, went back off, and she came out, a pillowcase-sized bag in each hand.

"Whatcha got?" I said.

She smiled. "Mostly dog toys. I'll go through it later but I'm glad they saved them. I'm sure there're some things that Roxie likes."

We were quiet when we pulled into the drive at Kira's townhouse. "Help me get Roxie in?"

"Sure."

She leaned toward me as she unbuckled so that her hair hid her eyes before she looked up. I don't know if I kissed her or she kissed me, but what I remembered most was the feeling of her hair falling around my face and her hand on the back of my neck.

A little later, she said, "There might be something good on Netflix too."

I nodded. "Let's see."

~

THE NEXT MORNING, we both had to get moving early. We were in the kitchen waiting for the coffee to finish brewing and Kira was already shooting texts to all corners of Carrefour. Roxie was splayed on her dog bed, unconcerned with auctions or cases.

"A lot going on the next few days?" I said.

"Uh-hmm," Kira said, thumbs flying.

I looked over at the dog bed. "Want me to take Roxie for a while?"

Kira looked up. "Would you?"

I nodded. "I've got a couple of weeks yet before things really heat up. Seems like you're in it now."

She nodded. "I'm going to have to visit both vacation properties again. The Sanibel inspection went bad and the Harbor Springs..." Kira stopped, smiled, then said, "Taking Roxie would really help."

"No problem." I paused. "Want to get some dinner later?"

The corner of Kira's mouth turned up. "Nate Shepherd, are you angling for a movie night?"

"No, I just was offering—"

"Are you saying you don't want to watch a movie with me?"

"Not at all, I just know you're busy—"

"Because it seemed like you enjoyed watching movies with me."

"Of course, I just—"

She laughed. "Good. Just checking. I'd love to tonight, but I can't, I'm going to be at the house until late then I have to hit the road north in the morning."

"Sure."

"When I get home though?"

"Love to. Looks like you're stuck with me, Roxie."

"Poor girl," said Kira.

We scrambled around then, juggling phones, coffee, and some more things to take to my house for Roxie. I took one load out to my car and, when I returned, found Kira, now motionless at the kitchen table where she'd been a whirlwind just a moment before. The table was covered in dog toys, the now empty bag she'd picked up from the Plutides house draped over a chair-back.

"What's up?" I said.

She handed me a piece of metal about the size of a stick of gum. It was covered in small punctures and scrapes and circular dents. It was pretty scratched up, but I could make out some letters. My heart sank. "Does that say 'Ledger?'"

"It does."

I played with the metal hinge and a mangled black stump of plastic rotated out. Only about a third of it was there.

"In the dog toy bag?" I said.

"Yep."

I stared at the mangled black stump, then stared at Roxie, snoring with the sleep of innocence in her dog bed.

Roxie had eaten a cold wallet with five million dollars in it.

"Bad dog," I said.

48

We both had more pressing things to handle that day than to mourn Roxie's adventures in gastronomy so, when we left the townhouse, Kira headed back to the Plutides house to prepare for the auction, and I took Roxie to my place to get her settled. When she plopped down in her bed, I was reminded that Fourth of July cookouts can wear a nine-year-old boxer out.

I was feeling a little tired myself, but I still had Olivia's discovery to deal with, and right away. I showered up, continued the coffee, and started to call Edge. Then I thought better of it and texted him to set up a meeting at Pillars.

I mentioned before that conversations about being charged with murder need to be in person.

So do conversations about affairs.

~

I FOUND Edge in his office on the phone. He waved me in and said, "I realize that but if you don't come in today, we'll lose more than that in food. Eleven o'clock is fine, I'll let him in. I understand. No, the weekend rate is the weekend rate. Thanks."

Edge hung up and sighed. "One of our refrigeration units went down, and of course, we had a food delivery last night."

"Weekend repairs aren't cheap," I said.

"They are not." He shook his head. "I can't tell you how grateful we are to Danny for referring us to Spencer Martel."

"He was able to help?"

Edge nodded. "He set us up with some credit lines," he winced and gestured at the phone, "which I have just tapped again. I don't know that we'd be open without him."

"I'm glad it worked out."

"He's even taking a look at the health clinic proposal. But that's not why you're here. What's up?"

"Edge, I don't need to know everything about your personal life, but I need to be prepared for anything the prosecutor could bring up when we're defending the case."

Edge nodded.

"And anything you tell me stays confidential between you and me."

"You've mentioned that."

"So I apologize for asking you, but I have to—is Carissa having an affair?"

Rather than come across the table, Edge smiled. "Is this the old Greg Kilbane rumor?"

"I don't know the rumor, only the name. And yes."

"The short answer is no, she's not. Would you like the long one?"

"Please."

"Carissa's mother died of complications from diabetes. She had always worked but between high deductible/high co-pay insurance and the cost of her medication and equipment, Carissa's mother couldn't afford the basic care she needed. Carissa only found out the full extent of it after her mother died." Edge shook his head. "While she was still in med school, which of course made it worse."

"You've been around us long enough to know that our philosophy is that if we see a need, we should strive to fill it. Well, Carrefour is filled with people just like Carissa's mom, Nate, so Carissa has wanted, from the jump, to open a free health clinic here. I completely support it."

"Last fall, we'd finally grown Pillars to a place where that was within our reach, so Carissa ramped up fundraising to get that drive off the ground. You've met Greg, right?"

I nodded. "A couple of times."

"Once we started the push for the health clinic, Greg and Carissa spent a lot of time together publicly at events and privately to strategize to get the clinic funded."

"And?"

"And people sometimes mistake passion for one thing for passion for another. And my wife is especially passionate about this clinic."

I studied him. "I have to say, Edge, you're being pretty calm about this."

He thought for a moment, then said, "There's a practice called *dana,* which is cultivating generosity for those in need without any expectation of return. It's embedded more in Eastern religions than the West, but it teaches that compassion as an abstract thought is useless. We need to develop the habit of actively going out and helping people in distress, understanding that we may not get a financial benefit or even gratitude. Viewed from that lens, peoples' comments about my wife aren't that surprising."

"No good deed," I said.

Edge smiled. "I like to finish that differently—'No good deed should go undone because someone might think the worst of it.'"

I smiled back. "Because they always will?"

"Exactly." He looked at his phone. "Now, if I can get this refrigeration unit going, I'll show some gratitude of my own."

"I'll leave you to it then. Thanks."

As I left the room, I said, "I'm going to have to talk to Carissa."

He nodded. "I understand. Tell her what I said."

"I can't. But you can. Where is she now?"

"She has a shift at St. Isidore's today. She might have a break later."

I thanked him and texted Carissa Carson-Fleece on my way to the car. She replied that she could meet me at the St. Isidore cafeteria if I could be there in thirty-eight minutes. I told her I would.

St. Isidore's was a small hospital on the outskirts of southeast Carrefour. I've mentioned before that I hadn't spent a lot of time on the south side, so I plugged St. Isidore's into my phone to find the shortest route there from the Pillars headquarters.

It took me right down Sunnyfield Drive. I drove past the Coulter intersection, past Mrs. Pepperstone's oak tree, past Theo's street, before driving another ten minutes to the hospital. As I was driving, I realized again that I had no explanation for why the other two Pillars vans had been on that road the night Benjamin Trane was killed, or even any indication who was in those vans or why. Supposedly, three vans were on routes with their regular drivers, one van was being cleaned after the car-sick vomit incident, and the driver of the sixth van, Greg Kilbane, said he didn't know where he was that night. That was besides Edge, of course, who was driving his van around, dented and covered in deer blood. The route itself didn't give me any more clues that day—there were cross streets every couple of hundred feet, at least, to take people on and off the road.

I arrived at the hospital with eight minutes to spare and went directly to the cafeteria. I grabbed two cups of coffee and found a place in the corner as far away from anyone else as I could. I wasn't thrilled about doing this in public, but there were only a few other people scattered about, so I was hopeful.

Dr. Carissa Carson-Fleece walked into the cafeteria and looked around. I caught her eye and raised both cups.

Carissa was in work mode—scrubs, white coat with ID badge, pulled back hair—and she strode up as if she were going to triage me. "Nate," she said. "I have about five minutes."

I slid a coffee over as she sat down. "Black okay?"

"Perfect. What is it?"

With anyone else, I would've said coffee. With Carissa, I said, "Do I have to worry about hearing at trial that you were in a relationship with someone other than Edge?"

Carissa didn't blink. "No. Why?"

"Because I need to know if there's anything else that the prosecutor might bring up."

"How's my marriage relevant to whether Edge hit Benjamin Trane?"

"It's not. That doesn't mean the prosecutor won't bring it up."

"Would you ask me this if I were a man?"

"Yes."

"Did you ask my husband if he was having an affair?"

I smiled. "Touché. No. But no one was mentioning him."

"Let me guess—someone strolled around on the internet and you're wondering about Greg and me."

"A perfect diagnosis, Doctor."

"Let me make it simple for you—I did not and am not having

an affair with Greg or anyone else. And my husband did not and is not having an affair with anyone else so you can eliminate that from your differential diagnosis and move on to the real problem, which is proving that my husband didn't run down Benjamin Trane."

I nodded. "I understand you spend a lot of time with Greg to work on building the health clinic."

"I do. That's how this nonsense started."

"Do you know where Greg was on the night Benjamin Trane was killed?"

She sipped. "I told you before, I was on shift here. I don't know where anyone was, including my husband." Carissa checked her smartwatch. "So now that you know I'm not an adulterer, how are you going to save my husband? And I have about one minute."

"I'm going to argue they can't prove that he was actually there at the accident. Have you been able to find any other evidence of the deer accident?"

"No."

"No texts of him telling you? No call?"

She shook her head. "No. I was on shift when he hit the deer. He's good about not bothering me at work unless it's an emergency that's greater than what I'm dealing with here."

Her watch dinged, and she stood. "Speaking of which."

I stood with her and shook her hand.

"Edge and I do a lot of good together, Nate. Keep it that way."

She didn't wait for my reply as she left.

49

Roxie and I were sitting on the couch late that evening when Kira called.

"Hey, you home yet?" I said.

"On the way. I told Manny Amaltheakis about the cold wallet today."

"What did he say?"

"He says there's no way to know if it is *the* cold wallet but, as far as he knows, the cold wallet with the Bitcoin is the only one that's missing so he suspects that's the one."

"Or what's left of it."

"Right."

"How'd he take it?"

"Actually, he wasn't worried about it at all. Which brings me to the good news—apparently, we can still get whatever was in the destroyed wallet."

"Really. How?"

"Each wallet comes with a recovery sequence. We can buy a new wallet, enter the recovery sequence from the old wallet, and then we have access to everything that was in the old, dog-eaten wallet."

"That's fantastic! Wait, why didn't we just do that in the first place then?"

"That's the bad news—because we don't have the recovery phrase for the eaten wallet."

I thought about Theo's inventory in his will. "But we have the pin number, right?"

"That's not the same thing. The PIN is the eight-digit number that gives you access to the wallet. The recovery sequence is a series of words that comes with the device that allows you to recover the contents of the device if it's ever lost or destroyed."

"So why wouldn't Theo just write that down?"

"Because if someone has your recovery sequence, they can access your account from anywhere, take your money, and then you're screwed."

"And we don't know where that is? The recovery sequence?"

"No, but I'm less worried than I was."

"Why?"

"I was worried someone had stolen the wallet and had the PIN, which would mean the money was gone. But now that we know the wallet was destroyed, we just have to find the recovery sequence and Manny will be able to get access to the money again to distribute it."

"I take it Manny didn't know what it was? The recovery sequence?"

"No, but now he and I can look through Theo's documents for the phrase rather than his houses for the hardware."

"That is good news."

"Sorry," said Kira. "I know it's late but I had to share."

"Of course. Thanks."

"Roxie okay?"

I scratched Roxie's ears, her eyes stayed closed, and I said, "Tearing up the place as usual."

"See you when I get back."

"Have a safe trip."

As we hung up, I thought about the wallet. After so many weeks of looking for it, well, Kira looking for it, it was a relief to know where it was and know there was a way to get the accounts back.

"See what you've done?" I said.

Roxie snored.

50

About three weeks later, right at the end of July, Danny and I were meeting to organize our last preparations for trial.

As I looked at our calendar, I said, "I think the time has come for you to push any more estate planning meetings until after the trial."

Danny nodded. "I'm squeezing in five more this week then they all go to September."

"Can you manage it?"

"I can, but Martel is just burying me with these clients."

"That's a good problem. I'm working on the witness examinations. Can you start uploading the exhibits into the document management software?"

Danny nodded. "I've already started. I'm still waiting on the final Pillars financials from Dawn Blackwell."

"That should be pretty straightforward. The numbers are the numbers."

"Speaking of numbers," said Danny. "Has Pompeo mentioned the 120-hour rule yet?"

"No. As far as I know that trap is still set. If Pompeo spends a bunch of time talking about Edge's five-million-dollar motivation to kill Trane, we'll be able to douse it with the rule that Pillars doesn't get any of it."

"And Amaltheakis hasn't mentioned it either?"

"Not that I know of. I haven't even told Kira. As far as I know, we're the only ones who have figured it out so far."

I checked my list. "Last thing—when you draft the jury instructions, we're going to need the instructions for murder, for vehicular homicide, and for failure to stop at the scene of an accident along with all the standard instructions."

"Got it."

"Thanks."

Danny left to go back to his office, and I moved on to the next thing on my list—Olivia. I called. "Hey, Liv. Any luck with the auto body shops?"

"Good and bad," she said. "The good news is that over the last three weeks I was able to get into every auto body shop on the south side of Carrefour and they were all willing to take a look at their repair records around the time of the accident."

"How in the world did you manage that?"

"Let's just say that I have a range of approaches that I tailored to the particular man, or woman, behind the desk."

"And?"

"And the bad news—nothing matches the kind of damage we're looking for. Drivers in south Carrefour were surprisingly safe that week."

"Well, it was a medium shot. Thanks for taking it."

"I have better news, though."

"Yeah? What?"

"I hit on our traffic light camera requests."

"Why didn't you say so?"

"Because you asked about the body shops and I am nothing if not compliant."

"That's exactly the word I think of when I think of you. What'd you get?"

"A Pillars van that ran a red light on Sunnyfield Drive."

"When?"

"At six twenty-five p.m. on February 17th."

"That's right before the accident!"

"It is."

"Where?"

"At Sunnyfield and Coulter."

"The intersection right before! Did it get a shot of the plate?"

"That's how they issue the ticket."

"Can you send it?"

"Check your inbox. Need anything else for the trial?"

"Nothing urgent. Maybe just keep an eye on the Alert Shield Network to make sure nothing pops up at the last minute. Pompeo's been playing things a little loose."

"Done. Kick ass. Take names."

"Thanks, Liv. I'll check out the ticket and call you back."

"We can discuss it when you come to the gym tonight."

"I might have to—"

"When you come to the gym tonight." She hung up.

My phone buzzed. "I forgive you," I answered.

"Uhm, Nate?"

I looked at my phone. "Sorry, Edge, I thought you were someone else."

"I have a new problem, Nate."

"What is it?"

"The bank is completely dropping the financing on our health clinic."

"Did they say why?"

"They say it's the drop in our cash flow but we both know it's the murder trial. I want you to meet with them."

"The bank? Why?"

"So you can tell them that we'll win the trial and, when we do, we'll get the five million dollars from Trane's estate."

"Edge, I can't do that for a whole bunch of reasons."

"Why not?"

"First, like I've told you, I'm not Pillars' lawyer. Second, as your lawyer I'm not going to talk to anyone about our case before the trial."

"But if I win and we lose the financing anyway then what's the point of all this?"

"The point is keeping you out of prison."

Edge was quiet for a moment before he said, "Fine, Dawn and I will just have to explain it to the bank on our own."

I thought. I was going to have to trust Edge. A little.

"Edge, there are all sorts of obstacles to getting that five million dollars. Like I told you before, I don't think you can rely on it at all and I certainly don't think you should be telling a bank you're going to get it."

"Obstacles? Like what?"

"Like the fact that the Bitcoin is missing for one. And if it's found, who knows what it will be worth, it's fluctuating every day. And Edge, we just don't know how things will go at trial—things could happen that will prevent Pillars from receiving any of that money."

"Like what?"

"I can't say right now. It could impact your defense."

"Well, you're going to have to because I need to know, now!"

"I am serious, Edge. I can't say."

"Then how am I supposed to save Pillars?"

"The first step in doing that is saving you."

There was silence at the other end of the line.

"I need you to trust me, Edge."

"My life's work is falling apart, Nate. Over something I didn't do."

"I understand that. But if we don't win your case first, then we can't save your work."

Silence again, then, "I'll handle it myself then," he said, and hung up.

I knew I was right, but that didn't make a conversation like that any easier—Edge had just expressed more distress at Pillars' potential collapse than he'd ever shown to me about the murder charges against him. I felt bad about the health clinic financing but that really wasn't my problem right now. I had to keep Edge out of jail; if I did that, the rest of this would take care of itself.

Or maybe it wouldn't.

I remembered my conversation with Olivia and pulled up her email with the citation for a red-light violation involving a Pillars van at the intersection of Sunnyfield and Coulter. Olivia was right, the time stamp was six twenty-five p.m. on the night of the accident. It included a clear, blown up shot of the license plate. I pulled up the vehicle log for the six Pillars minivans to match up the license plate. Once I found it, I re-checked, then checked it again.

The license plate belonged to Van No. 5—the van that had been being cleaned that day to get the car-sick vomit out. The van that didn't have a driver on the log sheet because it had supposedly been at the Pillars facility all afternoon.

I thought. Van No. 5 wasn't damaged so it couldn't have been the one that hit Benjamin Trane. But what if it were the last van to pass? Wouldn't the driver have seen what had happened? Or at least the accident site? Yet, as far as the Pillars logs were concerned, this van had no driver. And no witness. Which left me with no leads.

As I was wrestling with where this most recent discovery left us, I realized that I couldn't focus anymore on things that weren't part of my responsibility. So, I decided that—until the trial was over—I'd have to let Kira look for the missing Bitcoin on her own.

Right on cue, Kira called.

"Hey," I said. "How's the auction prep going?"

"Nate, I need you to come over here."

"Where's here?"

"The Plutides house."

"Are you okay?"

"I'm fine. I'm pretty sure I found the wallet's recovery phrase."

51

"I'm an idiot," Kira said as she opened the front door.

"Only for dating me," I said. "What did you find?"

"Come with me."

There were more people in the house than I'd ever seen there, at least ten or eleven, moving things around and arranging them in rows and generally putting things together.

Kira took my hand, which I didn't mind at all, and pulled me through, around, and over furniture, art, and stuff of all sorts that was set up more like a warehouse store than a home. "We're keeping the things that are going to be auctioned online here at the house," she said as we walked. "We moved the ultra-high value items to our facility, both for extra security and so that we can auction those in person for qualified buyers."

"Makes sense," I said.

She pulled me into the library. "We've already moved most of the original art—all of the paintings and a few sculptures—to the auction house. The prints and other less valuable pictures we stored here."

"Got it."

"So remember the old wallet, the one that was destroyed,

came with a recovery phrase. If that wallet was ever lost, or your dog eats it, all you need to do is go buy a new wallet and enter the recovery phrase into the new wallet and you'll have access to all of the accounts from the old wallet again."

"I remember."

"The recovery phrase is a sequence of twenty-four words."

"Okay."

"And that's when I remembered this." Kira dragged me to a row, bent down, and picked up a piece of slate hanging from a frayed rope. As she handed it to me, I recognized the wine-glasses in the corner and the painted words.

"The live-laugh-love poem?" I said. "What about it?"

"Count the words, Nate."

I looked at the poem again:

Seek hope, young orphan.
Reject despair, old father.
Grow wisdom, innocent youth.
Guard wonder, wise age.
Play music, make love,
drink wine, toast life!

I counted. I looked at Kira. "Twenty-four."

Her eyes were alight. "This poem was hanging on the same wall as three paintings of maritime battles from the War of 1812 and two classic Renaissance landscapes. Does this poem fit with any of the other artwork you've seen here? At all?"

"Nope."

"Nate, the recovery phrase for the wallet is twenty-four words long. This has to be it. It's the only thing that makes any sense."

"How do we find out?"

Kira held up a small two-inch drive with a metal case. "We

enter the words and see what happens."

"Let's do it."

There was banging in the hallway as two men carried an end table between the rows of furnishings. Without thinking, I went and shut the door as Kira took a seat at Theo Plutides' old desk.

As she flipped the metal case off the wallet, I put the slate in front of her.

"What do we do?" I said.

Kira was prepared. She had her laptop up and running and a small cable sticking out the side. She inserted the cable into the wallet and a green LED screen lit up.

"That's the new wallet?" I asked.

"It is. Let me just enter the pin to get it running."

I watched over her shoulder. The wallet looked like a regular two-inch thumb drive except there was a small screen with green LED letters and numbers on the side. There were two buttons on top of the wallet that Kira used to control the cursor on the little screen. A cursor blinked on the first blank and Kira began to press the buttons on top. The numbers cycled from zero to nine and Kira moved them up by hitting the right button and down by pressing the left. When she got to the number she wanted, she hit both buttons together, which locked the number and moved to the next blank. It took a bit of time, but she whizzed through the eight-digit pin number and unlocked the device's menu.

"Now we need to go where we can enter the recovery phrase." She picked the option for a twenty-four-word recovery phrase. "And if these are the right twenty-four words, it'll give us access to the original Bitcoin wallet."

Kira was prompted to enter word number one. It was a painstaking process. She went to the first letter, scrolled through the alphabet until she got to "s," then locked it with both buttons. Then she moved on to "e," then scrolled through to the second "e," then entered "k," and locked it all to complete the word "seek." Then she was prompted to move on to the second word and scrolled through each letter until she had locked "h-o-p-e." Then she moved to the third word—"young."

Scrolling through all the letters to spell twenty-four words took forever, or at least seemed to. Add the fact that we double-checked each one to make sure we had spelled it right, and it took quite some time. Finally, though, we had entered them all.

Kira looked up at me, I nodded, and she hit both buttons to validate the final word.

Error message.

"Let's check the spellings again," I said.

We navigated through, button by button, and checked all twenty-four words but they were spelled correctly.

We stared.

"Let's double check the order," Kira said. "You read them to me, and I'll scroll through."

I did, starting with "*seek*" and "*hope*" and continuing all the way through "*toast*" and "*life.*"

Kira followed along with the buttons. "It's the right order."

"Try again?"

Error message.

I thought, then asked, "Do they have to be in a specific order too?"

"Yes."

"So let's just try these in a different order."

Kira gave me a wry smile. "There are over sixteen million possible combinations."

"But if we cleared the weekend?"

Kira's smile faded as she looked down at the wallet. Then she swore and slammed her palm on the desk. I couldn't blame her; the entire process had been a pain the ass.

"I thought for sure that was it," Kira said.

"Me too," I said.

She sighed. "I'd hoped with all that's going on, I'd at least have this problem out of the way."

"Yeah, what's up?"

"Another delay," Kira said. "We're going to have to push the auction back another three or four weeks."

"I bet Rory Dennison is happy."

"The only one who wants this done more than him is me."

"I bet. When does that put it?"

"Right now, we're looking at August 27."

I laughed. "Won't we be a pair?"

"Why?"

"That's the week of my trial."

"Nice. How's the trial prep going?"

"High gear. We'll be rolling for the next month."

"Can you keep Roxie for the next week? I can take her again after that."

"That'll work just fine."

Kira tapped the cold wallet on the desk. "Working every day now?"

"Pretty much. You?"

"Same."

"Sorry, but I won't be able to break free much for a while."

"Don't apologize. I'm in the same boat."

I smiled. "Pencil in Labor Day?"

"Permanent marker." Then we exchanged some comments about movie marathons that you would find corny and I would find embarrassing before Kira said, "Call me tomorrow?"

"Definitely."

We said goodbye and I thought, in that moment, that Labor Day seemed an awfully long way away. At the same time, August 22nd felt like a freight train, so I went back to my office and got to work.

PART V

BRACE

52

When people think of the northern Midwest, they tend to think of cold winters, but it can be sweltering in Michigan in the summertime and on the August Monday morning when Edgerton Fleece and I entered the courthouse for his murder trial, the air was thick with humidity, the kind that sat in your lungs and clammed up your shirt on the short walk from the parking lot to the security desk.

It was only supposed to get worse.

When we stepped out of the elevator, Ryan Pompeo was waiting for us outside the courtroom. He was wearing a tight black suit and a thin black tie that looked more like he was angling to be named Mr. Black in *Reservoir Dogs* than to try a murder case. His black hair swooped up with particular flare that morning as he grinned and said, "A minute before we start, NATO?"

"Sure." I pulled Edge aside. "That's our courtroom. Danny's already in there. Go ahead and I'll be right there."

Edge looked at Pompeo, nodded, then went into the courtroom.

"Your guy cleans up well for a murderer," said Pompeo.

"What do you want, Ryan?"

"It's hot as balls, NATO. I want to be at Put-in-Bay, sitting in the pool at the Sand Bar with a Corona, instead of being cooped up all week convicting a guy we all know is guilty anyway."

"So dismiss and you can get there by three."

Pompeo barked a laugh. "Good one. What I'm going to do instead is offer you murder with a prosecutorial recommendation for fifteen years instead of life, so take me up on it so we can get out of here."

"I feel like we've had this conversation before."

"We have, and it's so rare to get a chance to make up for your mistakes in this business that you should take advantage of it. Your guy gets fifteen, he gets out of prison while he's still on the back nine, and he has a chance to sit in the sun again, which is exactly what we should be doing."

"Forget it, Ryan."

"Ah, ah, ah. You know the rules, NATO. I'll be waiting out here because once I go through those doors, the deal is off."

I stared at Pompeo for a moment, then went into the courtroom.

Danny was pulling exhibit books out of a briefcase while Edge sat at the defense table. I realized that in all the time we'd known each other, I had never seen Edge in a suit because he was always in his Pillars pullover, working. He wore a well-tailored, dark blue number with a faint pattern of stripes and a dark blue tie. His hair, which was normally in disarray from whatever activity he was doing, was neat and thick and for the first time, I thought he looked like a preacher you might see in an arena on TV as opposed to the man I saw constantly unloading trucks and paying bills. He raised his eyebrows as I approached.

I didn't bother to sit. I bent over, rested my arms on the chair back next to him, and said, "The prosecutor's offering a deal—

plead guilty to murder and he'll recommend fifteen years. You should reject it."

Edge nodded. "I agree."

I put a hand on his back, then went back out to Pompeo. "No deal," I said.

Pompeo pointed at the doors. "Sure?"

"We're sure."

"Didn't work out so well last time, you know."

"We don't know how it's worked out yet."

Pompeo waved. "Like that's in doubt. All right, your funeral. Well, I guess it's Trane's funeral, but you know what I mean. Let's go get your client off to jail."

As we went back into the courtroom, Bailiff Mickey Fields came out of the judge's chambers. She gave us a quick wave and said, "The judge wants to see you before we get started."

I looked around the courtroom. There were some spectators, most likely a few reporters, but no family members for Trane, obviously, and none for Edge either. "Is Carissa still coming?" I asked.

Edge nodded. "Her shift ended at seven. I told her to get a little sleep first."

I nodded and looked at Danny. "Probably arm-twisting time. Why don't you stay with Edge."

Danny nodded, and I went in to see the judge.

Judge Stephanie Jurevicius's office had a new feel to it. Sure, the furniture was old, but one wall was plastered with degrees—Ohio State and Ohio Northern by the look of it—along with other framed evidence of academia like a Moot Court award, an Order of the Coif key, and two certificates showing she had received the highest grade in her law school class in ethics and public law. Below those hung a picture of her in a legal cap and gown with her father the councilman and her mother, and another of her judicial swearing in where her father held the Bible as Judge Anne Gallon did the honors.

Judge Stephanie Jurevicius sat up straight behind her desk with hands folded, already wearing her robe along with the incongruous lace collar and pearls. Bailiff Fields followed us in as Pompeo and I said good morning and took our seats.

"Good morning, Mr. Pompeo, Mr. Shepherd. Before we begin today, I wanted to inquire as to whether there had been any further plea negotiations?"

"We made a generous offer just a moment ago, Judge," said Pompeo. "But Shepherd here rejected it out of hand."

Judge Jurevicius looked at me. "Is this true, Mr. Shepherd?"

"They offered murder, Your Honor. That made the decision pretty easy."

She looked back at Pompeo, who shrugged. "We offered a lenient sentencing recommendation, too."

"How lenient?"

"At the bottom end of mandatory."

"That seems reasonable, Mr. Shepherd."

"The bottom end of mandatory for murder, Your Honor. Which my client did not commit."

We sat there for a moment.

Bailiff Fields cleared her throat.

Judge Jurevicius said, "Would you consider a lesser charge, Mr. Pompeo?"

"No, Judge, my boss would have my as—my rear end. Besides, the offer was withdrawn once Shepherd rejected it."

Bailiff Fields coughed again.

Judge Jurevicius said, "Mr. Shepherd, have you considered that your client is facing life in prison if convicted?"

"We understand the seriousness of the charges, Your Honor."

"You think you can prove that your client is innocent?"

"We don't think the state can prove he's guilty, Your Honor. And fifteen years in the face of that isn't even tempting."

Judge Jurevicius sat there for a moment, straightening her lace collar with both hands. "Very well. Bailiff Fields, shall we send for a jury?"

Mickey Fields nodded once. "Already done, Judge."

"Thank you, Bailiff Fields. Counselors, let's seat a jury for your case."

53

The process when people are questioned to find out if they can serve as jurors on the case is called voir dire. The judge seats twenty-four or so people at a time in the jury box and then usually asks some basic questions to get things started. Some judges do all the questioning, but most let the attorneys follow-up and ask their own questions too.

That morning, Bailiff Mickey Fields rattled through twenty-four names and had the potential jurors seated in the jury box in short order. Judge Jurevicius greeted them, explained what voir dire was and that they shouldn't be offended by any personal questions, then read a thorough, if unexpected, description of the role the jury plays in the American judicial system. Then she smiled, straightened some papers, and said, "Let's begin."

Judge Jurevicius put a piece of paper in front of her, picked up a pen, and said, "Panel member number one, please state your full name for the Court, indicating your middle name with an initial."

As the person answered, Judge Jurevicius nodded, made a check on her paper, and said, "Please state your address for the Court." A nod, a check, a pause, and then, "Please state whether you are married for the Court and, if so, please state your spouse's full name." A nod, a check, a pause. "Please state whether you have any children and, if so, whether those children live with you at your indicated address or at a separate address."

You get the idea.

Ten minutes later, Judge Jurevicius finished with potential juror number one. When she did, she nodded, shifted her papers, readied her pen, and said, "Panel member number two, please state your full name for the Court, indicating your middle name with an initial."

By the time we hit our midmorning break, Judge Jurevicius had completed the initial questioning for eight jurors.

Pompeo was fidgeting as the potential jurors left the room, turning what looked like some sort of class ring on his right hand. As Judge Jurevicius stood and straightened her papers, Pompeo added knee twitches to the mix. Finally, when Judge Jurevicius went into her chambers, Pompeo shot over to Bailiff Fields and said, "You've got to move her along, Mickey."

Bailiff Fields did not look up from an entry she was making in the judge's calendar. "I don't know what you mean."

"She's taking forever!"

Bailiff Fields kept writing. "The judge is thorough."

"We're going to take a week just picking a jury!"

Bailiff Fields looked up, her worn face like stone. "If you have a problem with the judge, you can take it up with her directly."

Pompeo looked at me. "NATO, tell her!"

Bailiff Fields turned to me.

I shrugged. "Looks like I'll clear my calendar."

She went back to writing.

Pompeo flicked his hands, snorted, and left the courtroom.

I turned to Edge, who was looking at me, eyebrows raised.

"We're going to be a while."

IF BAILIFF FIELDS talked to Judge Jurevicius during the break, I didn't see it, but the pace of the judge's questions picked up noticeably after the break. I caught Pompeo grinning over at Bailiff Fields a couple of times, but she never looked away from her computer screen and just kept typing. Within half an hour, Judge Jurevicius was finished with the preliminary questioning of the potential jurors and said, "The attorneys now have the opportunity to question you as well. Please give them your full attention. Mr. Pompeo, you may question the venire."

"Thanks, Judge." As Pompeo sauntered over to the jury, he said, "My name is Ryan Pompeo. I'm a prosecutor and I'm representing the State of Ohio in this murder case we've brought against Edgerton Fleece, the man who's sitting right over there in the blue suit. Do any of you know Mr. Fleece?"

Twenty-four shaking heads.

"Great. Now Mr. Fleece is the head of an organization called Pillars Outreach of Carrefour. Have any of you heard of Pillars?"

Twelve hands went up, but Pompeo wasn't fazed at all. Instead, he smiled and said, "I'm surprised it wasn't more. Let's start with you, Mrs. Swarski, wasn't it?"

"That's right," she said.

"How do you know Pillars?"

"I've donated to their food bank before."

"Marvelous. That's generous of you. And you, Mr. Harrison, how about you?"

"My daughter takes my granddaughter to their daycare when I can't watch her."

"Nothing is better than grandpa, though, I imagine?"

Mr. Harrison smiled. "No, sir. Not when it comes to making waffles."

Pompeo put his hand on his stomach. "Don't start, please. We still have awhile to go until lunch. And Mrs. Zilba, did you have your hand up?"

"I did."

"How do you know Pillars?"

"I'd rather not say."

Pompeo nodded. "I understand, Mrs. Zilba, but you see, Mr. Fleece is being prosecuted for murder, so he has the right to know anything about your experience that might be relevant to our case. So you just go ahead and tell us how you know Pillars."

Mrs. Zilba raised her chin. "I get the food there from time to time."

"From the Pillars food pantry?"

She nodded. "During some of these housing slowdowns when carpenters don't work so much."

"Well, that's exactly what it's there for, isn't it? Carrefour is filled with beautiful houses to live in because your family builds them, so it's only right to set up stores for your family when not so many are being built."

Mrs. Zilba nodded.

Pompeo put his hands on his hips, pushing his suit coat back. "Tell you what, let's see if we can cut through this a little. How many of you know Pillars because you've used their child-care services?"

Four hands went up.

"And how many of you know Pillars because you've used their food pantry?"

Three hands went up.

"And how many of you haven't used Pillars yourself, but you have a friend or family member that has, like with Mr. Harrison's daughter, so you've heard about it that way?"

Five hands went up.

"Have any of you volunteered there or donated, like Mrs. Swarski?"

Mrs. Swarski and one other hand went up.

"Have I missed anything?" said Pompeo. "Is there some other service that Pillars provides that any of you have used or heard of that I haven't mentioned?"

Two hands went up.

"Yes, Mr. Peete?"

"I've taken my son to their mobile clinic before."

"I see. And you, Ms. Birch?"

"My neighbor is in her nineties. I see a Pillars van at her house two or three days a week. I think they deliver food and check in on her."

"Very good. Anything else? No? Okay. So let me ask you all this—do you think that you can listen to this case fairly and impartially and decide it based solely on the evidence?"

Twenty-four nods.

Pompeo smiled. "I suppose I should ask it the other way—raise your hand if you think you would not be able to hear this case fairly and impartially."

No hands went up.

"So it works like this—Judge Jurevicius is going to tell you that you can only decide this case based on things that are put into evidence. You can't consider all the things that Mr. Fleece may have done at Pillars. That has nothing to do with this case. Instead, you can only evaluate the evidence that Mr. Shepherd and I show you and that Judge Jurevicius lets in."

He paused and twenty-four heads kept nodding.

"So I'm going to present you with evidence that Mr. Fleece

hit Benjamin Trane with his Pillars minivan, then drove away and left Mr. Trane to die. If I prove that to you beyond a reasonable doubt, will you be able to put aside all of these services that Pillars has provided and find Mr. Fleece guilty of murder?"

There were twenty-four nods, though some not quite so strong.

"Is there anyone who thinks they can't do that, that they can't act on the evidence we present of this murder?"

No hands, no nods.

"Good. Because you see that's the interesting thing. I know Mr. Fleece's organization does a lot of good things in our community, but that doesn't mean that someone within the organization can't do something wrong." He held up his right hand and wiggled the ring. "I went to a university just down the road that's part of one of the biggest charitable organizations in the world, an organization that does an awful lot a good. But people within that organization who do something wrong still have to be held accountable, they don't get a free pass because of good things they've done. Take for example—"

I stood. "Your Honor, may I approach?"

Judge Jurevicius look startled. "Certainly, Mr. Shepherd."

Pompeo and I went to the bench. "Your Honor, Mr. Pompeo's talked quite a bit about charitable organizations, but I don't think he should be permitted to start listing people who worked for charities that did or didn't commit crimes."

"Seems relevant, Judge," said Pompeo.

"It's way too far afield and prejudicial."

Judge Jurevicius nodded, and we waited. And waited. And waited a little more before she said, "I think you've gone far enough, Mr. Pompeo. We don't need specifics."

As I went back to my table and Pompeo went back to the panel, he said, "By the way, that's going to happen from time to time. You shouldn't think Mr. Shepherd is trying to hide something or delay the proceedings when he asks to talk to the judge. He's just doing his job."

I restrained the urge to stand and object, which would just emphasize the comment, and kept a straight face. An experienced judge would excoriate Pompeo for that without my prompting.

Judge Jurevicius nodded in agreement.

Pompeo nodded too. "Anyway, what I was getting at is, the fact that someone is the chief officer of a charity doesn't mean that he can't kill someone. If we present you with evidence that meets the standard the judge describes, can you render the verdict the evidence requires?"

Twenty-four nods.

"Even if the verdict is guilty of murder? Can I have that commitment from you?"

Twenty-four more nods.

"Well, I don't think there's anything more we can ask of you. Thanks, then. I'll be talking to you more in a little while, but Mr. Shepherd gets to ask you some questions now."

Pompeo strolled back to his seat as I approached the jury.

"Good morning." I smiled, and I received more smiles back than I usually did in a murder trial. "My name is Nate Shepherd and I represent Edgerton Fleece. My associate Daniel Reddy is the other gentleman at the counsel table. Do any of you know me or Mr. Reddy?"

Twenty-four shaking heads.

"How about Mr. Pompeo? Do any of you know him? Yes, Ms. Birch, you know Mr. Pompeo?"

"He doesn't remember me, but I remember him."

"And how is that?

"My nephew, he got robbed at an ATM last year. Mr. Pompeo put away the jerk who did it."

"I see. Were you grateful to Mr. Pompeo for doing that?"

"You bet your—I was."

"Were you pretty sure that the guy who robbed your nephew had done it?"

"They had a picture of the guy at the ATM, so yeah."

"You bring up a great point, Ms. Birch. This case is going to involve some video evidence. Mr. Pompeo is going to show you videotape of some vans, several vans actually, but he's not going to show you any video of the accident itself and he's not going to show you any video of my client at or around the scene of the accident. Are you, all of you, willing to commit to reviewing all of the evidence, every single bit of it, before arriving at your verdict?"

Nods, except for one. Ms. Birch frowned.

"Ms. Birch, you don't seem too sure."

"Are you saying they have video of your client at the scene of the accident?"

"No, Ms. Birch, I'm saying they *don't* have video of him at the scene of the accident—they have video of several vans like my client's van before the accident and some video of my client and his van after the accident but there's no video of the accident itself. So what I'm asking is if you all are willing to examine all of this evidence and then hold the state and Mr. Pompeo to its burden, which the judge will describe to you, of proving his case beyond reasonable doubt."

"Oh," said Ms. Birch. "That's okay then."

I smiled. "You know, Ms. Birch, your question reminds me of another point. The state gets to go first in this case. That means Mr. Pompeo gets to present evidence for several days, maybe even a week, before we get our turn to put on our case. Now that's only fair because Mr. Pompeo has the burden of proof, and his case fails if he can't produce evidence to meet it, but what I ask is that all of you keep an open mind and wait until both sides present you with evidence before you make up your mind? Can you do that?"

Twenty-four nods.

"Speaking of sitting here this week, the judge asked you earlier whether any of you had anything that might make it difficult for you to be here this week and Mr. Sherman, you mentioned that you have some difficulty seeing?"

"I do, sir."

"This case is going to involve reviewing some documents and some video. Forgive me for prying, but will you be able to see it?"

"Well, I can see your left ear ain't the prettiest if that's any help."

I laughed and about half the jurors laughed with me. "Then I expect you'll be able to manage just fine. If you are seated on the jury, will you please raise your hand and tell us if you're having trouble seeing something?"

"I'll be sure to holler."

"Thank you, Mr. Sherman." I looked at all of the jurors. It was time to inoculate them against some of what they were going to hear.

"This case involves the tragic death of Benjamin Trane. You're going to hear evidence about Mr. Trane, about how he worked for Pillars helping folks right here in our community, about how he was killed while walking the service dog of one of the men he had cared for. You're also going to hear evidence about the terrible, painful way that Mr. Trane died."

"It's natural for us to have sympathy for Mr. Trane. How could you not? But the issue here isn't whether Mr. Trane died because, unfortunately, he did. The question is whether my client, Edgerton Fleece, killed him. Will you commit to us that if the prosecutor does not meet his burden, if Mr. Pompeo does not prove to you beyond a reasonable doubt that Mr. Fleece killed Mr. Trane, will you commit to rendering a verdict in favor of Mr. Fleece even though you might have sympathy for Mr. Trane?"

The nods came, but they were slower.

"Thank you then. I look forward to speaking to you again in a little bit."

As I sat, Judge Jurevicius looked at the clock and said, "Members of the venire, we will now break for lunch. The Court will call you back a little later than usual as I will be meeting with counsel to select our jury. Please plan on being back at one-thirty p.m."

Then Judge Jurevicius smacked her gavel, and we broke for the morning.

54

At two o'clock that afternoon, we were still in Judge Jurevicius's chambers arguing about the jury. When picking a jury, an attorney can ask the judge to remove a juror for cause if it's apparent that the juror can't be impartial. An easy example is if the juror was related to the defendant. The reason "for cause" challenges are so important is that after all the jurors are excused for cause, each side can remove a few jurors for any reason at all. Those are called peremptory challenges but, since you only have a limited number of them, you want to remove as many jurors for cause as you can and save the peremptory challenges for the ones you just have a bad feeling about.

We were stuck on Ms. Birch.

"You can't strike her just because she knows me," said Pompeo. "Three quarters of the jury knows your client's charity."

"That's not why she should be removed, Your Honor," I said. "She should be removed because she has a strong connection to someone who was a victim of a crime and she specifically said she was grateful to Mr. Pompeo for putting the defendant away."

"Oh, come on," Pompeo said. "You saw her—she nodded

every time you asked her whether she could be fair and impartial and whether she'd wait until the end of the case and whether she'd hear all the evidence and all of that other commitment garbage you were slinging around out there."

"It is a close call," said Judge Jurevicius. She glanced at Bailiff Fields, who was scrolling disinterestedly through her phone on a couch over to one side.

"Your Honor," I said. "She also showed a predisposition to guilt because there's video involved."

Pompeo snorted. "Everyone's going to be predisposed to guilt when they see him washing the blood off his car."

"We're not talking about her conclusions *after* she sees the evidence. We're talking about what she said her preconceptions are *before*."

"And she said she could be fair and impartial."

Judge Jurevicius raised one finger and we stopped. Then she put both hands on her lace collar, straightened it, smoothed it, then straightened it again before she said, "Defense counsel's request to dismiss juror number eleven for cause is denied. If you would like her excused, you may exercise one of your peremptories."

I nodded. Pompeo grinned.

"Are there any others?" Judge Jurevicius said.

"Yes, Judge," said Pompeo. "We want to excuse juror number seventeen, Mr. Peete, the one who had taken his kid to the Pillars' mobile clinic."

"That does not seem sufficient, Mr. Pompeo," said Judge Jurevicius.

"The mobile clinic is run by the defendant's wife, Carissa Fleece. That means his child has a protected physician-patient relationship with the defendant's wife. He can't be an impartial juror, so he needs to be excused."

"Your Honor," I said, "Mr. Pompeo didn't put any of this into the record and he didn't ask any questions about this protected relationship with Dr. Carson-Fleece or whether it would affect Mr. Peete's ability to serve as a juror."

"Are you denying that Mrs. Fleece runs the mobile clinic?" said Pompeo.

"It's Dr. Carson-Fleece and whether I admit it or deny it doesn't matter—you didn't enter evidence of it and because you didn't enter evidence of it, no one could follow-up with questions on it."

"Mr. Shepherd," said Judge Jurevicius. "Does Mr. Fleece's wife run the mobile clinic?"

"She does, Your Honor. But we have no evidence of whether she actually saw this man's child."

"But regardless, she runs it and manages it for Pillars?"

"Yes."

Judge Jurevicius nodded, straightened her lace collar again, and said, "The Court finds that the physician-patient relationship is a protected and confidential one and so excuses juror number seventeen for cause."

I kept my face straight as Judge Jurevicius said, "Are there any other challenges for cause?"

"That's it for me, Judge," said Pompeo.

"No, Your Honor," I said.

"Very well, we will proceed with the peremptory challenges."

We each exercised all three. I struck the woman who knew Pompeo, a man who had recently lost his wife to a drunk driver, and a young man who worked in an animal shelter who had me concerned about the role Roxie was going to play in all this.

Pompeo used his three to knock out the jurors who had utilized Pillars' services the most. When we were done, we had twelve jurors and two alternates. Only five of them had a connection with Pillars. I'd hoped for more, but Pompeo had managed to knock out four.

Judge Jurevicius said, "Very well, Mr. Pompeo, Mr. Shepherd. We have our jury. Bailiff Fields, will you please assign them seats?"

Bailiff Fields didn't look up from her phone as she waved a piece of paper. "All set."

"Excellent," Judge Jurevicius nodded and smiled. "Gentlemen, let's go bring in our jury and proceed with opening statements."

WHEN WE WENT BACK into the courtroom, there were two new people in the gallery that caught my eye. The first was Carissa Carson-Fleece, who was sitting in the first row behind the banister, leaning over and whispering to Edge. The second was Manny Amaltheakis. He sat in the back row on the aisle and made a point of catching my eye and nodding, once. I nodded back then leaned down and said hello to Carissa.

"When do we start?" she said.

"Right now."

Judge Jurevicius entered, and Bailiff Fields brought in the members of the venire and organized our jury. When Bailiff Fields had the jury situated, Judge Jurevicius excused the people who weren't selected and welcomed the twelve jurors and the alternates who were. Then she read the jury a series of standard instructions introducing them to the case (which were rarely understood) and prohibiting them from looking up anything on their cell phones (which were rarely obeyed).

When she was done with the instructions, Judge Jurevicius said, "Mr. Pompeo, you may present your opening statement."

Ryan Pompeo rolled on up to the jury without a note or a projector or an assistive device of any kind, put his hands on his hips, and said, "Edgerton Fleece over there hit a man named

Benjamin Trane with a company minivan and killed him. It's that simple."

"Now that by itself would be vehicular homicide, but we've charged Mr. Fleece with failure to stop at an accident and with murder. Here's why. After Mr. Fleece smashed into Benjamin Trane, he didn't stop, he didn't get out of his minivan, and he didn't try to help Mr. Trane. He didn't even have the decency to hit three digits on his phone and call an ambulance. No, Edgerton Fleece took off, leaving Mr. Trane in a crumpled heap at the bottom of an oak tree."

Ryan Pompeo's hands stayed on his hips as he shook his head. "Getting crushed by a van and smashed into a tree causes massive internal injuries and bleeding. As Edgerton Fleece sped away, Mr. Trane lay dying on the freezing ground in agonizing pain, struggling to breathe. It took witnesses some time to get out there and find Mr. Trane. One of them did the decent, humane thing and called an ambulance. The paramedics came as fast as they could, but Mr. Trane died as he was being wheeled into St. Wendelin's hospital that night, deprived of crucial minutes he needed to get medical care."

"Now you may be thinking to yourself, Ryan, is that murder? Cruel, inhumane, scandalously unchristian maybe, but murder? Why in the world would a good man like Edgerton Fleece do such a thing? I'll be honest with you, I didn't think it was murder at first either, because we can all get taken in by first impressions and reputations like the slick advertising they are. But as we dug into this case, we discovered a motivation for murder—money. A massive amount of money."

"You see, Mr. Trane left everything he had in the world to the charity he worked for—Pillars Outreach of Carrefour, the charity founded by that man, Edgerton Fleece. I can tell you that for most of Benjamin Trane's life, everything he had in the world would not have amounted to very much. But less than a week earlier, Benjamin Trane had inherited a huge sum of money. The man Benjamin Trane had taken care of for many years, a wealthy man named Theo Plutides, had died and left five million dollars to Benjamin Trane. Five. Million. Dollars. And all of that money, all five million dollars, was left to Pillars the moment that Benjamin Trane died."

Pompeo flipped a hand. "Once we learned that, once we learned that Edgerton Fleece's company profited massively from Benjamin Trane's death, we dug deeper and discovered more of the evidence that we're going to show you. You'll see Pillars is overextended and struggling financially, so much so that Edgerton Fleece's company is in danger of closing its doors. You're going to see that Pillars helped Mr. Trane draft this will that left everything to itself, that Edgerton Fleece himself right over there begged Mr. Trane and others like him to leave Pillars their money. You're going to hear that the folks at Pillars knew this—they knew that Benjamin Trane had just inherited money and a fancy car from Theo Plutides and they knew that Benjamin Trane's money went to Pillars if he died. Heck, the evidence is going to show you that Mr. Fleece's own secretary was the executor of Benjamin Trane's will!"

Pompeo shrugged. "I suppose Mr. Shepherd might argue that the inheritance thing is all a coincidence, just a series of fortunate events for Pillars, but we're going to show you that Edgerton Fleece had the opportunity to do exactly what we said. The evidence will show that the defendant decided to 'work from home'"—Pompeo put air quotes around the phrase—"the day Benjamin Trane was killed so no one saw him during the day. The evidence will show that everyone knew that Benjamin Trane walked Theo's dog, Roxie, right down Sunnyfield Drive every day between six and six-thirty. And the evidence will show that the defendant arrived at Snyder Funeral Home at seven o'clock that night, right after Benjamin Trane had been killed, in a van that had been in an accident; a van that was dented and streaked with blood."

Pompeo pointed a thumb at me over his shoulder. "Personally, I can't wait to hear Mr. Shepherd's explanation for that. I think he's going to tell you that Edgerton Fleece hit a deer, so I ask you to give Mr. Shepherd your full attention when he presents you with evidence that this convenient, elusive deer exists. If he can."

"I suppose Mr. Shepherd might try to convince you that this is all circumstantial, that there's an explanation for all of these incriminating events. But we're going to show you a last bit of evidence that will change your mind, evidence that shows Edgerton Fleece knew what he was doing and knew that he was guilty. We're going to show you evidence that the next morning, the very next morning after Mr. Trane was killed, Edgerton Fleece tried to hide the evidence of his crime."

"We will show you that on the morning after the defendant hit Benjamin Trane, Edgerton Fleece took his company minivan to a car wash and tried to scrub the blood off of it, over and over and over again. Then Edgerton Fleece took the minivan to an auto body repair shop to get the dents fixed, dents that were all over the front right quarter panel and hood. He tried to scrub out the blood and repair the van to hide his crime, to disguise the rotten interior of a man who would kill his own employee so he could get millions of dollars for his failing company."

Pompeo shrugged again, hands back on his hips. "It's heinous and it's murder. That's why at the end of the evidence, we're going to ask you to convict Edgerton Fleece of murder and of failing to stop at the scene of an accident. I look forward to showing it all to you."

Pompeo strolled back to his seat and slouched into his chair as I approached the jury. I got some hard looks and some questioning looks, but no one looked angry, which was something. I took a moment until I had all of their focus, then said, "Benjamin Trane is dead. Edgerton Fleece didn't kill him."

"Mr. Pompeo says that he has evidence that Mr. Fleece hit Mr. Trane with a minivan and then fled the scene. Look for that evidence and hold Mr. Pompeo to what he claims. Does he have any witnesses to the accident itself? Does he have any witnesses or videos who saw Mr. Fleece or his van at the scene of the accident? He doesn't have any, by the way, or at least he hasn't shared any such evidence with the court or us. And if he can't put Mr. Fleece at the accident, he can't prove beyond a reasonable doubt that Mr. Fleece killed Mr. Trane."

"The same is true of this supposed motive Mr. Pompeo was talking about—he says my client wanted to kill Mr. Trane so that Pillars could collect five million dollars which would save the company. Hold Mr. Pompeo to that—examine the evidence he gives you because if he doesn't prove that Pillars would receive five million dollars from Mr. Trane's death, then the State's supposed motive goes right out the window."

"Now when Mr. Pompeo was talking to you in voir dire, he mentioned Mr. Fleece's long history of working for those in need in the Carrefour community and he asked you to look beyond it. On this we agree—the fact that my client founded and runs one of the largest charitable organizations in Carrefour, an organization that provides outreach services to thousands of underserved residents in our community has nothing to do with this case. Nothing. I wouldn't even bring it up except that Mr. Pompeo did earlier because it doesn't matter at all. What matters is whether the State has evidence beyond a reasonable doubt that my client killed, no murdered, Benjamin Trane, and I am telling you that it does not."

"It has evidence that there were a number of vehicles in the area on the night of Mr. Trane's death, but it can't prove that any of them were my client's van. It has evidence that there were drivers in the area, eight to be exact, but can't prove that any of them were the vehicle that hit Mr. Trane. When you hear it, I ask you to consider whether the state's case makes any sense at all. We think it does not."

"Now, we don't have to put any evidence on because the State has the burden here. But we will. We'll be calling witnesses that further point out that the prosecution isn't anywhere close to meeting its burden. And when we're done, after you've had a chance to scrutinize the prosecution's case and take a look at ours, we think you're going to come to the same conclusion that we did—that Edgerton Fleece did not kill Benjamin Trane. So when all of the evidence is in, we'll be asking you to return a verdict that Edgerton Fleece is not guilty of murder and not guilty of failing to stop at the scene of an accident. And if the State decides on its own that it can't meet its burden for murder and tries to convince you that Mr. Fleece should be convicted of aggravated vehicular homicide, we'll ask you to return a verdict of not guilty on that too. Thank you."

I sat back down. Pompeo remained slouched back in his chair, shuttling his knees open and closed. We looked at Judge Jurevicius. She nodded, turned the page in a notebook, nodded again, waited, then said, "Mr. Pompeo, you may call your first witness."

"Thanks, Judge. The State calls defendant's wife, Carissa Fleece."

55

I stood. "May we approach, Your Honor?"

Pompeo put his hands out and said, "You're not going to object to his wife testifying, are you?"

I kept my face straight. "Your Honor."

"I mean, it seems to me that if anyone knows where Mr. Fleece was that night—"

"Your Honor!"

Judge Jurevicius's eyes were wide. Then her computer dinged, and she said, "Counsel, please approach."

I strode up, Danny right behind. Pompeo took his time with innocent eyes and a grin he could not quite contain.

"Your Honor," I said. "As we briefed before the trial, Dr. Carson-Fleece cannot be forced to testify in this proceeding against her husband."

"And as we opposed," said Pompeo. "We'd like to put her on to find out what she knows."

I shook my head. "Your Honor has already ruled that Dr. Carson-Fleece cannot be required to testify against Mr. Fleece under Ohio's spousal competency laws. You also ruled that no one could bring up the matter of her testimony without first speaking to you and getting permission."

"Did I say permission?" said Judge Jurevicius.

Danny had the order in his hand and pointed to the passage at the end. I took it and said, "Yes, Your Honor. It's right here."

Judge Jurevicius stared at it for a moment before she said, "It does indeed say that, Mr. Pompeo."

"Does it?" said Pompeo. "My bad. Sorry."

I shook my head. "Your Honor, this completely prejudices the jury. They now know that Mrs. Fleece has been called and will not be testifying as is her right."

"That's not necessarily true, Judge," said Pompeo. "I'm sure a curative instruction will do the trick."

"That will just emphasize the fact that she's not testifying," I said. "It's completely inappropriate and we move for a mistrial."

"That seems excessive," said Pompeo. "And a waste of taxpayer resources."

Judge Jurevicius nodded, then said, "Mr. Pompeo, you will abide by the Court's rulings and seek our permission before calling any witness whom we have said cannot be called."

"Will do, Judge."

"The Court finds that there is not sufficient prejudice to warrant a mistrial and will issue a curative instruction. Mr. Pompeo, you will not mention Dr. Carson-Fleece testifying or not testifying again."

"I certainly won't, Judge. Again, my apologies."

"But Your Honor—"

"Your motion for a mistrial is denied, Mr. Shepherd."

Danny and I went back to the table. I looked at Carissa, shook my head, then sat down.

Judge Jurevicius smoothed her lace collar and said, "Ladies and gentlemen of the jury, under the law, a person may not be forced to testify against her spouse in a criminal proceeding. Mr.

Pompeo and the state are not permitted to call Dr. Carson-Fleece to testify regarding what she knows, if anything, about the facts of this case. You are not to assume anything from her assertion of this right as her decision not to testify is entirely within the bounds of Ohio law."

Sweet Jesus, I thought, keeping my face straight. As I feared, the cure was worse than Pompeo's offense.

"Mr. Pompeo, you may call your first witness."

"Certainly, Your Honor, and my apologies to Mrs. Fleece." He looked over and gave her what I'm sure he believed was his most remorseful look. Carissa Carson-Fleece returned it impassively.

"Your Honor, the prosecution calls Mr. Robert Snyder."

Robert Snyder was a small man in his fifties who walked with a slight stoop that seemed as much an effort to avoid attention as it was a matter of posture. He ducked his head to Pompeo as he passed and, after he sat, straightened his thick, black glasses with one hand, cleared his throat, and nodded.

"Mr. Snyder," said Pompeo. "Could you please introduce yourself to the jury?"

"My name is Robert Snyder," he said. "I own Snyder Funeral Home."

"That's here in Carrefour?"

"On the south side, yes."

"Do you know the defendant, Edgerton Fleece?"

"Yes, I do."

"How?"

"Mr. Fleece has been to our facility many times."

"Your funeral home? Why's that?"

"Mr. Fleece makes it a point of visiting when patrons of Pillars pass away."

"Pillars is his charitable corporation?"

"His outreach ministry, yes."

"I see. And Mr. Fleece makes a point of coming to visitations?"

"And funerals, yes. He's very compassionate."

"I bet. Mr. Snyder, we're here about the death of Benjamin Trane. Did you know him?"

Robert Snyder nodded. "I spoke with him just the day before he passed."

"That would February 16?"

"Yes."

"Why did you speak with him on February 16?"

"He was at our facility for the funeral of Theo Plutides."

Pompeo nodded. "Now the jury doesn't know all these people, Mr. Snyder. Who is Theo Plutides and how is he related to Benjamin Trane?"

Robert Snyder cleared his throat, glanced at the jury, then stared straight ahead and said, "Theo Plutides was a prominent Carrefour businessman. As he got older, he needed a little help at home, so I understand that Benjamin Trane looked in on him and helped out with Roxie."

"And Roxie is?"

"Mr. Plutides' service dog. Mr. Plutides had epilepsy and Roxie helped him know if a seizure was coming on."

"When did Mr. Plutides pass away?"

"Some days before. February 12, I believe."

"How?"

"Natural causes. He was well into his eighties so, while it was sad, I don't think anyone was surprised."

"So Theo Plutides' funeral was on February 16, you said?"

"Yes. That was when I saw Benjamin Trane. He came to pay his respects to Mr. Plutides. And to bring Roxie of course."

"Benjamin Trane brought Roxie to the funeral?"

"Yes, we all thought it was appropriate. She...she was devoted to Theo."

"Mr. Snyder, you seemed to hesitate there."

"I did."

"Why?"

Robert Snyder cleared his throat. "I was just recalling that at the end of the service, Roxie would not leave. Benjamin wound up carrying her. It made an impact on all of us."

"I'm sure. I take it since Mr. Plutides had passed away, Benjamin Trane was taking care of Roxie?"

"That's what he told me, yes."

"That was the last time you saw Mr. Trane."

"It is, yes."

"You're aware that Benjamin Trane died the next day, February 17?"

"I am, yes."

"Did you speak with the defendant Edgerton Fleece on February 17?"

"I did, twice."

"Tell us about the first time."

"I called Mr. Fleece that afternoon."

"About what?"

"Mr. Plutides had directed that in lieu of flowers, donations be made to the Pillars Independent Living Outreach program he'd benefited so much from. A number of people left checks, so I called Mr. Fleece to ask how he'd like them delivered."

"What did he say?"

"He said he would pick them up that evening like al—that he would pick them up that evening."

"Mr. Snyder, were you about to say, 'like always?'"

Robert Snyder ducked his head for a moment, then said, "Yes."

"What do you mean by that?"

"It was common for Pillars to be named as the recipient of memorial donations. Mr. Fleece would often pick them up."

"And did he swoop over for the checks that night, February 17?"

"He stopped over, yes."

"What time?"

Robert Snyder thought. "About seven o'clock. That was the only day we didn't have a visitation that week, so I was there late catching up on paperwork."

"And did you see Mr. Fleece?"

"I did. He came into my office and I gave him the checks."

"Did you talk?"

"Yes."

"About what?"

"About the funeral, of course. And about how generous Mr. Plutides had been."

"In what way?"

"Oh, just a general sort of way."

"Right. How did he seem to you?"

Robert Snyder cleared his throat. "What do you mean?"

"How was he acting? How did he seem?"

Robert Snyder shook his head. "Fine. I mean, we were all sad from Theo's funeral the day before, but fine."

"Not distraught?"

"No."

"Not upset?"

"Not that I could see, no."

"What happened next?"

"He left and I peeked out the window as he went back outside. I saw that he'd parked in one of the far spots, which seemed unusual since the lot was empty. Then I watched as he backed out of his spot and left."

"When Mr. Fleece left, did that bring his van closer to your view?"

"It did."

"What did you see?"

Robert Snyder shifted in his seat, then said, "I saw that the front right side of the van was dented."

"Anything else?"

"There were two dark streaks that ran from the headlight to the wheel."

"Was it blood?"

"Oh, I couldn't say that."

"But two dark streaks?"

"Yes."

"And dents?"

"Yes."

"And this was just around seven p.m. on the night of February 17?"

"It was."

"The night Benjamin Trane was killed?"

"Yes."

"Thank you, Mr. Snyder. Mr. Shepherd might have some questions now."

I stood.

"Mr. Snyder, it's not unusual for someone to pick up donations, is it?"

"Not someone local, no."

"It saves you the trouble of mailing them, right?"

"That's right."

"Mr. Snyder, I'm going to hand you what's been marked as Joint Exhibit 1. Can you identify that for me?"

"It's a map of southern Carrefour."

Danny put the map up on the screen for the jury. I put the red dot of a laser pointer on a square. "This is the address for your funeral home, isn't it?"

"That's the proper location, yes."

"I'm going to represent to you that this is Edgerton Fleece's address, okay?" I put the laser pointer on another square.

"Actually, I know that to be the case. I've sent him correspondence many times."

"Great. Based on this map, would you agree with me that the shortest route between Mr. Fleece's house and your funeral home is taking Orchard to Winterhaven?"

"It is."

"That route would not put a driver on Sunnyfield Drive at all, would it?"

"No, not taking that route."

"You didn't ask Mr. Fleece about the dent on his van, did you Mr. Snyder?"

"No, Mr. Shepherd. I didn't see it until he was leaving."

"So he didn't have a chance to tell you about a deer accident, did he?"

Pompeo stood. "Objection."

Judge Jurevicius nodded. "Sustained."

I moved on. "And based on what you just told Mr. Pompeo, Mr. Fleece wasn't upset when he spoke to you, was he?"

"No more than you'd expect the day after a funeral."

"He did not give you the impression that he'd just been in an accident, did he?"

"No. Not at all."

"Thank you, Mr. Snyder."

Pompeo was right back up. "Mr. Snyder, take a look at the map Mr. Shepherd put up there for you."

"Okay."

"I see at least two routes that could use Sunnyfield on the way to your business. How about you?"

Robert Snyder stared at the screen through his thick glasses. "Actually, I see three."

"Oh, there you go, I missed that one. You don't have any idea how Mr. Fleece got to your place, do you?"

"No, I don't."

"No idea if he stopped to get milk, went to the bank, ran over a guy."

"No, I don't."

"Now, we both asked you how Mr. Fleece was acting, and I get the impression that he was cool as could be, right?"

"Like I said, he was a little upset from the funeral."

"But he certainly didn't seem bothered by anything that had just happened, did he?"

"No, not really."

"From your perspective, it seemed like Mr. Fleece's night was going according to plan, wasn't it?"

I stood. "Objection."

"Sustained."

"And there's no question that Mr. Fleece parked on the far side of your lot when he arrived?"

"That's true."

"And that you saw dents when he left?"

"Yes."

"And streaks that may or may not have been blood?"

"Yes."

"Thanks."

Judge Jurevicius looked at me. I'd gotten all I needed and didn't want to give Pompeo another chance to bang the dented-van drum—he'd be doing that enough as it was and I could already see that the jury wasn't reacting too well to it.

"No further questions, Your Honor," I said.

"Very well, we have time for one more witness. Mr. Pompeo?"

"Your Honor, the prosecution calls paramedic Kevin Donald."

56

A man rose from the back row and lumbered up the aisle. He was dressed in a dark blue paramedic uniform that said "CFD" in a yellow circle on his left chest. He was of average height but his uniform strained to contain a massive chest and arms. His head was shaved, and he looked as if he would be just as comfortable tearing someone apart as putting him back together.

After the paramedic sat down and nodded to the jury, Pompeo said, "Could you state your name please, sir?"

"Kevin Donald."

"What you do, Mr. Donald?"

"I'm a paramedic for the city of Carrefour."

Pompeo took Kevin Donald through his education and his fourteen-year experience responding to auto accident calls, reaching diagnoses, and treating conditions like broken bones and internal bleeding. Then Pompeo said, "Mr. Donald, on February 17 of this year, were you called on a run to 5436 Sunnyfield Drive?"

"Yes, sir, I was, along with my partner."

"Mr. Donald, I'm going to hand you what's been marked as State's Exhibit 6. Can you tell me what that is?"

Paramedic Donald glanced at the paper. "It's a copy of our run report for the incident you just asked me about."

"Tell me what happened."

"I was at station house 32 when we received a dispatch of an auto accident victim at the address you mentioned. My partner and I went immediately to the scene."

"About how long did that take?"

"You can see from our report that it took approximately eleven minutes for us to get there from the time that we were dispatched."

"What happened next?"

"When we arrived, I found a victim at the base of a tree laying on his side."

"Would that person be Benjamin Trane?"

"I would come to learn that, yes, sir."

"What condition was Mr. Trane in?"

"He was seriously injured, sir. It appeared to us that he had a fractured shoulder and likely broken ribs, but our real concern was that he had internal hemorrhaging."

"That means he was bleeding inside?"

"Yes, sir."

"And why was that a concern?"

"It's one of the first things we look for when we have a vehicle versus pedestrian accident."

"Did Mr. Trane have any symptoms of internal hemorrhaging?"

Kevin Donald nodded. "Some of the signs were obvious—he was bleeding from the mouth and nose and had significant bruising on his left shoulder and abdomen. He was in significant pain and, as I began to assess him, he lost consciousness."

"What did you do?"

"We immediately started an IV in the hopes that we could replace the fluids to stabilize him. We then evaluated him for neck fracture, put him on a backboard, and placed him in the ambulance."

"Did you drive or stay with Mr. Trane in the back?"

"I stayed with Mr. Trane and managed his condition."

Pompeo put his hands on his hips and then raised one hand. "You know, just to go back for a second, you mentioned that Mr. Trane lost consciousness while you were evaluating him?"

"He did, yes, sir."

"So he was awake and conscious when you first saw him?"

"Yes, he was."

"Was he aware of what was going on?"

"Mr. Trane was in shock, and he was in terrible pain but yes, he knew what was going on."

"How do you know he was in pain?"

"Because he was screaming when I pulled up."

"Screaming?"

Kevin Donald thought. "That might be too strong a word. I was told he'd been screaming. By the time I saw him, Mr. Trane was moaning in a way that people do when the pain is overwhelming."

"Were you able to do anything for his pain?"

"I administered pain medication."

"Did it work?"

"I believe so, but it was hard to tell. He became unconscious shortly after."

"From the medication?"

"From blood loss."

"Was Mr. Trane aware of his surroundings until he became unconscious?"

"He was."

"How do you know?"

Kevin Donald paused, stuck out his lower jaw, then said, "Because he kept asking us to take care of his dog."

Pompeo nodded and stood there for a moment as if thinking, then said, "You were telling the jury about taking Mr. Trane to the hospital?"

"Yes, sir. We were transporting Mr. Trane to St. Wendelin's hospital when his blood pressure and vitals dropped."

"At the time, did you know why?"

"I suspected it was internal blood loss."

"And now?"

"And now I know that was the case because of the coroner's investigation."

"What did you do?"

"I continued to push fluids and my partner notified the hospital that we had an emergent surgery case coming in."

"And then what happened?"

"Mr. Trane's vitals crashed completely as we arrived at the hospital."

"Did you attempt to resuscitate him?"

"I did until the ER code team came out to meet us and took over."

"Do you know what happened?"

"Yes, sir. I understand that the code team worked on him for approximately ten minutes before pronouncing him."

"Do you know why they stopped so soon?"

"Yes, sir. Mr. Trane had essentially died en route. When a patient shows up without vitals, the hospital primarily checks to make sure that the person has indeed passed away before pronouncing him."

"And was that the case here?"

"Yes sir, it was. Mr. Trane died in the ambulance."

"Mr. Donald, do you have an opinion as to whether earlier intervention by you could have saved Mr. Trane's life?"

I stood. "Objection, Your Honor. Mr. Donald is not a medical doctor and so is not qualified to make that determination."

Pompeo raised a hand. "I withdraw the question, Your Honor. Mr. Donald have you in your fourteen years of experience ever treated patients with internal bleeding sustained in an auto accident?"

"Yes, sir, I have."

"Have you ever been able to stabilize them so that you can get them to surgery at a hospital?"

"Many times, sir, yes."

"Do you have an opinion, as a paramedic, as to whether you could have stabilized Mr. Trane if you had been called to the scene sooner?"

I stood. "Same objection, Your Honor."

Pompeo held out his hands. "I'm asking him his opinion as a paramedic who has treated this exact injury before, Judge."

"Your Honor," I said. "Medical causation opinions have to be rendered by a physician."

Judge Jurevicius smoothed her lace collar before she said, "Overruled. The witness may give his opinion as a paramedic."

"Do you remember the question, Paramedic Donald?" said Pompeo.

Kevin Donald nodded. "I'd like to think that a patient always has a better chance the earlier I can intervene and help him."

"How about here?"

"I think if I had been able to give him fluids sooner, I could have stabilized him."

"Would fifteen minutes have made a difference?

"I think so. Remember he died just outside the hospital."

"Thank you, Paramedic Donald. Mr. Shepherd might have some questions for you."

I stood. "Mr. Donald, the time of death listed on the run report is 6:52 p.m. on February 17. Do you see that?"

"Yes sir, I do."

"Are you the one who entered that time onto the report?"

"I did, yes, sir."

"Are you sure about that time?"

"Yes, sir."

"Is that a rough estimate or is that the exact time?"

"It's the exact time, sir. I checked the strips for when he lost rhythm and those strips are time marked by the computer."

"So there is no question that Mr. Trane passed away at 6:52 PM on February 17?"

"No, sir, that was absolutely the time."

"Were you able to talk to any of the witnesses while you are there treating Mr. Trane?"

"Briefly. My focus was on Mr. Trane."

"Of course it was. As far as you knew, this was a hit-and-run accident?"

"That's right."

"And as far as you knew, no one had seen the vehicle or the driver that hit Mr. Trane?"

"Not that I ever heard."

"And you didn't see the vehicle or driver that hit Mr. Trane, did you?"

"Obviously not. I was called after the accident."

"I understand, Mr. Donald. So it's fair to say that you know that Mr. Trane was hit and killed by a vehicle, but you have no information that would help us determine what kind of vehicle that was or who was driving it, right?"

"That's fair, sir."

"That's all I have, thanks."

Pompeo stood. "Paramedic Donald, it wasn't your responsibility to investigate the accident, was it?"

"No, sir. My job was to treat Mr. Trane."

"Exactly, your job was to treat Mr. Trane's horrible injuries as he lay moaning in pain on the cold wet ground, not to find out who put him there, right?"

"Yes sir, that's right."

Pompeo sat down.

When I shook my head, Judge Jurevicius said, "Thank you, Mr. Donald, you may step down. Members of the jury, that will be all that we have for today. Please return tomorrow at eight-thirty a.m." Judge Jurevicius gave the jury a last instruction not to discuss the case among themselves or with others, then banged her gavel with a sharp rap and court was dismissed.

The judge had barely left the bench when Carissa Carson-Fleece walked up to me, her face straight, her voice quiet but filled with fury. "What are you doing?"

"What do you mean, Carissa?"

"There's no way that paramedic could have saved Trane's life. He's no doctor. He has no right to give those kinds of opinions."

"That's why I objected."

"He said it anyway."

"I was overruled."

"So that just stands?"

"Yes."

We were keeping our voices down, but that didn't keep Pompeo from giving me a wave and a grin as he left. I nodded to him as Carissa continued.

"Then we need to call a thoracic surgeon to show that there was no way he could have operated on Trane in time to save him and then we need—"

"No."

Carissa stopped, blinked, then said, "Why?"

"We're not going to spend a bunch of time proving that Mr. Trane would have died no matter what once he was hit by the car. What we are going to prove is that your husband wasn't the one who hit him. Do you understand why?"

It took Carissa less than a second to process it. "Yes. Sorry, I got caught up in the medicine."

I shifted so that I was talking to both Carissa and Edge. "I know the paramedic was stretching things, but it's not worth our time to prove that. All we would be emphasizing is that fleeing the scene of the accident didn't cause Trane's death. But the vehicle impact still did so we're better off spending our time proving that it wasn't you."

Edge nodded. "Got it." He smiled at his wife. "Ready? I need a ride."

She didn't smile back, but she did take his arm and the two walked out.

When Danny and I left the courtroom a short time later, Manny Amaltheakis was still sitting in the back row with his legs crossed, scrolling through his phone as if he were waiting for a plane. He looked up as we passed and said, "Interesting opening."

"Hi, Manny."

He stood. "I am just a business lawyer, but it certainly sounded like you were setting up motive."

I kept walking as I said, "You know, just want the jury to keep an open mind."

Manny Amaltheakis walked with us. "It sounded like more than that."

"Have to keep the prosecutor honest, make sure he meets his burden."

Manny Amaltheakis stopped. "I know you know that we are having trouble recovering the funds in the wallet."

"Hmm."

"But it still goes to Trane when we do."

"That's what I hear."

"Which means it then goes to Pillars."

There was no way I was discussing our 120-hour strategy

with Amaltheakis, not until Pompeo had committed himself to the jury. "I'm just a defense lawyer, Manny. I leave the big estates to experts like you."

Manny nodded. "I still have not decided yet. Whether he did it."

I nodded back. "I hope the jury feels the same way."

57

On Tuesday morning, Judge Jurevicius straightened her lace collar, cleared her throat, and said "Mr. Pompeo, the State may call its next witness."

Pompeo stood. "Your Honor, the State calls Ms. Sharon Pepperstone."

Mrs. Pepperstone rose from her seat in the front row and strode up to the witness stand, her cane punctuating every other step with an authoritative thump despite the carpet. She wore an electric blue dress with a matching suit coat and her hair was a slightly deeper shade of gold than the last time I saw her. She thumped her cane in front of her as she sat, then rested both hands on the handle. Her eyes narrowed when she saw me, then she turned back to Pompeo and said, "Let's get on with it, Pompeo. I'm not getting any younger."

Pompeo stood and smiled. "Could you state your name, please?"

"You just said it. Did you forget already?"

"No, Ms. Pepperstone, I need you to say it for the record—"

"Don't you dare disrespect my Johnny like that, Pompeo. It's

Mrs. Pepperstone and has been for all twelve years since my Johnny passed."

"Of course, Mrs. Pepperstone. Could you please state your name?"

"It is *Mrs.* Sharon Pepperstone."

"Now Sharon, may I call you Sharon?"

"You may call me Mrs. Pepperstone."

"Mrs. Pepperstone, do you live at 5436 Sunnyfield Drive?"

"You know that," she said. "You came to my house."

"Mrs. Pepperstone, there are things that I know but the jury hasn't heard yet. So I may ask questions that seem stupid to you—"

"They don't *seem* stupid," said Mrs. Pepperstone.

"—but they are necessary for the case."

Mrs. Pepperstone sighed. "Can we do the stupid part faster then?"

Half the jury lowered their heads or covered their mouths.

Pompeo continued. "You live at 5436 Sunnyfield Drive, right?"

"Right."

"Were you home on the night of February 17?"

Mrs. Pepperstone made a rolling motion with one hand. "Yes, yes, yes. I was home, I heard a commotion, I heard the barking, and I came outside to find Benny Trane crumpled up against my oak tree and Roxie barking like the dickens."

"I'm sorry, Mrs. Pepperstone, but we need to slow that down just a little."

"I imagine you say that a lot. How slow do we need to go?"

"You were home on the night of February 17?"

Mrs. Pepperstone took a deep breath. "Yes."

"What did you hear that made you go outside?"

"It was a thump or some sort of commotion but what I really heard was the barking and the barking didn't stop, and it was right outside so I went to my window and saw Roxie standing there barking by my oak tree."

"Mrs. Pepperstone, did you hear the sound of brakes squealing?"

"Did I say I heard brakes squealing?"

"No."

"Then why would you think I heard brakes squealing?"

"I'm not saying you did, Mrs. Pepperstone. I'm confirming that you did *not* hear any brakes."

"If I had, I would have said it."

"So you heard Roxie barking and saw her at the tree?"

"That's what I said."

"Do you know what time that was?"

"Not exactly, but Benny and Roxie always passed by between six and six-thirty. When I went outside, the news was switching from local to national, so I'd say it was around six-thirty."

"That's six-thirty p.m.?"

"We're going to go that slow?"

Pompeo didn't say anything. I didn't blame him.

Mrs. Pepperstone thumped the cane. "Yes, six-thirty p.m."

"Did you go right out as soon as you heard it?"

"Out as fast as I could make it, but it was cold, so I needed to get bundled and of course my third leg here doesn't make it any easier in the snow. But I got out there eventually."

"And what did you find?"

"I found Benny Trane and a lot of blood."

"Could you describe that for the jury please?"

"More?"

"Yes, please."

"That's kind of ghoulish, isn't it?"

"Please, Mrs. Pepperstone. It's necessary for the jury to hear."

Mrs. Pepperstone thought, rapped once with her cane, then said, "Benny was crumpled around the base of the oak tree. His one arm didn't look right. He was bleeding out of his nose and mouth and had some cuts that were bleeding more, on his forehead for sure and you know how those bleed like a rushwater storm. As soon as Roxie saw me, she laid at attention just like she used to do if Theo had one of his seizures."

"What did you do?"

"I tried to get to him, to Benny, but it had snowed a couple of days earlier, so I had some trouble getting there because of this damn hip but I made it eventually."

"What happened next?"

"Once I got close, I could see things were twisted every which way and there was blood everywhere. My Johnny, he fell a lot at the end, so I know how to get someone up, but I also knew enough not to move someone who was in a way like Benny was right then."

"So what did you do?"

"I didn't want to leave him but, in my rush, I'd left my phone inside like an all-fired moron, so I told Benny I'd be right back and told Roxie to stay and went back inside."

"How long did that take?"

"I'm not sure." Mrs. Pepperstone lifted her chin. "I'm not as fast as I used to be, and I fell once on the way. I called 911, then I found a blanket and went back outside."

"What was the blanket for?"

"Didn't you just hear me say that Benny was lying bleeding in the snow?"

"I did."

"Then what do you think the blanket was for?"

"Was it for Benjamin?"

"Cripes-sakes-alive, no wonder these trials take so long. Of course."

"What did you do next?"

"I went back out there. By then the Collinsworths were there too so they helped me put the blanket on Benny and we tried to calm him while we waited for the ambulance."

"Calm him?"

"Benny was in pain and showing it and I didn't blame him a bit."

"What do you mean showing it?"

Mrs. Pepperstone stared at Pompeo. "Really?"

"Yes. Please."

"He was screaming, Pompeo. Screaming like his voice would break."

Pompeo nodded, then said, "Mrs. Pepperstone, you mentioned it had snowed a couple days earlier?"

"Congratulations! You remembered!"

"Did you notice anything else about the accident scene?"

"Like what?"

Pompeo glanced at me, then picked up a hard copy of a picture, handed it to her and said, "Mrs. Pepperstone, this picture is State's Exhibit 31. Can you tell us what it shows?"

"My front yard and oak tree."

"Is that a true and accurate representation of what your yard looked like on February 17?"

"After the accident, yes."

"And what can you tell me about the ground?"

"There was blood on it. And the tire tracks of course." She looked up. "Is that what you were trying to get me to say? That I saw tracks in the snow? Why in the world wouldn't you just ask me?"

Pompeo ignored her question. "So you saw tire tracks in the snow?"

"I just said that!"

"Where did they go? The tire tracks."

"They angled up my drive over to the sidewalk then took a sharp turn back to the left over the curb and onto the street."

"Did the car hit your tree?"

"Not that I could see."

"And did it look like the tracks stopped and backed up at all?"

"No. It looked like they made a smooth 'U' from my driveway over the sidewalk and back into the street."

"Eventually the ambulance came?"

"Yes."

"Was Mr. Trane still alive when it got there?"

Mrs. Pepperstone was quiet and then she nodded. "He was still moaning and moving now and again. Not long after though, I think."

"You stayed with him? Until the ambulance arrived?"

"Yes."

"Why?"

Mrs. Pepperstone gave Pompeo a look that was intense but no longer a glare as she said, "Everybody deserves to have someone with them."

"They sure do, Mrs. Pepperstone." He stood there in the center of the courtroom, quiet, nodding. After a moment, he said, "Mr. Shepherd might have some questions for you now."

As I stood, the lines at the corners of Mrs. Pepperstone's eyes deepened and she squeezed the head of her cane with both hands.

"You," she said.

I realized Pompeo had been getting her good side.

"Hi, Mrs. Pepperstone. We've met before, haven't we?"

"If you call traipsing around my front yard uninvited meeting, then yes."

"Mrs. Pepperstone, you didn't see my client in your yard, did you?"

"No, he had skittered off by then."

"You never saw the car that hit Mr. Trane either, right?"

"No, he had hightailed it right out of there before I got outside."

"You can't describe anything about the car that hit Mr. Trane, can you?"

"I just said that."

"Mr. Trane was a friend of yours, wasn't he?"

"I'd say that if you're with someone when they're about to die in your front yard, that qualifies."

"You were his friend before the accident too, weren't you?"

"We'd talk during the warm months when he walked by with Roxie and Theo."

"So you want to see whoever did it put away, right?"

"For forever and a day, Mr. Shepherd. In a hole so deep you can't see out."

"But you don't have any information for the jury to help identify that person, do you?"

"Just that Pompeo says that's the man right there. That's good enough for me."

"You're taking Mr. Pompeo's word for it?"

"I don't know why I wouldn't."

"I don't have any more questions, Mrs. Pepperstone. Thank you."

Pompeo stood. "Mrs. Pepperstone, you just told Mr. Shepherd that you didn't see the person or the car that hit Mr. Trane, right?"

"We were all sitting right here."

"Please, humor me, Mrs. Pepperstone."

She sighed. "That's right."

"In the days after the accident, no one called you to tell you they had driven up on your property, did they?"

"No."

"No one stopped by to pay for any damage they did?"

"Not a one."

"No one reached out to you to find out how the man who had been struck in your front yard was doing?"

"Nobody."

"Whoever it was just ran away and hid, right?"

She looked at Edge. "Not far enough."

Pompeo raised his hand. "Now, Mrs. Pepperstone, Mr. Shepherd could object to that because you don't know who hit and killed Mr. Trane. But you know that no one called you or reached out to you or contacted you in the days after the accident to find out how you or Mr. Trane were doing, true?"

She stared at Edge. "They didn't have the decency. Or the guts."

"Now, you told Mr. Shepherd that, during the warm months, you would talk to Benjamin and Theo when they walked by your house with Roxie, right?"

"I said that."

"And you told me that they usually passed by your house between six and six-thirty, do I have that right?"

"Darn near every day."

"So if you were looking for Mr. Trane one day, you'd know right where to find him, wouldn't you?"

"I would."

"That's all Mrs. Pepperstone. Thank you."

I stood. "Mrs. Pepperstone, you said that no one reached out to you after the accident to see how you were doing, right?"

"Cripes-in-a-cocktail, you lawyers. I said that thirty seconds ago."

"But you talked to my client, Mr. Fleece, didn't you?"

"Wait, what? Not that I..." A light dawned. "Well, I guess I did."

"At Benjamin Trane's funeral, right?"

"Yes."

"The two of you spoke, and he extended his sympathy that you had to go through this experience, didn't he?"

"I didn't know at the time that he'd done it."

"You mean you hadn't been told at the time, by Mr. Pompeo or someone else, that he'd done it."

"I suppose that's right."

"But Mr. Fleece asked how you were doing in all this, true?"

Mrs. Pepperstone paused, then nodded. "That's true."

"Thanks, Mrs. Pepperstone," I said, and sat.

Mrs. Pepperstone turned to the judge. "Is that it?"

"It is," said Judge Jurevicius. "You may step down."

Mrs. Pepperstone stood and waved her cane. "You need to make these two get to the point."

Judge Jurevicius smiled and nodded.

Mrs. Pepperstone squinted. "Lose the pearls, keep the jabot." She pointed her cane back and between Pompeo and me. "And don't let these two nimrods call it a lace collar."

Judge Jurevicius's hand went to her lace collar—er, her jabot—while Mrs. Pepperstone made her way out of the courtroom, thumping her cane like a military parade.

We all, Pompeo, Judge Jurevicius, and I, took a collective breath before Judge Jurevicius took her hand off her jabot, and said, "The State may call its next witness."

Pompeo stood. "Judge, the State calls Officer AJ Hackett."

58

Officer AJ Hackett came in from the hall. He was in his early forties and had blonde hair that was a little longer and a little floppier than was usual on the Carrefour police force, but his blue uniform was neat and pressed and he held himself straight as he walked briskly to the stand.

"Could you introduce yourself to the jury, please?" said Pompeo.

"My name is Alan James Hackett, but most people call me AJ."

"And what you do Officer Hackett?"

"I am a police officer for the city of Carrefour."

"And how long have you done that?"

"Coming up on nineteen years now."

"You don't look old enough for that."

Officer Hackett grinned. "I took my test right out of college and entered the Academy as soon as the city had a class."

"And do you have a specialty with Carrefour police force?"

"I investigate vehicular accidents in Carrefour that cause serious injury or death."

"Does that keep you busy full-time?"

"Fortunately, no. The rest of the time, I'm a patrolman."

"So over the course of your career, how many accidents involving serious injury or death would you say that you've investigated?"

"Somewhere in the area of seven hundred and fifty to one thousand."

"And did you get called to the scene of the accident involving Benjamin Trane on the night of February 17?"

"I didn't know that was his name at the time but yes."

"What happened?"

Officer Hackett described arriving at the scene, investigating by taking photos, taking measurements, and interviewing witnesses, and determining how the vehicle came up Mrs. Pepperstone's drive and onto the sidewalk before striking Benjamin Trane. His description was methodical, detailed, and far less colorful than Mrs. Pepperstone's.

Then Pompeo said, "Officer Hackett, what else could you determine from your investigation?"

"It appeared to me," said Officer Hackett, "to a reasonable degree of probability, that the driver of the vehicle never braked, stopped, or slowed down."

"Now how can you make that determination?"

"A couple of ways. First, we know the car didn't stop completely because there were no signs of piled snow, ripped dirt, or of backing or changing direction after stopping."

"Okay, I can see that, but how do you know the driver didn't slow down?"

"It's possible the driver took his foot off the accelerator, but we know he didn't brake because he would have slid and left different marks in the snow. These just kept on going."

"All right, what else could you determine?"

"It's my opinion that the driver of the vehicle drove up onto the sidewalk on purpose."

I stood. "Objection, Your Honor. Officer Hackett can't testify as to someone else's state of mind."

Pompeo shrugged. "His opinion is based on physical facts, Your Honor, which he'll explain in just a moment."

Judge Jurevicius straightened her lace jabot, then said, "Overruled."

Pompeo turned back to Officer Hackett. "What makes you think the driver did this on purpose?"

"Well, you can see for fifty yards on either side of this driveway there's a curb so it would be very difficult for a vehicle at speed to pop up onto the yard without damaging the vehicle and potentially making it undrivable. But you see here, by running up onto the driveway first, the driver eliminated the curb as a barrier and was able to run right into the victim before popping back into the street."

I stood. "Continued objection and move to strike, Your Honor. Again, there was no basis for that speculation."

Pompeo shrugged. "Counsel is free to cross on the issue, Your Honor. It's based on the facts Officer Hackett observed."

Judge Jurevicius nodded slowly, then said, "Counsel is free to cross-examine on this issue. Overruled."

"Very good. Now Officer Hackett were you able to find anyone who saw the accident right then?"

"No, sir. By the time Mrs. Pepperstone and her neighbors got out there, the vehicle was gone."

"Were there any other witnesses driving by who saw the accident?"

"If there are, no one has come forward.

"You arrived some twenty minutes to half an hour after the accident, is that right?"

"That's right."

"There's no question that whoever caused the accident didn't stick around, did they?"

"No, sir, they did not."

"Not a very charitable thing to do, is it?"

"Not the way I was taught, no, sir."

"I ask because one of the charges here is failure to stop at an accident. Whoever caused this accident did not stop, correct?"

"No question, sir, he did not stop."

"Now were you able to determine anything else from your investigation of the accident site?"

"No, I think that's about it."

"Anything at all?"

Officer Hackett thought. "I don't think so."

"About the point of impact, maybe?"

I stood. "Objection, Your Honor. Leading."

"Oh, right, right, right," said Officer Hackett.

"Your Honor," said Pompeo. "If I don't help a little, we'll be here all day just like Mrs. Pepperstone said."

"That's not the standard, Your Honor," I said.

Judge Jurevicius smoothed her jabot. "Overruled. Let's move things along, please."

Pompeo turned back to Officer Hackett. "So you were going to tell us about the point of impact?"

"Right, based on the tracks and the angle to the tree, I concluded that the vehicle struck Mr. Trane with its right front side."

"Very good. And after you inspected the site, did you continue your investigation?"

"I did. We learned a couple of hours later that Mr. Trane had died so we treated it as a homicide investigation and, along with Chief Detective in Charge of Serious Crimes Mitch Pearson, we investigated this as both a traffic accident and a killing."

"What did you do?"

"Chief Detective Pearson checked the Alert Shield network, and I started checking auto body shops."

I stood. "Objection as to what Detective Pearson did, Your Honor."

Before Judge Jurevicius could reply, Pompeo raised a hand and said, "I agree, Your Honor. Officer Hackett, I don't want you to tell me anything about what Detective Pearson did but was there a time when Chief Detective Pearson brought you the results of his work, whatever that might be?"

"Yes, he did."

"And what was that?"

"He brought me video from the Alert Shield Network. He went onto the app—"

Pompeo raised his hand. "Let's keep it to just what you know. So he brought you a video?"

"Yes."

"And what did the video show?"

I stood. "Objection. Foundation."

"We are not offering the video right now as evidence, Your Honor. We will do that through Chief Detective Pearson. Right now, we just need to show how it impacted Officer Hackett's investigation."

"Overruled."

"So what did the video show?" said Pompeo.

"It showed a silver 2015 Grand Caravan minivan with the Pillars logo on the side."

"I will show the jury the video a little later when Chief Detective Pearson testifies. Why don't you tell us what you did with that information?"

"Knowing that a Pillars vehicle was involved in the accident, I canvased local auto body shops to see if any of them had performed repairs on a silver Pillars minivan around the time of Mr. Trane's death."

"And what did you find?"

"I found that Carrefour Collision, an auto body shop in South Carrefour, had repaired the front right corner of a silver 2015 Grand Caravan minivan owned by Pillars on February 18."

"February 18? That's the day after Mr. Trane was killed, isn't it?"

"It is."

"What else did you find?"

"The man who did the repair was Rick Dalton and he said—"

I stood. "Objection, Your Honor. Hearsay."

"Judge, we are offering it for the impact on the investigation."

"Your Honor," I said. "This is classic hearsay. The witness never saw the unrepaired van and is just relaying the findings of someone who did."

Pompeo flipped his hands. "I'm just trying to move things along, Judge."

Judge Jurevicius sat there. We watched. Her computer dinged. She looked at it then said, "The objection is sustained."

Pompeo turned back to Officer Hackett. "What did you do after you learned that the auto body shop had repaired a Pillars minivan?"

"I obtained a search warrant for Pillars' vehicle logs and registrations and found that Mr. Fleece had possession of the subject vehicle during the time in question and that he was listed as the primary driver on that vehicle's insurance policy."

"So Mr. Fleece was listed as the primary driver of the silver minivan with damage to its right front quarter panel?"

"And hood. Yes, he was."

"Thank you, Officer Hackett, you've been very helpful. Mr. Shepherd might have some questions for you."

I stood. "Officer Hackett, you never found any evidence linking my client to the scene of the accident, did you?"

"We found evidence of a Pillars van in that area—"

"Pardon me, Officer Hackett, but that's not what I asked. You did not find any evidence linking my client, Edgerton Fleece, to the actual scene of the accident, did you?

"Well, we found the tire tracks."

"Yes, you certainly did. And I noticed in your testimony you did not link those tire tracks to a particular vehicle, did you?"

"No, I did not."

"That's because you couldn't, could you?"

"No, the snow was too sloppy and the prints too indistinct to make a definitive match."

"And the ambulance had spoiled a portion of the tracks with its own tires, right?"

"That's right."

"So that the jury is clear, you could not identify the type of vehicle which made the tire tracks at the scene, could you?"

"We could not."

"So, circling back around to my original question, Officer Hackett, you don't have any evidence putting Edgerton Fleece at the scene of the accident, do you?"

"But we know—"

"Tell you what, Officer Hackett, let me make this easy for you. You don't have any eyewitnesses that put Mr. Fleece at the scene of the accident, do you?"

"We do not."

"You don't have any pictures or video of him at the actual scene of the accident at 5436 Sunnyfield Drive, right?"

"That's true."

"You don't have any footprints or fingerprints or any other physical evidence linking Mr. Fleece to 5436 Sunnyfield Drive that day, do you?"

"Not that I have found, no."

"You mentioned a video that Officer Pearson found, right?"

"Detective Pearson. And that's right."

"So we should talk to Detective Pearson about how that video was obtained?"

"Yes."

"So the jury is clear though, that video of the Pillars van you testified about was not taken at 5436 Sunnyfield Drive, was it?"

"It was not."

"It was taken more than a mile away."

Pompeo stood. "Objection, Your Honor. Mr. Shepherd can't have it both ways."

"Sustained."

"Officer Hackett, it's fair to say that you're assuming that Edgerton Fleece hit Benjamin Trane because he took his van to Carrefour Collision the next day, isn't it?"

"It was damaged on the front right. It seems like an obvious connection."

"I'm sure it does. Did you check all of the auto body shops in Carrefour, by the way?"

"What?"

"Did you check all the auto body shops in Carrefour for vehicles with damage to the right front quarter panel?"

"Well, no, once we found this one..." Officer Hackett trailed off.

"Once you found Mr. Fleece's vehicle you stopped, right?"

Officer Hackett pursed his lips. "We did."

"Because in your mind, you'd found what you were looking for and could stop?"

"That's right."

I handed Officer Hackett a paper. "Officer Hackett, I'm handing you an insurance claim form that's been marked as State's Exhibit 47. Did you review this as part of your investigation?"

"I did."

"This is a claim form submitted by Pillars to its insurance company for the repairs done at Carrefour Collision, right?"

"Yes."

"It says that van's damage was caused by a collision with a deer, correct?"

"That's what the form says, sure."

"You told Mr. Pompeo that you've investigated hundreds of serious accidents, right?"

"Maybe as high as one thousand, yes."

"Some of those were accidents where a car hit a deer, weren't they?"

"They were."

"Accidents with deer are common in this state, aren't they?"

"They happen now and again."

"Now and again? You keep up with the research in your field, don't you, Officer Hackett?"

"I do."

"The State Highway Patrol is a good source of information, isn't it?"

"It is."

"It recently published a study showing that over a five-year period, there were 100,672 automobile collisions involving deer in the state of Ohio. That's more than now and again, isn't it?"

"I suppose."

"And those collisions can cause significant damage to a vehicle, right?"

"They can."

"Damage that needs to be fixed by an auto body shop, true?"

"Sometimes."

"Almost always, right?"

"That's right."

"Thanks, Officer Hackett. That's all I have."

Pompeo stood. "Officer Hackett, did you find any record that

Edgerton Fleece ever reported his supposed accident with the deer to the police?"

"No, I did not. No such report was filed."

"Thank you, Officer. Oh, and don't most deer crashes happen during the rut in October, November, and December?"

"Yes, sir, they do."

Pompeo waved a hand and sat down.

I stood. "Officer Hackett, a driver is not required by law to report a collision with a deer if there's no injury or property damage to anyone else, right?"

Officer Hackett shifted. "That's right."

"So if the damage from the deer accident was only to Mr. Fleece's vehicle, he would not have been obligated to file a report with the police, would he?"

"He would not."

"Now you just testified that most deer related crashes happen in October, November, and December. Do you remember that?"

"Well, it was just a second ago."

"Good. I'm glad you remember. The same Highway Patrol study we talked about says that only forty-seven percent of deer related crashes happen in those three months."

"Okay."

"So that means the majority of all deer related crashes, more than half, happen outside of those three months, right?"

Officer Hackett shrugged. "If that's what the study says."

I picked up a stack of papers. "Would you like to read it and refresh your memory?"

"No. I guess I might've gotten that detail wrong."

"You and Mr. Pompeo both had that detail wrong, didn't you?"

"Maybe but that hardly matters."

"Really? Details matter in murder investigations, don't they, Officer Hackett?"

Officer Hackett stared at me.

I stared back.

"Yes," he said.

I sat down, Judge Jurevicius dismissed Officer Hackett, and we broke for lunch.

59

When I came back to the courtroom for the afternoon session, Ryan Pompeo was the only one sitting there, leaning back in his chair and staring at the ceiling, rotating from side to side.

As I put my trial notebook on the table, he said, "The deer ate my homework? You're really going with that, NATO?"

"It's easy to go with the truth, Ryan."

He stopped circling and rolled his head over toward me. "So easy you're going to put the Fleeces on the stand to tell us all about this horrifying Bambi incident?"

"Don't need to. The jury knows all about it."

"But do they believe it? The timing seems kind of funky to me."

"I'm glad you're not on the jury then."

"True. I suppose they could be a gullible bunch, but they seemed pretty sharp to me. I think they'll see through the phantom deer defense."

He sat forward and pulled a little tin of mints out of his pocket. "Want one?"

"No, thanks."

"I need three," he said and popped a handful into his mouth. "Ruben breath. Nobody wants that."

"You ate a Ruben?"

"Hell, yeah. Went over to The Gavel. I know people like the triple-decker club but I'm telling you, their Ruben is the best in town. The afternoon breath is killer though."

I noticed that Pompeo had his iPad and that was about it. He didn't have an associate, he didn't have a trial notebook, and, if he was to be believed, he had spent lunch waiting in line and wolfing down a Ruben.

It was also very possible that he was winning. It was enough to annoy a guy.

"Speaking of The Gavel," said Pompeo as he put the mints back in his pocket. "How about the way our judge is rapping that thing? Goes right through my head every time."

There was the sound of a throat clearing. I looked over at the bailiff's desk where Mickey Fields had appeared and was typing.

Pompeo gave an "oops" shrug and smiled. "Of course, I mean that in the most authoritative and judgey sort of way."

Then Danny and the Fleeces returned from lunch, and we settled in for the afternoon session.

POMPEO STOOD, put his hands on his hips, and said, "Judge, the State calls Rick Dalton."

Rick Dalton walked into the courtroom and stopped just inside the door before Pompeo said, "Right this way, Rick. The chair up here."

Dalton's hesitation, along with his dark jeans and red button-down shirt with "Carrefour Collision" in bright yellow on the pocket, made Dalton seem like a fish out of water. It also screamed auto body expert. I had no doubt that Pompeo had set it up on purpose. It was a good move.

"Could you state your name, please?" said Pompeo.

"Rick Dalton."

"What do you do, Rick?"

"I run Carrefour Collision. It's an auto body shop on the south side."

"What does an auto body shop do?"

"We repair the bodies of cars, the outside. Mechanics repair thc inside."

"Are the repairs you do usually from accidents?"

"Usually. It can be rust or wear and tear too."

"Do you know Edgerton Fleece?"

"I do. He brings cars in from time to time."

"Did he bring a car to you in February of this year?"

"He did."

"What happened?"

"Mr. Fleece brought in a 2015 Grand Caravan with damage to the right front quarter panel and hood. We provided him with an estimate and then fixed it."

"When was that?"

"I would have to look at my paperwork."

"Here you go. I'm handing you what's been marked as State's Exhibit 51. What is that?"

"That's a copy of our estimate and invoice."

"And when is that dated?"

"Looks like the estimate is dated February 18."

"What does that mean?"

"It means that Mr. Fleece would have brought the van in on February 18, and we would've given him an estimate to repair it."

"What did you do? Feel free to look at your estimate."

"Actually, that's on the invoice. Yeah, we replaced the right front quarter panel, pounded out some dents on the hood, and replaced the right headlight."

"Was the headlight still functioning?"

"It was. It looks like the casing was cracked so we switched it out."

"Mr. Dalton, did you do the work on Mr. Fleece's minivan?"

"Some of it. I took the original quarter panel off and pounded out the hood. The boys did the rest."

"Okay, I just want to make sure we have the timing right for the jury here. Mr. Fleece brought the minivan in on February 18?"

"That's what the estimate says."

"And you completed the work by February 20?"

"That's what the invoice says."

"You replaced the front right quarter panel and headlight casing and pounded out the hood."

"That's right."

"Did Mr. Fleece tell you what had happened?"

Rick Dalton nodded. "He said he hit a deer."

"Did that make sense to you when you did the repair?"

"What do you mean 'make sense?'"

"Was the damage to the van consistent with hitting a deer?"

"Yes."

"How so?"

"It's pretty common to have damage to the front or side and we see dents on the hood when the deer tumbles over the top."

"I see. Was there anything else that was consistent with damage from hitting a deer?"

"Well, yeah, there was the blood."

"What blood?"

"In the folds of the dents and in the gaps around the headlight."

"There was blood in those spots?"

"There was blood."

"Mr. Dalton, had the car been washed when Mr. Fleece brought it to you?"

"It looked like it. There wasn't much grime or salt for winter."

"But there was still blood in the crevices of the van?"

"Yeah, it can be pretty hard to get out of the cracks."

Pompeo scratched at the back of his hair without messing it. "A two-day turnaround is pretty quick for a job like this, isn't it?"

"It is. We put a rush on it."

"Did Mr. Fleece ask you to do that?"

"He did."

"He wanted it done as soon as possible?"

"Yes. And we wound up having access to everything we needed, so we were able to turn it around pretty quickly."

"Last thing, Mr. Dalton. Was the damage you saw on Mr. Fleece's van consistent with hitting a man as well as a deer?"

"Well, Mr. Fleece said that he hit a deer."

"I understand that. My question, though, is, was the damage the same as you might see if the van had hit a man?"

Rick Dalton shifted in his seat. "I suppose the damage would be similar for anything that weighed a couple of hundred pounds."

"And that bleeds?"

"Sure, and that bleeds."

"Thanks, Mr. Dalton. I'm sure Mr. Shepherd has some questions for you."

I stood. "Mr. Dalton, you see auto body damage from deer accidents all the time, don't you?"

"I do."

"It's pretty common here in Carrefour and in the outlying areas, isn't it?"

"It is."

"You see deer accidents at all times of the year, right?"

"We do."

"In fact, you've seen so many that you've said collisions with deer have practically built your business, is that right?"

"We have seen a fair bit of them, yes."

"So you did not find it unusual for Mr. Fleece to tell you that he had struck a deer, did you?"

"No, I didn't."

"And the damage you found on the minivan was consistent with hitting a deer, wasn't it?"

"You can have a whole range of damage. This was a middling one, not too serious but not something you could ignore either."

"People wash their cars sometimes before they bring them to you, don't they?"

"If the accident isn't too bad, sometimes. Especially in winter so we can assess the damage."

"Now you said that Mr. Fleece asked you to put a rush on the repair, do you remember that?"

"Yeah."

"Did that surprise you?"

"Not really."

"Why not?"

"Well, I know they transport a lot of people to different appointments and such and they don't have that many minivans to do it, so I figured that they would want it done before the weekend."

"And you know this because you have serviced their vehicles before?"

"Yeah. Not too often, but whenever they had a fender bender or some rust damage and what not, they would bring the vehicle over to us and we'd take a look at it."

"A number of people drive their vehicles, right?"

"I don't suppose that one person can drive them all at once, no."

"Mr. Dalton, we've met before today, haven't we?"

"We have."

"I came by your shop to ask about this estimate and invoice, didn't I?"

"You did."

"Did any police officers come by? An Officer Hackett or a Detective Pearson?"

"I remember one man in a uniform and another man in a suit."

"And they were both police officers?"

"That's what they said."

"Did the police officers ask you if the damage to the minivan could've been caused by a person instead of a deer?"

"They did."

"And what did you tell them?"

"What I told you today—it was possible, but that Mr. Fleece had told me it was a deer and it looked like it was from a deer."

"And what about Mr. Pompeo? Did he talk to you about your testimony today?"

Pompeo stood. "Objection, the witness can't be asked about my conference with him."

"Your Honor, Mr. Dalton is a fact witness. Any discussion the state had with him is open to discovery."

Judge Jurevicius stared. I heard some rustling to my left but didn't take my eyes off the judge as she glanced over my shoulder, then said, "Overruled. The witness will answer the question."

Rick Dalton nodded. "Mr. Pompeo asked me to say that the damage was more likely caused by hitting a man than a deer. Wait that's not fair, he asked if I *could* say that and if I wanted to see justice done."

"I see. And I take it your response to Mr. Pompeo was the same as what you testified to today, that the damage was consistent with a deer, but it was possible it could be from hitting a person as well?"

"That's right."

"Thank you, Mr. Dalton. That's all for me."

Pompeo popped to his feet. "Mr. Dalton, I didn't ask you to lie, did I?"

"No, sir, you did not."

"I simply asked you if it was more likely that the damage was from a person than a deer, true?"

"That's true."

Pompeo turned and made like he was going to sit down, then turned back and said, "Mr. Dalton, you knew Mr. Fleece before this, right?"

"Right. Like I said, I've fixed some of his other vehicles."

"Well, it is more than that, isn't it?"

Rick Dalton shifted in his seat. "I'm not sure what you mean."

"You've used some of Pillars' services, haven't you?"

"I've used the childcare there for my daughters now and again when my mom is busy."

"Sure, but that's not what I was thinking of. What else?"

Rick Dalton raised his chin and stared at Pompeo for a moment before he turned and looked at the judge. "Do I have to answer that, Judge?"

Judge Jurevicius glanced at Pompeo.

"Goes to bias, Judge."

Judge Jurevicius glanced at me and, when I didn't say anything, looked at Rick Dalton and said, "Yes, sir, you do."

Rick Dalton shifted, glanced at Edge, then said, "Four years ago we had a fire in the garage. It took us some time to fix it and get the business running again and the insurance payments were slow." He raised his chin a little further and said, "I do believe my wife went to the food pantry on two occasions during that time."

He looked at Edge. "For which I thank you."

"Right," said Pompeo. "That's all then."

When I indicated I had no questions, Judge Jurevicius dismissed Mr. Dalton and, as soon as he'd left, dismissed the jury for the day with a sharp rap of her gavel that caught me off guard once again. The judge had just gone into her office when I felt Edge jostle me.

Startled, I looked up as Edge leapt around me. His eyes were wide, his lips snarled, and he jabbed his finger within an inch of Pompeo's chest.

"There was no reason to do that," Edge said. "There was no reason to attack his pride."

Pompeo stepped back, both hands up, a slight smile on his face. "Hey, hey, hey," Pompeo said. "No reason to murder anybody here."

Spit flew from Edge's lips as he said, "His family had no *food*! That's what it's there for!"

I shouldered my way between them as Pompeo said, "Don't lose control, Mr. Fleece. Someone else could get hurt."

"People don't want to need help!" said Fleece driving his shoulder into my chest.

I held Edge back. "Pretty big when I'm in the way," I said to Pompeo.

Pompeo shrugged. "So step aside."

"Haven't you ever tried to help people?" yelled Edge.

Pompeo smiled faded. "Every day. I put killers away."

"Edge," said a woman's voice. "That's enough."

And just like that it was gone—the rage dropped out of Edge's face, his body relaxed, and the same affable man I had known stood before me. “You’re right, Carissa,” he said as she took his arm. “Sorry about that.”

“That’s a switch,” she said and kissed his cheek. “Usually I’m the one who can’t tolerate assholes.”

Carissa took Edge by the arm and led him out.

“He’s not wrong,” I said.

“Neither was I,” said Pompeo.

60

It was Danny's pick for sandwiches that night so he went with West of Philly cheesesteaks, although he ordered his without. Philistine.

Danny chewed, swallowed, then said, "So what's up with Judge Jurevicius? She's letting Pompeo get away with mur—you know what I mean."

I nodded. "She's new is all. Remember your first murder trial?"

Danny smiled. "Hank Braggi leaves an impression."

"Now imagine if something had happened to me and you had to step in."

Danny's smile faded at the thought. "Gotcha."

"I think she's scared of making a mistake. We have to take all the guess work out of this for her."

"How?"

"We need to have bench briefs for her on every evidence issue we think is going to come up. I know we have some on major topics ready, but you saw what happened today."

Danny nodded. "We need them on basic trial issues too."

"Let's make a list."

A bench brief is just a quick one-page summary of the law on a topic for the judge to support your objection. Danny and I spent the next half hour putting together a list of topics. When we were done, it was long.

"We need to have these by tomorrow," Danny said.

"I'm sorry," I said.

"Don't be. It has to be done and you need to get ready for Pearson and the videos. Speaking of which, when are we going to drop the 120-hour rule?"

"As soon as Pompeo commits to the five million dollars with the jury. He mentioned it in opening but hasn't pulled it from a witness yet. I'm guessing it'll be with Pearson."

Danny nodded.

"Thanks. Jenny holding up okay?"

"No problems at all. Ruth has been sleeping great."

"Small favors, Danny, small favors." After we crumpled our wrappers, Danny made his shot into the waste basket across the room, and I missed mine. As I properly disposed of my failure, I said, "Touch base with me before you go?"

"Yep," said Danny.

We had just gone to our respective offices when my phone buzzed.

"Hi, Mrs. Horvath."

"Mr. Shepherd, hello. Is this a bad time?"

"I have a few minutes. What's up?"

"I was calling to see if I can help in any way."

"No, you've helped plenty, Mrs. Horvath. We're all set."

"Are you sure? If you need any documents or anything else, I'm sure I can find it."

"If I do, I know who to call."

"Well, I'll be there tomorrow if you change your mind."

I thought, then said, "Mrs. Horvath, I'd really prefer that you not come tomorrow. Or the rest of this week for that matter."

Silence, then, “Why, Mr. Shepherd?”

“So far, Ryan Pompeo hasn’t indicated that he’s going to try to call you as a witness. If you’re there, and especially if you speak to Edge or Carissa—you have been speaking to Edge and Carissa, right?”

“I support them both, of course.”

“Then it would be no problem for Pompeo to hand you a subpoena and put you on the stand. I don’t want to give him the opportunity or the idea.”

“Are you certain, Mr. Shepherd?”

“I am.”

“Then that’s what we’ll do—I’ll stay away unless I hear otherwise from you.”

“Thank you, Mrs. Horvath.”

“I’ll let you get back at it.”

I hadn’t been working more than half an hour after we hung up before my phone buzzed again. Olivia.

“What’s up, Liv?”

“My suspicions.”

“How now?”

“A new video has been uploaded to the Alert Shield network. It shows a Pillars van a couple of miles away from the accident. Not on Sunnyfield though, on a street almost out of Harvest Township, near the EveryGround Coffee.”

“I know the place. Is it Edge?”

“No. This video is taken from the passenger side, the right side, and there’s no dent on the van. That’s not what’s strange.”

“What is?”

“This video is much closer to the street. Between that and the streetlights, we have a pretty clear view of the van.”

“Can we see the driver?”

“No. But we can see the passenger on the camera side.”

“Do you recognize him?”

"Her."

"What?"

"I recognize her."

"Who?"

"Dr. Carissa Carson-Fleece."

"Carissa? This video is at what time?"

"Six-forty p.m."

"But she was working a shift at St. Isidore's then."

"Apparently not."

"That doesn't make any sense."

"Hence my call."

"How did you find this?"

"I'd been checking the Alert Shield Network regularly since Pearson made his original request. There were no new responses, so I checked less and less often. I realized today that the trial may have gotten people's attention, so out of paranoia I checked again tonight. This video was uploaded Monday night. I'm at Brad's so I saw the video on my phone through the app. I'm sending it to you now."

"Great. I'll let you go."

"It's on the way."

"Thanks, Liv. You're the best.

"True words, Shep. Talk to you tomorrow."

By the time I hung up, the video had come in. I clicked on it.

It showed a front, passenger side view of a silver minivan approaching. I paused. The front right corner of the vehicle was undamaged. Between the overhead reflection of a streetlight and the glare of the headlights, I couldn't see through the front windshield. I hit play then paused when the van was directly opposite the camera. The woman in the passenger seat was visible.

There was no question it was Dr. Carissa Carson-Fleece, looking up and to her right, laughing. I let the video run, stopped it, backed it up, and stopped it a little closer so that I could read the license plate. I pulled out the vehicle log and ran down the list.

It was the license plate for Van No. 6. The one signed out to Greg Kilbane.

I thought about it and thought some more. Then I went back to preparing my cross-examination of Mitch Pearson.

61

There were familiar faces in the courtroom the next morning—Manny Amaltheakis was sitting in the back row and nodded when I entered, Danny was leafing through a Bankers box of new bench briefs that he'd drafted overnight, and Bailiff Mickey Fields was sitting at her desk typing away, ignoring us all. Ryan Pompeo was sitting at his counsel table, feet up on the adjacent chair while Mitch Pearson leaned on the banister that separated the counsel table from the gallery, arms crossed, telling a story to Pompeo who laughed in a way that annoyed me but shouldn't have.

What I did not see was my client. Or his wife.

As I went to my table, Pompeo said, "Your client hasn't buggered off, has he NATO?"

"Probably just looking for a container for his joy to see you, Ryan," I said as I put my laptop on the table.

"You may have to get that criminal you call a bail bondsman to look for him," said Mitch Pearson.

Pearson was a tall, blond, athletic detective who handled all the serious crimes in Carrefour, Ohio. He was also an officious prick. While that may seem overly harsh, we had a long history that bore it out. For what it's worth, Pearson felt the same way about me.

"Still fit in your lucky court suit, Pearson? Good for you."

I took more satisfaction than my mom would've been proud of as Pearson looked down, caught himself, then folded his arms.

I heard Mickey Fields clear her throat behind me and I was about to make an excuse for my client's absence when Edge and Carissa hurried through the courtroom door. Carissa kissed Edge on the cheek and slid into the front row while Edge took his place between me and Danny.

"Sorry, Nate," he said. "Carissa's shift went long."

"No problem," I said, "Are you ready—"

"Everyone is here?" said Bailiff Fields.

"For half an hour," said Pompeo.

"All set," I said.

"I'll get the judge," said Bailiff Fields.

"COULD you state your name for the jury, please?" said Pompeo.

"I am Chief Detective in Charge of Serious Crimes for Carrefour, Ohio Mitchell Pearson."

"I take it from your job title that you investigate serious crimes as a police officer for the city of Carrefour?"

"I do."

"Were you involved in the investigation of the death of Benjamin Trane?"

"I was."

"Please tell us how, Chief Detective Pearson."

"I was approached by Officer AJ Hackett about an accident that had caused the death of a pedestrian. The driver of the vehicle had fled the scene. Officer Hackett asked me to get involved to see if we could find the perpetrator."

"What did you do?"

"I reviewed the witness statements but saw pretty quickly that no one at the scene had identified the vehicle or the driver. So I put in a request to the Alert Shield Network asking residents in the area to check their video to see if they would voluntarily assist our investigation."

"Chief Detective Pearson, let's slow down just a little so that the jury knows exactly what you're talking about."

Pearson explained the Alert Shield camera system, then described the Alert Shield Network and his belief that recording each other all the time fostered a sense of community between neighbors.

Then Pompeo said, "As a law enforcement officer, can you tap into this network directly?"

Pearson said, "If we know the location where a crime happened, like if Mrs. Pepperstone had installed a camera in this case, we would. But if it's checking a general area, we just ask residents to take a look. The community, the neighbors, have taken the excellent step of installing these cameras themselves so we want them to be comfortable with what is being produced."

"So you put out a request in the Alert Shield Network for video in this case?"

"Yes, we requested people in a ten-block area of 5436 Sunnyfield Drive check their videos from six to seven p.m. on February 17 of this year."

"And did you receive any replies?"

"We did. We received a video from one of the Sunnyfield residents who lives about near the accident site."

I stood. "Your Honor, may we approach?"

She paused, then waved us up.

When we were out of hearing of the jury, I said, "Your Honor, for the reasons we cited in our pre-trial motion, we renew our objection to the use of this video."

"We still oppose that, Judge," said Pompeo. "We've submitted adequate foundation and have provided you with rulings from other courts allowing admission of doorbell video evidence."

Judge Jurevicius methodically took a piece of paper out of her pile, looked at it, and said, "And for the reasons set forth in our pretrial order, we find that this video is admissible. Mr. Shepherd, your objection is noted for the record."

I nodded. "Just to be clear, Judge, are you ruling that all Alert Shield videos uploaded into the network in response to Detective Pearson's request are admissible?"

"Right, right, right, the short one and the long one," said Pompeo.

Judge Jurevicius nodded. "I am."

I nodded. I glanced at Pompeo, but he was already talking as we headed back to our tables. "Chief Detective Pearson, I've taken the liberty of loading this video into my iPad so we can play it. Let me pull it up—there we go. Chief Detective Pearson, this is State's Exhibit 48. Tell me what we are looking at.

"This video was taken from an Alert Shield camera at 3901 Sunnyfield Drive, just down the road from the accident site."

"And you mentioned that this camera is installed on the front of the person's house?"

"It is. Normally, it's triggered when a person gets within thirty feet or so of the front door, but we were fortunate here."

Pompeo nodded. "How so?"

Pearson smiled. "You will see once we start rolling that a cat spends a good deal of time on the porch."

"I see. And when was this video taken?"

"According to the timestamp, the video was taken from 6:18 to 6:25 p.m. on February 17."

"And when was the accident?"

"We estimate the accident occurred at 6:28 p.m."

"Officer Pearson, I'm going to hand you my iPad here. It has the controls up so you can play and pause the video whenever you want. Why don't you describe what you are seeing and stop it whenever you think it's appropriate."

"Very well. 3901 Sunnyfield is an odd number address, so it's on the opposite side of the street from 5436 Sunnyfield where the accident occurred. We will be looking at the driver's side or the left side of the vehicles." Pearson hit play. "You can see that traffic is not heavy. You can also see our tabby cat here in the foreground."

"Can't you set the camera so that pets won't trigger it?"

Pearson smiled. "The owner enjoyed watching them. Apparently, there are a couple of cats in the neighborhood that drop by."

"I'm sorry, Detective Pearson, go ahead."

"We don't have to watch the whole thing; I can take you to the relevant part." Pearson dragged a finger across the screen and fast-forwarded. "This is it here." He hit play, a van rolled into the picture, and he hit pause. "You can see the Pillars minivan come onto the screen."

"Why is that important, Officer Pearson?"

"Because this puts a Pillars minivan on Sunnyfield Drive just before the accident."

"Can you see the license plate?"

"Unfortunately, you cannot."

"How about the driver?"

"No, the camera is too far away."

"Well, surely you can blow up the video or perform some video magic like we see on TV, can't you?"

"Unfortunately, no. When you blow this video up, it just gets blurrier. We don't have the resolution to see either of those things."

"So all we know is that a Pillars minivan went by right before the accident."

"Actually, we know that two went by right before the accident."

"Two? What do you mean?"

Pearson rewound the video. "Here. You can see that another Pillars minivan passed first."

"And I assume you can't see the driver or the license plate on this one either?"

"That's right, you cannot."

"Now Chief Detective Pearson, Mr. Shepherd here is an awfully clever attorney. I expect he's going to ask you why that isn't reasonable doubt right there. After all, we have two Pillars minivans driving by, how can you possibly know which one hit Mr. Trane?"

"Two reasons," said Pearson. "First, our assumption is that it had to have been the second minivan. Presumably if it had been the first, the second one would've stopped to help. Or come forward as a witness."

"Presumably."

"Second, like I said, the video alone doesn't tell us who was driving. What was important about the video was that it led us to investigate local auto body shops looking for Pillars minivans."

"I see. What did you do next?"

"I showed Patrolman Hackett the video and had him check the auto body shops."

Pompeo nodded. "We've had Officer Hackett and Rick Dalton of Carrefour Collision testify for the jury already. Did Officer Hackett relay his findings to you?"

Pearson nodded. "He did. I learned that the defendant Edgerton Fleece brought his Pillars minivan to Carrefour Collison on the day after Mr. Trane was killed to fix damage which was consistent with hitting a pedestrian. I also learned that the vehicle had been washed prior to the repair, so I investigated local car washes."

"Did you find anything?"

"I did."

"How in the world did you do that?"

"I started with car washes that were near Carrefour Collision and the Pillars headquarters. We eventually found the footage of the defendant from the U-Wash just down the road."

Pompeo walked over and pulled up a new video. A car wash bay appeared on the big screen for the jury, one of those that was open on both ends with a spray gun and brush mounted on one wall next to a box for quarters.

"Chief Detective Pearson, I just cued up a video that's been identified as State's Exhibit 54. Could you tell the jury what that is?"

"That is video I obtained from the U-Wash two miles away from Carrefour Collision."

"And what are we going to see?"

"We are going to see the defendant Edgerton Fleece wash his van on the morning of February 18."

"The day after Mr. Trane was killed?"

"That's correct."

"Go ahead then."

Pearson hit play and, a few seconds later, a Pillars minivan pulled in. The car wash camera was mounted so that it gave a view of the front passenger side of the van, which was dented and had two long, dark streaks that swooshed from the front corner by the headlight, up to the hood, then down to the front wheel well.

"What are we looking at there?" said Ryan Pompeo, although we could all see it.

"Just a moment," said Pearson. He waited until the driver's door opened and a man went over to the coin box, dropped in some quarters, and pulled the spray gun out of its holster. The man then circled around to the front of the van so that the camera had a clear view of him.

Pearson paused the video. It was framed perfectly: Edgerton Fleece, the spray gun, and the dented, bloody van.

"That is defendant Edgerton Fleece holding the spray gun," Pearson said. "If you look closer—and you can blow this up just a little without losing resolution—there we go, you can see the dents on the front right of the vehicle like Mr. Dalton of Carrefour Collision described. And do you see these two dark streaks running from the front corner to the wheel well?"

"I do."

"That's blood."

"I see."

Pearson hit play and Edgerton Fleece began to spray the blood off his van.

The two of them didn't say anything for the next ten minutes. Instead, we watched as Edge sprayed the van, spending most of his time on the front right. Then he activated the foam brush and spread soap over the whole vehicle, although the way he finished at the front right and scrubbed repeatedly was a sharp contrast to the way he lightly ran the brush over the rest of the van. No, on the front right, Edge scrubbed in and around the bumper, on the hood, in the crack where the hood met the quarter panel, on the dented side, in the gap between the quarter panel and the front bumper, in the wheel well, and on the wheel and hubcap itself. The timer ran out at one point. He fed it some more quarters and kept going.

Edge eventually switched to the spray gun and rinsed the

whole van. Again, though, he spent most of the time on the front right, shooting the powerful sprayer in and around and all along the gaps and nooks and crevices in that part of the van.

When he was done, he holstered the spray gun and went back to check the right side of the van. You could see that the two streaks were gone. Edge squatted down next to the wheel well and looked back and forth.

"You can pause it there, Chief Detective Pearson," said Pompeo.

Pearson did.

"My, that was thorough," said Pompeo.

"Oh, he's not done," said Pearson.

"What?" said Pompeo as if they hadn't rehearsed it.

"Watch," said Pearson, and hit play.

Edge was squatting down next to the wheel well, looking. Then he went back to the box, fed it some more quarters, clicked over to the foam brush, and started scrubbing again. Just the front right side.

He ran through his allotted time, fed more quarters into the box, picked up the spray gun, and stood there, blasting the damaged part of his van with water until it ran out.

I snuck a glance at the jury. They were all watching except for when they snuck a glance at Edge.

The video finally stopped.

It was damning.

"What did you do after you saw this video, Chief Detective Pearson?"

"We subpoenaed the vehicle records from Pillars."

"And what did you find?"

"That the subject vehicle here was registered to Pillars and that Edgerton Fleece was the dedicated, primary driver of that vehicle."

"Did you speak to Mr. Fleece?"

"Briefly."

"And what did he tell you?"

"He told us that he had in fact driven the vehicle on the night of February 17."

"Did he have an explanation for the dent?"

"He said he hit a deer the night before."

"And that was his explanation for the blood?"

"Yes."

"Was any report filed regarding this supposed deer-minivan collision?"

"No. There was an insurance claim filed, but that was it."

"I see. What did you do next?"

"At this point, we believed there was sufficient evidence to consider charges, so we referred the matter to your office."

"And did that conclude your investigation?"

"No, it did not."

"What did you do next?"

"We learned that Benjamin Trane was an employee of Pillars, which surprised me given Mr. Fleece's involvement. I wanted to further explore that connection, if any, so I searched the victim's apartment."

"Did you find anything relevant to this case?"

"Yes, we did. Among his papers, we found the victim Benjamin Trane's will."

"Chief Detective Pearson, I'm handing you what's been marked as State's Exhibit 66. Can you identify that for the jury, please?

"Yes. That is a copy of Benjamin Trane's will."

"Was there anything in the will that was relevant to your investigation?"

"Yes."

"What is that?"

"Mr. Trane left everything he had to Pillars."

"His employer?"

"Yes. Mr. Trane had worked at Pillars for years."

"Was that fact relevant to your investigation?"

"It seemed unusual but not significant at first. Mr. Trane appeared to live a fairly modest life and we found the will in a plastic file box in his small apartment."

"Did your impression eventually change?"

"It did."

"How so?"

"We inventoried Mr. Trane's correspondence as part of our search and in it we found a letter from attorney Manuel Amaltheakis indicating that Mr. Trane had inherited a bequest from the man he was working for, Theo Plutides, and that Mr. Trane should contact attorney Mr. Amaltheakis."

"What did you do?"

"I contacted Mr. Amaltheakis."

"And what did you learn?"

"I learned that Benjamin Trane had inherited approximately five million dollars from Theo Plutides the week before Mr. Trane died."

I felt the jury sit up but didn't look at them as Pompeo continued.

"How was that fact relevant to your investigation?"

"It meant that when Mr. Trane died, Pillars inherited five million dollars from him."

"Five million dollars?"

"That's correct, five million dollars."

"Was that significant to your investigation?"

"Yes. It meant, to me, that Edgerton Fleece stood to profit from Mr. Trane's death. By a substantial amount.

I stood. "Objection, Your Honor. Move to strike."

Before Judge Jurevicius could speak, Ryan Pompeo raised his hand and said, "I'll correct the record, Judge. Chief Detective

Pearson, Edgerton Fleece didn't directly receive any money from Mr. Trane's death, did he?"

"No, he did not."

"Instead, the charity he founded and has run these many years is the entity that will receive the money, right?"

"That's right."

"Did you investigate the financial health of Pillars at all?"

"No. I advised your office of this finding and I believe other witnesses will be testifying regarding how much Pillars needed this money."

"All right, you've been very patient, Chief Detective Pearson. I have just one more area to discuss with you. Did you do any further investigation of Pillars or Edgerton Fleece?"

"I did."

"And what was that?"

"After I learned about Mr. Trane's will, I did some internet research on Pillars."

"And what did you find?"

"I found a variety of things about their services. But I also found a video on a couple of platforms that solicit donations and specifically explain how you can donate to Pillars by remembering it in your will."

Pompeo walked over to the iPad again. "Chief Detective Pearson, I'm putting up what's been marked as State's Exhibit 67. Can you identify that?"

"I can. It's the video I just mentioned."

"And, after you watched it, did it have any significance to you?

"It did. It showed that Edgerton Fleece was actively soliciting funds for Pillars and was aware that people were putting Pillars in their wills."

"Please show us what you found."

As Pearson moved to play the video, Pompeo glanced at me,

anticipating an objection. When I didn't make one, he raised his eyebrows and looked back at the screen.

Edgerton Fleece appeared and, for fifteen minutes, he talked about all of the services Pillars provided, including an appearance by Dr. Carissa Carson-Fleece to talk about the plans for the new health clinic.

At the end, Edge said, "But we can't do this without your help. Every donation keeps these vital Pillars programs alive and supports our brothers and sisters right here in Carrefour. You can donate now by clicking the button below this video. And, if you can't donate now, consider remembering Pillars in your will. We have sample language that your attorney can use to specify a donation to our outreach programs or, if you don't have a lawyer, you can contact us to put you in touch with someone who is familiar with making these kinds of bequests. Together, we can lift each other up and continue the Pillars mission of 'Support for All.'"

They stopped the video, a frozen Edge smiling above the big red donation button.

"Why was that video important to you, Chief Detective Pearson?"

"Because the video shows that Edgerton Fleece not only knew about people making donations to Pillars in their wills, he was actively soliciting them."

"And did you investigate how Benjamin Trane came to have such a will?"

"I did. He attended a Pillars planned giving seminar in the months before his death and went to one of their recommended attorneys, who drafted the will that we found."

"From your investigation, was Mr. Trane a wealthy man?"

"No. From what we can see in examining his bank records, Mr. Trane had very modest means until shortly before his death."

"You're talking about when he inherited the five million dollars from Theo Plutides?"

"Yes. Unfortunately, he died before he could enjoy it."

"Because he was killed less than a week later?"

"Exactly."

"Thank you, Detective Pearson. Mr. Shepherd might want to talk to you."

I stood. "Detective Pearson, you just mentioned that Benjamin Trane died less than a week after Theo Plutides, is that right?"

"That's right."

"I have here what's been marked as State's Exhibit 61. That's a copy of the death certificate of Theo Plutides, isn't it?"

"Yes, it is."

"And the death certificate indicates that Mr. Plutides died on February 12 at 8:55 p.m., correct?"

"Yes."

"And this is the copy of the death certificate of Benjamin Trane, correct?"

"Correct."

"This document indicates that Mr. Trane died at 6:52 p.m. on February 17. Am I reading that correctly?"

"Yes. Like I said, Mr. Trane died less than a week after Mr. Plutides."

"Okay. We'll come back to those in a bit. Let me first ask you about the street video that you showed the jury."

"Fine."

"You showed us the part of the video where two Pillars vans passed the camera, true?"

"You saw it."

"There are more vehicles shown on that video, aren't there?"

"Yes."

"The video shows a total of eight cars passing, doesn't it?"

"I don't recall the number."

"Let's take a look at it, then."

As Danny cued up the video, Judge Jurevicius said, "Counsel, will you please approach."

I looked over at Pompeo, but he seemed just as surprised as I did as the two of us walked up to the bench.

Judge Jurevicius straightened her jabot and said, "Counsel, as you know, I take criminal docket on Wednesday afternoons. I have just been informed that, on top of that, there is another issue I must attend to. We are coming up on lunchtime, so it seems to me that this is a good time to break for the day. Detective Pearson can resume his testimony tomorrow morning."

Just so you know, it's common for a judge to have to take a break in trial to handle other matters, but Judge Jurevicius hadn't told us that Wednesday afternoon was going to be off limits. I thought I'd missed something, but Pompeo seemed just as irritated. "Judge, we only have Detective Pearson committed for today."

"How long do you have yet, Mr. Shepherd?" she said.

"A ways, Your Honor. I'm just starting."

"Detective Pearson will just have to return tomorrow, Mr. Pompeo. I will inform him. Thank you, Counselors."

After we went back to our tables, the judge went back on the record and told the jury that she had another matter to attend to and they had the rest of the day off. When she ordered Pearson to return the next morning, he didn't look any happier than the rest of us. Then Judge Jurevicius dismissed the jury, banged her gavel, and dismissed us. Bailiff Fields typed away.

I looked at Pompeo. "Did you know?"

He looked irritated for the first time during the trial. "If I had, I would've called him on a different day. See you tomorrow."

I gathered Danny, Edge, and Carissa over to us, told them to head back to the office and that I'd pick up lunch and meet them there. I took a little longer to gather my things and was the last one out.

Manny Amaltheakis was waiting for me at the door. The man apparently had an endless supply of light gray suits, white broadcloth shirts, and pocket squares. "That looked unexpected," he said.

"It was."

"Interrupts the flow of an examination."

"Some, but these things happen."

"You emphasized the time of death right out of the box."

I nodded.

"Is it important?"

"Seemed like a logical place to start."

Manny stared at me for a moment, then said, "I will be interested to see where it goes tomorrow."

"You and me both."

Then we took separate paths out of the courthouse.

62

I was halfway to my car when I realized I'd left an exhibit book, the one I had highlighted, in the courtroom. I turned around and trudged back through the August heat, through court security, and back up to Judge Jurevicius's courtroom. I expected there to be a proceeding going on but there was no one there. Even Mickey Fields was gone from her desk. I saw the exhibit book right there where I'd left it and was heading through the swinging door to the counsel table when I heard the shouting.

"You're making me look like an idiot!" came a deep voice. A man's voice.

"But the city didn't—"

"What do you think it looks like when a councilman's own daughter shuts him down?!"

"I didn't shut you down, Dad. I denied the city attorney's motion—"

"Who do you think told him to file it? Who do you think came up with the idea to take that property in the first place?!"

"But the law says the city has to—"

"I don't give a rat's ass on a sinking ship what the law says!

How do you think you're on that bench in the first place? How do you think people know the name Jurevicius?"

"I have to follow the law, Dad."

"Not for long, you don't. Not if you lose in November."

I heard shuffling, and I hopped to the other side of the swinging gate and acted like I was just coming through it as Councilman Jurevicius stalked out of his daughter's office. I nodded, held the gate to the side, and he stomped out. I gathered my exhibit book, waited a moment, then left.

I was back on the first floor and walking out when I ran into Judge Anne Gallon. "Hey," she said, looking over her wireless glasses, "Aren't you supposed to be in trial?"

"Judge Jurevicius has criminal docket this afternoon."

"Ah, right. How's Stephanie doing?"

Normally I would just say fine, but Anne and I went back to our days in the prosecutor's office and had come up together. So I said, "Thoughtful, but a little uncertain sometimes."

Judge Gallon gave me a smirk. "It can be a pain in the ass to work with someone in their first murder trial, can't it?" Anne had been my judge in the Hank Braggi case.

"Fortunately, I had a very wise judge."

She scoffed. "A wise judge who could see through your bullshit."

I thought about what I had just seen. "You know, she might appreciate spending a little time with a perceptive, wise judge."

"Oh?"

"Especially with some of the...stuff that City Council slings around."

Anne Gallon peered at me over those clear glasses, then nodded. "After the trial. Boy, is it hot. Stay cool, Nate."

"You too, Anne."

~

When I got back to the office with four deli sandwiches, Danny was sitting at the conference room table working on his laptop and Carissa was checking her phone while Edge was talking in his.

"Is the repair service still there, Lynn?" he said. "How long?" Edge covered the phone and looked at me. "Do you need me?"

"Only if you have questions," I said.

"I'll be there in half an hour," he said back into the phone. "Thanks."

He hung up. "The refrigeration is down again, and we have to decide whether to repair or replace and they want to show me something."

"Go."

"Replacement wouldn't even be an option if you hadn't referred us to Martel Financial, Daniel. Thanks again."

"Glad it worked out, Edge."

Edge looked at Carissa. "Drop me at work?"

She nodded. "I can't stay though. I need to sleep."

Edge held her hand, kissed it, and said, "I'll find a ride."

They started to leave, so I said, "Edge, can I talk to Carissa a moment before you go?"

"Sure," he said without blinking and was back in his phone and left.

"Danny, will you excuse us for a moment too?"

Danny looked a question but when I didn't answer, he grabbed his sandwich and his laptop and left. I closed the door.

"What?" said Carissa.

"You know part of our defense is that the prosecutor can't prove that Edge was the one who hit Benjamin."

"Right."

"As part of that, I'm going to show that there were a number of cars in the area that could've done it."

"Nate, I haven't slept in thirty hours. I know the case. What's your point?"

"You know there were two Pillars vans in the area."

She motioned for me to move along.

"I don't know who was driving those vans. But I know who was a passenger in one."

Carissa stared at me. "How?"

"Another video has been uploaded. The prosecutor hasn't mentioned it. I might."

Carissa nodded. "I see."

"The van you were in was signed out to Greg Kilbane. Was he driving it?"

Carissa only paused a moment before she said, "Yes."

"Did you see anything that night?"

Carissa's eyes flashed. "Don't you think I would've told you if I had?"

"I don't know what you'd do, Carissa. We don't know each other."

Carissa stood. "Obviously, we didn't hit anybody."

"Obviously."

"We didn't see the accident either. I would've said something if we had."

"How about the other Pillars van, did you see it?"

"Not in front of us. I wasn't looking behind us."

I nodded. "I don't know how this is going to go over the next few days. But I'm going to emphasize that the other vehicles were there. And, now that I have this information, I'm going to try to prove that the two Pillars vans weren't Edge."

"You should." She paused. "Does who was in them matter?"

"I'm still deciding."

"We weren't doing anything and then when all this happened, there was enough trouble for Pillars and us and..." she trailed off.

"That part doesn't matter to me. Either way."

Carissa stared at me for another moment. "I need to get Edge to Pillars," she said, and walked out.

I took my pastrami on rye to my office and ate it while I fine-tuned my examinations for the next day. I heard Danny working and taking calls but was focused on my own thing and didn't pay attention until the middle of the afternoon when Danny walked into my office.

"I just got a call from Spencer Martel," he said.

"Did you tell him you have to wait to take on any new estate clients until after the trial?"

"He wasn't calling to send me a client. He was calling to say he might pull them."

"A client? Which one?"

"All of them."

Danny had my attention. He looked pale.

"Martel said that?" I asked.

"He implied it."

"Tell me."

Danny sat down. "Martel said he enjoys working with me but that, as a new lawyer, I probably don't fully understand the nuances of arcane estate planning laws.

"Okay."

"He also said that, since I'm young, I might not appreciate how estate planning and business can intersect."

"I see."

"So I should probably just leave the application of laws about how bequests pass to the Probate Court and to seasoned attorneys."

I stared.

"Because he needs to be able to refer clients to lawyers who make rational business decisions and can see the big picture."

Danny was clearly shaken. Unfortunately, there wasn't a lot I could do to make him feel better.

"You understand what he's saying, right?" I said.

"Of course! Martel's company has extended financing to Pillars. If we bring up the 120-hour rule and Pillars loses the five million dollars, it's more likely that Pillars goes under. Losing the money affects Martel Financial almost as much as it does Pillars."

I thought. "I warned Edge not to bring up the potential five million dollars with the banks. He must have told Martel about it to secure the financing."

Danny shook his head. "What I don't understand is how Martel figured out that we're going to bring it up. I haven't said anything."

"I know you haven't. Manny Amaltheakis figured it out today."

"What? How?"

"He asked me about emphasizing the times of death at the beginning of my cross of Pearson this morning. I bet he knows about the rule. Once I set it up, he figured out what we were going to argue next."

"Wouldn't he have known the whole time?"

"I'm not sure but I get the impression that Amaltheakis has a large practice and delegates a lot."

"But what's the link to Spencer Martel?"

I thought, then said, "If Spencer Martel was taking a financing interest in Pillars that was related in part to the five million dollars, he probably confirmed it was out there before extending the financing."

"And if Amaltheakis told Spencer Martel that the Plutides bequest was valid—"

"Then Amaltheakis might feel obligated to tell Martel that it was in jeopardy."

We sat there. I knew that might not be exactly right, but it didn't matter. What mattered was Spencer Martel's call and the result for Danny.

"Well, I'm glad I found out now," Danny said finally.

"Why's that?"

"Because I don't want to refer people to someone who would screw one client to make money off another."

"We can distance you from this, say it's my decision."

"No way. We owe Edge the best defense we can give him, you and me, and that includes sticking it to Pearson and Pompeo because they didn't figure out the motive evidence."

"It could set your practice back. By quite a bit."

"Then it sets it back. I'll explain it to my boss."

"I heard he's a prick."

"He is, but he'll get it."

"Are you going to call Martel back?"

Danny shook his head. "Let Manny tell him after trial tomorrow." Then he walked out of the conference room and went back to work.

Daniel's parents would probably never know what he had just done, but if you ever run into Mr. and Mrs. Reddy, tell them that you hear their son is doing a great job.

63

I met Danny in the office the next morning before we went over to court.

"Did you sleep on it?" I said.

"No," Danny said.

"Did you talk to Jenny?"

"There's nothing to talk about, Nate."

I nodded, and we left.

~

By eight forty-five, Mitch Pearson was back in the witness chair, and I was re-starting my cross.

"Detective Pearson, we were talking yesterday about the fact that the Alert Shield video shows eight cars going by, do you remember that?"

"I remember that you said that was the case."

"We're going to run the video now, Detective Pearson. Why don't you count the number of cars that go by."

"You don't have to. There are eight."

"Well, let's make sure. Go ahead, Danny."

The video ran, all eight minutes of it. Pearson didn't watch. The jury did.

When it was done, I said, "I counted eight there, Detective Pearson. How about you?"

"There were eight, like I said."

"Like you eventually said, that's right. There were two Pillars minivans in there, right?"

"I mentioned that yesterday, yes."

"And two more minivans and a truck?"

"Yes."

"And three cars."

"Yes."

"There is nothing in this video that tells us which of these vehicles struck Benjamin Trane, is there?"

"We know from their presence in this video that these vehicles had the opportunity to strike Mr. Trane. We used that as a lead to discover the evidence which showed us that Mr. Fleece's vehicle hit Mr. Trane."

"That's a great way to say it, Detective Pearson—you know from their presence in this video that all of these vehicles had the opportunity to strike Mr. Trane, don't you?"

"That's not what I said."

"That's exactly what you said. All eight of these vehicles were in the window in which they could've hit Benjamin Trane, weren't they?"

"Except we know that they didn't all hit Benjamin Trane."

"Of course not. In fact, we know that at least one of these Pillars vans didn't hit Benjamin Trane, don't we?"

"We think it's likely that the second vehicle struck Mr. Trane."

"You can't tell the jury that for sure, though, can you?"

Pearson sighed as if he were being patient. "The importance of this video, Mr. Shepherd, is that it set us on the trail to discovering the damaged and bloodied Pillars van driven by your client."

"We'll get to that in a few seconds, Detective Pearson. For now, though, you would agree with me that this video shows eight vehicles that appear on Sunnyfield Drive in the time window right before Mr. Trane's accident, doesn't it?"

"I've already mentioned that."

"So each of these vehicles had the opportunity to hit Mr. Trane, didn't they?"

"The vehicles appear in the video."

"The red Camry had the opportunity to hit Mr. Trane, didn't it?"

Pearson pursed his lips then said, "There is a red Camry in the video."

"The black Altima had the opportunity to hit Mr. Trane, didn't it?"

"There is a black Altima in the video."

"The first Pillars minivan and the second Pillars minivan each had an opportunity to hit Mr. Trane, didn't they?"

"Two Pillars minivans appear in the video."

"And the blue F350 and the white Sebring and the black BMW and the red Town & Country all had the opportunity to hit Mr. Trane, right?"

"Those four vehicles all appear in the video. But none of those lead us to your client's vehicle."

"Okay, Detective Pearson, since you'd like to talk about my client's vehicle, you never inspected my client's van while it was damaged, did you?"

"No, he repaired it and scrubbed it before I had the chance."

"That's right, you never saw blood on Mr. Fleece's van, did you?"

"No, but Mr. Dalton did."

"I'm not disputing that the blood was there, Detective Pearson. You never tested it to determine whether it was deer blood or human blood, did you?"

"Your client had washed it off by the time I saw it."

"So the answer is 'no?'"

"Your client had washed it off."

"You know, Detective Pearson, Mr. Pompeo has been real anxious to move things along here, but I'm still going to ask this question until you answer it. You did not test the blood on my client's van to determine whether it was deer blood or human blood, did you?"

Pearson looked at Pompeo, who slouched in his chair and shrugged.

"No. We were not given the opportunity to test it."

"You weren't here when Mr. Dalton testified, Detective Pearson, but he stated that the damage to Mr. Fleece's van could just as easily have been caused by a deer as any other source. Were you aware of that?"

"I am."

"So it is reasonable to assume that the damage could have been caused by a deer, right?"

"No, it's not."

"Why not?"

"Why would Mr. Fleece have scrubbed it off if it was just a deer?"

"I don't know, Detective Pearson, has a bird ever pooped on your car?"

Pompeo stood. "Objection."

"Your Honor, Detective Pearson appears to be taking the position that it is unreasonable to wash animal products off your car. I think I'm entitled to ask about it."

Judge Jurevicius straightened her lace jabot with one hand and covered her mouth with the other before she said, "Overruled."

"Has a bird ever pooped on your car, Detective Pearson?"

"Yes."

"Have you ever driven up north so that your windshield was covered in bugs when you got there?"

"Yes."

"Did you wash them off afterward? Or will we look outside into the parking lot and see a car covered in bird poop and bug guts?"

Pearson ground his jaw, then said, "I washed it."

"So it was reasonable for Mr. Fleece to wash his car on February 18 if he hit a deer a couple of days before, wasn't it?"

"If he hit a deer."

"Do you have any evidence, any evidence at all, that Mr. Fleece did not hit a deer?"

"I have Mr. Trane's body."

"Oh? And did you look for a deer carcass? I have not heard any evidence from Mr. Pompeo of your failed search for a dead deer."

Pearson didn't say anything.

"You did not search for a dead deer, did you, Detective Pearson?"

"Of course not."

"Let's talk about some other things you didn't search for. Once you discovered my client's vehicle at Carrefour Collision, you stopped searching auto body shops for damaged vehicles that were consistent with the Trane accident, didn't you?"

"Once we found evidence of your client's bloody vehicle, yes."

"Your office didn't look for Camrys or Altimas or Town & Countrys or BMWs or F350s at any other auto body shops after you found Mr. Fleece's van, right?"

"We searched until then."

"That's right, but you stopped once you found Mr. Fleece's van, true?

"That's true."

"And you never searched the Carrefour body shops on the Michigan side of the line, did you?"

"We thought it unlikely the driver would be from the north part of town."

"Really? You know where I'm from, don't you, Detective Pearson?"

Pearson stared. "I do."

"Where?"

"Michigan."

"Huh. Yet here I am. So you only partially searched the auto body shops in Carrefour, Ohio and you didn't search any of the auto body shops in Carrefour, Michigan to find out if there were any vehicles matching those in the video which had damage which was not deer related, did you?"

"That was a pretty convoluted question, Mr. Shepherd."

"Fair enough. You stopped searching once you found my client's vehicle, didn't you?"

"I already testified to that. It was pretty obvious."

"Mr. Dalton didn't think it was obvious. He said it was just as reasonable for the damage to be from hitting a deer as from anything else, didn't he?"

Pearson smirked. "Your client wasn't going to get five million dollars for hitting a deer."

"That's right, you concluded from your investigation that my client's organization, Pillars, inherited five million dollars upon Benjamin Trane's death, is that right?"

"I did not conclude that. Mr. Trane's will expressly provided that."

"That's right, you testified yesterday with Mr. Pompeo that

you believe Mr. Trane's will left five million dollars to Pillars, right?"

"It's not my belief, it's true."

"And it is your belief that this provided Mr. Fleece with a motive to kill Mr. Trane, right?"

"I think it provided five million motives."

"I know that's what you think, Detective Pearson, so I want to circle back around to your answers to my first questions yesterday. The death certificate shows that Theo Plutides died on February 12, at 8:55 p.m., true?"

"I already said that's true."

"And the death certificate for Benjamin Trane indicates that he died at 6:52 p.m. on February 17, right?"

"It's right there on the documents."

"So, I'm right?"

"You're right."

I turned to Danny. "Could you put those up on a split screen please, Danny?"

Danny winked at me and hit the button. The two death certificates popped up on the screen right next to each other.

"Are you aware of the 120-hour rule, Detective Pearson?"

"The what?"

"The 120-hour rule. You were aware of it before you gave your theory on motive to the jury, weren't you?"

"What are we talking about?"

"I mean, you're here as an officer of the law. You do know the law, don't you?"

Pompeo stood. "Objection, Judge. Argumentative and defense counsel is arguing some sort of legal theory here for the first time."

I shrugged. "The law is always the law. I assume the State and Detective Pearson know it."

"Approach," said Judge Jurevicius.

Without my asking, Danny came with us and brought a handful of manila folders with him.

"What is this, Mr. Shepherd?"

"Your Honor, under Ohio law, if a testator leaves something to a beneficiary under a will and the beneficiary dies within one hundred and twenty hours of the testator, the beneficiary is presumed to have predeceased the testator and does not receive anything under the will."

"What are you talking about?" said Pompeo.

"Your Honor, here's a bench brief on the 120-hour rule, here are copies of the cases that have applied the 120-hour rule, and here is a bench brief on the death certificates establishing the time of the deaths. Here are copies for you, Mr. Pompeo."

Judge Jurevicius took the bench briefs and the cases, then said, "Boil it down for me, Mr. Shepherd."

"Mr. Trane died one hundred and eighteen hours after Mr. Plutides. As a result, Mr. Trane didn't inherit anything from Mr. Plutides. The motive that the state has claimed to this jury isn't true."

"Mr. Pompeo?"

"I'll have to look at these cases, Judge, but I've never heard of this rule."

"I hadn't either, Mr. Pompeo. But that doesn't mean it isn't true."

"Judge," said Pompeo, "I would ask that Mr. Shepherd not be allowed to question this witness on this so-called rule until we've had an opportunity to fully review and brief it."

I shook my head. "We already had to take a half-day break with this witness, Your Honor. I should be permitted to ask these questions. This issue is going to be decided as a matter of law one way or the other. I'm either right on this rule or I'm not. You will establish it, one way or the other, and if I'm wrong, the jury will know it."

"Give me a moment please, gentlemen." Judge Jurevicius read through the bench brief on the 120-hour rule, then the brief on the death certificates. Pompeo scanned quickly at the same time. His face fell a moment before Judge Jurevicius set the cases aside and said, "The Court preliminarily finds that the 120-hour rule is a valid doctrine under Ohio law and that Mr. Shepherd may ask these questions of Detective Pearson. I will make the final determination of whether it applies here after I have a chance to review the cases this evening. I will tell you both, however, that it appears that it does. Thank you for indulging the Court."

Pompeo stared at me, eyes hooded, with the most deliberately indifferent look I'd ever seen on his face. He walked back and slouched into his seat as I faced Pearson and said, "Detective Pearson, you've never heard of the 120-hour rule, have you?"

"No."

"Don't feel bad, I hadn't either before I actually dug into this case. The judge is going to instruct the jury on the details, but essentially Benjamin Trane wouldn't get the five million dollars if he died within one hundred and twenty hours of Theo Plutides."

Pearson looked from me to Pompeo then back to me.

"There are two death certificates up on the screen, Detective Pearson. How many hours passed between the death of Theo Plutides and the death of Benjamin Trane?"

"I don't know."

"Would you like me to do the math?"

Pearson ground his teeth. "One hundred and eighteen hours."

I nodded. "That's the same answer I got, one hundred and eighteen hours. We haven't agreed on a lot, but we can agree that one hundred and eighteen hours is less than one hundred and twenty, right?"

"Of course."

"So if the 120-rule applies here, Pillars does not receive the money from Benjamin Trane, does it?"

"I don't know how that rule works."

"I see. And if the 120-rule applies, the death of Benjamin Trane on the night of February 17 actually *deprived* Pillars of the chance to inherit five million dollars, didn't it?"

"I don't know the answer to that."

"Shouldn't you, though? Shouldn't you know the answer to that if you're going to claim to this jury that the money was a motive for my client to commit murder?"

"You figure it out."

"I have, Detective Pearson. My question was, before you tell this jury that my client's company stood to gain five million dollars from killing Benjamin Trane, shouldn't you know that that's true?"

Pearson was silent. I didn't speak. The jury waited.

I leaned back on my counsel table and crossed my arms.

"Yes," said Pearson.

"No further questions, Your Honor," I said, and sat down.

Pompeo was up immediately. "Detective Pearson, Benjamin Trane's will says that his money goes to Pillars, right?"

"Right."

"Anyone who looked at it would think that Trane's money goes to Pillars, right?"

I stood. "Objection as to what other people thought."

"Sustained."

"When you read Trane's will, it says right in it, in black and white, that all of his money went to Pillars when he died, right?"

"That's right."

"That's a reasonable interpretation of the will?"

I stood. "Objection. A reasonable interpretation of the will is consistent with Ohio law."

"Sustained."

"Now this 120-hour business that Mr. Shepherd is talking about, that comes from this monstrosity here, right? Mr. Plutides' will?" He held up the thick binder for the jury to see.

"Yes."

"And that appears to give Mr. Trane one hundred Bitcoin that was worth about five million dollars when Mr. Plutides died, right?"

Pearson nodded. "That's how I read it."

"In your experience investigating serious crimes and murders, a motive can be wrong but still be the motive, true?"

I stood. "Objection. Facts not in evidence."

"Overruled."

Pearson thought. "That's true, people do things for a mistaken reason all the time. Or based on a misunderstanding."

"That's right. For example, a wife might shoot her husband because she thought he was having an affair even though he wasn't in fact having an affair, right?"

"Objection."

"Sustained."

"Now let's put all that 'hours' business aside for a moment and get back to the blood and the damage. Mr. Shepherd made a lot of about this so-called deer accident. Did you find any evidence, at all, at any time, that Mr. Fleece struck a deer?"

"We did not."

"No body, no horns, no police report?"

"That's correct."

"And why did you stop searching for damaged vehicles once you found Mr. Fleece's vehicle at Carrefour Collision?"

"We had a vehicle with damage to the front right which matched the pattern of the accident scene, with blood, that was brought in the morning after the fatal accident. To us, to me, that matched far too well to be a coincidence."

"And this business about washing bugs and bird poop off your car, does that have anything to do with this case?"

"No, sir."

"What was significant to you about Mr. Fleece washing off his car?"

"That it happened the morning after Mr. Trane's death. That he paid in cash so that there wasn't a transaction record. And that he took painstaking care, washing his car over and over and over, to try to remove every bit of blood. If he'd just run it through a car wash, I might not have thought the same. But I don't know how you can watch that video and not think he was hiding something."

"Thank you, Detective Pearson. We've taken enough of your time."

I stood. "Detective Pearson, we can agree that you were wrong about Pillars getting five million dollars from Benjamin Trane, right?"

"I don't know that for sure, but if the Judge says so, I would abide by that."

"In which case you would have been wrong about the motive, right?"

"If Mr. Fleece thought that Pillars was going to get the five million dollars, whether it actually did or not isn't relevant."

"You were mistaken, weren't you?"

"If the judge says so."

I was almost back to the table when I turned and said, "What if neither of the Pillars vans in the video is Edgerton Fleece's van?"

Pearson's brow furrowed. "What?"

"I said, what if, hypothetically, it is subsequently demonstrated that neither of those Pillars vans were my client's van? Then he would have no connection to this accident at all, would he?"

Pompeo stood. "Objection, Your Honor. This is outrageous."

"I'm asking the witness a hypothetical, Your Honor. It's only applicable if I prove what I just said."

Judge Jurevicius thought. The computer dinged but she didn't look at it. Instead, she thought some more and then said, "Overruled."

"Do you need me to repeat the question, Detective Pearson?"

"No, Mr. Shepherd. If you can prove that neither van in the video was Mr. Fleece, then the only connection to the scene would be that he brought a bloodied, dented van in to be repaired the next day."

"In that situation, hypothetically, you would be mistaken again, right?"

"Your hypothetical is nonsense."

"I guess we'll see. No further questions, Your Honor."

Then Judge Jurevicius dismissed Detective Pearson and gaveled us out for a break.

64

It was all I could do to keep Edge and Carissa calm until we got to the stairwell.

The moment the heavy metal door clicked shut, Edge turned on me. "You just destroyed everything I've worked for!"

"How's that?"

"That five million dollars would've saved us."

"No Edge, that five million dollars would have saved Pillars. You're facing jail for the rest of your life. I'm trying to save *you*."

"Not by destroying Pillars!"

"I didn't destroy Pillars. I didn't kill Theo Plutides or Benjamin Trane and I certainly didn't make them die one hundred and eighteen hours apart. And I didn't invent the rule either. It's the law. It would've been applied eventually. I just pointed it out at a time that would help us."

"But you didn't have to tell them."

"Of course I did! Pompeo kept saying that Pillars stood to gain five million dollars with Trane's death, and it didn't. He was wrong. You were wrong. Anyone who was counting on the five million dollars was wrong because Pillars wasn't entitled to it. So let's stop worrying about something you were never supposed to have and start worrying about how to keep you out of prison!"

A realization dawned. "You told me not to use it for financing."

"I did."

"You've known for weeks and didn't tell me."

"Do you think it would've played out this way if I had?"

I can't say Edge took my point, but he did calm down, especially when Carissa put a hand on his arm. "He's right, Edge. We have to see the whole picture." She looked at me. "That bit at the end. Can you really prove that the two vans in the video aren't Edge?"

I stared at her. "I can prove that two Pillars vans were in the area of the accident that were not Edge's."

"The other one too?"

I nodded. "The other one too."

Carissa got her triage look and turned back to Edge. "We have some work to do."

"I have to call Lynn and Dawn to let them know about the money."

"Dawn is testifying this afternoon," I said.

Carissa nodded to me. Edge already had his phone out as they left. I took a deep breath, waited for a few moments to give them a head start, then went back to the courtroom to grab my lunch.

Before we started after the lunch break, Judge Jurevicius called us up to the bench. I noticed that she wasn't wearing the pearls.

"Gentlemen," she said. "I have reviewed the bench briefs submitted by Mr. Shepherd and Mr. Reddy and have concluded that the 120-hour rule does, in fact, apply in this case. I will be ruling accordingly to the jury and directing them that, as a matter of law, Pillars would not have received money as a result of Benjamin Trane's death."

"Judge, I would like the opportunity to file briefs on this," said Pompeo.

"You've made your argument, Mr. Pompeo, and it does not affect the clear application of the statute here. You're welcome to put your objection on the record. While you may not argue that Pillars would receive five million dollars as a result of Benjamin Trane's death, you are permitted to argue that Mr. Fleece thought that Pillars would receive five million dollars."

"If he shows that Mr. Fleece knew about the will?" I said.

"Exactly."

"But I don't—" Pompeo caught himself. "Thanks, Judge."

I waved to Danny. "Your Honor, we have a proposed limiting instruction for the jury on this issue if you would like to consider it."

"I would, thank you, Mr. Shepherd."

Danny handed a copy of the instruction he drafted the night before to Judge Jurevicius and then to Pompeo.

Judge Jurevicius glanced at it, then said, "Finally, I don't want half-cocked motions right now. If there are going to be motions for a mistrial or an amendment of the indictment or anything else like that, I want them in writing first thing tomorrow. In the meantime, we will finish out the day. Am I understood?"

We nodded.

"All right. Mr. Pompeo, are you prepared to proceed?"

"Yes, Your Honor. We are calling Scott Swayze, our cryptocurrency expert."

"Let's get him in here then."

~

CARREFOUR IS NOT EXACTLY a hub of international finance, but it has very competent professionals in all sorts of specialties. Scott Swayze was a financial planner and a former banker who had been on the cutting edge of cryptocurrency. Before this morning, he was going to be a big part of Pompeo's case, teaching the jury all about cryptocurrency and Bitcoin and how Theo Plutides' modest investment some years ago had exploded into five million dollars.

Now though, it didn't much matter. You could see that the wind was pulled entirely out of Pompeo's sails on this particular issue. Swayze got up there and explained what Bitcoin was, which I'm pretty sure was a waste of the jury's time. He did a good job, though, of walking the jury through the math, which in the end was pretty simple—Theo Plutides had bought one hundred Bitcoin in 2015 for $22,3310.00. On the day Benjamin Trane died, each one of those Bitcoins, which Plutides had bought for $223.31 a piece, was worth $52,173.50. That meant Benjamin Trane would have inherited $5,217,350.00. The luck and the sum were both staggering.

Pompeo did a good job of summarizing it in the end. He told Swayze that he, as a simple prosecutor, didn't understand how all this cryptocurrency worked but was it true that you could really cash that Bitcoin in for a value at or near five million dollars? Swayze told him that he could, day or night.

I stood. "Your Honor, perhaps in light of the arguments that have been presented to the jury, a limiting instruction regarding the Court's finding would be in order?"

Judge Jurevicius nodded. "It would. Members of the jury, you have heard argument from counsel that Pillars would have received a sum of approximately $5,217,350 on the date of Benjamin Trane's death. The Court has reviewed this matter and found that Pillars could not have inherited this sum from Benjamin Trane. Specifically, because Mr. Trane died within 120 hours of Mr. Plutides, Mr. Trane was not entitled to inherit from Mr. Plutides as a matter of law. You will disregard any argument that Pillars stood to profit from Mr. Trane's death as this is not true under the law. You may, however, consider any evidence that Mr. Fleece believed that Pillars could profit from Mr. Trane's death at the time he was killed."

"You may question the witness, Mr. Shepherd," said Judge Jurevicius.

"Mr. Swayze, you don't have any evidence that Mr. Fleece knew about this Bitcoin account or the value of it, do you?"

"No, I don't."

"Are you aware that this money is not accessible to anyone right now?"

"I was not aware of that, no."

"Yes, the cold wallet containing the keys to the Bitcoin account was destroyed."

Mr. Swayze nodded. "That's unfortunate but if the recovery phrase of BIP39 words is used, the money can still be recovered."

"It's my understanding that the recovery phrase can't be located either."

Scott Swayze grew solemn. "Then I'm afraid no one will be getting access to those funds."

"Thanks, Mr. Swayze."

That was the last we spoke about Bitcoin at the trial.

65

It was almost three o'clock when Dawn Blackwell entered the courtroom. It took me a moment to figure out what looked different about her, and then I realized she didn't have a big binder in her arms. She wore a dark blue suit and strode up the aisle in a way that was familiar—purposeful, swift, and determined. As she passed me, I saw a second figure slip through the door and take a seat in the back row opposite Manny Amaltheakis.

Mrs. Horvath.

I suppressed my irritation that she was there and turned my attention to Dawn Blackwell as she planted herself in the witness chair. Before Pompeo could say anything, she turned to Judge Jurevicius and said, "Will we be done by five, Judge?"

Judge Jurevicius looked up. "I don't know how long your examination will take Ms. Blackwell, but I hope to be."

"Can we make sure? My day care closes at six."

"There's no one else?"

"No. Just me. And I didn't fill out the forms for someone to stay later."

"Very well. I can't say how long your examination will take, but if it needs to continue, we can break and bring you back tomorrow. Is that acceptable to counsel?"

Pompeo was smart enough not to complain about that accommodation. "That's fine with me, Judge, but I don't think it will be necessary. We can get Ms. Blackwell out of here by five."

When I nodded, Judge Jurevicius said, "Very well. Proceed, Mr. Pompeo."

"Could you state your name, please?"

"Dawn Blackwell."

"You are the chief financial officer of Pillars Outreach of Carrefour, aren't you?"

"I am."

"You are not here voluntarily today, are you?"

"I drove myself, if that's what you're asking."

"No, what I meant was, I subpoenaed you to be here today, didn't I?"

"You did. While I was holding my daughter's hand in the Pillars parking lot, so thank you for that."

Pompeo took her through her qualifications—an accounting degree from LGL University, passed the CPA exam on the first attempt, then worked in a couple of local companies before coming on board at Pillars.

"Why did you go to Pillars?"

"Because I believe in its mission."

"Which is?"

"Support for all."

Pompeo turned to the judge. "Judge, given Ms. Blackwell's long relationship with Pillars, I'd like permission to lead."

I stood. Judge Jurevicius waved me back down. "Granted, Mr. Pompeo."

"Ms. Blackwell, Pillars maintains a number of outreach programs, doesn't it?"

"It does."

"This includes meal service, ride service to medical appointments, independent living visits, and a food pantry, right?"

"That's right."

"It provides on-site seven-day a week childcare?"

"Yes."

"Incidentally, is that where your daughter is today?"

"It is."

"Pillars is also seeking to expand the services it provides, isn't it?"

"It is."

"You mentioned that your daughter's day care closes at six today. Is one of the expansions to provide twenty-four-hour daycare?"

"Second and third shift workers need childcare too."

"Especially single parents?"

"Any parent who works has childcare provided by a spouse or someone outside the home."

"Pillars has a monthly mobile clinic?"

"That's right."

"It's run by Dr. Carissa Fleece?"

"Carissa Carson-Fleece, yes."

"That's Edgerton Fleece's wife?"

"Yes."

"Those programs all take money, don't they?"

"Obviously."

"How does Pillars raise money to provide these services?"

"A few ways."

"Such as?"

"We apply for grant funding whenever we can. We receive contributions from local churches and charities. We also receive monetary contributions from those churches and charities to fund specific projects such as the proposed healthcare clinic or childcare expansion."

"Do you also receive bequests from wills?"

"We do."

"Are they substantial?"

"Any gift is important."

"Have you ever received a gift in a will of five million dollars before?"

"No. And it is my understanding that we haven't received one now."

Pompeo put his hands on his hips. "Ms. Blackwell, did people at Pillars know that Benjamin Trane had inherited a car from Theo Plutides?"

Dawn nodded. "He was very excited about the car. He told all of us at Theo's funeral."

"What about the money? Did people know about that?"

"He mentioned he was getting a little money. He never mentioned five million dollars, I don't think he knew it was that much. He mostly talked about the car."

"You said 'he told all of us' about the car at Theo's funeral. Does that include Edgerton Fleece?"

Dawn shifted in her seat, glanced at Edge, then said, "I can't say what Edge heard."

"Of course you can't. Ms. Blackwell, how is Pillars structured?"

"It's a charitable corporation. Edge started the company as a vehicle for people to help others and eventually set up a board of directors."

"Edgerton Fleece is the CEO?"

"Yes."

"You're in charge of the financials of the company?"

"I keep track of things."

"Let's go through them then."

Pompeo spent the next forty-five minutes going through the Pillars financials. He went through annual statements and monthly statements and tax returns and financial proposals, picking and choosing items that highlighted how Pillars was operating at a deficit and that the number had been growing each year.

"So Pillars was in the red early this year?" said Pompeo.

"That's what operating at a deficit means." Dawn Blackwell rolled her eyes and continued. "Listen, is all this necessary?"

"What do you mean?"

"Yes, Pillars was operating at a loss—our community is filled with needs, and we try to fill them. Yes, we could have used five million dollars, who wouldn't? But no, Pillars hasn't received five million dollars as a result of Benjamin Trane's death and Edge certainly didn't kill him for it. Can I go pick up my daughter now?"

"Not yet, Ms. Blackwell. Thank you for your patience. You weren't with Mr. Fleece that night, were you?"

"No, I was not."

"You weren't driving one of those Pillars vans, were you?"

"No."

"But you have worked with Edgerton Fleece for a long time, haven't you?"

"I have."

"You believe Mr. Shepherd when he says Edgerton Fleece isn't guilty, don't you?"

"Of course."

"But your organization might collapse if it doesn't receive an infusion of capital like the one Benjamin Trane's death might have provided if it had happened just a few hours later, right?"

Dawn Blackwell raised her chin. The circles under her eyes looked darker than when she'd entered the courtroom, as though the weight of the numbers from the last hour had exhausted her even more. "It might."

"And if Pillars collapses, a number of people will lose its services, true?"

"True."

"Including you?"

"Yes."

"You said, you've known Mr. Fleece a long time?"

"Yes. Several times."

"Would you say he would do anything to help people?"

"Yes. That's what he does."

"And that he would do anything to save Pillars."

"Yes, I mean, anything within reason. Not murder, of course."

"Of course. No further questions."

I stood. "Ms. Blackwell, I have a couple of questions, but we'll be able to get you out of here in time to pick up your daughter."

"Thank you."

"Pillars has been operating at a deficit for the last few years, right?"

"That's right."

"And it's been able to survive?"

"Yes. It's difficult at times but it has been for everybody."

"And I know you said this, but just so the jury is clear, so far, Pillars has not received the five million dollars from the estate of Benjamin Trane, right?"

"It has not, that's right."

"Okay. Last topic. In your role as the accountant for Pillars, do you pay certain expenses for the organization?"

"I do."

"Does that include traffic tickets that are incurred by Pillars vehicles?"

"It does when the tickets are issued by traffic light cameras."

"Will you explain that to me, please?"

"Sure. If a Pillars vehicle runs a red light or is caught on a speed camera, the ticket comes to Pillars headquarters because that's who the vehicle is registered to. I pay the ticket and then charge it back to whoever was driving."

"Ms. Blackwell, I'm going to hand you what's been marked as Defendant's Exhibit 4. Can you identify that for me, please?"

"Sure. It was a ticket issued to one of our Pillars vans the night of February 17."

"Where was the ticket issued?"

"At the traffic light at the intersection of Sunnyfield and Coulter. It was for running a red light."

"And what was the time on the ticket?"

"Six twenty-five p.m."

"And that was approximately half a mile from the scene of the accident here?"

"I don't know. If you say so."

"So you paid this ticket for Pillars?"

"I did."

"Did you then charge it back to the driver?"

"I tried, but I was unable to."

"How do you mean?"

"I checked our vehicle log and was unable to identify a driver."

I popped the vehicle log up on the screen. "So the ticket was issued for this van right here?" I pointed to the column for Van Number 5.

"That's right. You can see that no driver is logged in after two p.m., so I didn't know who drove it."

"Did you investigate any further?"

"For a one-hundred-dollar ticket? No. I put it into the general expenses."

"By the way, just so the jury is clear, Van Number 5 is not Edgerton Fleece's van, is it?"

"No, that would be Van Number 1, in that column over there."

"And to your knowledge Van Number 5 was not damaged and has not had any repair work done?"

"Not that I've approved, no."

"No further questions."

Pompeo stood and I could see him think. He knew the ticket showed a Pillars van in the area of the accident, knew that it wasn't Edge's van, and knew that it had to be one of the two Pillars vans on the Alert Shield video. Which meant that I only had to prove the existence of one more van in the area that wasn't Edge's to make the hypothetical I'd given Pearson true. Questioning Dawn Blackwell about the ticket would just emphasize that to the jury.

Pompeo came to the same decision I would have.

"No more questions for me, Judge," he said.

"That will be it for the day, then," said Judge Jurevicius. "Ms. Blackwell, I think we have you out on time." Then she banged the gavel and sent us home.

66

As the courtroom cleared, Pompeo caught my eye. I asked Edge to wait for me and stepped over to talk to Pompeo. We moved a little farther away before he said, "You are one sand-bagging motherfucker."

I shrugged. "I thought you knew."

"Oh, bullshit. You were just waiting for me to commit myself. Nice play."

I shrugged again.

"Listen, I still think I have him dead on vehicular homicide and I think I can still prove intent with all of the other stuff he did, but I'll take a look at everything tonight and let you know where my head's at tomorrow."

"We'll do the same," I said. "I think your representations were enough for a mistrial."

Pompeo waved. "Hardly."

"And a dismissal would get you to Put-in-Bay."

"That's the best argument you've made this whole trial, but no. In the a.m., then." Pompeo scooped up his iPad and left.

Mrs. Horvath came up to me from the gallery the moment

he stepped away. "Mr. Shepherd, can I borrow the Fleeces for a moment?"

I waved and kept packing. "Sure, Mrs. Horvath."

"Is there somewhere private I may speak with them?"

I looked up. "Why?"

"We've had another issue come up with our company financing that I need to speak with them about right away."

"Do you want to go back to my office?"

"I'd rather talk to them now."

Edge was looking at Mrs. Horvath curiously while Carissa scrolled through her phone.

I snapped my trial case shut. "Follow me. Danny, I'll meet you back at the office."

We left the courtroom and walked down the hall to the Wellness Room that had been installed during the last renovation. It was intended for breast-feeding or resting or meditating, none of which was going on right then. It was also the only room that wasn't about to be locked up by judges' bailiffs anxious to get home for the evening. I opened the door and let the three of them pass and was about to follow them in when Mrs. Horvath stopped and turned.

"I really need to speak with them alone, Mr. Shepherd," she said.

I was not a fan of anyone speaking to my clients alone in a courthouse. "Why?"

"This is a matter related to Pillars' financing of the health clinic and you've made it very clear that you're not the company's attorney on that matter."

"It really can't wait until you get back to your office?"

Mrs. Horvath's meticulously styled hair did not move as she shook her head. "I'm afraid it needs to be acted upon right away. Thank you, Mr. Shepherd." And she closed the door.

I considered leaving, but I could see the courtrooms being

locked one by one as staff went home for the night so I figured I would have to stay until they were done to keep them from getting kicked out or locked in. I took a seat on one of the benches in the hallway, opened my phone, and began to catch up on emails I'd missed during the trial that day.

It had been about ten minutes when I heard a door rattling, followed by a curse. I looked up to see Dawn Blackwell trying, and failing, to open the locked door to Judge Jurevicius's courtroom.

I stood. "Dawn? Down here."

She saw me, put her head down, and hustled down the hall. She had both arms around her binder, which had returned, and her long green coat was spotted with rain.

"What are you doing back?"

"Where are they?" said Dawn.

"Right here." I opened the door and said, "Dawn's here," as she barreled in.

There was one small table with four chairs in the room. Edge and Carissa looked up, serious.

Mrs. Horvath smiled. "Good, you brought the financials. Here, take my seat," she said as she stood. "I'll leave the three of you to it. Let me know what you decide and I'll see to it."

Mrs. Horvath walked out, taking my arm for support, and guided me away as she shut the door. "Thank you so much, Mr. Shepherd. I have some other things to take care of. Can you make sure they get out okay?"

I stared at the woman who was unflappably managing a charitable emergency in the middle of a murder trial and decided I really needed to rethink the whole not hiring an administrative assistant thing. Then I said, "Of course."

Mrs. Horvath smiled and patted my arm. "You are a dear. And really quite brilliant today. Thank you."

"Don't thank me yet."

"A good job is a good job no matter how things turn out."

I smiled. "I don't necessarily find that to be reassuring."

"You should," she said. "See you soon." Then she hustled off to the elevator.

I shook my head and resumed my place on the bench.

An officer wandered by a little while later saying he needed to lock up. I told him we had a wellness emergency and asked if we could have a little more time. He recognized me from the trial and said he could give me fifteen more minutes. Ten minutes later, the door to the wellness room opened and Dawn Blackwell hurried out. She had both arms wrapped around the binder, tight, like a child, and her head was lowered as she hustled past me in that particular high-heeled run of a woman in a hurry.

She was also crying.

Edge and Carissa walked out then. I looked from them to a retreating Dawn Blackwell and back.

"Is everything all right?"

"Yes," said Edge.

"I don't know," said Carissa.

Edge put a hand on Carissa's arm. "We had a development with the health clinic and childcare financing that needed Dawn's input. Unfortunately, we've now made her late to pick up Dana. I think between the financing and the rush after testifying today, it was all just a little too much."

"Don't give me any detail but did you figure it out? The financing thing?"

"I think so." Edge put his wife's hand into his arm then put his own over it. "Do you need me any more tonight, Nate? I have to say I'm a bit tired."

"No, of course you are. Go home and get some rest. We'll be back at it tomorrow."

Carissa shifted from looking at Edge to me. With her full

diagnostic stare, Dr. Carissa Carson-Fleece said, "We had a good day today, didn't we?"

"We did."

"Is there a chance we can win?"

"Of course."

"How much?"

I thought. "We made a lot of headway today. We knocked the legs out from under their motive theory today and I'm going to go after the two vans when it's our turn to put on evidence."

"Can you give me a percentage?"

"No."

"Better than even?"

There was no way that Dr. Carissa Carson-Fleece told her patients what their odds of a cure were and here she was asking me for the same opinion. My hesitation and my expression must have told her what I was thinking because she said, "I understand, it's just an educated guess. Please."

It seemed as if Carissa was trying to peer through me like an x-ray machine.

Against my better judgment, I said, "Yes. Better than even. By a good bit."

She nodded thanks, then pulled on Edge's arm and said, "Let's get you home."

"No shift tonight?" he said.

"No shift."

The security officer came around again, and we all agreed to be hustled out so he could get home for the meatloaf his wife had just pulled out of the oven. We left the courthouse, three of the last ones by the look of the parking lot, then the Fleeces went to their car and I went to mine and I headed for the office.

When I arrived, I went to Danny's office. He looked up, weary, and said, "I thought I'd lost you."

I sighed and sat. “Our clients had a meeting. So how do you think the jury took the motive evidence today?”

Danny nodded. “I think they understood it. You could see some of them scowling at Pearson and Pompeo when it came out. Now, explain this two-van business you were talking about with Pearson today.”

“Okay. You know the original Alert Shield video showed two Pillars minivans in the area of the accident?”

“Right.”

“And that’s what led Pearson to check the body shops and find Edge’s van.”

“Yes.”

“The police have always assumed that one of those vans belonged to Edge.”

Danny nodded. “So if we can prove that neither of those two vans was the one that Edge was driving, we have doubt.”

“Exactly. On the vehicle log, Edge’s van is Van Number 1.”

“Okay.”

“The traffic light ticket we entered into evidence with Dawn was for Van Number 5.”

“So that eliminates one. Can we really prove that the other one wasn’t Edge either?”

“Yep.” I told him about the new Alert Shield video Olivia had found, the one with Carissa Carson-Fleece in the passenger seat.

“And that wasn’t Edge’s van?” Danny asked.

“No. It was Van Number 6.”

“Who was driving?”

“Greg Kilbane.”

Danny’s eyes widened. “Carissa was with Kilbane? But I thought they weren’t...”

I raised a hand. “I don’t know why they were together, but they were. If we need to, we can call Greg to say he was driving —that way we still won’t have to put Carissa on the stand. But the judge has already ruled that any video produced in response to Pearson's request to the Alert Shield network is admissible."

Danny worked through it. "So we have an undamaged van that got a traffic ticket and a second undamaged van with Greg and Carissa in it."

I nodded. "Which means neither of the vehicles in the original Alert Shield video were Edge. Combine that with Pompeo screwing up the motive evidence..."

Danny nodded. "Sounds like reasonable doubt to me. Speaking of screwing up motive evidence, I did some research while I was waiting—it's not clear if we'd win but we should move for a mistrial based on Pompeo's inaccurate statements about Pillars getting the money."

I nodded. "Draft one up. I'm supposed to talk to Pompeo before we start tomorrow. Let's see if he dismisses or amends. If he doesn't, we'll move for the mistrial."

"Even if it's denied, I think we can win anyway."

I knocked on the desk. "Today was a good day."

I was still keyed up, but fatigue was nibbling at the edges of my adrenaline wall. I made it for another four hours or so at the office, then decided to head home early and get some rest before the next day's testimony. I made something bland, ate it without thinking, and was in bed within forty minutes.

I WOKE up at 3:00 a.m. but it wasn't Roxie this time. It was me. A piece of the day's testimony had finally wormed its way through my subconscious to the surface.

I went to my computer. I pulled up the document I was looking for and it said what I had remembered. Then I researched one other thing, and that made sense too.

I was pretty sure I was right, but I still needed to double check it.

I couldn't call anyone about it, not at this hour and maybe for longer than that, so I went back to bed. I didn't worry about writing it down before I fell back asleep.

I knew I'd remember.

67

When I arrived at court the next morning, Ryan Pompeo was sitting on a bench in the hallway waiting for me.

"NATO!" he said. "Have a seat."

I went over, dropped my trial case, and sat.

Pompeo was slouched back, his legs crossed, jacket open. "So me and my girl have a place over at Put-in-Bay. Actually, her family gave it to her as an early wedding present and we'll both own it next year but that's beside the point. You ever go out there?"

"Put-in-Bay? It's been a while. I'm more of a northern lakes guy."

"Well, it's a bitch of a drive to our marina and even worse on a Friday afternoon."

"I'm sure."

"And then you still have the boat trip over after that."

"Sounds like quite the haul."

"Bah, her family's from Cleveland so you have to make compromises sometimes. Anyway, here we are at the end of August, and I would much rather wring the last bit of summer out of that place than spend another week cooped up here with you."

"Every job has a sacrifice."

"I suppose they do. But needless sacrifice? That's just stupid. So I have a deal for you."

"What do you mean?"

"A plea deal, NATO. Keep up."

I leaned forward to stand up. "We're not pleading to murder, Ryan."

"That's why I am not offering it. Vehicular homicide with a negligence stipulation and a second-degree felony failure to stop at an accident. We'll recommend the minimum for both, served concurrently. Your client would be looking at two years."

I stared at Pompeo. His offer made no sense.

"That's less than what you offered back when this all started."

"Things change."

"You know you've lost motive. Why don't you just dismiss?"

Pompeo smiled and shook his head. "Now is that the kind of attitude to take with someone who's trying to free up the end of your summer?"

"You can't make your burden."

"On murder? Maybe, maybe not. But on aggravated vehicular homicide for a guy with a bloody van who was trying to hide it? No sweat."

"I don't think so."

"No matter what you think of it, you're obliged to take my offer to your client. I'll wait."

I checked my phone. "It's about time to start."

"The judge will wait. I will too, right here. The offer stands until I walk through that door." Then he slouched a little more and started scrolling through his phone.

I stared at him for a moment, picked up my case, and went

into the courtroom. The usual crowd was there—Manny Amaltheakis in the back row, Danny, Carissa, and Edge all sitting at the counsel table.

Danny stood as I approached. "What's going on?" he whispered.

"A last-minute offer from Pompeo. We'll reject it and then get going."

Danny nodded as I bent down and whispered to Edge and Carissa, "The prosecutor has offered another plea deal that I am technically required to present to you—"

"We'll take it," said Edge.

Carissa grabbed his leg. "What is it?" she said.

Edge glanced at her, then said, "Right, what is it?"

I stared at Carissa. She stared back.

I straightened and walked over to where Bailiff Fields was typing away on the computer. "Mickey, I'm going to need a few minutes—"

Bailiff Fields never stopped typing as she said, "Pompeo told us. The judge said take all the time you need. The Wellness Room is open."

I motioned for Edge and Carissa to follow me and they did, with Danny bringing up the rear. Manny Amaltheakis adjusted his white pocket square as we walked by.

I wasn't crazy about walking past Pompeo, but he kept his head down, flipping through his phone.

We entered the Wellness Room with its short couch, small round table, and four plastic chairs. No one sat.

"What's going on?" I said.

"You were going to tell us about the prosecutor's offer," said Edge.

"You already said you would take it."

"What is the offer, Nate?" said Carissa.

"Vehicular homicide, which means you admit you negligently caused the accident, with an F2 level failure to stop at an accident, which means that you failed to stop after an accident when you knew the accident had resulted in death. He'll recommend the minimum sentences which would be six months for the vehicular homicide and two years for the failure to stop."

Edge looked at Carissa, shook his head, and said, "That's not what—"

Carissa put her hand on Edge's arm and said, "The testimony was that Mr. Trane died *after* the accident. Edge couldn't have known that there was a death if it hadn't happened yet."

I nodded. "Failure to stop for an accident that ultimately results in death is a third-degree felony."

"And what's the sentence for that?"

"A minimum of one year."

Carissa turned to Edge and nodded.

Edge said, "Tell Pompeo that we would accept a plea deal for vehicular homicide with a year for failure to stop so long as he recommends the minimum sentences."

"You mean *you* would accept that deal?"

"That's what I said."

"No, it's not. You said *we* will accept. You're the one who'll be going to jail, Edge. For at least a year."

He took Carissa's hand. "I understand," he said.

I looked around the room. Silence. Then I jerked my thumb and said, "Everyone out. Except you, Edge."

Carissa didn't budge. "You can't make me leave."

"I'm going to confer with my client."

"You have to convey our counteroffer to Prosecutor Pompeo."

"I do. But I won't until I have an opportunity to confidentially confer with my client."

Carissa stared at me. I sat down at the table and crossed my legs. Carissa looked down at me and crossed her arms.

Edge laughed. "Look at all these people trying to protect me.

I've never felt safer." He gave Carissa a kiss on the cheek and sat down. "Go. I'll be out in a minute."

I didn't have to say anything to Danny. He followed her. As soon as the door snicked shut, I said, "What's going on?"

"What do you mean?"

"You were going to accept the offer before I even told you what it was."

"And it's a good thing I didn't because then we wouldn't be making this counter."

"Why plead at all? We can win!"

"Oh?" It was Edge's turn to lean back in his chair and cross his legs. "Can you guarantee that for me, Nate?"

"No, but you heard the evidence—we have a really good chance of winning this case."

"Which, if I understand all the arguments that you've been making this week, means that there is also a chance I'm going away for fifteen to life."

"But the likelihood is that you're not."

"I've had a good teacher this week, so let me ask you how he would—Mr. Shepherd, there is a chance that I could be convicted and get a sentence of fifteen years to life, isn't there?"

"Yes, but—"

"And if I make this deal, I'll be out in a year, true?"

"Yes, but—"

"Nate, I think you made the very fine point just a moment ago that I'm the one who will be serving the time, aren't I?"

"Of course."

"So I'm the only one who can weigh the certainty of one year versus the risk of life."

I leaned forward. "Edge. We can win."

Edge gave me a smile that was calm and peaceful. "And we could lose, Nate. Make the offer."

"I don't recommend it."

"I understand that. Please make it anyway."

I thought of one more tack. "Won't this hurt Pillars?"

"The sooner this is resolved, the sooner Pillars will recover."

"There's no way they'll ever let you be part of it again."

"Maybe not. No, probably not. But Pillars will survive the actions of one man."

I took my last shot. "We don't know each other well, Edge, but it seems to me that your whole life has been about helping others."

"I try."

"You're going to be admitting that you wouldn't stop to help Benjamin Trane."

Edge's smile didn't change, but his eyes flickered, and I thought I had him. Then he said, "I understand. Please go make the offer."

I stared at him. He didn't flinch, just waited. Finally, I said, "Do I have your permission to try to improve it?"

"As long as you don't lose it entirely. But I want to get this done so we can end this madness."

I stood.

"And if you don't mind, Nate?"

I looked at him.

"Please send Carissa back in. I'd like to wait with her."

I nodded and left. When I passed Carissa in the hall, I pointed at the door, and she went in. I went back to where Pompeo sat on the bench, toying with his phone. He didn't look up as he kept scrolling and said, "Well?"

"We can't accept your deal."

He kept scrolling. "What did you have in mind?"

"Two things. Drop the failure to stop to an F3 and recommend the minimum sentence so that my client serves a total of one year."

Pompeo smiled faintly. "I suppose I could make that work. What's the second?"

"My client enters an *Alford* plea."

Pompeo looked up now. "That's not—"

"That's not what?" I said.

Pompeo set his phone down. "That's not what I had been considering."

"It makes sense here. My client agrees to be found guilty without admitting he committed the crime."

"It has the same effect as a guilty plea, you know."

"I do."

"So it doesn't really matter."

"It matters to me. And to him."

"You know they don't even allow *Alford* pleas in some states?"

"I guess we're lucky to be in Ohio."

Pompeo stared at me for a moment, then checked his phone. "It's seventy-six degrees already at the Bay." He held out his hand. "Done."

I shook it, and we went to tell the judge.

JUDGE JUREVICIUS MET us in chambers first. She had accepted many plea deals in her young career so I could see her increased confidence in managing that process, all of which evaporated when we brought up the *Alford* plea. I suggested that Judge Gallon might have the forms and a quick call by Judge Jurevicius confirmed that she did. When Pompeo told Judge Jurevicius his sentencing recommendation, the judge said that she was inclined to agree so long as everything checked out in the sentencing report.

Because we had a jury seated, Judge Jurevicius wanted the plea agreement on the record before she let them go. She told

Bailiff Fields to order breakfast for the jury and tell them they would have to wait while the Court handled some issues. In the meantime, she downloaded the forms from Judge Gallon, and we put together a plea agreement that could be read into the record.

It took a while and included some back and forth with Edge. He was stoic about the whole thing until I explained what an *Alford* plea was.

"What?" he said.

"You agree to be found guilty without admitting you committed the crime," I said for the second time.

"The prosecutor agreed to that too?"

"Yes."

He clasped his hands together and looked down. "Thank you."

"Legally, it has the same effect as a guilty plea."

"But not to me," he said.

When we finally had everything put together, we went back into court. By that time, more people had shown up, including the folks from Pillars—Mrs. Horvath, Dawn Blackwell, and Greg Kilbane—who all sat in the front row with Carissa.

There are a lot of details that go into putting a plea bargain on the record, details that are boring to read if it's not your ass on the line and vitally crucial if it is. Essentially, Judge Jurevicius read what Edgerton Fleece was accused of, told him the effect his plea would have, and asked him a long series of questions which were the legal equivalent of, "Are you sure?"

Edge never blinked. He was.

Judge Jurevicius then ordered an officer to take Edge to the electronic monitoring office. Carissa, Mrs. Horvath, Dawn Blackwell, and Greg Kilbane followed. Manny Amaltheakis gave me a look, then left.

Judge Jurevicius then told Mickey Fields to bring the jury

back. After a five-minute delay while they finished their food, the jury filed in, clearly curious about what was going on. Judge Jurevicius thanked them for their patience and told them that a plea agreement had been reached. Juror Number Four gasped, put her hand to her mouth, and looked at me with an accusation that I could feel across the room.

It hurt.

Most of the rest of them looked relieved to have their Friday back and were out the door as soon as the judge had discharged them with thanks for their service. With that, Judge Jurevicius grabbed the handle of her gavel, let it go, then said, "Thank you, gentlemen. Court is adjourned."

We gathered our things. Pompeo was done first, as usual, since all he had to do was slip his iPad into his case. He came over and offered his hand.

"See you next time, Shepherd," he said.

I waved at the empty courtroom. "It's over now," I said. "Why'd you do the deal?"

Pompeo grinned. "I told you, I love Put-in-Bay." He walked away but stopped at the swinging gate. "And I hate to lose." Then he left.

As I picked up my things, Mickey Fields looked at me from behind her desk. "He's not wrong," she said and went back to typing.

PART VI

BUCKLE

68

Danny and I talked for a moment in the parking lot, then split up to head back to the office. As I walked to my Jeep, I saw a group at the other end—Greg Kilbane, Mrs. Horvath, and Dawn Blackwell. The three of them broke up as I watched them get into separate cars—Greg Kilbane into a Pillars minivan, Mrs. Horvath into a Chevy Impala, and Dawn Blackwell into her white Kia Sportage. Greg Kilbane talked on the phone, Mrs. Horvath waved, and Dawn Blackwell fiddled with her radio as they passed.

The three cars stopped in line at the pay gate, giving me a clear view of each of their license plates. As the three vehicles left, one by one, I wondered whether we would have had a trial at all if the original Alert Shield video had given us a clear view of the license plates of the Pillars minivans on Sunnyfield Drive that night. I took a deep breath, making a conscious effort to turn off the case now that it was done, then climbed into my Jeep and headed back to the office.

~

I'VE OFTEN TOLD people that the mindset of preparing for trial isn't much different than getting ready for a football game—you prepare for weeks for a contest that you're trying to win, and someone is working just as hard on the other side to beat you. The contest will take place for all to see and if you want to avoid a very public embarrassment, you have to be disciplined and you have to work hard and you have to plan for every possible thing you can imagine that your opponent might throw at you.

The biggest difference between the two, though, besides the fact that courts frown upon tackling opposing counsel, is that you always know the football game will take place. You might win, you might lose, but you always get to play so there's no doubt that the weeks of preparation were worth it.

Settling a case during a trial is the worst because you've prepared for weeks, months even, and right as you're about to find out if you win or lose—nothing. Don't get me wrong, you only settle a case if that's what's best for your client so there's still a feeling that you've done your best job. But in the visceral part of you, in the part that drives you to step into the courtroom and try cases in the first place, you're left with a sudden emptiness and random adrenaline with nowhere to go.

It also apparently leads to long-winded introspection.

Danny and I were back in the office by noon. We found ourselves a little adrift as we set our trial cases and computers and exhibits on the conference room table with no real next task to take on.

Finally, Danny said, "What just happened?"

I shook my head. "I know. Edge said the risk was too much, that he couldn't risk fifteen to life when a year was on the table."

"But if that's what he wanted, we could have tried to plead out before all"—he waved at the piles on the conference table—"this."

"Preaching to the choir, man."

"Now, there's no way he can go back to Pillars, in any role."

"Charities don't normally make felons their CEOs, no."

"So why would he take the deal? I mean, service is his life's work. I don't understand how he could give that up without a fight."

I shook my head. Danny had far more exposure to Fleece than I did, but what he was saying was consistent with everything that I had seen. "I don't understand the other part of it either," I said.

"Which part?"

"Why Pompeo would make the deal. He had a murder charge pending, and he lets Fleece walk with a year? Something that supports ten, even five years I would understand, but a year?"

"You did raise a lot of doubt yesterday. And the deal still counts as a conviction on Pompeo's trial record."

"Going from murder to one year seems like a loss."

"But you'd have to look pretty close at the raw numbers to see it."

Danny and I stood there, staring at the table, at the piles of paper and files that represented a significant portion of the last few months of our lives.

"We should probably wait a month before we throw them in the shredder," I said. "Feel like lunch?"

Danny shifted. "If you don't mind, I told Jenny—"

I waved. "Go. Don't come back until Monday."

"Thanks for taking this on, Nate."

"I have to pay your exorbitant salary somehow."

"Anything else before I go?"

"No, that's it. Tell Jenny I said 'hi' and that—"

"Yeah, yeah, yeah, this was all my idea."

"Perfect. Have a good weekend."

As Danny left, I thought about what to do.

I texted Kira to find out her plans. She texted me back that she would be busy until late finishing preparations for the auction the next day. I asked if she minded if I stopped by tomorrow and she said Saturday wouldn't work but late Sunday would. I said perfect and let her be.

I sat there, adrift, then decided that, since I had the whole afternoon, I might as well go take my medicine.

CADE WAS WORKING behind the desk at the Brickhouse so instead of Olivia's amazement that I could roll my soft ass in there or offer to give me the new member tour, I got a grunt, a swipe of my card, and a terse, "You pled?"

"You heard already?"

"Word spreads. I thought you were winning?"

"It looked that way. Client made a risk decision."

"I assume you need a beer?"

I lifted my gym bag. "After this."

Cade nodded. "I'll meet you across the street at three."

"In two hours?"

Cade stared at me blankly. "You need at least that."

"Ah, there's the customer service I've come to know and love."

Cade stared.

"Right. See you at three."

IT WAS hot but not oppressive when Cade and I went across the street to the Railcar, so we grabbed a table out on the covered patio. I'm not saying that sitting in the shade listening to a creek and looking at the woods with a cold beer is better than sitting in a stuffy courtroom talking about dead bodies, but it's not a bad change of pace either.

"So why did he take it?" said Cade.

"Certainty of one year versus the risk of fifteen. That's what he said, anyway."

He grunted. "Risk calc makes sense."

"I have a feeling that you might view that year a little differently than Edgerton Fleece."

Cade shrugged. "A cage is a cage no matter the animal. If he chose it, he must think he can handle it."

I wasn't as sure, but Cade knew more about that end of the business than I did. We were a couple of beers in, and Cade was telling me about the ridiculous amount of money Molly made as a fitness influencer—because, of course—when Olivia showed up. We stood and rearranged the chairs so that all three of us had a view of the woods. She gave me a hug, confirmed with Cade that we had earned our beers across the street first, then sat down between us.

"No Dr. Brad?" I said.

"He's on call this weekend. Do I say congratulations?"

I shrugged. "I don't think so, but you know how it is."

Another round came, which included a vodka concoction for Olivia, and we clinked all the way around.

Olivia demanded a recap, and I gave her one, and she especially liked using Pearson to eliminate motive. "Were you going to use the Alert Shield video of Carissa in the van?"

I nodded. "During my case. And I used the traffic light ticket with Blackwell, so thanks for all the leg work."

She smiled. "It's my best feature."

"I didn't say it like that."

"No, I did." She took a sip. "It sounds like you had reasonable doubt."

"Maybe so," I said. I pointed outside with the top of my bottle. "But that's water past the Railcar now."

"I suppose it is."

That was about all I had to say about the case, so instead I asked, "So, what's up this weekend?"

It turned out Cade was supporting Molly at a fitness expo and Olivia had finally had enough of her Bronco breaking down, so she was going to shop for a new one instead of fixing the old one yet again.

Dr. Brad was on call and Kira was preparing for the Plutides auction and Molly was influencing, so the three of us stuck around for a while.

I CAME HOME, changed, started to fill Roxie's water bowl, then remembered she was at Kira's. That made the place seem a little emptier than it had as I grabbed a beer and plopped down on the couch and flipped around on TV until I found a show where four guys were forging swords out of car parts.

They were sorting through the junk looking for the parts with the best tensile strength (apparently old springs are a hot blacksmith commodity) when it hit me. I called Olivia.

"Hmm. I was not expecting a late-night call from you."

"Sorry."

"I didn't say I minded. What's up?"

I told her what I was thinking. I asked if it fit in with her plans.

She said, "I can do that."

"Thanks, Liv."

"Does it matter?"

"To me, I think."

"Then I'll take care of it."

A beep. "That's Brad. Talk to you later."

"Thanks."

As I hung up, the fatigue of the week finally caught up with me. I remember the second guy's sword breaking on a coconut before I fell asleep.

69

I waited until late in the day Sunday to go over to the Plutides house. There were a few cars and one truck in the circular drive when I arrived but overall it didn't seem too busy. The front door was open, so I walked in. I was amazed. The house was empty—all the rows of furniture, pieces of art, and boxes that I had grown used to were gone.

Which made the voice from the back of the house echo all the louder.

"Three weeks?" said a man's voice. "Just what the hell have you been doing all this time?"

"This house didn't clear itself, Rory," I heard Kira say.

"But it's clear now," said Rory Dennison. "So what's the holdup?"

"There's still some paperwork that needs to be done. Just talk to Manny, and he'll let you know—"

"He said we're waiting on you!"

"For the sale, Rory, not the closing paperwork."

"I'm closing on a place in Jackson Hole, so I need the money moving through this estate by next week. Get it done!"

"We will get it done but I just don't think it will be next week."

"File your shit with the court and get me my money! It's not that hard!"

Kira rounded the corner with a thin young man with overly long, overly floppy hair that fell into his eyes. He stopped, looked at me, and said, "What the hell do you want?"

I ignored him. "Excuse me, Ms. Freeman?"

Kira's mouth twitched. "Yes?"

"Another truck just arrived. They said they're looking for the douche canoe?"

She kept her face straight. "Tell them it's in the garage."

"They said they already checked there. They're wondering if it might be in the house?"

"Who keeps a canoe in the house?" said Rory Dennison. "No wonder this is taking so long." Then he stomped out.

Kira punched me, not in a playful aw-shucks kind of way, but a full out punch straight to the sternum. "You're going to get me fired."

"Too late. You already sold everything. Do you have some time?"

She sighed. "Not anymore. Looks like I'm going to have to scramble to get this all accounted for so we can have a hearing next week to distribute some assets." She smiled and looked a little tired. "There's a property in Jackson Hole to close on, you know."

"There's certainly a hole somewhere. Give me half an hour. It'll be worth it."

I could see she was curious now. "What?"

"Do you have your computer and the wallet?"

She straightened. "Do you have something to tell me?"

"I might."

We went into the kitchen where her laptop sat on the island.

She flipped it open. "Well?"

"Do you have a picture of the 'live-laugh-love' poem?"

"Sure. It sold during the online auction." She pulled it up. "But we already know that doesn't work."

"Humor me."

As she pulled up a picture, I said, "You're right, it's too great a coincidence that the recovery phrase is twenty-four words and this poem is twenty-four words. I was hung up on the recovery phrase part of it but then, Thursday, an expert said that the recovery phrase is twenty-four BIP39 words."

Kira looked up. "Wait, what's a BIP39 word?"

"Turns out these recovery phrases aren't made of just random words. All of the words are part of what's called a BIP39 word list—essentially, they're words that are approved to be part of the code."

"How does that help us?"

"Do you have a copy of the Plutides estate plan here?"

She tapped the top of her computer.

"Can you pull it up?"

She typed, then said, "Got it."

"Go to the inventory."

"I'm there."

"Go to the cash and currency section."

"Got it."

"Go to BIP39."

Kira looked at me and wondered how, in the name of a righteous supreme being, her brains had been replaced with the results of defecation.

"There was no context for it," I said. "I didn't catch it either, not even when the expert said it right to me. Not until later."

She clicked to the section labeled BIP39 which I had assumed was an account like a 401(k).

Kira's eyes darted back and forth, then she slouched. "There are no words there."

"No," I said. "Just three strings of numbers. I thought they were account numbers. Three sixteen-digit account numbers."

I looked over her shoulder as she stared at this:

BIP39—
10 08 04 05 21 15 07 01
23 24 12 22 17 03 06 16
14 09 20 02 19 11 13 18

Kira frowned. "Okay."

"Instead of three sixteen-digit account numbers, look at them instead as a series of two-digit numbers. What do you see?"

Kira's eyes widened. "The numbers 1 through 24. In a random order."

I smiled. "Let's enter the poem in this order and see."

Kira looked from the slate to the computer screen. "The first number is 10 so the first word we should enter is...'*wisdom*'." She grabbed the wallet and started hitting buttons. It took a while to get back to the first word and enter it. "The next number is 8 so we enter—"

"'*Father*'," I said.

It went faster then. "The next number is 4, so the word is—"

"'*Orphan*'."

We continued on like that—Kira looking at the number from the inventory, me giving her the word from the poem, then her hitting buttons on the wallet to spell it.

"Finally," she said, "the last number is 18."

"'*Music*'," I said.

She entered the word, then looked at me and said, "Here we

go." Kira pressed both buttons on the wallet to validate the sequence.

Success.

She tilted her head, then remembered out loud that the contents of the wallet would be shown on the computer screen. She clicked once, twice, a third time, then pulled up the account the wallet was linked to.

I looked over her shoulder. We stared.

"Well," I said.

70

We kept staring.

Finally, I said, "One hundred Bitcoin."

"Millions of dollars," said Kira.

We stared some more.

"That's portable, fungible currency, you know," said Kira.

I nodded. "Did you tell anybody about the poem?"

"No."

"There are a lot of people with access to the BIP39 code in the estate planning inventory."

Kira nodded. "And there are a lot of people with access to the poem. But not many with access to both."

"Well, we know nobody has figured it out yet."

"How?"

I pointed at the screen. "The money is still sitting there." I thought. "Does Manny know? He drafted the inventory."

Kira shook her head. "He doesn't know about the poem. That's the genius of Theo's little system."

"You know, I should tell you, there's a dispute over who this money goes to now." I told her about our day in court, the 120-

hour rule, and the agitation of various parties who may or may not be getting the money.

Kira's eyes widened as she said, "Then I don't like the idea of this information, and access to the money, just floating around." She frowned. "Technically, this new wallet wasn't Theo's property. What I have is knowledge." She thought, then nodded. "I'm going to give it directly to the Probate Court when we have the hearing to approve the sale and distribution of Theo's property."

I nodded. "That's probably safest. What are you going to do with the wallet in the meantime?"

Kira smiled. "You're thinking in old money terms."

"What do you mean?"

"The individual wallet isn't really what's necessary. Now that we've figured out the recovery phrase, we can access the currency from any wallet. I can store this wallet in the safe at our auction house or in our safe deposit box at the bank, but there's nothing that would prevent you or me from buying another wallet and accessing the cash."

I smiled. "And dropping the other one a postcard from Fiji."

"Fiji has extradition. I suggest the Maldives."

"I do look amazing in a sarong," I said, and ignored my concern that she had a working knowledge of extradition treaties.

Kira turned and looked at me full on and said, "Nate, we are literally walking around with millions of dollars in cash until this is taken care of."

"I get it."

"We have to trust each other."

There was no way I was skipping the country to a tropical island with millions of dollars, but I realized that Kira had only known me for a few months so she might not be sure.

And, of course, I didn't know her that well either.

"I trust you, Kira. We'll keep this to ourselves until you go to probate court. Can you use the hearing you were just telling Dennison about?"

She nodded. "I'll include 'wallets' in the list of items I'm accounting for to the Court but leave the cash amount blank. I'll tell the Court what we found at the hearing."

I nodded. "That should give you cover so that the money gets in the right hands. Want me to grab some takeout?"

"I'm tempted but I'm still going to have people in and out of here for a few hours yet. I'm sorry this is so hectic."

"Trial lawyer, remember?"

"Thanks." She put her hands on my cheeks and pulled me down for a kiss. "Could you watch Roxie for a few days?"

"Of course. I should've volunteered yesterday."

She took a key off a ring and gave it to me. "Just leave it on the kitchen table. Oh, and ignore the suitcase I have packed. I'm going up to Harbor Springs tomorrow."

"Not the Maldives?"

"Not as far as you know."

"I'll see you in a few days."

"I'll call you from a burner phone when my plane lands."

I decided she was mostly joking, gave her another kiss, and went to get Roxie.

71

The probate court hearing to approve the distribution of the assets of Theo Plutides was scheduled for that Thursday. The day before, Danny walked into my office, head down.

"What's the matter?"

"I just sent the last of the estate plans to new counsel. Martel convinced just about all of them to go with a new firm."

"We'll get more."

"Do you think?"

"For sure."

"Martel's referrals just really jump-started my practice."

Danny really seemed down about the whole thing, so I said, "You're perfect with these clients. I've watched you—you're patient, you explain things well, and you're good at figuring out the complex stuff. Don't worry."

"Thanks, Nate. It's just so frustrating. Even my own church referred an estate plan somewhere else this week. To Manny Amaltheakis, of all people."

That caught my attention. "What do you mean?"

"I mean there was an older couple in our church who volunteers at the Pillars food pantry and our pastor referred them to Manny Amaltheakis to do their will."

"Maybe your pastor has always referred people to him?"

Danny didn't look convinced. "Maybe. But I don't remember hearing Manny's name before this case."

"Just let him know, your pastor I mean, that you're doing that kind of work now too. You're too good a lawyer, too good a man, to not get referrals. And this time, when you've built your practice, you won't owe anybody."

Danny nodded. "Thanks, Nate. You've been super patient."

"You're welcome. And if it doesn't work out, there's always murder."

"You're a prince."

72

The next day at promptly nine a.m., Danny and I went to the Carrefour Probate Court for a hearing on the estate of Theo Plutides. Probate court is different than the common pleas court where we try criminal cases—it handles things like estates and guardianships and adoptions, and it generally moves at a decidedly slower pace. Today, though, the courtroom was filled, which lets you know just how many people had an interest in the way Theo's money was going to be distributed.

The hearing was public, so we didn't need a reason to be there, but I went in case Kira needed anything from me on the cold wallet and Danny went because he knew the most about the probate process and was curious to see what happened with such a big estate. Manny Amaltheakis was running the show as the estate lawyer and Rory Dennison was sitting next to him as the executor, his hair floppy as ever. Kira was sitting toward the front and gave me a little wave. Mrs. Horvath sat in the middle of a crowded row and smiled and nodded when she saw me. The rows were filled with people, but I didn't recognize any of the rest of them.

As Danny and I sat, I noticed another man on the far side, hair slicked back, wearing an expensive gray suit. He glanced at us and looked away.

"Spencer Martel," said Danny.

"Turd," I said.

Danny smiled. Court wasn't in session yet, but he spoke softly anyway. "The main purpose of this hearing today is for the Court to start approving the distribution of assets. The cash account transfers will all be approved, then Manny will present Kira's sale of the physical assets and approve those distributions."

"That'll take forever."

"They submitted most of it in writing ahead of time. They're primarily here to answer any questions from the Court."

My phone buzzed, which was of course frowned upon. I reached down to silence it and saw a text from Kira.

It was the palm tree emoji, the one with a little sand and water around it.

The bailiff told us to rise as Judge Wayne Stackhouse entered the courtroom.

"*Too late*," I texted back.

Judge Stackhouse was a heavier guy in his early sixties with a reddish face and puffy cheeks. I knew he'd been Carrefour's only probate judge for at least twenty years but little else. He settled into his seat and said, "Good morning, Mr. Amaltheakis."

Manny Amaltheakis stood. "Good morning, Your Honor."

"We're here this morning for the approval of administration of certain assets of the Estate of Theo Plutides, Case Number 202P—2196." Judge Stackhouse put his hand on a stack of papers that was easily a foot high and said, "Counsel may assume that the Court has reviewed the inventory and disclosures. Counsel may further assume that the Court's wife was irritated that it occupied the Court's attention late into the last two evenings. Is there a reason we are looking to expedite this matter?"

"Your Honor," said Manny Amaltheakis, "Mr. Plutides died six months ago and very little has been moved through his estate. His heirs and beneficiaries have requested that we move things along.

Judge Stackhouse nodded. "Meaning they've spent the money already?"

Rory Dennison straightened and scowled.

Manny Amaltheakis didn't blink. "There are some very worthy charities that could use the bequests, Your Honor, so if there was anything we could do to expedite that process, we were happy to."

"I see. Well, then why don't you guide me through it."

"Certainly, Your Honor. We can start with the disposal of the physical assets because that will be added to the pool of cash and securities that then fund a variety of Mr. Plutides' bequests."

Judge Stackhouse waved a hand and Manny Amaltheakis gestured at Kira. "The estate engaged Northwest Auction to assemble and liquidate assets here and in other states. Kira Freeman managed the effort and can summarize it for the Court."

Judge Stackhouse pulled a binder off the pile, opened it, and made a motion to proceed.

Kira stood up and joined Manny at the table. She ran through a general overview, then said, "We have disposed of three homes, Your Honor, one in Carrefour, Ohio, one in Harbor Springs, Michigan, and one in Sanibel Island, Florida. Those sales have all now been closed, and you can see the schedules for the net sales proceeds for each."

"I see them, Ms. Freeman. The Court approves those sales and the addition of the net funds to the estate."

"We also held auctions for the contents of each home and

the physical property of Mr. Plutides. You can see the items sold thus far, which is most of them, along with a backup appraisal for specialty items such as artwork or vehicles."

"The Court has reviewed the schedule and approves it," said Judge Stackhouse.

"The market for artwork is more fluid, Your Honor, so there were several pieces which we did not receive sufficient opening bids for. We've retained those items and are continuing to look for buyers."

"Understood, Ms. Freeman. Approved."

Kira led Judge Stackhouse through specific categories of assets that she had sold and, without even seeing the lists, I was amazed by the sheer volume of things she had moved and the broad range they covered. Her traveling around all the time suddenly made a lot more sense; I was surprised I had been able to see her at all.

It took the better part of an hour, and, with each approval, Rory Dennison would scowl or wince or shake his head, especially when Kira would say the amount she received. Finally, after a particularly loud sigh, Judge Stackhouse said, "Is there something you'd like to say, Mr. Dennison?"

"She should have gotten more."

"For which thing?"

"For all of it."

Judge Stackhouse's bored air vanished, and he focused completely on Rory Dennison. "Do you have any competing appraisals to present to the Court today, Mr. Dennison?"

"No."

"Did you assist in the sale or marketing of the assets in any way?"

"I kept an eye on it."

"I'm sure that was very helpful. Do you have any research on the value of any of these assets that you'd like to submit today?"

"I didn't really have time to look anything up. But I know it should be more."

Judge Stackhouse sat back and waved a hand. "Very well, Mr. Dennison, you may request a re-appraisal of all assets to determine whether fair market value has been obtained by Northwest Auction. Given the unique nature of many items and the sheer volume of the estate, the Court would allow you one year to obtain those appraisals and will hold all funds in the original estate accounts until that time. Of course, you will pay for any additional appraisals out of your own pocket as the estate has already paid for one round. Is that what you wish to do?"

"Wait," said Rory Dennison. "What do you mean you won't distribute for a year?"

"That's what you want, isn't it? To make sure Ms. Freeman sold the assets for full value?"

"No, no, I didn't mean that."

"You don't want to make a formal motion for a second appraisal of the assets?"

"No, I was just...it just seemed like...,"

"You were just complaining?"

"I guess."

"Then the Court directs you to keep quiet unless it is to thank Ms. Freeman for obtaining such an extraordinary amount of money for you in such an exceedingly short time. Ms. Freeman, you may continue."

Kira ran through a few more categories of items. When she was done, the judge closed a folder and said, "Very good, Ms. Freeman, if that's all we will move on to—"

"Actually, there's one more thing, Judge."

Judge Stackhouse frowned and re-opened his folder. "Did I miss something?"

"No, Judge. I have something that sort of falls between categories that needs your specific attention."

"I see. What's that?"

"Some property related to one of the currency bequests."

"I see. And what is that?"

"Mr. Plutides left a cold wallet filled with Bitcoin to Benjamin Trane. It's in the inventory section under 'currency.'"

I couldn't see everyone but I'm telling you, the entire courtroom sat up. Everyone except Manny Amaltheakis, who sat there, legs crossed, straightening his white pocket square.

"I take it you found this wallet in liquidating the property?"

"I did, Your Honor. But it had been destroyed."

"Destroyed?"

Kira smiled. "Chewed would be more accurate, I suppose."

I believe, but I'm not certain, that Rory mouthed, "That fucking dog."

Fortunately for him, Judge Stackhouse didn't see it as he said, "Well, that's too bad. So it was not functional?"

"It was not, Judge. But it was possible to replace the wallet with the proper tools."

"And did you, Ms. Freeman? Have the proper tools?"

"Not at first, Judge. But there was something I came across in the house that let me figure it out."

"What was that?"

"I would rather not say in open court, Judge."

For the first time, Judge Stackhouse looked impatient with Kira. "Why not?"

"Because the way this works, whoever has that information can obtain access to the funds."

"How much are we talking about?"

Kira told him the current worth of the Bitcoin.

Judge Stackhouse stared. "Was that a million with an 'M?'"

"Yes, Judge."

"I knew you were holding out on me!" said Rory. "Give me my money!"

"Sit down, Mr. Dennison," said Judge Stackhouse, pointing. "Mr. Amaltheakis, control your client!"

Manny pulled Rory down as he stood up.

"Did you know about this?" said Judge Stackhouse.

"I did not, Your Honor," said Manny. "I assume Ms. Freeman had a good reason for not telling us until now."

All eyes turned back to Kira as she said, "I was concerned that the nature of the information gave anyone who knew it access to the money. We believed that the safest way to handle this was to get the information to the Court directly so that it could decide what to do."

"We?" said Judge Stackhouse.

Kira looked back at me. I nodded.

"Attorney Nate Shepherd helped me figure out how to recover the information."

Judge Stackhouse sat back. "And who is Nate Shepherd?"

I stood and raised my hand.

"You're an attorney?" Judge Stackhouse said.

"I am."

"How are you involved in all this?"

"I was involved in the criminal case related to the death of Benjamin Trane."

"Who is Benjamin Trane and why do I care?" said Judge Stackhouse.

"Mr. Trane worked for Mr. Plutides," said Manny Amaltheakis. "The Bitcoin we are talking about was all left to him."

"But this Benjamin Trane is now dead?" said Judge Stackhouse.

"Exactly, Your Honor," said Manny Amaltheakis.

"And you're involved how?" said Judge Stackhouse to me.

"My client pled to causing the auto accident that killed Mr. Trane," I said.

"So how do you two know each other?" He pointed between Kira and me.

As I stuttered, Kira said, "His sister-in-law set us up on a blind date."

Judge Stackhouse sat back and gazed at the ceiling. "Can't people just die and leave their kids the house anymore?"

No one had a response to that.

Judge Stackhouse took a breath, then looked at us all. "Boil this down please, Ms. Freeman."

Kira nodded. "Mr. Plutides left this wallet with millions of dollars in Bitcoin to Mr. Trane. Mr. Trane has since died. Though the wallet was destroyed, I have the information that will let the proper person have access to those funds."

Judge Stackhouse rocked forward. "That's simple enough, then. We will give the information to the executor of Mr. Trane's estate. Do we know who that is?"

I heard a throat clearing and Mrs. Horvath stood. "That would be me, Your Honor."

"And you are?"

"Lynn Horvath."

"And you are the executor of Benjamin Trane's estate?"

"I am."

"Okay, so the Court will review the wallet information from Ms. Freeman and will then provide it to Ms. Horvath for administration out of Mr. Trane's estate."

Ms. Horvath stood there, hands crossed, eyes down. Danny looked up at me.

I raised my hand. "There's another issue, Judge."

"Of course there is. What?"

"In handling the case related to Mr. Trane's death, the Court found that the death of Mr. Trane occurred one hundred eighteen hours after the death of Mr. Plutides. We understand that may impact whether the money passed to Mr. Trane."

"That was relevant to your case?"

"It was."

"What was that finding based on?"

"The death certificates for both men."

"Mr. Amaltheakis, who does the money pass to if it doesn't pass to Mr. Trane?"

"If that were true, it would pass with the rest of the estate to Mr. Dennison, Your Honor," said Manny Amaltheakis.

"To me?" said Rory Dennison. He practically cackled it.

I put my hands out. "That's why I agreed that Ms. Freeman should provide the information directly to the Court, Your Honor. So that the funds weren't taken before the Court could decide where they should go."

Mrs. Horvath remained standing, hands crossed. Spencer Martel stared at me from across the room. Rory Dennison grinned.

Kira lifted a sealed envelope. "May I, Judge?"

He nodded and waved. Kira walked up to the bench and handed it to him. "That has everything needed to unlock the funds. We can file it under seal if you'd like."

"Let's just leave it here for now," said Judge Stackhouse.

There was a general undercurrent of chatter as everyone tried to understand what was going on. Finally, Judge Stackhouse said, "Mr. Amaltheakis?"

The courtroom fell silent.

"Can you clarify any of this?"

"I think so, Judge," said Manny Amaltheakis stood. "It is true that during the trial of Edgerton Fleece, the Court determined that the death of Benjamin Trane occurred approximately one hundred and eighteen hours after the death of Mr. Plutides. It is also true that Ohio law requires Mr. Trane to have survived Mr. Plutides by one hundred and twenty hours in order to inherit from him."

"After I heard the testimony in the Fleece case, I investigated further to confirm the times of death for Mr. Plutides and for Mr. Trane. During that investigation, I learned that the death certificate of Mr. Plutides had been filled out erroneously and listed the wrong time of death. I have here the affidavit of Nurse Amanda Pattinson, along with a copy of her original nursing note, which indicates that Mr. Plutides died at 3:55 p.m., not 8:55 p.m. I also have here an Affidavit to Correct Certificate of Death executed by her supervising physician which lists 3:55 p.m. as the correct time of death. Finally, I have Nurse Pattinson here if the Court wishes to take her testimony."

All eyes turned to a young woman in the back of the courtroom who raised her hand.

Judge Stackhouse did not look at all interested in having a mini-trial. "You have the proper Department of Health correction form?"

"Yes, Your Honor."

"Has it been filed?"

"Here's a filed-stamped copy, Judge," said Manny as he handed it to him.

Judge Stackhouse glanced at it, then said, "The Court finds that the appropriate correction affidavit has been duly executed and filed which establishes the time of death of Theo Plutides at 3:55 p.m. on February 12. As a result, Benjamin Trane survived Theo Plutides by 123 hours and so can inherit from him. The contents of this envelope," he held it up, "will be delivered to the executor of Benjamin Trane's estate for subsequent disposition in accordance with Mr. Trane's estate plan. Are there any other questions?"

"Wait, did I just get jobbed out of all that money?" said Rory Dennison.

Manny Amaltheakis shrugged. "That part of the estate was

never yours. I'm sure the Court will schedule another hearing if you like."

"Will that delay the distribution?"

Manny Amaltheakis shrugged again.

"Fine," said Rory Dennison.

"Is there anything else from you, Ms. Freeman?"

"No, Your Honor."

"Then why don't you meet with Mr. Trane's executor, Mrs. Horvath, was it?"

"Yes, Your Honor," said Mrs. Horvath.

"And explain to her how to access the funds. Here." He held out the envelope and Kira retrieved it.

Judge Stackhouse continued, "The Court has reviewed the inventory submitted by Northwest Auction, finds that the marshaling of assets and valuations were appropriate, and that it has obtained a fair market value. Therefore, Mr. Amaltheakis, you are hereby authorized to distribute—"

"What about the dog?" said Rory Dennison.

"Mr. Dennison," said Judge Stackhouse, "I've had just about enough—"

Rory Dennison plowed on. "The dog that ate the wallet was a thirty-thousand-dollar service dog. It's not listed anywhere in the inventory."

Judge Stackhouse sighed and turned to Kira. "Ms. Freeman?"

"Mr. Plutides did have a service dog, Your Honor, but Roxie is too old to be put back into service. She does not have a current value of thirty thousand dollars and so I am looking for an appropriate home for her."

"You're not supposed to be looking for a home for it," said Rory. "You're supposed to be selling it. Just like all the rest of my uncle's property."

Judge Stackhouse frowned. "Pets are deemed to be property under the law, Ms. Freeman. If you can find—"

"I'll pay the estate one thousand dollars for Roxie," I found myself saying.

"It's worth twenty thousand at least," said Rory.

Judge Stackhouse ignored him. "The court finds that one thousand dollars is fair market value for a retired service dog. Are you sure, Mr. Shepherd?"

"Yes, Your Honor."

"Then pay Ms. Freeman so that it can be included in the estate reconciliation."

"Absolutely, Your Honor."

The judge looked at the clock. "We are going to take a break because that concludes the property section of the estate and because I need more coffee. When we return, I will deal with Mr. Amaltheakis and Mr. Dennison about the cash portion of the estate. The rest of you are free to go."

As the judge left, there was muttering and mingling as people gathered in groups. Beside me, Danny was quietly furious.

"They're making that up."

"We don't know that."

"All this time? All this time, including a murder trial and they never correct the death certificate? Why didn't he do it before?"

I shrugged. "I don't know that Manny Amaltheakis cares where the money goes; he just hands it out."

"He has to have made it up."

"If the nurse says it was really a three and not an eight, no one's going to prove otherwise."

I could see Danny wasn't satisfied with that, but it was still true. As we joined Kira in the aisle, Mrs. Horvath walked up and said, "Excuse me, Ms. Freeman, Mr. Shepherd, could you show me what to do? To access the funds?"

Before Kira could answer, Spencer Martel barreled up and

said, "Do you have an attorney for Benjamin Trane's estate yet, Mrs. Horvath?" Spencer Martel was a tall man, tall enough to look down at Danny as he said, "I can recommend one who gives excellent, *rational* advice."

Danny practically growled.

Mrs. Horvath smiled. "I have already made arrangements, Mr. Martel. Thank you."

"Have him call me when you access the account. My company will want to have someone there, too."

"I'll have the lawyer contact you when we're ready, Mr. Martel."

"You have my card?" Martel said.

She nodded.

Spencer Martel walked away.

We waited a moment for the stench of superiority to pass before Kira said, "Here's what I suggest, Mrs. Horvath. Let's go over to your bank and get a safe deposit box in the name of the Trane estate. We'll put this in it and when you have everything set up and you and your lawyer are ready to receive and distribute the funds, we can walk you through how to do it. You can't just drop this amount of money into a checking account so, for now, the wallet is the safest place for it."

"If you think that's best."

"I do."

"Then that sounds just fine."

As we left, Kira stopped to tell Manny Amaltheakis what they were doing. He was busy getting his ear chewed off by Rory Dennison but nodded his agreement that it was a good plan. Then, as we left the probate court together, Kira gave me a smile and said, "So you bought a dog."

73

As part of his deal, Judge Jurevicius had granted Edge one week to put his affairs in order before he needed to report to the jail and await sentencing there. Since the time would count toward his sentence, Edge was anxious to get it started. I arrived at his house that Friday morning to take him in and make sure everything went smoothly.

The Fleeces' neighborhood was squarely on the nice end of upper middle class—large lots uniformly fenced holding two-story houses with irregular roof lines, surrounded by sidewalks that had an awful lot of people walking on them in the middle of the day. I walked past mildly neglected flower beds and knocked on the door. Edge opened it, smiling far brighter than one would expect of someone on his way to jail, and invited me in. When I hesitated, he said, "You wouldn't deny a condemned man one last cup of coffee with a friend now, would you?"

"Not when you put it that way," I said and went in.

"We have time, right?" he said as he led me to the kitchen.

"We do." I didn't tell him that I usually baked in a little extra time just because you don't know how these things are going to go.

The house was just as nice on the inside, with wood floors, granite countertops in the kitchen, and the precise neatness that comes with an absence of dogs and kids. He waved me to a high-top chair at the island and poured me a cup of coffee which he left black because you don't spend a week in trial with someone without learning their coffee preferences.

I looked around. "Carissa?"

"We said our goodbyes last night. She had call early this morning."

"How's she doing?"

"Better since we heard about the probate hearing yesterday. Is the Trane bequest really going to come through?"

"It looks that way." I took a sip. "I meant, how is she doing with you going to jail?"

"Oh, right, that."

"Yes, that."

"She's fine. I mean, she's not, but she's used to compartmentalizing her worry. She'll be busy practicing and once we get the Trane bequest, it will be full steam ahead on the health clinic." Edge took a sip himself before he smiled. "She'll hardly notice I'm gone."

"What about you?"

"Me? I'm fine now that Pillars is secure."

"It means that much to you?"

He smiled. "Compassion as an abstract thought is useless, remember?"

It took me a moment, but then I remembered our conversation about the practice of *dana.* It seemed like a long time ago. "Practice generosity without reward, right?"

Edge pointed, seemingly pleased that I had remembered. "There are a lot of people in distress in Carrefour, Nate." He paused before he said, "Hopefully, with my case over and our funding secure, we'll give *dana* a chance to thrive."

Edge drained his coffee. "Sooner started, sooner finished. Ready?"

"Ready," I said.

That was as close as Edge ever came to telling me what he knew.

But of course, he was wrong too.

THAT NIGHT, Roxie and I went for a walk just after sunset. It was dark, but it was warm and the stars were out and it was altogether pleasant.

When we came back home, I had just replaced her water and filled her food bowl when Kira knocked at the door. She was carrying a box of toys, a bag of treats, and an extra dog bed for Roxie. "That's great," I said. "I won't have to move the one back and forth between the living room and the bedroom."

"Does she still insist on sleeping in there?"

"She's happy to scratch a hole in my door instead."

"Old service habits, I suppose. Speaking of old service dogs—"

"Awkward segue."

"—you owe me one thousand dollars."

"Let me do it before I forget. Can I Venmo it to you?"

"Paper's better, since it's for the estate."

I went into the kitchen and found my checkbook. "Estate of Theo Plutides?"

"That's fine."

"Are you done?"

"Just about." She bent down and scratched Roxie under both ears. "Then it's on to the next one."

"I know the feeling."

"About the next one—it's in Harbor Springs."

I paused, then filled out the last of the zeros. “That’s good news.”

“And I have a line on two more—one in Petoskey and one in Suttons Bay.”

“Many more of those and you’ll have to move up there.”

When Kira didn’t say anything, I looked up. She was staring at me. I smiled. “You *are* moving up there.”

Kira nodded. “The Plutides estate was the breakthrough—it created some connections and gave me credibility handling high net worth sales. And once word got out that I knew boats too...”

I nodded. “There are some beautiful properties up there.”

Kira nodded again. “Vacation and year-round, with a lot of connections to other parts of the country. There’s just a lot more money floating around up there than in Carrefour.”

“I get it. And you’ll be close to Glen Arbor again.”

“I’ve always wanted to be back up there.”

I shook my head. “Makes total sense.” I smiled. “Northwest Auction. You won’t even have to change the name.”

“I know, right?”

Kira scratched Roxie’s ears. “I’m glad you’re taking her.”

“We’ll be fine.”

“It’s only about four hours away.”

I didn’t say anything about the time it takes to jumpstart a new business or to practice law. Instead, I hesitated, then said, “Sure.”

She smiled as Roxie closed her eyes. “That’s what I thought too.”

The sound of tearing the check out of the book seemed loud. I set it on the table and said, “It’s official.” We both looked at Roxie to commemorate the occasion.

Kira stood.

“Want to grab some dinner?” I asked.

Kira glanced at the TV. “Let’s order in,” she said.

So we did.

74

Roxie and I had just come home from my parents' cottage on Sunday night when my phone buzzed. Olivia.

"Hey, Liv."

"So I stopped by Tri-State Auto Store today like you said."

"And?"

"How did you know?" she said.

"A vague feeling that turned into a suspicion that morphed into a hunch."

"Do you want me to be like that when I report to you?"

"That would be annoying."

"Exactly."

I paused, then said, "It was a bunch of things. She was awfully upset at the trial last week. Then, when she was leaving, I noticed the license plate holder again, and I remembered that when I had helped her to her car a few months ago, she was struggling with the car seat and her daughter wanted it back on the side it used to be on."

"Like it had been moved?"

"Exactly. Was I right?"

"Dawn Blackwell traded in a damaged vehicle when she bought her Kia Sportage."

"When?"

"On February 19th."

"How in the world did you find that out?"

Olivia chuckled. "Tri-State Auto Store might have been under the impression that I was a transparency inspector from Carfax in the process of giving gold certifications to used car dealers who meet its very high disclosure standards."

"Is there such a thing?"

"The weekend sales manager certainly believes there is."

"Which car was it?"

"The red Town & Country."

"The last car on the video."

"Yep. Anyway, Tri-State took the minivan in trade, fixed it up, and sold it three weeks later, complete with a report disclosing the damage and the repair."

I swore. "I don't know why I didn't think about the person *selling* the car."

"Apparently, no one did. Well, except Dawn Blackwell and her mom."

"Her mom?"

"The sales manager actually remembered the deal, said Dawn's little girl accidentally knocked a picture off the wall and broke the glass so that Dawn's mom had to take her outside while they finished. She looked so frazzled, Dawn I mean, and he felt so bad for her, that the sales manager gave her an extra hundred bucks on the trade-in."

"You got all of this information out of him?"

Olivia chuckled. "How else would Tri-State get its gold certification?"

"Remind me never to piss you off."

"Just make sure you're back in the gym now that this trial is over, and I might let you live a peaceful life."

We hung up, and I spent the rest of the night reshuffling my perception of what had happened to Benjamin Trane and, even more, what had happened in the last week.

I WAS AGITATED when I arrived at the office on Monday morning. I pulled Danny into the conference room and told him why.

"Dawn Blackwell hit Trane," I said. "And Mrs. Horvath helped cover it up."

Danny blinked. "How do you figure that?"

I told him about Olivia's car dealer reconnaissance over the weekend, then said, "The car salesman told Olivia that Dawn's mother helped watch Dana when they were finalizing the deal. If there's one thing that's been clear, it's that Dawn's on her own here."

"But why Mrs. Horvath?"

"One—there's no one else it could be. Two—think about all of the meetings we had the night before the plea deal. Mrs. Horvath met with Edge and Carissa, she brought Dawn in to speak with them, and then she left. My guess is she contacted Pompeo."

Danny looked skeptical. "Mrs. Horvath isn't negotiating plea deals."

I shook my head. "No, but there's nothing to prevent her from dangling bait in front of Pompeo and letting him know Edge would accept one."

Danny thought. "But why would Mrs. Horvath hang Edge out to dry?"

"I don't think she intended to. She couldn't know that Edge had hit the deer or that a video would pick up two Pillars vans near the scene. Originally, she was just trying to hide that Dawn did it. Then it was too late."

Danny frowned. "Let's say this is true and Mrs. Horvath helped hide the accident and then convinced everyone to have Edge accept a plea deal. Why would they all go along with it?"

"Think about it from their perspective. The trial was destroying their life's work. They were already losing donations and then our defense strategy costs them five million dollars and Carissa knows I was about to put on evidence to show that she and Greg were tooling around in the other Pillars van on the same night Edge supposedly ran a man down. It was turning way too messy."

"But to agree to plead? That seems extreme."

"Maybe, until you think about what they all got. I think Mrs. Horvath convinced Edge to sacrifice himself for Dawn and Dana if she could deliver Trane's money and save Pillars. I think she convinced Carissa that she could get her health clinic and they could prevent evidence coming in that she and Greg were together that night. Dawn's easy, she avoids jail, keeps her daughter, and gets the extended child-care. I couldn't figure out Manny Amaltheakis at first, but once you said your church was referring clients to him, I was reminded that Pillars works with dozens of churches and Mrs. Horvath led a concerted effort to refer him cases. That's an awful lot of estate plans. Maybe there was some Bitcoin in it for him too, I don't know, but it's the only thing that makes sense."

Danny nodded. "That still leaves Pompeo. Why would he agree to the plea?"

"Pompeo didn't do anything unethical. He'd overcharged Edge from the start and always wanted to plead out. Once it looked like we might win, I'd bet the conviction was more important to him than the crime and once he heard Edge might plead out, he jumped on it."

Danny shook his head. "You really think Mrs. Horvath put all this together behind the scenes?"

"While we were preoccupied with winning the case, yes."

"Why?"

"My guess is it started as a way to rescue a friend and it ended as a way to rescue Pillars."

"So what do we do?"

"I have some thoughts."

Danny and I had a long discussion then, about the ethical duties of lawyers to the Court and to their clients and a longer one about the difference between suspecting something and proving it. The more we spoke, the narrower our options seemed. Since Danny had spent so much time volunteering with Pillars, there was one thing he was adamant about.

I thought, then nodded. "We can do that. How long do you think it would take?"

"I can talk to my pastor this weekend. Maybe two weeks?"

"Let me know when it's set up."

We both sat there.

"It doesn't seem like enough," he said finally.

"It's not. But it's all they've left us with."

75

Two weeks later, I was in the Pillars corporate offices on the third floor. I had only been waiting a couple of minutes when Mrs. Horvath hurried out of a conference room. She wore a royal blue dress that came just below her knees, a matching coat that came just below her waist, and a long string of pearls around her neck. Her hair didn't move as she ducked her head and said, "I am so sorry to keep you waiting, Mr. Shepherd. We just have meetings every which way today."

"No problem, Mrs. Horvath." I stood and picked up the box of corporate file materials we'd used in the case. "Let me carry it for you."

"That would be wonderful. You can just bring them right in here to Mr. Fleece's office and I'll go through them later."

"Sure."

The office of Edgerton Fleece remained exactly as I had seen it last; not a thing that I could see had been moved.

"Over by the desk is fine," she said, and I followed her instructions.

"You're a dear. You know I could have picked those up from your office, Mr. Shepherd."

"I was in this part of town. A friend was getting ready to move, so I was dropping some things off anyway."

"I see. It's really all done?"

"Yes. He's reported, so now he just has to serve his year."

"This is all such a tragedy. It just breaks my heart."

"You certainly were there to support Edge, especially there at the end."

Mrs. Horvath nodded. "I think taking that plea must have been the hardest thing Mr. Fleece has ever done, but maybe now we can all just move on with things."

"That was nice of you all to come. You. Greg. Dawn."

Mrs. Horvath nodded solemnly. "He certainly needed all of our support and encouragement."

"I think encouragement is just the right word."

"Well, Mr. Shepherd, thank you for dropping these off, but I'm afraid I must get things ready for another meeting."

"Sure. Sorry to keep you. I'm sure you're swamped with all the Board's changes."

Her smile stayed, but her head tilted. "Excuse me?"

"The Board's changes. To take a more active management role in Pillars."

"What do you mean?"

"Oh, haven't they announced it yet? The Board is forming a special committee to oversee management of the Benjamin Trane donation. Directly."

"I haven't been informed of that."

I nodded. "I'm sure you will be. Apparently, the member churches were worried—you know, with the donation being so large and cryptocurrency being so new and now having the Pillars leadership in flux—they want to make sure Pillars turns square corners."

Mrs. Horvath's ever-present smile stayed plastered on. "That's wonderful news," she said.

"So they want to keep a closer eye on things to make sure."

"We've always given our best efforts here."

"Your efforts for Pillars haven't gone unnoticed, Mrs. Horvath."

"Oh?"

"Like encouraging Edge with his plea deal."

Mrs. Horvath nodded. "He certainly needed our support."

"Securing donations for Pillars."

"They are our lifeblood."

"Arranging referrals to counsel."

"We need good relationships with many professionals."

"Following spouses."

That was a guess, but when the smile left her face, I knew I was right.

"Trading-in cars," I said.

Mrs. Horvath stepped closer. "I'm not sure what you're saying, Mr. Shepherd, but I'm just doing what any good assistant would do. Support for all, you know."

I shrugged. "I suppose *support* is one way to describe it."

Mrs. Horvath leaned forward and spoke softly. "What do you call it when one of your friends is stretched so thin that she falls asleep, Mr. Shepherd? Do you help your friend put things back together? Or do you offer *legal* solutions like prison and foster care? Is that how *you* define support?"

"I'm not defining anything, Mrs. Horvath. I just hope your next boss ends up in a better place than your last one."

Mrs. Horvath straightened. "I built my last boss's dream, alongside people who worked themselves to exhaustion doing the same."

"That's certainly one theory."

"We don't have a theory at Pillars, Mr. Shepherd, we have a practice—Support. For. All."

I nodded. "I think the Special Committee will be keeping a closer eye on the way Pillars practices."

"There's only one way to practice support."

"Then it sounds like you might have some decisions to make, Mrs. Horvath. Take care."

I was glad that Mrs. Horvath hadn't killed Benjamin Trane. If she had, I'm not sure I would've turned my back on her as I left.

ON MY WAY OUT, I sorted through what Mrs. Horvath had said. It sounded like what we had was a tragic circumstance that spiraled out of control until Mrs. Horvath tried to rein it all in—Dawn Blackwell had fallen asleep at the wheel and somehow Mrs. Horvath had discovered what had happened and stepped in. I didn't agree with Mrs. Horvath's logic, but I understood why, with Dawn facing prison and the loss of her daughter, she might have done what she did. Mrs. Horvath couldn't have known that her solution would lead to Edge being accused and bring Pillars to the brink of ruin, but then she'd fixed that problem too.

Given the punishment Dawn would have been facing for the crime of falling asleep, I'm not surprised that everyone went along with Mrs. Horvath's solution.

As I crossed the parking lot, I saw Dawn Blackwell and Dana a few rows over going home for the day. Dana was holding a treat bag while Dawn wrestled with her ever present ledgers to open both car doors to her used Kia Sportage. Dawn opened the driver door, put down the ledger, opened the passenger door, lifted Dana into the car seat, put the treat bag on the floor in front of her, buckled Dana in, took a sippy cup off the roof and handed it to Dana, closed the door, moved the ledger to the far seat and threw her purse after it, then climbed in, buckled up, and took a deep breath. Moments later, Dawn Blackwell drove by, reaching into the back seat to hand Dana something. She didn't notice me.

I stood there for a full minute after she had passed. Then I went back inside.

A YOUNG WOMAN with sunny hair and a bright disposition met me at the desk of the Pillars Childcare Center.

"Good afternoon, sir," she said. "If you're picking up, I'll need your barcode bracelet and information, please."

I glanced at her nametag and said, "I'm not here to pick up, Amanda. I'm here for Mrs. Horvath. She needs copies of the childcare logs for February 17."

"Certainly, sir. What were you looking for?"

"The pick-up log and any late pick-up request forms."

"No problem. Just a moment." Amanda typed and a moment later there was a whirr, and she gave me a handful of papers. "Should I email them to her as well?"

I glanced at the log, then read the second late pick-up request.

"Do you have to fill out the late pick-up requests in advance?" I asked.

"Yes, sir, that's how we know to schedule someone to stay later."

"And you normally close at six?"

"We do."

"Then yes, please, email Mrs. Horvath a copy too."

"Right away."

"Thank you, Amanda."

Mrs. Horvath wasn't at her desk when I arrived back on the third floor. I found her in Edge's office, sitting in a chair, resting her perfectly coifed head in her hands. She looked up, saw it was me, then put her head back down before she said, "She didn't fall asleep."

"No," I said. "She filled out the late pick-up form at four-thirty that afternoon."

"She told me she fell asleep."

"Dawn made arrangements to leave Dana here, found Benjamin where he always was between six and six-thirty, ran him down, then came back here and picked Dana up at seven-ten."

"She told me she fell asleep and swerved off the road."

"She didn't though."

Mrs. Horvath straightened and dabbed the corner of her eye with a handkerchief. "We were all so upset about Benjamin that I wasn't surprised when Dawn didn't come to work the next day. When she didn't come in the day after that, I was worried and went out to check on her. Dawn was a mess, barely making any sense, and Dana hadn't eaten all that day so I got Dawn into the shower and fed Dana before tucking her away to bed, then put a meal in Dawn too before she told me that she'd fallen asleep at the wheel and hit Benjamin, then panicked and drove away."

Mrs. Horvath wiped her other eye. "I believed the whole thing."

"Did Dawn know about the inheritance?"

"We all did. But he must have told her about the Bitcoin. I'm sure he didn't know what it was worth."

"But she would."

We were quiet for a moment before I said, "Did she dislike him so much?"

Mrs. Horvath barked an un-Mrs. Horvath-like laugh. "She killed him, didn't she?" I thought she was going to lose it then but she gathered herself and said, "She didn't think much of him for leaving his wife and thought even less of his criminal record and I'm certain she had opinions about whether such a man deserved to have all that money when she knew a better use for it. I'm such a fool."

Mrs. Horvath dabbed her eyes once more, then put her handkerchief away, folded her hands, and sat up straight. "What do you intend to do, Mr. Shepherd?"

"I'm not sure yet, Mrs. Horvath. I'll need to tell Edge, of course, but after that, I'm not sure. I have to sort out what my obligations are."

Mrs. Horvath nodded. "Me too. Thank you for showing this to me."

I nodded and stood. I was halfway out when I turned back. "Why were you following Carissa and Greg in the second van?"

Her face went from sad to disdainful. "Dr. Carson-Fleece called for him at the office that night and Mr. Kilbane left immediately. I did not like the tone of the conversation I could hear from Mr. Kilbane's end. So, I followed them." She barked another laugh. "I even ran a red light to keep up, so I could interrupt them if I needed to."

Her face fell. "But I didn't. They just went to EveryGround Coffee. And if neither of us had driven vans past the camera that night, Edge wouldn't be where he is now."

Mrs. Horvath looked as if she might break down again. It wasn't my place to comfort her.

"Good night, Mrs. Horvath," I said and left.

76

I didn't sleep much that night as I tried to figure out what I was obliged to do with the information of what had really happened to Benjamin Trane. I had duties of confidentiality to protect Edge and duties to the judicial process itself and I just wasn't sure yet where my conversation with Mrs. Horvath intersected with all of that.

I was resigning myself to a day of research when my phone buzzed.

It was Mitch Pearson. I answered.

"Hi, Pearson."

"This is low even for you, Shepherd."

I started at that. "What?"

"I expect these stunts from you at trial, but this crosses the line."

"What are you talking about?"

"I'm talking about you sending Fleece's secretary in here."

I blinked. "Mrs. Horvath?"

"She was sitting right outside my office this morning at seven a.m. with a bullshit story about how Benjamin Trane died."

"I didn't tell her to do that, Pearson."

"Right, it's a complete coincidence that your client's secretary magically appears after your client's trial with a story to muck up his plea."

"I had nothing to do with that."

"Sure. And you know, it's bad enough that you're sacrificing the secretary, but blaming someone who's mentally incompetent is beyond chickenshit."

"Mentally incompetent?"

"Blackwell. The woman Horvath blamed. I tried to follow up on Horvath's story and found Blackwell is in the psychiatric unit at St. Wendelin's. She's had a total breakdown."

"Did you talk to her?"

"Of course not! What good is her statement going to be now? Besides, you and Pompeo just had her on the stand and none of this came up."

"I see."

"This investigation dies here, Shepherd. Your client rots for his year and he's not getting out by blaming these women."

"If you say so."

"I won't forget this, Shepherd."

"Me either," I said.

And that was it.

I MET with Edge at the jail the next day. I told him what I knew and offered to find a way to reopen the case.

He looked surprised at first, then listened. When I finished, he said, "Would that process take more than a year?"

"Probably," I said.

"Then leave it alone. We're all better moving on."

"I'm sorry I didn't figure it out sooner."

Edge shook his head, then said, "I'm sorry I didn't realize her burden was so great."

That's not the view I would have taken, but I'm not Edge.

Later that afternoon, Carissa confirmed that they didn't want me to do anything.

Then she fired me just to make sure.

77

The following week, I went with Kira to the conference room of the bank where the cold wallet and the recovery phrase were being stored. Mrs. Horvath, a lawyer for the Trane estate, a lawyer for Pillars, three members of the brand-new Trane Fund Oversight Committee from the Pillars Board, and Spencer Martel met us there. Kira and I unlocked the cold wallet, showed all of them how to get access to the Bitcoin, and got the heck out of there while they were arguing about how to transfer the money to a joint account held by Benjamin Trane's estate, Pillars, and Martel's financing company.

Mrs. Horvath dealt with me professionally the entire time.

Kira left for Harbor Springs for good a few days later. She was under the gun to close out the sale of one house and two boats before the season closed and it was already September. She made it down twice that fall, and I made it up once in early winter, but then it turned out that several of the estates she had picked up also had properties in Florida and she had to spend a good part of her time there.

We had each seen that it might go this way and there was no big breakup, just slowly dwindling contact. I wanted to see her but our schedules just didn't line up and neither of us made the extra time. I still think of her, though, and how important she was for me, and every once in a while, my dad will ask what happened to that girl who could ski.

I checked in with Edge one more time in the early days of his sentence. He didn't want to revisit the case but instead wanted to tell me all about how Pillars had brought in an outside CEO who had gotten the financing for the health clinic approved. Carissa was spearheading the effort to break ground on it that spring.

Edge was sad to report that Dawn Blackwell was still receiving in-patient care. Mrs. Horvath had stepped in, like always, as the temporary guardian for Dana while her mom got well. It gave Mrs. Horvath a reason to reduce her hours at Pillars.

Edge thought the situation was terrible, all of it, but what got him through was knowing that the future of Pillars Outreach was secure and that it would be supporting the Carrefour community for years to come. Edge wasn't sure what he was going to do after he got out, not exactly, but he knew there were plenty of people who needed help and not enough people to give it.

Danny's estate planning practice took a giant step backward. Spencer Martel was true to his word and not only yanked all of Danny's cases but bad-mouthed him around town besides. The thing about bad-mouthing Danny, though, is that if you spend any time with him at all, you know it isn't true. Danny was able to hold on to a couple of cases because the clients didn't believe Martel and that in turn led to a couple more, but it was a slow process and wasn't anything like the flood it had been before. He never complained.

And Roxie settled in with me just fine. She's getting old and she's pretty tired and it's about all she can do to walk half a mile with me at night, but she's sweet and she's happy to see me when I come home. It's nice to leave the lights on for her.

THE NEXT NATE SHEPHERD NOVEL

Lost Proof is the next book in the Nate Shepherd Legal Thriller Series. Click here if you'd like to order it.

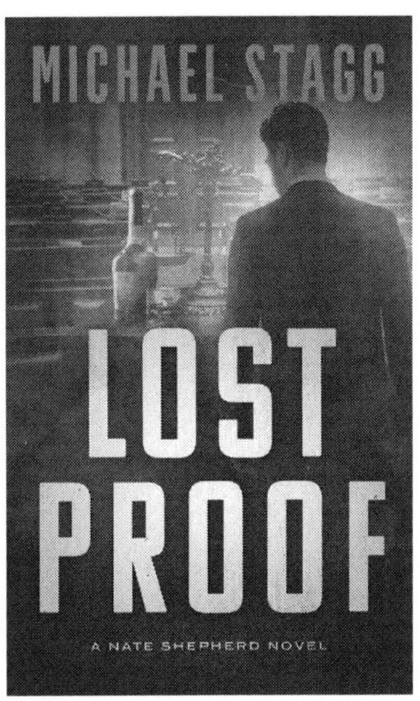

FREE SHORT STORY AND NEWSLETTER SIGN-UP

There was a time, when Nate Shepherd was a new prosecutor and Mitch Pearson was a young patrol officer, that they almost got along. Almost.

If you sign up for Michael Stagg's newsletter, you'll receive a free copy of *The Evidence,* a short story about the first case Nate Shepherd and Mitch Pearson ever worked on together. You'll also receive information about new releases from Michael Stagg, discounts, and other author news.

Click here to sign up for the Michael Stagg newsletter or go to https://michaelstagg.com/newsletter/

ABOUT THE AUTHOR

Michael Stagg was a civil trial lawyer for more than twenty-five years. He has tried cases to juries, so he's won and he's lost and he's argued about it in the court of appeals after. Michael was still practicing law when the first Nate Shepherd books were published so he wrote them under a pen name. He writes full-time now and no longer practices but the pen name has stuck.

Michael and his wife live in the Midwest. Their sons are grown so time that used to be spent at football games and band concerts now goes to writing. He enjoys sports of all sorts, reading, and grilling, with the order depending on the day.

You can contact him on Facebook or at mikestaggbooks@gmail.com.

ALSO BY MICHAEL STAGG

Lethal Defense

True Intent

Blind Conviction

False Oath

Just Plea

Lost Proof

Made in the USA
Las Vegas, NV
09 July 2022

51287614R00305